Murder on Madison Street

MURDER
ON MADISON STREET

Baltimore City - August 18, 1922

JOHN VONEIFF II

Westphalia Press
An Imprint of the Policy Studies Organization
Washington, DC

Dedication
December 2023

James Patrick "Jim" O'Conor, who passed away in December 2023 at the age of 94, was the reason I wrote *Murder on Madison Street*. Jim was a dear friend and an irreplaceable source of information. This picture of Jim and his wife Betty, who died in 2015, was taken in the summer of 2010. Although Jim will never see a finished copy, he very much enjoyed reading earlier drafts. *Murder on Madison Street* is dedicated to Jim and Betty.

TABLE OF CONTENTS

Scene of the Crime

From an article courtesy of the *Baltimore Sun*:

1. Location of the Commonwealth Bank at the southeast corner of Howard and Madison Streets.

2. Site of the robbery on Madison Street (just west) of the Park Avenue intersection.

3. The getaway car (a 1919 dark-blue Hudson Cruiser) accelerating, as it weaves between vehicles, speeding eastward on Madison Street.

Recognition:

Many thanks to the *Baltimore Sun* for making articles, pictures and testimonies available for use in *Murder on Madison Street*.

INTRODUCTION

For the December 2012 issue of *Lifestyle Magazine*, a local publication, I wrote a short story about Jim O'Conor, who was a son of Maryland's 51st Governor, Herbert R. O'Conor. Herbert O'Conor served as Governor of Maryland from 1939 until 1947, and as a United States Senator from 1947 until 1953. Governor O'Conor, who enjoyed a distinguished political career, passed away at Mercy Hospital in Baltimore City on March 4, 1960.

My 2012 story was about the last Christmas the O'Conor family shared together at Government House in Annapolis, Maryland. Since 1870, Government House has been the social heart of Annapolis and epicenter of executive authority for Maryland governors.

Jim told me, "Christmas at Government House was always glorious."

Herbert O'Conor was in office during the most consequential years of the 20th century (Great Depression and Second World War). He was Maryland's war time governor who additionally played a national role, as a United States Senator, during America's remarkable ascendancy following the Second World War.

This story is not about politics. There is no intent to favor one political party over the other or espouse any political point of view. Nevertheless, from his Loyola High School days, Herbert O'Conor aspired to become a lawyer and hold political office. For 30 years, politics (with the exception of his Catholic faith) was the hub of his everyday life. Because Governor O'Conor was a Democrat, there is an unavoidable Democrat side to this story. When he retired from the Senate in 1953, tributes (from the President of the United States and both sides of the aisle) measured him an exceptional governor and United States Senator.

This narrative is told largely through the remembrances of his son James P. "Jim" O'Conor who was 91 years of age in 2021 when I began to write *Murder on Madison Street*. Jim, who passed away in December 2023, was the last of his four siblings. Between 1939 and 1947, Jim, his sister Patricia and brothers Herbert Jr., Eugene and Bobby had the good fortune to call Government House their home. During those youthful years in Annapolis, Jim was often with his father—in the Governor's office, on trips throughout Maryland, and even the White House where he found himself in the company of President Franklin D. Roosevelt.

As a profession, Jim founded and ran one of the largest real estate brokerage companies in the mid-Atlantic—O'Conor, Piper, Flynn.

I met Jim O'Conor, who was 17 years my senior, some 25 years ago. We were members of the same club. In the locker room, after a workout or playing racquet sports, Jim and I would chat about various subjects, but rarely politics—and never the years he grew up in Annapolis. Until I wrote "*Christmas at Government House*" in 2012, I was not aware Jim's father was Maryland's 51st Governor. In the course of a casual conversation in December that year, when I was considering a topic for a Christmas story, Jim told me he had just returned from visiting Government House, where he had lunch with then Governor Martin O'Malley, his wife Katie, and the O'Malley's four children, who wanted to know what Christmas at Government House was like when he lived there.

Hearing about his afternoon with the O'Malley family was the first time I learned that like Governor and Katie O'Malley's four children—Grace, Tara, William, and Jack—Jim O'Conor spent his childhood at Government House. Throughout the holiday season, Herbert and Eugenia O'Conor opened the doors to Government House to welcome Marylanders who came to view the decorated grounds and public rooms. It was a festive time when during the bleak days of the Great Depression and through the war years, Christmas at Government House was an occasion for the O'Conor's to provide gifts and treats to children and greet Maryland's veterans. Christmas Day, however, was reserved for the family.

While interviewing Jim for my story *"Christmas at Government House,"* I learned more about his father's life and how he came to choose a political profession. One event, in particular, stood out.

On August 18, 1922, during the Prohibition era, five gangsters robbed and, in the process, shot and killed a well-known businessman in broad daylight on Madison Street in Baltimore City. That murder triggered the largest nationwide manhunt in decades.

At the time of the robbery, Herbert O'Conor was a 25-year-old unknown Baltimore City Assistant State's Attorney who had been on the job for less than a year. By Christmas 1922, he was the most famous district attorney in America. I titled the (short) story, written for the October 2013 issue of *Lifestyle Magazine,* *"Murder on Madison Street."*

During the pandemic that began in 2020, I rewrote and expanded *"Murder on Madison Street"* to include more details about the crime and many of the individuals involved. For Herbert O'Conor, it was the genesis of his political career .

Baltimore City – Summer 1922

It was a safe harbor protected from unobstructed winds and turbulent seas. No storm could impede a ship that docked there. Baltimore town would begin upon the western bank of a small cul-de-sac on the Patapsco River close to where it empties into the Chesapeake Bay atop the fall line between the Piedmont Plateau and the Atlantic Coastal Plain. The climate was moderate; the precipitation was generous and evenly spread throughout the year. The vast bay to the east was navigable and rich in marine life. The higher ground of the plateau was forested and ideal for farming. Maryland's colonial General Assembly selected this place as the perfect spot for the port they believed indispensable to the ever-increasing tobacco trade. On a strip of low land on the north shore of Locust Point, in 1706, Maryland built a port.

The City of Baltimore was not officially founded for another 23 years. By then, merchants, shipwrights, teamsters, and farmers and their families erected their homes, stores, and warehouses to the west and north around the cul-de-sac that has become Baltimore's well recognized Inner Harbor. Charles Street, Baltimore's first street, began as a simple carriage path that year by year extended further north, following the rising slope of the topography, toward Pennsylvania. The town was named in honor of the 2nd Baron Lord Baltimore (Cecilius Calvert) the first Proprietary Governor of the English Provence of Maryland. By 1922, when this story "Murder on Madison Street" begins, Baltimore was America's eighth largest city and the center of commerce for the mid-Atlantic region. It was a bustling, vibrant and expanding metropolis that, like all American cities, suffered the opportunistic crime and political corruption that mutated amidst burgeoning prosperity.

1

August 18, 1922

For Bill Norris, Friday began like every other weekday—up at 5:45 a.m., shaves with a straight-razor, showers and puts on one of his three-piece dark business suits. He winds his gold pocket watch, a treasured inheritance from his father, and slides it into his vest pocket. Before heading downstairs, he wakes up his eleven-year-old son Edward and encourages him to get a move on. Today Eddie is already up and raring to go.

At 8:30, Eddie, a member of Mount Washington Boy Scout Troop 220, is being picked up for a weekend camp jamboree at Cox Creek on Kent Island. Troop 220 will embark from Sandy Point. It will take thirty minutes to travel the 4.3 miles across the Chesapeake Bay, on a steam powered ferry, to Maryland's Eastern Shore. Open coaches will transport the boys another three miles to their campsite.

Bill asks his second oldest son, "Is your knapsack packed?"

"Sure Dad—all packed—ready to go!"

Bill adds, "Better get a move on, Mom has breakfast waiting."

Mabel Norris is in the kitchen mixing oatmeal with raisins and honey, frying country bacon, turning bread into toast, and brewing coffee. The Norris' youngest son, six-month-old Albert (Bill affectionately calls Bertie), is in his highchair with more oatmeal covering his face and hands than is going into his mouth. Bertie looks up and beams at his father. Bill leans down and kisses his little son on the forehead—then looks up at Mabel, smiles and says, "I'll take Gracie for her run."

Gracie, the Norris' twelve-year-old Labrador retriever, is wagging away in anticipation of her morning outing. A little blind and hard of hearing, Gracie knows every inch of the way. Bill follows his elderly four-legged companion's probing nose from one well-known tree and bush to another, three blocks east to Deweese Park, in the north Baltimore neighborhood of Govans, where Bill sets Gracie loose to sniff at will. In earlier days, it was ball fetching time, but Gracie is too old for that. So long as she knows her life-long buddy is nearby, Gracie is content to wander.

At 6:40, Bill and Gracie are back. Bill unfastens Gracie's leash, scratches her head, and gently pushes her forward, urging his dependable old pal to fetch the newspaper. Gracie, as if the paper were a fallen mallard from some bygone Eastern Shore hunting expedition, responds by scooping up the *Baltimore Sun* and carrying it into the house where she eagerly gives it up for a strip of bacon.

Eddie, dressed in his Scout uniform, is at the kitchen table wolfing down oatmeal and drinking a glass of milk. As he puts Gracie's leash back in the cupboard, Bill tells his son to slow down. "Your bus won't be here for another thirty minutes."

Bill ladles himself a bowl of oatmeal, grabs several strips of bacon, a piece of toast and sits down between his sons.

Mabel hands her husband a cup of coffee then fills a bottle of milk for Albert who is shaking his spoon as if it were a rattle. Before taking a sip of coffee, Bill leans over and wipes oatmeal from Bertie's sticky hands.

Bill and Mabel are both excited about seeing Billy. William Norris, Jr., the Norris' oldest son, will be home in a few days from his summer job at a bayside beach resort in Southern Maryland where he is a lifeguard during the day and waiter at dinner.

In nine days, Billy Norris, who just turned 16, begins his junior year at Loyola High School. Bill is looking forward to spending a few early mornings, with Eddie and Billy, fishing on the

Gunpowder River before school starts and Billy begins football practice.

At 7:25, Bill tucks the newspaper under his arm and tells everyone to have a great day. Looking at Eddie, Bill says, "this will be an exciting weekend for you. I want to hear all about it when you get back—can't wait."

Bill reminds Mabel that he is taking the afternoon off to play golf at the Baltimore Country Club. He won't be home until seven or eight o' clock.

Mabel says, "You told me that last night."

She hands her husband a bag containing four chocolate brownies, part of a batch she baked the day before. Then adds, "we have plenty of leftover meatloaf. If you're hungry when you get home, I'll warm it up.

Giving his wife an appreciative kiss, Bill says, "Thanks Mabs."

As he turns to leave, Bill pauses and looking back at his wife and two sons declares, "See you tonight!"

Gracie is right there too, waiting by the front door—wagging away. Bill stoops over to reward her enthusiasm with a brisk goodbye scratch.

Forty-four-year-old William B. Norris turns and leaves the house.

He will never return.

Eddie Norris –
Mt. Washington Troop 220

3

2

BOTTOM FEEDERS

Baltimore, like most big cities during the prohibition era, is rife with crime and corruption. The Baltimore Crew, an offshoot of New York's D'Aquila Family, ruled by [godfather] Salvatore D'Aquila, is led by Vincenzo "Jim" D'Urso. D'Urso is the king-pin of Baltimore's not so enigmatic underworld. Members of the Baltimore Crew live open and large, controlling their felonious empire through bribery, extortion, and force. Their influence over corrupt politicians, judges, and police is hardly a secret.

Murder among criminals—waging war over territory—goes unsolved. If racketeers stay clear of respectable citizens, there is little public outrage. Thugs dressed like dandies, openly packing guns, run Baltimore's gin mills, brothels, and numbers' racquets with apparent impunity. Everyone answers to Jim D'Urso, who doesn't mind a little infighting, as long as he is kept out of the illicit spotlight.

Thursday night, August 17, 1922, ten members of the Broadway Gang (also known as the Hart-Saperstein-Carey-Smith-Lewis Gang) gather in a brick row house, rented by John "Wiggles" Smith, at 909 Broadway, on Baltimore's east side.

Jack Hart

Charles P. "Country" Carey

Benny Lewis

John "Wiggles" Smith

Frank "Stinky" Allers

Allen N. "Buddy" Blades

George Heard

John "Fatty" Novack

Walter "Noisy" Socolow

John "Squeaky" Keller

Hart called the meeting but Buddy Blades, who works as a truck driver for the Fulton Laundry Company (a truck he also uses to deliver bootleg whiskey), does most of the talking. Blades explains that one of his regular stops is the Hicks Tate and Norris Construction Company. Making small talk while smoking rollups with Johnny Jubb, a bricklayer employed by the company, Blades learned that every Friday morning, one of the owners, William Norris, withdraws the company payroll from the Commonwealth Bank at the corner of Howard and Madison Streets. "Norris," Blades informs his cronies, "is an average size middle-aged dupe who wouldn't be hard to take out. He's stupid enough to walk to the bank and back alone. He will be unarmed. Norris walks to the bank on the north side of Madison and returns on the south side. I watched him make the trip twice."

Pleased with himself for outing the gang's next job, Buddy rocks back in his chair and lights a cigarette then adds, "Norris is an easy mark."

Hart asks, "How much dough will Norris be withdrawing?"

Buddy responds, "I'm not sure. According to Jubb, there are 60 or 70 employees. It's got to be thousands."

Benny Lewis says, "Maybe we should hit the office after Norris returns. It might be easier than taking him on a busy street?"

Hart asks Blades, "Have you ever been inside the building?"

Blades shakes his head—"No—never been there."

Hart says, "Too much can go wrong. We'll take him on Madison Street." Hart instructs Stinky Allers and Wiggles Smith to take his motorcar, a bright yellow 1917 Mercer Raceabout, and head over to Hicks Tate and Norris, instructing them to "case the

Hicks building then check out the Commonwealth Bank. Look for trouble spots and pick the best place for the hit. There's a big Hudson, stored in an East Highland Avenue garage. It's covered up—hasn't been driven in months." Smiling he adds, "I don't think the owner will mind if we borrow his motorcar for a few hours."

"Noisy, Wiggles, Country, Stinky[1] and I will head to Madison Street in the Hudson. Noisy and I will take Norris. If something unexpected happens, Country and Wiggles are backup."

Hart tells Benny Lewis, Fatty Novack, John Squeaky Keller, and George Heard they will not participate. Lewis, Novack, and Heard are suspects in a July shootout with a rival gang at the Belle Grove Inn, an unsavory roadside hangout south of Baltimore. The youthful Squeaky Keller is considered unreliable.

Buddy Blades, the newest member of the Hart-Carey-Smith-Lewis crew, is out because he might be recognized. Blades has been bugging Hart to give him a larger role in the gang's bootleg-ging activities. A big payoff tomorrow might be what it takes to get Jack's attention.

Lewis, Heard, Keller, and Novack will drive to a farmhouse locat-ed in a remote area called Back River, a few miles south of Essex, a small town just east of the city line.

The farm belonged to George Heard's parents. Since the passing of Heard's father in World War I and his mother two years later, the twenty-acre property has gone uncultivated and overgrown.

The gang uses the farmhouse as a hideout and the barn as a place to hide whiskey. Hart tells his gang, "We'll split up the payroll at Heard's place."

---

1   Walter "Noisy" Socolow, John "Wiggles" Smith, Charles "Country" Carey, and Frank "Stinky" Allers

Late that night, the gang meets again in Smith's Broadway house to nail down the details. Allers speaks up, "We (pointing to Smith) think the corner of Madison Street and Park Avenue, across from the First Presbyterian Church is the best place. The curbside will be open."

"If there's trouble," Smith points out, "we can get away in any direction."

Hart agrees. "But if there's a motorcar or truck parked at the corner, we'll pull-over mid-block, on the west side of Park, and wait for Norris there."

August 18, 1922

At 7:45 a.m., the gangsters gather around a large dark-blue Hudson in front of Smith's 909 Broadway rowhouse. At five o' clock that morning, Jack Hart swapped his Mercer for the Hudson. He camouflaged his car with the canvas that covered the Hudson.

Jack Hart made a name for himself as a trigger man for New York's D'Aquila Family. After a stint in prison, he relocated to Baltimore in 1917. It didn't take long for Hart to hook up with D'Urso's Baltimore Crew. Determined to run his own gang, with Jimmy D'Urso's blessing, Hart took over the Saperstein-Carey-Smith-Lewis gang after Leo "The Butcher" Saperstein was shot dead on Lombard Street in June 1920.

Charles Carey has never been happy with the arrangement, but with D'Urso backing Hart, he had little choice. The elimination of Leo Saperstein was a message Country Carey understood.

Before heading out, Hart insists they go over the plan one more time. Then, with Stinky Allers and Country Carey in the front seat (Allers driving) and Jack Hart, Wiggles Smith, and Noisy Socolow in the back, they drive south on Broadway. In two blocks, Allers turns west on Madison Street and motors across town to Howard Street and the Commonwealth Bank. At the intersection of Madison and Howard Streets, Allers makes a U-turn and heads back east. He pulls over to the curb, on the south side of Madison Street just west of Park Avenue, and kills the engine .

The five mobsters settle in to wait for Norris.

It is 8:15 a.m.

Minutes after the Hudson pulled away from Smith's Broadway house, Buddy Blades headed for his Fulton Laundry truck parked in the alley behind the house. Blades will drive his regular Friday route. It doesn't include the Hicks Tate and Norris Construction Company.

Lewis, Heard, Keller, and Novack set out, in Novack's Ford, for Heard's Back River farm where the gang, except for Buddy Blades, will join-up after the heist.

1919 Hudson Cruiser

3

HICKS TATE AND NORRIS

At 7:50 a.m., Bill Norris steers his Packard into his parking space behind Hicks Tate and Norris at 106 West Madison Street, two blocks east of the Commonwealth Bank.

Fred Kuethe, the company's head bookkeeper, and his staff are already there pre-marking employee pay envelopes and figuring out denominations: 20s, 10s, 5s, 2s and 1-dollar bills, plus all the coins needed to make change.

Bill Norris and Bob Hicks catch up in the lunchroom on the second floor. Fresh coffee is brewing. Robert Holiday "Bob" Hicks[2] is an animated, short-stocky, round-faced 55-year-old with few hairs on the top of his head offset by an oversized mustache.

Bob Hicks, a fastidious construction engineer, just finished adding a half teaspoon of sugar to his coffee. When Norris arrives, Hicks sets his cup on the counter and turns to greet his partner. He is anxious to tell Bill about yesterday's meeting with Dr. Frank Goodnow, President of Johns Hopkins University, and several members of the Board of Trustees.

---

2   Robert Holiday "Bob" Hick's grandfather, the late Thomas Holiday Hicks, was Governor of Maryland during the American Civil War. Although Governor Hicks' early sympathies were for the South, he was instrumental in stopping Maryland from seceding. After his term as Governor ended in 1862, Hicks was appointed then elected to the United States Senate. He endorsed Abraham Lincoln for reelection in 1864 but died soon afterward in February 1865.

Governor Hicks was twice widowed. His third wife, Jane Wilcox, was a widow. She had been married to Governor Hicks' cousin. Their son was the founder of Hicks Construction Company—now Hicks Tate and Norris Construction Company. Bob Hicks (President of Hicks Tate and Norris) is the grandson of Governor Thomas Holiday Hicks and Jane Wilcox Hicks. In 1922, Governor Hicks was still a well-remembered politician and a reason Hicks Tate and Norris remained well connected in Maryland.

"Bill," Hicks announces, "We won the contract to build the Marburg addition."

Bill Norris, who was in the process of grabbing his favorite mug decorated with the moniker *My Golf Handicap is Me,* answers, "That's terrific."

After filling his golf mug with coffee (black—no cream or sugar) the two partners sit down at one of the lunch tables to talk about fitting the Hopkins job into a demanding schedule.

Fred Kuethe enters the kitchen to pour a refill. He sits down with Hicks and Norris. "Goodnow," Hicks continues, "wants us to start construction in October. Can we do it? I told Dr. Goodnow I would get back to him Monday or Tuesday."

Norris answers, "Ed[3] and I have already gone over the architectural plans. October is possible, but no later than November first," adding, "When I get back from the bank, Ed should be here. He's stopping by our construction site in Arbutus. Ed should show up around ten-thirty. We can get together then."

Bob nods his head in agreement, "Okay, sounds good."

Bill reminds Bob and Fred: "I'm leaving early today to play golf at the Baltimore Country Club. I should be out of here around noon."

Norris, who is Secretary and Treasurer, turns to Kuethe and asks, "What's the number this week Fred?"

Kuethe responds, "Seven thousand, two hundred sixty-three dollars and change. I've already notified the bank of the cash breakdown."

Norris replies, "It's good to be busy. I'll head out after I check my mail."

---

3   Ed Tate is Vice President of Hicks Tate and Norris Construction Company.

Kuethe adds, "I need to join you today to sign loan papers for the City Hospital job."

Norris responds, "Glad to have the company. I'll only be a few minutes."

Pausing on the way back to his office, Hicks tells Kuethe, "It will be helpful Fred, if you join us when Ed returns."

Kuethe replies, "Yes, sir."

At 8:30, Norris and Kuethe exit the front door. Norris is carrying the brown leather briefcase he uses to hold the payroll. The two men leisurely walk west on the north side of Madison. Fred Kuethe tells Bill Norris that he and his family are looking forward to going to Ocean City at the end of the month. "I've leased a three-room family suite at the Plimhimmon Hotel. It's right on the ocean."

Norris asks, "Let me know how your family enjoys the beach. It's a place Mabs and I have been thinking about taking the boys."

Norris and Kuethe don't notice the blue Hudson parked on the south side of Madison.

Hart and his cronies, however, spot Norris (at least they think it's Norris). He's not alone.

"Who's that?" Hart asks Allers.

Allers, shrugging his shoulders, answers, "I don't know."

None of them recognize Kuethe. In fact, there're not quite sure who's who. The hoodlums quickly decide—no change in plans except that Wiggles Smith will join Socolow and Hart when they make the hit. Socolow will take the man with the satchel—Smith the other.

Norris and Kuethe, still chatting about Ocean City, reach the northeast corner of Madison and Howard Streets. They wait for several passing motorcars, cross Madison, and enter the Commonwealth Bank through a set of elaborately engraved brass doors.

Commonwealth Bank

Southeast Corner of Howard Street and Madison Street, looking east on Madison where the police traffic booth is shown on the left side of the photograph. Bill Norris and Fred Kuethe accessed the bank through the Howard Street entrance. They returned on the south (right) side of Madison. Park Avenue is two blocks east. The building is presently an M&T bank branch.

It is nine o'clock.

Seven thousand, two-hundred sixty-three dollars and change is a pile of money. The bank tellers have banded the currency in bundles of 25 notes each. The branch manager, Alex Baker, shows up with the loan document Kuethe needs to sign. It only takes a minute. As Baker organizes the papers, he thanks Fred for stopping by and tells Bill Norris how much Commonwealth appreciates Hicks Tate and Norris's business. After shaking hands, Baker heads back to his office.

Kuethe counts each bundle of cash as Norris packs them into his briefcase. A teller hands Kuethe a bank tin full of rolled change—quarters, dimes, nickels, and pennies. Norris signs the receipt and thanks the tellers.

"See you all next week."

Kuethe and Norris leave the bank and head back to the office on the south side of Madison. Talking about putting together a financial spreadsheet for the Hopkins project, they are unmindful of pedestrians or parked motorcars.

Twenty-feet short of crossing Park Avenue, Norris and Kuethe are rushed from behind.

4

THE HIT

"HAND IT OVER!"

Bill Norris and Fred Kuethe, surprised and stunned, instinctively turn around to see what they're facing.

"Noisy" Socolow presses the barrel of his snub-nosed .38 against Bill Norris' chest and again bellows: "HEY STUPID - HAND OVER THE GODDAM CASH."

"Wiggles" Smith levels his .38 at Kuethe's head.

Jack Hart directs the muzzle of his revolver at two passing women and roars, "Get the hell out of here!"

Refusing to let go of his briefcase, Norris backs up.

Socolow doesn't hesitate. He shoots Norris in the thigh.

As Norris agonizingly reaches for his leg, with his right hand, he continues to hold onto the briefcase with his left.

Kuethe, traumatized by the gun shot and Norris' frightful reaction, reaches for his collapsing boss.

Smith smashes Kuethe across the temple with his revolver, causing Kuethe to drop the cash box and collapse bleeding and unconscious to the sidewalk.

Noisy Socolow grabs the briefcase. Norris won't let go. Socolow steps back and pumps three slugs into Bill Norris' chest.

As Norris recoils to the pavement, Socolow rips the briefcase from Norris' grasp and tosses it to Hart.

Smith bends over and retrieves the cash box from the sidewalk.

Allers starts the Hudson and pulls up next to the curb where Bill Norris was just gunned down, shouting "Hurry up; get the hell in! Let's get the (shit) out of here!"

Hart and Smith jump in with the blood-stained briefcase and cash box.

From inside the Hudson, "Country" Carey fires several shots across Madison Street, toward the church, scattering onlookers who dive for cover.

Allers steps on the gas, revving the engine.

Socolow, despite the two motionless victims lying in a pool of blood on the sidewalk, rifles through their coat pockets stealing Norris' and Kuethe's billfolds. It's a delay that nearly prevents him from reaching the Hudson in time to escape. Socolow leaps onto the running board at the last second, then dives in.

The Hudson, belching exhaust and weaving between cars, accelerates east on Madison Street.

Back at the southwest corner of Park and Madison, several bystanders race to the aid of the two fallen businessmen. Walter Kuethe, although badly injured, will recover. Nothing can be done for Bill Norris. He is dead at the scene.

5

THE GETAWAY

As the Hudson speeds east with the band of villains hooting and howling over their newfound loot, Sergeant Charles S. Orem, a Baltimore City policeman, thinks the big blue cruiser looks out of place as it roars past him (heading east) at the corner of Eager Street and Patterson Park Avenue. Orem is sure he recognizes Noisy Socolow carrying on in the back seat next to a thug he thinks is Wiggles Smith. Orem isn't sure.

Orem jots down the license number: 85-065.

When he reaches a call-in box, two blocks away, he notifies the desk sergeant, Shawn Campbell, that he spotted Walter Socolow and a bunch of ruffians speeding east on Patterson Park Avenue in a dark-blue Hudson. "I'm not sure," he tells Campbell, "But I think John Smith was also in the Hudson."

Orem tells Campbell: "Socolow looked surprised when he saw me and tried to cover his face. It doesn't look right." Orem repeats the license number twice. "Have you heard anything?"

Campbell answers, "I haven't. I'll keep an ear out for any news."

Orem responds, "Okay—I'll bet something's up with that bunch. Send out the license number just in case." Orem closes the metal call box and resumes his beat.

By four o'clock, the afternoon newspapers are on the streets with newsboys shouting:

BANDITS KILL CONTRACTOR ON MADISON STREET
ESCAPE WITH PAYROLL – MANY WITNESS CRIME!

As mob boss D'Urso feared, the brazen murder of a distinguished citizen on a busy street in broad daylight ignites widespread

MURDER ON MADISON STREET

public outrage. The murder of William Norris triggers the largest manhunt in decades. By evening, the reward for the apprehension of the killers reaches $10,000. Maryland Governor Albert Richie contributes $250 out of his own pocket.

While all this is going on, nine of the ten mobsters split up the take at Heard's farmhouse in Back River, situated a mile south of Guttenberger's General Store. Located east of the city line, at the corner of Eastern Avenue and Mace Avenue in Essex, Guttenberger's is a local landmark.

By eleven o'clock, all except Benny Lewis, Wiggles Smith, and Jack Hart head back to Smith's Broadway house in Novack's Ford. Buddy Blades will collect his share there. The gang is oblivious to the escalating public fury and the ensuing dragnet that will track each of them down.

Because he doesn't want to take the chance of being recognized, Hart dispatches Lewis and Smith to drive the Hudson back to the Highlandtown garage and bring back his Mercer. He instructs Smith and Lewis, "Make sure you cover up the Hudson like I left it. Stretch the canvas over the bumpers so no one will know it's been used. Come straight back. Be careful with my car."

After switching out the Hudson for the Raceabout, Lewis and Smith head for Heard's farm. Before leaving the farmhouse, Smith told Hart, "We'll be back by two o'clock."

"After you return," Hart tells Smith,[4] "I'll drop you and Benny[5] off at your house. I'm taking Noisy[6] to New York for a few days until things cool off. The kid's never been to the big city."

On Eastern Avenue, however, as Lewis and Smith reenter Essex,

4   John Wiggles Smith rents and lives at 909 Broadway.

5   Benny Lewis (waited at Heard's farm for Heart, Smith, Socolow, Carey, and Allers to return).

6   Walter Noisy Socolow (the man who murdered William Norris).

17

the Mercer stalls. Lewis and Smith, who have been drinking all day, get into a fistfight over how to get the Mercer running. The brawl attracts the attention of Baltimore County police officers— Sergeant Wade Walter and officer Tom Hagerty.

Sergeant Walter and Officer Hagerty had just left the Essex Jail where they read Sergeant Campbell's dispatch identifying Socolow as part of a gang heading east in a dark-blue Hudson with license number (85-065).

A yellow Mercer Raceabout is not a blue Hudson Cruiser, but Lewis and Smith are recognized by Sergeant Walter and Officer Hagerty as Baltimore gangsters known to hang-out with Noisy Socolow.

Lewis and Smith are arrested at gun point and searched.

Baltimore County Police Officers Sergeant Wade Walter and Tom Hagerty, assigned to the Essex Station, arrested Benny Lewis and John Smith who were returning to Heard's farm with Hart's Mercer Raceabout on August 18, 1922, at 1:15 p.m. on Eastern Avenue.

MURDER ON MADISON STREET

The two heavies, banged up from scuffling over trying to get
Hart's Mercer started, don't resist. Walter and Hagerty seize guns
and $690.00 in new bills. Some of the currency is two-dollar
notes, rarely distributed except when put out by banks as part of
a company payroll.

Lewis and Smith are cuffed and transported to the Essex Jail.

Hart's Raceabout is left on the side of the road.

6

GUTTENBERGER'S GENERAL STORE

Jack Hart, growing impatient and suspicious (Lewis and Smith should have returned hours earlier), decides to walk to the general store to find out if anyone knows anything.

It's 7:45 p.m. when Hart enters. Mr. Guttenberger, behind the counter, gestures a welcoming wave to the stranger dressed in a blue-grey suit, white shirt with a gold collar pin, topped with a tan fedora.

A group of men wearing work clothes are sitting in tatty wooden chairs, under a fog of cigarette smoke, surrounding an unlit wood stove, gabbing away. They don't bother to look up.

Guttenberger asks Hart, "Can I help you?"

Hart responds, "I'd like a pack of Camels."

Jack Hart

As Guttenberger hands over the cigarettes, he cheerfully says, "That will be fifteen cents."

Hart passes Guttenberger the coins, opens the pack and lights a smoke by igniting a match on the surface of the counter. Pointing to the men surrounding the stove, Hart asks, "What's up with them?"

"Didn't you hear," Guttenberger replies. "There was a robbery in the city today. A man was shot and killed. It's everywhere—on the radio and in the paper. There's a big reward for the killers."

Hart, showing no emotion, exhales a draw from his cigarette then glances back at the men gathered around the stove. Guttenberger responds, "They're regulars, here every Friday after work."

Guttenberger pointing to one of the patrons, a carpenter named Harry Long, continues, "Harry Long, over there, wearing the black and red shirt, told us that two men driving in from the city were arrested earlier this afternoon. They were fighting over something and hauled off to jail. Maybe they were involved in the murder. Their machine was left down the road. It might still be there."

Hart, showing little curiosity, answers, "It's probably gone by now."

Hart thanks Guttenberger for the Camels and then decides to purchase a carton. As Guttenberger deposits Hart's $1.80 into his cash-register, he thanks the visitor with his ruddy mustache and gold capped front teeth adding, "Come again anytime."

Hart, tipping his hat to the genial Guttenberger, casually walks out of the store.

With the carton of Camels under his arm, Hart walks west along Eastern Avenue. A few motorcars, with headlights glowing, pass by in both directions. In the humid obscurity of a mostly empty summer nightscape, Hart goes unnoticed. In a quarter mile, he comes across his abandoned Mercer.

Hart walks around his machine looking for damage and to see if anyone is watching. He closes the engine hood and climbs into the driver's seat. The key is in the ignition. He pulls out the choke, adjusts the timing and throttle, presses the clutch with his left foot, pumps the gas pedal with his right, turns the key, and pulls the starter knob. The Mercer's 4.9-liter engine comes to life.

Given what he learned from Guttenberger, Hart realizes he can't return to the Back River farmhouse or Smith's Broadway Street rental. He never did trust Lewis or Smith, a couple of simple-minded thugs, he thought, as he turned west on Eastern Avenue. If they're outed by the cops, those two dummies will talk. Hart can't take his Mercer to the Highland Avenue garage either. A flashy yellow Raceabout is easy to spot.

D'Urso keeps a warehouse on East Lombard Street near the outskirts of Little Italy where he stores whiskey. Hart decides to take a chance and drive there. D'Urso's boys are always on guard. Hart, who has several sources of whiskey, made a deal with D'Urso to store some of his spirits there. The Baltimore Crew keeps nondescript delivery trucks and spare motorcars inside. It's a good place to hide his Raceabout until the heat's off. Hart knows most of D'Urso's henchmen. He'll cover the Mercer there, maybe borrow one of Jimmy's Fords.

The detention of Benny Lewis and Wiggles Smith is quickly reported to Baltimore Police Commissioner, Charles D. Gaither. Gaither verifies there is a good chance Lewis and Smith took part in the robbery and murder. He requests that the two hoods are transferred to Baltimore City police headquarters.

Baltimore County Police Captain, Andrew Coppin, complies. Benny and Wiggles, handcuffed in the back of a police motor-wagon, are whisked away to the Baltimore City police building on Fayette Street, where they are turned over to Charles H. Burns, Captain of Detectives.

Burns signs the transfer papers and has two detectives, backed up by police officers toting shotguns, drive Lewis and Smith to City Jail on East Madison Street, where the two feuding and befuddled crooks are booked and locked in separate cells.

Jack Hart's 1917 Mercer Raceabout

Guttenberger's General Store was located at the corner of Eastern Avenue and Mace Avenue in Essex. At the time, Essex was a mostly immigrant farming community just east of Baltimore City. Guttenberger's was a regional landmark for more than three-quarters of a century.

7
ABSENCE OF HONOR

The following morning, August 19th, Smith is identified by Sergeant Orem as being in the Hudson next to Walter Socolow. He tells Captain Burns that Smith lives in a three-story rowhouse on Broadway, a few blocks north of the hospital.

Charles "Country" Carey, Fatty Novack, George Heard, and Buddy Blades are scooped up the following day. Carey, Novack, and Heard are unearthed hiding in the basement of Smith's Broadway house.

The same day, Buddy Blades is pulled off his laundry truck claiming he "hadn't done nothing" despite the recovery of several hundred dollars in new bills (including two-dollar bills) stuffed in the pockets of his coveralls.

Frank "Stinky" Allers

Four days later (August 22nd), with front-page stories about the robbery and murder of William Norris, the apprehension of Lewis, Smith, Carey, Novack, Heard, and Blades, and the nationwide dragnet for Walter Socolow and Jack Hart broadcast coast to coast, Frank "Stinky" Allers turns himself in.

Allers claims he was forced to drive the Hudson. He never wanted to be part of robbing Norris. He declares that Hart, Socolow, Carey, and Smith threatened to kill him if he backed out.

According to Allers, he had no choice. Hoping for a deal with prosecutors, Allers offers information about the robbery and killing.

Stinky fingers everyone in Hart's gang and gives up the details of how they planned the crime that resulted in the death of Bill Norris.

Meanwhile, locked up in the Maryland Penitentiary, seven of Hart's sidekicks are moaning about their innocence and blaming their boss, Jack Hart, and the trigger-happy Noisy Socolow for the murder.

When questioned about the robbery and murder, "The Boss," Jim D'Urso, vents outrage about such a heinous crime. Like any good citizen, he voices satisfaction that the bandits are apprehended. He doesn't know any of them. D'Urso never heard of Jack Hart or Walter Socolow. The next night, Hart's yellow Mercer vanishes from D'Urso's East Lombard Street warehouse.

The big question in the ever-expanding nationwide crime story is the whereabouts of Jack Hart and Walter Socolow. Squeaky Keller is reduced to a footnote. No one is looking for Squeaky. Up and down the East Coast, everyone is focused on finding Jack Hart and Walter Socolow and becoming $10,000 richer.

Governor Ritchie is incensed by a ruthless murder in broad daylight, on a busy street, in Baltimore City. He places calls to Police Commissioner Gaither and Baltimore City State's

Frank "Stinky" Allers 1922

Attorney, Robert Leach, offering his full support in tracking down, apprehending, and prosecuting Jack Hart and Walter Socolow.

He tells Gaither and Leach that he and his cabinet secretary (his closest adviser) Stewart Janney want to be kept in the loop. Colonel Janney, the Governor tells Gaither and Leach, is my point person for whatever you need.

Governor Ritchie and Colonel Janney met at the University of Maryland School of Law. They became close friends and law partners. In 1904, they formed the law firm of Ritchie and Janney, LLC. When Ritchie was elected Governor in 1920, Colonel Janney became his senior cabinet secretary and closest advisor. Janney was a U.S. Army captain during the Spanish American War. He volunteered to serve again when the United States entered the First World War. He took a leave of absence from his and Janney's law firm to be commissioned a Lt. Colonel in command of Maryland's 313 Infantry Division that fought along the Western Front in France. Ritchie asked Janney to represent the Governor's Office in supporting the apprehension and prosecution of the men who robbed and murdered William B. Norris.

Governor Albert C. Ritchie circa 1932

Colonel Stuart S. Janney (1918)

8

ROBERT F. LEACH, JR.
BALTIMORE CITY STATE'S ATTORNEY

Robert F. Leach, Jr. circa 1922

In 1920, Robert F. Leach, Jr., a 51-year-old, well known, and highly respected attorney was elected State's Attorney for Baltimore City.

Weary of the upsurge in crime and corruption related to the ratification of the 18th Amendment, in January 1919, which established the prohibition of alcohol in the United States, Leach is single-minded in becoming the "Elliott Ness" of Baltimore City.

No quarter will be given to criminals, from the likes of Boss Jim D'Urso and his Baltimore Crew, all the way down to the bottom feeders who grease themselves with the spoils of petty crime. In Leach's view, the Norris robbery and murder translates into the most despicable kind of malicious crime, a man's life for, in the scheme of things, not much money.

Leach tells his staff that it doesn't matter who the bad guys are. There is no difference between mobsters, like D'Urso's Baltimore Crew, and corrupt politicians, cops, or judges who provide protection. Leach considers all of them fair game.

Leach is an acquaintance of Maryland's Governor Albert Ritchie who was elected to his first term in 1920. Ritchie encouraged Leach to run for Baltimore City State's Attorney.

Vincenzo "Jim" D'Urso

Both lawyers turned politicians, consider the Volstead Act, enabling the enforcement of the 18th Amendment (Prohibition), an unconstitutional encroachment on States' Rights, the civil liberties of Americans, and a catalyst for criminality.

Governor Ritchie and Baltimore City State's Attorney, Robert Leach, believe the rise of the gangsters who thrive because of Prohibition and the Volstead Act, are the greatest threat to the American way of life.

Ritchie and Leach are determined to crush the mob bosses, their accomplices (in and out of government), and reverse the civic disorder and corruption they spawn.

9

HERBERT ROMULA O'CONOR
ASSISTANT BALTIMORE CITY
STATE'S ATTORNEY

Herbert R. O'Conor – 25 years of age in 1921

On February 3, 1921, Leach appoints 25-year-old Herbert R. O'Conor, Assistant State's Attorney for Baltimore City.

Herbert O'Conor has come a long way from the lowly Irish Catholic family of farmers who worked land they didn't own near the village of Raford, close to the town of Longhrea in County Galway, Ireland.

His grandfather, James Connor, (not O'Conor) immigrated to the United States around 1852. James relocated from New York to Texas, Maryland, north of Baltimore. He found a job in the Texas stone quarries where James reunited with other Irish immigrants and met his wife, an eye-catching young lass from Roscommon, Ireland, named Sarah Farrell.

29

Working the quarries was an arduous backbreaking way of life. But for Irish Catholic immigrants, like James Connor and thousands of similar Irish refugees seeking a better life in America, the Texas quarries represented freedom from the predetermined indentured trades they left behind in County Galway and a pathway to a richer future for their families.

James and Sarah Connor would raise eight children. They named their fourth child, born in 1865, James Patrick Augustine Connor. James and Sarah made sure all their children earned a useful secondary education and encouraged them to seek a vocation away from the Texas pits.

When he came of age, James Patrick followed his older brother Thomas to downtown Baltimore where they acquired entry level jobs in the flourishing hotel industry. James, who took business courses at a local college, learned to speak both German and French. After 18 years, working bottom up, he became a successful hotelier rising to manage the fashionable St. James, one of Baltimore's most exclusive guesthouses.

In 1889, 24-year-old James Patrick married his distant cousin, 23-year-old Mary Ann Galvin who everyone called Mamie. To distinguish himself from his agrarian Irish forebears, James changed his surname from Connor to O'Conor.

Jim and Mamie moved into a row house on Homewood Avenue in northeast Baltimore. On November 17, 1896, at their 1202 Homewood Avenue home, Mary Ann "Mamie" O'Conor gave birth to a third son that she and Jim christened Thomas Herbert O'Conor.

Herb O'Conor was an outgoing, industrious boy. In 1902, when it was time for school, he entered St. Paul's Parochial School on Caroline Street, an east-west city avenue that passes through Fells Point, named for one of Governor Hicks' two daughters.

MURDER ON MADISON STREET

His mentor and favorite teacher at St. Paul's, Sister Mary Romula, oversaw the parish altar boys. Sister Mary encouraged Herbert to endeavor, no matter his eventual occupation, to give back to his community—become a priest or policeman or perhaps a lawyer, a dutiful Catholic, striving to protect the disadvantaged.

While attending St. Paul's, out of admiration for Sister Mary, Herbert dropped the forename Thomas and added "Romula." He was never called Thomas or Tom anyway. When he entered Loyola High School (now Loyola Blakefield), the aspiring lawyer was listed in the school's register as Herbert Romula O'Conor.

In 1912, while at Loyola High School, Herbert O'Conor was offered the opportunity to be an intern for the National Democratic Convention held in Baltimore. He was assigned to the Belvedere Hotel where the party platform was being formulated. At the Belvedere, he met well-known United States senators and governors including William Jennings Bryan. In later years, O'Conor would tell biographers that it was this convention, preceding the election of President Woodrow Wilson, that first whet his political appetite.

By the time O'Conor graduated from Loyola (now Loyola University Maryland) as class valedictorian in 1917, he had made up his mind that he could best live up to Sister Mary's expectations by following a political occupation. He graduated from the University of Maryland School of Law in 1920. O'Conor met Bob Leach through his involvement with Maryland's Democratic Party.

Robert Leach, who was nearly 30 years older than O'Conor, was a highly regarded lawyer and law professor. In 1920, he ran for and was elected Baltimore City State's Attorney. During his campaign, Leach championed States' Rights and railed against political corruption and crime in Baltimore City.

Although fresh out of law school, O'Conor, who campaigned for

Leach and Ritchie, applied to be appointed an assistant Baltimore City state's attorney. Leach gave him the job.

O'Conor turned out to be a tireless worker, abstemious in his personal life, and in Leach's view, a smart, effective prosecutor who never misplaced his self-control. By the time of the Norris murder, Leach considered his personable young assistant capable, reliable, and trustworthy.

Believing in his boss' directive to fight crime and corruption, O'Conor is committed to being a fearless district attorney. When Robert Leach assigns O'Conor to the Norris Murder Case, job number one was to track down Jack Hart and Walter Socolow.

By now, "Stinky" Allers has given-up Socolow as the triggerman, the cold-blooded killer who ended Bill Norris' life, and Jack Hart as the gang's ringleader.

Pictures of the two outlaws are circulating nationwide—even in Canada. The whereabouts of Hart and Socolow have become a national obsession.

10

PRINCE OF DECEPTION
HARRY B. WOLF

Harry Wolf in 1922

On Wednesday, August 23rd (five days after the crime), Captain John D. Leverton of Baltimore's Southern Police District requests a meeting with Commissioner Gaither. Leverton informs Gaither that while following up on a lead about William Norris' murder, he met with Harry B. Wolf.

Leverton didn't need to tell Commissioner Gaither who Wolf was. The overly jocular Wolf had been a member of the Maryland House of Delegates from 1906 to 1907, and a United States Congressman from 1907 to 1909. After being defeated in the Democratic Primary for reelection to the U.S. House of Representatives, Wolf went back to be a defense attorney.

Wolf represents some of Baltimore's most infamous scoundrels including Benny Lewis, Charles Carey, political boss Frank Kelly, several of Jimmy D'Urso's henchmen, and even Boss Jim himself. Wolf, while in office, was suspected of being engaged in the shady political malfeasance that Leach vowed to stamp out during his campaign for Baltimore City State's Attorney. Wolf is a well-connected, omnipresent, intrusive fixture in and around City Hall, the courthouse, and police headquarters.

Wolf, through an anonymous source (Leverton tells Gaither), has uncovered the whereabouts of Socolow and Hart. Leverton also divulges that Wolf's informant claims Socolow is not Norris' killer. The actual murderers are two out-of-town gangsters who go by the names of Chicago and Boston. Leverton suggests it would be helpful if he were assigned to the case.

Leach and O'Conor, who mistrust the always convivial Harry Wolf, nevertheless tell Gaither they want to find out more about Leverton's relationship with Wolf and Wolf's unidentified source. They tell Gaither that Leverton's connection to Wolf is suspicious, and his insinuation that hitmen with the unlikely monikers of Chicago and Boston killed Norris is nonsensical.

Such an implausible story from Captain Leverton raises questions about Leverton's motivation. If Wolf's unnamed source becomes a witness for the defense, however, he or she might muddle the state's cases against Hart's gang, not to mention Socolow and Hart. Does Wolf intend to defend some or all the members of Hart's ring of hoodlums? Does he represent his so-called "unnamed source?" Is his source Socolow or Hart?

In the meantime, Leach and O'Conor want to know why Leverton bypassed Captain of Detectives Charles H. Burns, assigned to head up the Norris case investigation, and went directly to Commissioner Gaither.

Gaither, who knows that Leverton and Wolf have been friends since Wolf's early political days, has his own doubts about both men.

Leach asks Gaither to let Leverton, at least for now, remain on the case. "Tell him we need to know more. Who are Chicago and

Boston? What is Wolf's stake in this? And who is his mysterious informant?"

Gaither and O'Conor agree.

They'll find out what they can but will remain distrustful of both Leverton and Wolf.

Baltimore City Police Commissioner
Former U.S. Army Brigadier General
Charles D. Gaither

11

CHICAGO AND BOSTON

John "Squeaky" Keller

It didn't take long for Captain Leverton to stir the pot. On August 24th, the day after his meeting with Commissioner Gaither, Leverton showed up at the courthouse with 17-year-old John "Squeaky" Keller, a well-known shoplifter and aspiring want-to-be in Baltimore's underworld. Squeaky never carries a gun. The witticism of the beat police who routinely arrest Keller for petty thievery is that if Squeaky packed a pistol, he would shoot himself. In and around City Jail, Keller (who is sometimes called Kelly) is considered more of a nuisance than a hardboiled mobster.

Even though Allers has identified Keller as a member of Hart's gang, he isn't mentioned in any of the newspaper accounts. Those in the police department who know Keller, find it hard to imagine that this boy burglar has the wherewithal to be a key culprit in the Norris robbery and killing. The feeling is that Squeaky will, sooner than later, be arrested for stealing something, and the police can deal with him then.

Now here he was, unhandcuffed side-by-side with Police Captain John Leverton, standing in the lobby of the Baltimore City Courthouse asking for a meeting with Baltimore City State's Attorney, Robert Leach. The duty officer notified Leach's office manager, Martha Fitzpatrick, that [a] Captain Leverton is in the lobby with a young man named John Keller. They want to see Mr. Leach. Through Fitzpatrick, Leach sends back a message that if it has anything to do with the Norris case, to tell Leverton to go through Detective Burns. Visibly frustrated, Leverton instructs the duty officer to inform Leach (or Mr. O'Conor) that he has brought in Wolf's anonymous informant.

Minutes later, O'Conor appears in the courthouse lobby. Leverton introduces Keller. O'Conor asks Leverton if he has arrested Keller. Leverton replies that he has not. "Mr. Wolf," Leverton explains, "thinks you will want to hear what John [here] has to say."

O'Conor leads Leverton and Keller up the courthouse's ornate marble stairway to the second-floor offices of the Baltimore City State's Attorney. Robert Leach is waiting in the lobby. Ignoring Keller, Leach shakes Leverton's hand. He asks the police captain if this is regarding the whereabouts of Hart and Socolow. Leverton, ignoring Leach's direct question, replies that "the kid (gesturing toward Keller) has information about the killing."

Leach asks Leverton why Wolf isn't with his client. Leverton responds, "Keller isn't Wolf's client. Mr. Wolf encouraged John (pointing to Keller) to turn himself in and tell you what he knows. When Keller agreed, Mr. Wolf asked me to bring him here."

Leach asks the same question as O'Conor. "Have you arrested Mr. Keller?" Leverton says, "I haven't. Wolf thought you would want to hear what the kid has to say first."

Squeaky stares downward (nervous and puzzled) after hearing the exchange about his possible arrest.

Leach doesn't say anything more about arresting Keller. Looking directly at Leverton, he asks, "You're telling me Mr. Keller is not one of Mr. Wolf's clients."

Leverton answers, "That's right. That's why Mr. Wolf isn't here."

Leach informs Leverton that he has already called Police Commissioner, Charles D. Gaither, and Captain of Detectives, Charles Burns. Gaither and Burns arrive at 10:15 a.m. The six men gather in Leach's office.

Keller is directed to sit in a leather backed chair in front of Leach's desk. O'Conor, standing, leans against the window casing behind Leach's swivel chair while Gaither, Burns, and Leverton pull up armchairs. Mrs. Martha Fitzpatrick is there to record the proceedings.

Leach, halfway sitting on the front corner of his desk, looks down at Wolf's shaky informant and begins. "Well, Mr. Keller, tell us what you know."

Keller, fidgeting with his hands, begins to spin what seems to O'Conor and Leach to be an implausible yarn, but they let the 17-year-old small-time crook relate his account uninterrupted.

Keller tells Leach that he knows Jack Hart. From time to time, he runs errands for Hart (getting him cigarettes, cleaning his car, picking up his suits at the laundry) anything Jack might ask him to do. "Nothing wrong with that—right."

"I know for sure," Keller continues, "Jack and Squeaky had nothing to do with that robbery and murder on Madison Street. Jack was in New York, and Squeaky was asleep in bed with his girlfriend. Whoever said Jack and Squeaky did it is a liar."

"I guess by Squeaky," Leach asks, "you mean your friend Walter Socolow?"

Keller answers, "Yes—we call him Squeaky."

Leach questions, "How do you know all this?"

Keller explains that he and Walter were friends and that on August 17, the night before the robbery, he went to catch up with Walter at Wiggles Smith's house.

O'Conor asks Keller for an address. Keller responds that he thinks Wiggles lives at 909 Broadway. But he's not sure, just that Smith's house is on Broadway, a few blocks north of the hospital.

"I got there about four o'clock."

Keller continues: "Noisy (I mean Walter) was there with his girlfriend, Shorts. Shorts lives in the neighborhood. Her real name is Virginia Williams. Shorts, Walter, and me went to a picture show that night. We didn't return to Smith's house until after eleven o'clock. We didn't get up Friday morning until around ten o'clock."

"Walter," Keller swears, "couldn't have been in on the heist. He was asleep when that guy was shot—just ask Shorts."

"We will talk to Miss Williams," Leach replies as he looks toward Captain Burns (implying that he should look into this) then adds, "I guess by 'that guy' you mean William Norris?"

"That's right," Keller mutters, "Mr. Norris."

"Are you aware that we have a witness who identifies Walter Socolow and Jack Hart as Mr. Norris' killers?"

Keller answers, "Whoever that guy is, is lying. Walter was in the room next to me asleep with Shorts. She'll tell you."

Leach changing the subject, "Are you aware that Charles Carey, John Novack, and George Heard were arrested in the basement of the same Broadway house (rented by John Smith) where you claim you, Socolow and Williams spent the night of August 17th. Do you know any of them?"

"Yes. I know Wiggles [Smith]. I run errands for him too. Wiggles lets me use his house when I need a place to flop."

Keller quickly adds, "I don't know none of them others."

O'Conor becoming impatient interrupts. "Why are you here, Mr. Keller?"

"Like I said, Walter isn't the killer. He was with me!"

"Right," O'Conor sarcastically responds. "If it wasn't Jack Hart or your friend Socolow, then who robbed and murdered Mr. Norris?"

Keller now sweating profusely, retrieves a grungy handkerchief from his coat pocket. Mopping his brow, Keller begins to tell the rest of his story.

According to Keller, about eleven o'clock the morning of the robbery, he left Smith's Broadway house to get a haircut. Walter and Shorts were still inside. When Keller left the house, he was approached by two men. One of them jammed a pistol against Keller's ribs. The other grabbed his arm. They showed him a money box and two license plates.

The two men told Keller that he was going to help them dump the cash box and plates where they couldn't be found. They warned the seventeen-year-old teenager not to be stupid. Keller tells Leach that he had little choice. He suggested throwing the box and plates into the harbor.

The two heavies forced Keller to hike to a pier at the south end of Broadway (in Fells Point) where Broadway dead ends into Thames Street and the harbor. As they were climbing onto the wharf, two policemen appeared a block north. To evade being seen, Boston and Chicago grabbed Keller by both arms and raced to a nearby growth of trees. On the way, his two abductors told him to toss the stuff. Instead of landing in deep water, the plates and box ended up next to Thames Street. They hid in the brush until the cops cleared out. While camouflaged among the trees, Keller relates that his captors began to talk.

They told him their names were Chicago and Boston and were the ones who stole the Hicks Tate and Norris payroll. The man who identified himself as Chicago admitted that he shot Norris. They planned to blame the robbery and murder on Hart's gang as revenge for the Glennbrook Whiskey robbery in west Baltimore and the ensuing gunfight at the Belle Grove Inn.

"We can just frame the whole bunch," Keller tells Leach, "were their exact words. After the police left," Keller said, "I was turned loose. That's the last I saw of Chicago and Boston."

Leach interrupts asking Keller to identify Chicago and Boston's real names and who they work for.

Keller answers, "They didn't say."

Leach asks Keller how he knows Harry Wolf.

Keller explains that Mr. Wolf helped him out of a few jams. When Boston and Chicago let him go, he went to Wolf's office and told him everything.

Looking fearfully at Leach, Keller comes to the end of his tale, muttering, "Mr. Wolf told me it was my duty to come and tell you what I know and that I can identify Chicago and Boston."

Leach presses, "You just said you don't know their names."

"I mean," Keller answers, "if I see them."

Leach replies, "Is that it, Mr. Keller?"

Keller, mopping his forehead answers, "That's what happened."

Looking over at O'Conor, Leach evokes an expression that infers—why are we listening to this bullshit?

For a few minutes, while Mrs. Fitzpatrick completed her transcript, no one said anything. Leach breaks the silence asking Commissioner Gaither to follow up on Keller's claim that he tossed license plates and a moneybox into the harbor.

Gaither orders Detective Burns and Captain Leverton to drive Keller to the foot of Broadway and show them where he dumped the plates and box.

Gaither says, "We'll begin there!'

In 1773, Fell's Point was annexed into Baltimore, joining Baltimore Town and Jonestown as the pillars of the city, just before the start of the American Revolutionary War. Fell's Point had already become an essential hub for trade in the region. The American Revolutionary War would greatly accelerate the area's growth. No battles were fought in the Fell's Point area, but the territory served a huge role in securing America's independence. Although the shipbuilding and manufacturing industries are no longer active in the neighborhood, Fell's Point has retained the personality and unrepressed social culture it developed early on, resembling the crazy charm of centuries past, where "shipbuilders raised families and sailors raised hell."

12

EVIDENCE

Gaither, Burns, and Leverton, flanking an edgy Squeaky Keller, walk back to police headquarters on Fayette Street. With Burns, Leverton, Detective Sergeant William Murphy, and Squeaky Keller in one car, and four police officers following in a second, they drive Keller the several blocks east to Broadway and turn south to where Broadway dead ends into Thames Street. A pier extending from Thames Street leads to deep water. Where the pier begins, the water is murky and shallow. Accumulated rubbish propelled by the wakes of tugs flush in and out among the pylons.

It doesn't take long to recover the cashbox and plates. Submerged in less than a foot of brackish water, a yard from the edge of the pier closest to Fell Street, two license plates (one Maryland, one New York) and a copper-colored metal box are visible.

Detective Sergeant Murphy theorizes: "It's like they were dumped here for us to find."

Keller, visibly unsettled, begins to justify why the evidence was in shallow water. "After Chicago and Boston saw the cops, they became rattled. They grabbed me by both arms and rushed for cover. Chicago ordered me to 'chuck the stuff.' That's why the plates and box were easy to find."

Keller, pointing to a stand of scrubby trees poking out of a swath of underbrush where Fell Street intersects Thames, just east of Broadway, says, "That's where we were."

"So Squeaky," Detective Burns sarcastically asks, "after these two men you say you don't know snatched you off the street, forced you here at gunpoint, hid in those trees where they told you they shot Norris, they just let you go. Is that right?"

Keller looks to Captain Leverton for validation. Seeing the police captain turn away, Squeaky nods his head up and down (implying yes).

Burns responds, "Amazing! You really want us to believe that?"

Squeaky, sticking to his story, replies: "That's what happened."

"And then, after this Chicago fellow told you to keep your mouth shut and set you loose—you went to see Mr. Wolf. Is that right?"

"Mr. Wolf helped me out of a jam. I didn't know where else to go."

Anxious to leave, Keller pleads, "Captain Leverton told me after I met Mr. Leach, he would take me back?"

"Not yet," was Detective Burns' reply.

This isn't what Squeaky wants to hear. Feeling pressured by Burns and unsure about Leverton, he would like to be anywhere else.

Burns pulls Leverton aside.

"It's my understanding (Burns asks too softly to be heard by the others) Keller can identify the two hoods that kidnapped him— Chicago and Boston."

Leverton replies, "That's what the kid said."

"Well," Burns continues, "no one has ever heard of these hoodlums, at least, not in Baltimore. Maybe we have them in custody and don't know it."

Leverton shrugging his shoulders questions, "What do you mean?"

Burns responds, "No one named Chicago or Boston has ever been arrested. Who are these two outlaws we've never heard of? Why would they need a bumbler like Squeaky Keller to unload the plates and cashbox in such an obvious place. Why would they need to get rid of them at all? His story doesn't make a lick of sense."

Without saying anymore to Leverton, Burns speaks up. "We're done here. Let's head back."

Instead of returning to the courthouse, Burns instructs Murphy to head to the penitentiary (connected to City Jail). He instructs Police Sergeant Patrick Oberon, in charge of the men in the back-up car, to drive to the courthouse and deliver the evidence to Mr. O'Conor, and advise O'Conor that he, Leverton, and Murphy, with Keller, will be waiting for him at the jail's 400 East Madison Street entrance.

Burns jams Keller into the back seat of his squad car between Leverton and a tough cop named George Cummings. He informs Keller that before Captain Leverton takes him back to wherever he wants to go, they will be stopping by the penitentiary to see if he can identify Chicago and Boston.

Keller is visibly shaken by this unanticipated change in plans.

So is Captain Leverton.

Herbert O'Conor Calls on Harry Wolf

After Burns left Leach's courthouse meeting to recover the plates and cash box, O'Conor dropped in on Harry B. Wolf. O'Conor informed Wolf that Burns had taken Keller to Thames Street to recover evidence connected to the Norris robbery and killing. O'Conor wants to know about Wolf's relationship with Keller.

O'Conor asks, "Do you represent John Keller?"

Wolf, genial as ever, answers, I don't ."

"As a favor to a client," Wolf continues, "I helped Keller a few times. That's it. I sent Keller to see Mr. Leach to get him out of my hair. If what he told you is of any value then all the better. I'm always ready to oblige the District Attorney."

O'Conor asks, "So what client did you do this great favor for?"

Wolf, "I don't think that matters. Just an old friend who doesn't like publicity."

O'Conor let Wolf know that he arranged for Burns to take Keller to City Jail to see if he can identify Chicago and Boston.

Wolf replied, "Good. I hope he can be helpful."

O'Conor asked, "Would you like to accompany me when I meet Burns, Leverton, Murphy and Keller at the jail – you might find it interesting."

Wolf declined saying, "There's no reason. As I said, I don't represent Keller and I never heard of Chicago or Boston."

O'Conor asked, "What about Leverton?"

Momentarily thrown by O'Conor's question about Leverton, Wolf replied, "I've known Captain Leverton for years. We're friends. When I had Keller here in my office asking for help, I called John and requested that he pick him up and deliver him to your office. I thought I was helping you out. I'm not involved, and neither is John."

"I hope that's true," was O'Conor's reply.

13

BALTIMORE CITY JAIL

Baltimore City Jail (constructed in 1869) fronted by the Wardens House, that faces south. The Maryland Penitentiary was connected directly north.

At 1:45 p.m., when Sergeant Oberon turned the moneybox and license plates over to O'Conor, he informed O'Conor that Burns was on his way to City Jail.

At 2:30 p.m., O'Conor catches up with Detectives Burns and Murphy, Captain Leverton and their jittery charge, Squeaky Keller, at the entrance to Baltimore's gloomy City Jail, coupled to the even gloomier Maryland Penitentiary.

After welcoming Assistant State's Attorney O'Conor and his entourage, Warden Claud Sweezey, a retired army colonel, guides them to a room where, because of focused lighting, O'Conor's group can sit unidentifiable (15 feet away) and view the members of Hart's gang as they are brought in, under guard, one at a time. O'Conor directs his assemblage to say nothing until each suspect is out of the room.

Benny Lewis, who was arrested with Wiggles Smith when Hart's Mercer broke down in Essex, was the first ruffian identified by Frank "Stinky" Allers as taking part in the robbery and killing of William Norris.

To give Keller a good look, Lewis is asked to turn to the right, then to the left, then face forward and clearly state his name.

After Lewis is escorted out of the room, O'Conor asks Keller if he knows Benny Lewis.

Keller answers: "Nope—don't know him."

Keller's reply is the same for Buddy Blades, John "Fatty" Novack, Charles "Country" Carey, and George Heard.

When an officer brings in John Wiggles Smith, who was arrested in Essex with Lewis, Keller admits he knows Smith. "Like I said, I sometimes do errands for him. He lets me stay at his house."

O'Conor asks, "You mean the Broadway house where you stayed with Walter Socolow and his girlfriend the night before Mr. Norris was murdered?" Keller replies, "Yeah, that's right, but Wiggles weren't there. I have no idea where he was."

O'Conor questions, "Did you know Smith was arrested the night of the murder, in Essex, driving Jack Hart's car?"

Keller answers, "Yes—maybe he borrowed Jack's car. I told you; Jack was in New York."

O'Conor asks, "How do you know Smith was arrested in Hart's car? It wasn't reported."

Keller responds, "I can't remember."

To break the tension, O'Conor asks Keller if he would like a glass of water—maybe a cigarette?

Keller answers, "I'll take a smoke!"

Murphy pulls a pack of Camels from his vest pocket, taps the package on its bottom, and hands Squeaky one of the two cigarettes that extend from the pack. As Detective Sergeant Murphy cups his hands to light Keller's cigarette, Keller takes a protracted draw to fire up the tobacco—then exhales.

Murphy holds out the pack to the others. O'Conor says, "No thanks—cutting back." But Leverton, Warden Sweezey, Captain Burns, and Sergeant Murphy light up.

The cigarette break is a calming pause before the final suspect enters a room that is becoming saturated with the aroma and fog of ignited tobacco. Warden Sweezey signals to the guard.

Since he gave himself up four days after the Norris robbery and killing on Tuesday, August 22nd, Frank "Stinky" Allers has met with Robert Leach and Herbert O'Conor hoping to make a deal that would save him from the gallows. Leach offered Allers limited immunity if he gave up the others. Allers agreed.

Allers admitted that he was the driver, Noisy Socolow was the killer, and Jack Hart was the ringleader. He identified Charles "Country" Carey, John "Wiggles" Smith, George Heard, Benny Lewis, John "Fatty" Novack, and Buddy Blades as being in on the planning of the crime. Hart, Socolow, Carey, and Smith were in the Hudson. Hart, Socolow, and Smith made the hit.

Allers explained how Blades, working for the Fulton Laundry Company, had come up with the idea of robbing the Hicks Tate and Norris payroll. He disclosed that Squeaky Keller, always shadowing his buddy, Noisy Socolow, was mainly a gopher for

Jack Hart and Wiggles Smith. Keller was only given a few bucks when the payroll was divided up at Heard's farmhouse. Allers admits that after the money was divvied up, he, Carey, Socolow, Heard, Keller, and Novack crammed into Novack's Ford, returned to Smith's Broadway rowhouse, where they met up with Blades.

Around 4:30 p.m., when they learned about the impending manhunt, Socolow and Keller left Smith's Broadway house together. Blades left in his laundry truck. No one had any idea what happened to Smith and Lewis until the following day when they read about their arrest in the newspaper (the Mercer wasn't mentioned). "That's when we knew," Allers told Leach and O'Conor, "the rest of us would be identified." Allers swore that he had no idea what happened to Hart after they left the farmhouse or where Hart and Socolow are now.

Squeaky Keller becomes animated when an officer escorts Allers into the room. He points to Allers and in a low but excited voice says, "That's him!—That's him!"

O'Conor turns and orders Keller to quiet down until Allers is out of the room. Keller, obviously on pins and needles to say something, nonetheless obeys O'Conor and stops talking.

"Okay," O'Conor questions after Allers is out of ear shot, "What do you want to tell us?"

As Keller drops his cigarette on the floor and stamps what's left of it out with his shoe, he stands up and says, "That's him. That's Chicago!"

O'Conor counters, "You're mistaken. We know that man's name is Frank Allers. We think you know who he is too."

Undeterred, Keller refutes O'Conor's insinuation that he should know Frank Allers.

"All I know," Keller insists, "he's one of the two mugs who hooked me on Broadway. He told me he was Chicago. Until then, I never seen him before. That's Chicago all right. Don't know any Allers."

O'Conor instructs Detective Burns to arrest and cuff Keller. As Burns arrests Keller, Keller—almost in tears—wants to know why.

O'Conor answers, "For the robbery and murder of William Norris."

Keller blurts out, "I didn't kill nobody! I've told you what I know. Captain Leverton said he would drive me home."

O'Conor tells Keller that he doesn't believe his story. "As far as I'm concerned, you were identified by a witness who admits he was in on the crime, and so were you."

As Burns begins escorting a blubbering Keller to a holding cell down the hall where he will wait to be booked, O'Conor rotates to Captain Leverton, who during Keller's unexpected arrest has said nothing. O'Conor informs Captain Leverton he can go.

Leverton replies, "Okay, I'll wait to hear from you." Without saying anything more, Leverton leaves City Jail.

As O'Conor and Detective Murphy depart the jail, they catch up with Detective Burns. O'Conor tells Burns and Murphy that they will give Keller a chance to revise his story after a night in the cage. "We'll question him here at nine o' clock tomorrow morning. Mr. Leach will want to interrogate Keller himself. I want both of you here."

O'Conor instructs Burns to investigate the relationship between Harry Wolf and Leverton, and to see if he can match the license plates with owners and to try and locate Virginia Williams. He has little doubt that this episode involving two hoods named Chicago and Boston was concocted to discredit Allers and steer the police off track. "I'll bet a week's pay," he tells Burns and Murphy, "Keller knows Allers."

What O'Conor doesn't share with Burns and Murphy is that if Keller sticks to his story, it could damage the credibility of the State's main witness, Frank Allers, especially during a high-profile trial in Baltimore City. Allers, a notorious bootlegger with mob connections and an extensive rap sheet, is not the most trustworthy witness.

Keller's rebuttal of Allers' account could weaken the government's case. Convictions of the members of Hart's gang are tied to the believable testimony of Allers. The other gang members, locked up in City Jail, have gone silent.

O'Conor tells Burns and Murphy, "Aside from John Smith and Frank Allers, Keller doesn't seem to know anybody. And he only admits he recognizes Allers as Chicago. The idea that Allers (freelancing as Chicago) robbed and shot William Norris as payback amongst gangsters is ludicrous. Keller can't deny he knows Smith because Smith lets him stay at his house."

O'Conor continues, "I'm sure Hart or Socolow (or both) coached Keller what to say. And if both, they were together when newspapers began reporting that Allers was in custody on August 23rd."

Burns and Murphy believe that Hart and Socolow are holed up somewhere in the city. Burns questions, "Why would Hart come up with a story intended to frame members of his own gang? It doesn't make sense."

"Wolf," O'Conor speculates, "is somehow involved. I'm sure Leverton reported back to Wolf after he left City Jail. If Wolf doesn't have something to conceal, why would he be willing to provide cover for Jack Hart and Walter Socolow."

Wanting to learn more about Captain Leverton's relationship with Keller, and therefore Wolf, is the reason O'Conor included

Leverton on the trip with Burns to recover the cashbox and plates. Certain the plates and cashbox would be spotted, O'Conor asked Burns to zero in on the reactions of Keller and Leverton after the evidence was recovered.

O'Conor also wanted Burns to observe Leverton's and Keller's responses when they unexpectedly found themselves at City Jail, forced to deal with the identification of the men charged in the Hicks Tate and Norris payroll robbery.

That night, at the Baltimore City State Attorney's courthouse office, O'Conor reviews with Robert Leach his concerns about Allers being the only State's witness with firsthand knowledge of the crime, and his suspicions about John Keller, Captain Leverton, and Harry Wolf.

Captain of Detectives, Charles H. Burns

14

WITNESSES FOR THE PROSECUTION

The next morning at 8:30 a.m., August 25, Robert Leach, Herbert O'Conor, Detectives Charles Burns, and William Murphy meet at City Jail for the nine o' clock interrogation of John Keller.

Warden Sweezey informs Leach that Keller had an uncomfortable night. Sweezey recounts that Keller couldn't sleep. He was often ranting ("He didn't do nothing"). As Sweezey leaves the room to arrange for Keller to be brought in, he adds, "He's a pretty nervous kid."

Before Keller arrives, Leach introduces Courtenay Jenifer, Baltimore County State's Attorney, whose office will join the Norris prosecution team.

Leach invited H. Courtenay Jenifer, Baltimore County State's Attorney, to join the questioning of John Keller. Leach introduces Jenifer to Burns and Murphy. O'Conor and Jenifer, both politically active Democrats, already know each other. Leach informs everyone that Jenifer and his office will be assisting in the prosecution of Hart's gang. "Some of the trials," Leach reveals, "may take place in Baltimore County. We are not waiting for the capture of Hart and Socolow to begin prosecuting the Norris case. Courtenay and I will start by trying John Smith and Charles Carey, who were identified by Allers as complicit in the robbery and killing."

Waiting for Keller, Leach and O'Conor take a few minutes to update Jenifer—beginning with potential witnesses.

Mr. Albert Conley – Insurance Salesman

On August 19th, Smith was singled out by Albert Conley, a

48-year-old insurance salesman who was near the corner of Park Avenue and Madison Street on the morning of August 18th. Conley identified Carey as being in the Hudson when it sped away on Madison Street. Since then, Mr. Conley has had second thoughts. Fearful that he might put his family in danger, Conley is apprehensive about being involved. O'Conor doubts Conley will be a dependable witness.

Mr. Robert Tyler Johnson, Sr.

This was also Burns' and Murphy's assessment of Robert Johnson, a florist, who was in the Commonwealth Bank when Norris and Kuethe were picking up the payroll. Johnson followed Norris and Kuethe out of the bank. He was about a half block behind when he heard the shots that killed Norris. Johnson said that he was startled by the gunfire, saw several men waving pistols, and took cover in a doorway. He was too far away to identify anyone.

Dr. Clarence J. Grieves

Sixty-two-year-old Dr. Clarence J. Grieves was across the street in front of the First Presbyterian Church. Unlike others interviewed, Dr. Grieves noticed and was suspicious of the Hudson parked directly across the street. He told Burns and Murphy the machine was full of fishy characters, dressed in suits, just sitting there. Grieves, assumed they were bootleggers, asserting that since prohibition, Baltimore has too many of these oily gangsters roaming the streets.

Dr. Grieves, like other bystanders, was alarmed when the hoodlums started shooting. Assuming it was gang related and wanting to avoid being in the crossfire, Grieves took cover in the church vestibule. From there, he saw Mr. Norris recoil to the ground after being shot several times.

Dr. Grieves told Murphy that three men pulled off the robbery while two others stayed in the car. Because of losing his spectacles when he tripped on the steps, as he dove for cover, Dr. Grieves admitted that it would be difficult for him to positively identify any of the gun waving muggers. He would be happy to try.

Dr. Grieves was one of the first to reach Bill Norris and Fred Kuethe after the Hudson pulled away. He immediately realized Mr. Norris was dead. The other man (Kuethe), Dr. Grieves said was unconscious. He was bleeding profusely from a severe head wound but hadn't been shot. Grieves did his best to help Kuethe until the ambulance arrived.

The following day, at City Jail, Dr. Grieves was not able to identify Benny Lewis or John Smith. On Tuesday, August 22, Dr. Grieves was invited back to City Jail to have a look at Charles Carey, John Novack, George Heard, and Buddy Blades. The doctor thought he recognized Charles Carey as the man leaning out of the Hudson, firing his pistol at the church, but wasn't sure.

The one man who Dr. Grieves could identify, Jack Hart, was still at large. Grieves said he recognized Hart, from newspaper pictures, as one of the three men who assaulted Norris and Kuethe.

Loula V. Riley and Mrs. Sadie Egnatz

Loula V. Riley and Mrs. Sadie Egnatz were crossing Park Avenue (east to west) along the south side of Madison when Hart's gang attacked Norris and Kuethe. They couldn't have been more than 15 feet away when Hart aimed his pistol at them, ordering the two terrorized women to scram. Instead, Mrs. Egnatz froze in the middle of Park Avenue, dropped her packages, and screamed at the top of her lungs. A panicking Miss Riley turned around and raced for cover behind a mailbox on the east side of Park Avenue.

Miss Riley and Mrs. Egnatz both claimed that the attack was so sudden and frightful they could not identify any of the assailants. Both women refused to come to City Jail to see if they recognized the members of Hart's gang. Leach and O'Conor decided to scratch Riley and Egnatz from the witness list.

Mary Kisling and Edna Dorsch

O'Conor learned that John Smith's Broadway House was actually owned by Edna Dorsch, who neighbors thought was Smith's wife. Comen and Kahler arrested Mary Kisling and Edna Dorsch as they were boarding a steamer heading for Point Comfort, Virginia. Mary and Edna, regulars at the Belle Grove Inn, were favorites of the Saperstein-Carey-Smith-Lewis gang before Hart took over. Kahler suspected that both women were hiding some of the Hicks' payroll.

Kisling and Dorsch, toting overstuffed fabric satchels, were taken to the Northeast Police Station for questioning. The satchels were stuffed, but only with clothes. Some of the clothing (suit coat and trousers) in Edna Dorsch's satchel were inked with the initials "JS." When asked if "JS" stood for John Smith, Dorsch said, "Absolutely not." Edna claimed she purchased the suit, shirts, and pants in a secondhand shop for her father who lived in Port Comfort. Both women said they were leaving on holiday, trying to get out of the city for a few days before summer ended.

When questioned about the house at 909 Broadway, Edna admitted she owned the house and sometimes stays there. She rents it to Smith, who she says is a friend. She also shares an apartment on Boston Street with Mary Kisling. Kisling verified this. Detectives Kahler and Comen, checking Dorsch's story out, learned that Edna was at 909 Broadway more than she was willing to admit. However, they could not tie Dorsch or Kisling to the robbery.

Dorsch and Kisling were detained and interviewed by Herbert O'Conor the following day. At the courthouse interview, Dorsch and Kisling were represented by Eldredge Hood Young, an attorney who had represented John Smith. The day before, Young filed a writ of *habeas corpus* with the Superior Court claiming the women were being held without cause. After the interview, Leach decided not to challenge the writ. Mary and Edna were released. There was nothing to link Edna Dorsch and Mary Kisling to the robbery.

Baltimore Police Sergeant Charles Orem

O'Conor doesn't have any doubts about Baltimore Police Sergeant Charles Orem. Orem is certain he saw Noisy Socolow hiding his face as the blue Hudson sped by him on Park Avenue the day of the crime. After having a look at Hart's gang at City Jail, Orem told Burns, "John Smith was also in the Hudson."

Mr. Eckert's Hudson

Although Frank Allers admitted that he drove the Hudson, he swore he had no idea where it was. All Allers knew was that Hart appropriated the Hudson Cruiser for the robbery. None of the other members of Hart's gang were talking. Even Benny Lewis lost his memory.

The Hudson (License Plate 85-065) was registered to Paul Eckert, a vice president of the Calvert News Company. The police had been trying to track him down since August 19th. Not finding Mr. Eckert at his home in the north Baltimore neighborhood of Roland Park, Burns and Murphy visited the Calvert News Company at 5302 Winner Street, a block west of the Pimlico Racetrack (home of the Preakness Stakes – second jewel of the Triple Crown since 1873). They learned that Mr. Eckert was in New Jersey convalescing from what was described as a stroke.

Detective Murphy was given a Morristown, New Jersey, address only to learn that the house was closed for the summer. Because Mr. Eckert, one of the company's founders, was retired, he was not often in touch with Duncan Fowler, the company's president. Fowler told Burns and Murphy that Mr. Eckert, who never married, went to his sister's house, in New Jersey, to recuperate. No one at Calvert News knew the location of the family's summer home. They thought it was in Cape May, New Jersey.

Mr. Fowler verified that Mr. Eckert owned a blue Hudson sedan and had put it in storage while he was in New Jersey but did not know where. Murphy asked Fowler if he had heard that the car involved in the robbery and murder on August 18th (six days ago) was a dark-blue Hudson. Fowler said, "Yes—but I never thought for one minute it might be Paul's car."

When Mr. Eckert returned to Baltimore on Wednesday, August 23, Fowler notified him that the police were looking for his car. Eckert called police headquarters and got in touch with Detective Murphy.

Eckert told Murphy that 85-065 was his license plate number. "My Hudson Cruiser," he said, "is stored in a garage owned by Fred Marsden, an old friend." Eckert told Murphy the address is 606 Banks Street in Highlandtown. "It's been there since the first of June."

Yesterday afternoon (August 24th), Burns and Murphy met Mr. Eckert at the garage. Eckert realized his car had been used. The canvas cover he had so meticulously spread over his cruiser had been carelessly applied. The interior was full of dust. Several cigarette butts had been stomped out on the floorboards and the front seat was torn.

When Burns and Murphy checked the Hudson's interior, they found several dollars' worth of change between the seats and two torn currency bands stamped Commonwealth Bank. Burns inventoried the change and bands. The Hudson was eliminated as a vehicle used by Hart and Socolow to flee Baltimore.

Murphy added, "Detectives Kahler and Comen canvassed the neighborhood for individuals who use the garage. The garage had been a storage building for grain and other horse and carriage supplies. It can accommodate about 20 motorcars. Spaces are rented to local business owners or their employees. There is no attendant. Everyone interviewed has seen the covered Hudson. No one remembers it being missing or saw a yellow Mercer."

Fred Kuethe

O'Conor asks Burns about Fred Kuethe (Hicks Tate and Norris' head bookkeeper). Burns reported that Mr. Kuethe's head was split open. He suffered a fractured skull and concussion. Kuethe did not regain consciousness until Sunday, August 20th. He could not remember anything. Kuethe wasn't sure he would be able to identify his and Norris' attackers and never saw the Hudson. He might recall more with time. "Right now," Burns tells Jenifer, "Mr. Kuethe isn't much of a witness."

John Smith and Charles Carey

Leach explains that he, Mr. Jenifer, and Herb O'Conor have decided that John Smith and Charles Carey will be tried together in Baltimore City. They suspect Smith's and Carey's attorneys will seek a change in venue to Baltimore County—the reason Jenifer has been asked to join Leach's prosecution team. This goes for Jack Hart and Walter Socolow when they are apprehended. In any event, Burns and Jenifer have decided to unify as prosecutors. Jenifer and his staff, led by his deputy, Timothy Andrews, will work closely with O'Conor and Bernard Wells, who was recruited by Mr. Leach not long after O'Conor.

Leach informs the group that if Frank Allers' testimony leads to the convictions of Smith, Carey, Hart, and Socolow, then Allers will not be charged with murder. Leach and Jenifer are considering limited immunity with a prison recommendation in the range of ten years. Allers is also wanted for a robbery in the county. Jenifer will suspend disposition of this indictment until after the Norris case trials.

Allers agreed to the partial immunity deal. He will remain held in the Maryland Penitentiary. Leach asks O'Conor and Wells to bring Jenifer and Andrews up to speed on everything relative to the case. "Going forward," Leach explains, "Baltimore City and Baltimore County States' Attorneys will work together."

John Meyer and E. Milton Altfeld – Representing John Smith and Charles Carey

O'Conor informs the group that John Meyer, a criminal attorney, is representing John Smith. E. Milton Altfeld is representing Carey. Smith and Carey were denied bail and have been transferred from Baltimore City Jail to the Maryland Penitentiary. On Tuesday, August 22nd, Meyer filed a petition for a writ of *habeas corpus* on behalf of Smith for unlawful arrest and detention. Altfeld did the same for Carey.

Both writs contend that Smith and Carey are not guilty of any crime. They are being unjustly held in the Maryland Penitentiary. Meyer and Altfeld made the case that the only witness is a convicted felon, Frank Allers, who helped plan and execute the robbery and murder. Allers is attempting to avoid a first-degree murder charge.

Meyer contends that Smith's only crime is getting into an altercation with his drinking buddy, Benny Lewis. Smith and Lewis' arrest in Essex on August 18, 1922, is proof, Meyer argued, that neither his client or Mr. Lewis could have been involved in the robbery and murder of Mr. Norris. Smith was in Essex when the crime took place—so was Lewis. Meyer questioned why Smith and Lewis were transferred to Baltimore City Jail (the night of August 18th) for little more than having too much to drink and getting into a fight, at most a misdemeanor.

Beyond this, the car Smith and Lewis were driving, purported to be a 1917 yellow Mercer Raceabout, is missing. Both Meyer and Altfeld petitioned the court to compel the Baltimore County or Baltimore City police to produce the Mercer. It is, according to Meyer, evidial proof that Smith, who was obviously with Lewis, could not have been in the Hudson and therefore, not guilty of the crime.

Altfeld insists his client, Charles Carey, was with Lewis and Smith from the night of August 17th through the afternoon of August 18th (when Smith and Lewis borrowed Hart's car); this is proof, he claims, that Carey could not have been at Madison Street on the morning of August 18th. Smith and Lewis will vouch for the whereabouts of Carey. Meyer and Altfeld argue that the Mercer is being intentionally hidden by the police, ostensibly at the request of Mr. Leach.

Finally, Leach reveals that Governor Ritchie has communicated to both him and Courtenay Jenifer that nothing is more important—to counter the perception of unchecked gang related crime in Baltimore—than the apprehension and conviction of the gangsters who robbed and killed William Norris.

Since August 18, local and national newspapers have made the heartless murder of William Norris a front-page headline, creating uninterrupted speculation as to the whereabouts of Noisy Socolow and Jack Hart.

Katherine "Kitty" Kavanaugh

Moments before two penitentiary guards escort Keller into the City Jail anteroom, Detective Burns adds that he had dispatched Detective Lieutenant Charles Kahler and Detective James Comen to track down the assignments of the license plates recovered from the harbor.

One was a New York plate (626-401) reported stolen in 1917. The second plate was a Maryland tag registered to a Katherine Kavanaugh, whose address is 612 Glover Street, in East Baltimore.

Burns recounts, "When Kahler and Comen arrived at the row house, a young man about 18 years of age was sitting on the front stoop smoking a cigarette. He identified himself as Martin Kavanaugh and told Kahler and Comen that the house belonged to his mother, Mary Kavanaugh. When asked if he knew a Katherine Kavanaugh, Martin answered that Katherine was his sister and wanted to know why they were looking for 'Kitty.' Detective Kahler explained that a license plate registered in his sister's name was recovered from the harbor. He and Detective Comen wanted to find out why Katherine had not reported the plate missing."

Burns continues, "Martin Kavanaugh asked if they were talking about the Mercer. Kahler responded that they were—a 1917 yellow Raceabout. Kavanaugh said that the Mercer belongs to his sister's husband, James Connelly. He had no idea why Jim Connelly's car would be registered in his sister's name. Kavanaugh said that his sister doesn't drive and never has."

"Detective Kahler," Burns tells O'Conor, "asked if Mr. Connelly lived in the house and might be home." Kavanaugh's response was that Jim didn't live there anymore. He revealed that Jim Connelly left his sister last Christmas. Kahler asked Kavanaugh if his sister was home. Kavanaugh answered that she was at work. He explained that two of his three sisters live there, Kitty and Rachel. Rachel and his mother were in the house. He went on to reveal that Kitty works at Epstein's Department Store on Eastern Avenue. She wasn't expected back until dinner.

"Kahler asked if they could speak to his mother and sister (Rachel). Martin Kavanaugh stamped out his cigarette and went inside. A few minutes later he returned with Mary Kavanaugh, who appeared to be in her late forties and Rachel, who said she was 17. Kahler asked Rachel and Mary the same questions about the Mercer. Both women, were obviously uncomfortable and gave similar answers. "Kitty, or Katherine," Burns tells Leach, "is married to James Connelly who moved out last year. Neither the mother nor the sister understand why Connelly's car would be registered in Katherine's name."

Kahler told the Kavanaughs that the police were investigating a robbery where the Mercer may have been used. Rachel Kavanagh asked if Jimmy was involved in a robbery. Kahler answered that he didn't think so, but his car may have been stolen. They thought it belonged to Katherine.

Mary Kavanaugh told the detectives that the Mercer wasn't there and that there was no reason it would be. It was her son-in-law's motorcar, not her daughter's. Mary repeated that her daughter didn't drive and told our detectives, "If Jimmy's car was stolen, it wasn't stolen from here."

Martin Kavanaugh revealed that Jimmy sometimes left his car at his uncle's metal shop. Kahler reported that Mary Kavanaugh gave her son a nasty look as if to say—stop talking. According to the detectives, all three of the Kavanaughs insisted they had no idea where the Mercer was or why it was registered to Kitty.

Kahler wanted to know more about the uncle. Mary answered that Uncle Joe was her late husband's brother, Joseph Kavanaugh. Comen asked what Joe Kavanaugh did for a living. Mary Kavanaugh said that he was a metal worker who owns his own company in Sparrows Point. She let it slip that her brother-in-law may have done some work for Jimmy, then quickly added that she wasn't sure.

Kahler got the address of her brother-in-law's company. Comen gave Mary Kavanaugh one of his cards requesting that when her daughter (Katherine) got home to have her give him a call. Both detectives came away believing they weren't getting the whole story.

Burns tells Leach, "Kahler and Comen said all three Kavanaughs seemed edgy. Maybe Katherine Kavanaugh's husband knows Hart and lent him his car without her knowing."

Leach responds, "We need to know if there is a connection between James Connelly and Jack Hart. Let's bring in Mrs. Connelly for questioning."

As Keller is being brought in for the interrogation, Burns says, "I'll take care of it."

Lock Up – Baltimore City Jail, where John Keller awaited his interrogation on August 25, 1922

15

DODGING THE GALLOWS
THE INTERROGATION OF JOHN KELLER
AT CITY JAIL 9:15 A.M. – AUGUST 25, 1922

At 9:15 a.m., two guards escorted a distressed and untidy John Keller into the room. Leach pointed to a chair in the middle of an eight-foot rectangular oak table and ordered the 17-year-old to take a seat.

Everyone pulls up a chair. The two prison guards sit down on a wooden bench behind Keller. Fidgeting with his hands (like he did the day before in Leach's office), Keller nervously glances around the table at each of the five well-dressed grim looking men, dreading that they are about to lock him up forever.

Detective Burns begins by offering Squeaky a cup of coffee. Keller nods his head (yes) and asks for a cigarette.

Leach says that they will hold off on cigarettes.

Warden Sweezey has arranged for the penitentiary's kitchen staff to set up a coffee table in the corner of the room. Keller starts to get out of his chair to retrieve a cup. One of the guards stands up and orders him to remain where he is—saying: "We'll get it for you."

Squeaky sits back down, "I like mine black with lots of sugar."

As Murphy, Burns, and Baltimore County State's Attorney Courtenay Jenifer retrieve coffee mugs, Warden Sweezey enters the room to inform the group that Martha Fitzpatrick, who will record the meeting, has just arrived from the courthouse. Little more is said until Mrs. Fitzpatrick takes her place at a small desk next to Leach.

Leach begins by asking Keller if he understands why he was arrested.

Keller responds, "I ain't done nothing. I was trying to help."

Ignoring Keller's bluster, Leach begins: "You have been identified by a credible witness, as a member of Jack Hart's gang and that you participated in the robbery and killing of Mr. William Norris on Friday, August 18, 1922. Do you understand this!"

Keller looks down and mumbles, "I didn't do nothing."

Disregarding Keller's mutterings, Leach makes it clear. "We don't believe you were kidnapped on Broadway. We think Chicago and Boston don't exist. We are confident that Frank Allers has never gone by the name Chicago, and you know who he is."

Squeaky, barely audible, replies, "I don't know any Frank Allers."

"Sure, you do! You and Allers are in the same gang—Jack Hart's gang!" Leach finishes by asking, "Who put you up to this—Jack Hart, your buddy Socolow, Mr. Wolf or all of them?"

Keller, sweating profusely, answers, "No, no one told me to do nothing. That man was Chicago. I don't know Allers."

Leach, realizing Keller was about to break, presses on—"I'll tell you what we do know, Mr. Keller. You are going to be charged with the murder of William Norris. We will ask for the death penalty. If you're convicted, you'll be hanged. Would you like to have a look at where the gallows will be erected, Squeaky? That's what they call you, isn't it? The gallows, where you will squeak-out your last breath, is not too far from where you're sitting."

For a few minutes nothing more is said. Keller, shaking so hard he spilled what was left of his coffee in his lap, is back fidgeting with his hands. One of the guards passes Keller a towel to blot the coffee from his pants.

The silence is broken by Baltimore County State's Attorney, Courtenay Jenifer. Jenifer looking directly at Keller and in a friendlier voice, says, "John, I want you to listen to me."

As Keller stares fearfully over at Jenifer, Jenifer begins: "You're in a lot of trouble son. But if you help us by telling the truth, we'll do what we can to help you. Do you know Frank Allers?"

Keller, as if thinking about what to say next, glances at each of his inquisitors, all looking austerely back at him, and answers, "Yes."

Jenifer asks him to speak up.

Keller, regaining his voice, replies, "Yes, I know Stinky."

Leach asks, "You mean Frank Allers?"

Keller responds, "Yes. We call him Stinky."

"What do you mean, we?"

Keller replies, "You know," and rattles off the names of Hart's gang including Frank Allers who Keller confirms drove the Hudson.

Leach asks Keller, "Who came up with the Chicago-Boston fairytale."

Keller, changing the subject, "Am I going to be hanged?"

In a more approachable tone, Leach answers, "Not if you tell us what you know."

Keller sits back in his chair and asks if he can have a smoke. Leach says, "Okay."

Detective Murphy hands Keller a Lucky Strike then helps him light up. After a draw and exhale, Keller admits there are no mobsters named Chicago or Boston. "Jack came up with the idea to throw off the cops. If the cops are looking for Chicago and Boston," Keller explains, "Jack thought it would give him and Noisy time to get out of town."

Leach asks, "Do you know where Hart and Socolow are."

"I know where they were Wednesday."

"Where's that!"

Keller, still puffing away and tapping the charred tobacco remnants into an ashtray, begins to unravel what happened to Jack Hart and Walter Socolow after the gang learned about the manhunt and reward for their capture.

Keller explains that after they split up the payroll at Heard's farm, he along with Socolow, Novack, Carey, Heard, and Allers drove back to Smith's Broadway house where Buddy Blades was waiting for his share. "We didn't know what happened to Hart, Benny Lewis, or Wiggles Smith until later."

Leach stops Keller, "We need to know where Hart and Socolow are now. There will be time to go over the details later. Tell us where they are!"

Asking for another cigarette, Keller says, "Sure, there're holed up in an empty burial vault in a graveyard called Sweet Home Cemetery off Biddle Street near the railroad tunnel. Jack and Noisy have been there since August 19th. They wanted to get to New York but couldn't steal a car. Jack thought the cemetery was a safe place to hide."

"Jack gave me money to purchase food, water, cigarettes, matches, coffee, and newspapers. I only went to the vault at night when the cemetery was empty."

Burns interrupts. "I know the area. The entrance to the cemetery is at the end of Chase Street. It's a remote place. The railroad tracks are south. Biddle Street runs along the cemetery's northern boundary. Edison Avenue is east. The cemetery is surrounded by a fence. The keeper's house, at the Chase Street entrance, is unoccupied. We can be there in 30 minutes. If they're there, we'll get them for sure."

Leach instructs Burns to gather his detectives and ten well-armed police officers and get there "as quick as you can. Take Mr. Keller to identify where Hart and Socolow are hiding."

O'Conor suggests that he go along. Leach doesn't object.

Leach and Jenifer head back to the courthouse. Burns, Murphy, and O'Conor, with Keller handcuffed, head for the police building.

Following World War II, Sweet Home Cemetery was sold by the Archdiocese of Baltimore. The property became a stone quarry. Graves and mausoleums were relocated to the New Cathedral Cemetery in West Baltimore. When the quarry played out, the acreage was abandoned for two decades. Purchased by the city, the old quarry was converted into a community park. East Chase Street still dead ends into what was once the entrance to Sweet Home Cemetery. The keeper's house is no longer there.

16

Sweet Home Cemetery

By 11:00 a.m., 20 armed police officers have surrounded Sweet Home Cemetery. Lead Detective Burns, detectives Murphy, Kahler, and Comen, with John Keller and Assistant State's Attorney O'Conor, are behind the gatehouse outside the main Chase Street entrance.

Keller points to a granite crypt in front of a grove of pine trees 150 yards from the gate, in the southeast section of the boneyard. The tomb is among four other mausoleums surrounded by a host of headstones.

The police parked their motorcars on side streets and encircled the cemetery on foot. Detectives Kahler and Comen set out in opposite directions to pass the word as to which mausoleum is the objective. All wait for 11:30, the designated time to move in.

At 11:30, 20 heavily armed officers and four detectives, weaving among the gravestones, approach the mausoleum Keller has identified. As the police close within yards of the crypt, there is no indication anyone is inside. The vault's two bronze doors are slightly ajar.

Burns, in a booming voice, calls out, "Jack Hart—Walter Socolow—you are surrounded! Come out with your hands in the air!"

There is no response. Burns repeats his ultimatum. Still no reply.

Burns signals for two officers to pull the bronze doors open, ordering them to stay clear of the line of fire. It only takes seconds for the officers (using the heavy doors as shields) to pull them open. There is no reaction from within.

Burns shouts out, "John Keller is with us."

He instructs Keller to let Hart and Socolow know they are surrounded and should surrender.

Keller yells out, "Jack and Noisy, they know you're in there!"

No response.

Burns and Murphy, backed up by Kahler and Comen and several officers with shotguns, are the first to enter. The interior is dark, hot, and stuffy. But from the moment the detectives entered the vault (even before they entered) it was obvious that Hart and Socolow weren't there.

The mausoleum is a mess. Cigarette buts, charred matches, crumpled newspapers, and discarded containers of food litter the cell's ten by 12-foot stone floor. Remnants of a fire, set inside a milk can, is where the two hoods boiled coffee. A large tin container exudes the pong of urine. Several tousled blankets are flung across coffin slabs. Playing cards are scattered about the stone floor.

Burns recovers a train schedule. Departure times for Washington D.C., New York, and Chicago are circled. Clothing is heaped in one corner. Murphy digs through the pockets. He discovers some loose change and a grocery receipt dated August 23rd, the day before Captain Leverton brought Keller to Leach's office.

"It's pretty obvious" Burns comments, "[that] other than sweating to death in here, Hart and Socolow were trying to find out what the police were doing and a way to get out of town."

O'Conor adds, "It looks like they left sometime yesterday—during the hours we were interrogating Keller. If Hart's plan was to create a diversion, to buy time, he succeeded."

Burns predicts, "To avoid the police, I am sure Hart and Socolow have split up. My guess is they have made it out of Baltimore."

O'Conor asks Burns to circulate an (all-points) bulletin notifying law enforcement across the country that Hart and Socolow have, so far, eluded capture in Baltimore. "We suspect they have split up and are likely traveling to Washington D.C. or New York City—maybe as far west as Chicago or St. Louis."

Although already in circulation (descriptions and pictures of Hart and Socolow have been distributed nationwide), Burns says, "I'll resend their profiles along with the bulletin."

Because of the $10,000 reward, the police and Leach's office have been inundated with leads (from across the country—even Canada) that have collectively served to muddle the search. "The mausoleum raid if nothing else," O'Conor says, "resets the timeline. Let's have another sit down with John Keller."

Maryland Penitentiary, connected to Baltimore City Jail, circa 1922

17

THE REST OF THE STORY

The Second Interrogation of John Keller at City Jail

That afternoon, at 3:30 p.m., Friday, August 25th, in the same room at City Jail, O'Conor, Burns and Murphy sit down with John Keller, who is wearing prison clothes. Since returning from the cemetery, Keller has had a shower and something to eat. Burns offers Keller a cigarette. The single guard in the room removes Keller's handcuffs and lights his smoke. Robert Leach and Courtenay Jenifer arrive with Mrs. Fitzpatrick.

Leach, Jenifer, and O'Conor continue the questioning of Keller.

O'Conor opens, "We appreciate your cooperation. I need you to tell us everything that happened after you and the other members of Hart's gang returned to Smith's house on August 18th."

Keller, puffing habitually on his cigarette, confesses a more believable account.

"After we learned Mr. Norris was dead, there were witnesses who could identify us, and there was a huge reward for our capture, Noisy and I, thinking Smith's house would be raided, left."

"We walked to the corner of Charles and 22nd Street and hailed a cab to a stop on Reisterstown Road, a block west of Mr. Wolf's house. Wolf had represented Jack when he was part of the Baltimore Crew. Last year, Jack talked Wolf into helping me and Noisy out of a jam. There was the chance," Keller continues, "that Jack, realizing he couldn't return to Heard's Farm or Smith's house, went to Mr. Wolf's place."

"When Mr. Wolf opened the kitchen door, he didn't seem surprised. He invited us in. Noisy asked him if he had heard from Hart. Mr. Wolf said he hadn't. He learned about the robbery and shooting, like everyone else, through the newspapers."

"Wolf asked us if we wanted something to eat. His housekeeper had prepared a kettle of beef stew before leaving earlier. After filling bowls with stew, we sat down at the kitchen table. Mr. Wolf asked if we were involved in the Hicks Tate and Norris robbery."

"Socolow confessed, that we were. He told Wolf no one was supposed to get hurt. He didn't think Mr. Norris would fight back. Shooting him was an accident. Mr. Wolf wanted to know who pulled the trigger. Noisy admitted he shot Mr. Norris."

"While we were sitting at the kitchen table, there was a loud knock at the front door. Wolf told us to put our bowls of stew and spoons in the sink. He hid us in a small room off the kitchen where he stored groceries."

"While we were doing that, there was a louder knock. We, later learned that the man at the door was a police detective named Hammersla."

"Wolf said when he opened the door for Hammersla, he told him he hadn't been feeling well and was in the bathroom. He apologized for the delay."

"Detective Hammersla asked to come in. Wolf wanted to know why. Hammersla said there was a good chance two of his clients, Jack Hart and Walter Socolow, may have been involved in a robbery on Madison Street earlier in the day."

"Wolf told Hammersla that Jack and Noisy were no longer his clients. He didn't know anything about the robbery other than what he read in the newspaper. Wolf told the detective he hadn't seen or heard from either Hart or Socolow for at least a year. He wasn't feeling well and needed to go to bed. Wolf closed the door and left Detective Hammersla on the porch."

"Noisy and I," Keller confessed, "were in Wolf's pantry for quite a while. We didn't learn about Detective Hammersla until Wolf let us out of his pantry after Hammersla drove off."

"Mr. Wolf wanted to know what went wrong. I told him I didn't take part in the robbery. I was in Heard's farmhouse with Lewis, Heard, and Novack waiting for Hart, Socolow, Allers, Smith, and Carey to show up. They got there around ten o' clock."

"I told Wolf that Jack was pissed that Noisy went nuts with his gun. Noisy yelled at me to shut up. He told Wolf that the dummy wouldn't let go of the money."

"Wolf said he had heard enough. He didn't want to know any more. He told us to leave his house and find another place to hole up. We were putting him at risk. He was worried Detective Hammersla would come back. He couldn't get rid of us fast enough."

"As Wolf began pushing us toward the door, Noisy became miffed and pushed back shouting at Wolf to keep his hands off. Wolf backed away but insisted we leave."

"Noisy asked, where should we go."

"As he opened the kitchen door, Wolf told us to get out of Baltimore. There was nothing more he could do. He had just saved us from being arrested. 'Forget you were here,' were Wolf's final words. He slammed the door closed and switched off the lights."

Keller explained, "Walter and I walked to the same trolly stop on Reisterstown Road where we hailed a cab to North Avenue. From there, we boarded the electric car east to Harford Avenue. It was a two-block walk to Country Carey's Durham Street row house."

"At the time," Keller said, "We didn't know Benny Lewis and Wiggles Smith had been arrested in Essex. We assumed Carey had returned from Smith's house. When we arrived, the shades were drawn but lights were on. Walter knocked on Carey's front door."

"It wasn't Carey who answered. It was Jack. He ordered us inside, then shut and bolted the door. Jack told us he had to stash his car. 'A yellow Raceabout,' he said, 'is as easy to spot as a lightbulb on a moonless night.' Not wanting to wait around and fearful of returning to Smith's house, Jack told us he walked to Carey's house where, like us, he expected to find Country Carey. Carey kept a spare key behind a loose brick next to the top step. Hart used the key to enter."

"When we showed up," Keller revealed, "Jack was as surprised to see us as we were to see him. We told him that we had just come from Wolf's and that Wolf threw us out after a police detective showed up."

"Hart told us that Lewis and Smith were arrested in Essex and how he learned of their arrest after walking to a general store on Eastern Avenue. Hart said he was going to steal a car and head to New York. After thinking about it, he thought lifting a car would give the police something to look for. Expecting Carey to be home, Jack walked to Carey's, from where he ditched his Mercer."

O'Conor asks Keller where Hart's motorcar was hidden.

Keller replied, "Don't know, Jack didn't say."

O'Conor asks Keller how Hart came to own the Mercer. "Registration records show the car belongs to someone else."

Keller answers, "Jack bought that motorcar when he came to Baltimore from New York. I have no idea where he got it."

O'Conor doesn't press the issue but looking over at Detective Burns nods his head in a manner that implied it was time to bring in Katherine Kavanaugh Connelly.

Keller went on to explain that Hart thought it best to hunker down in Carey's house for a few hours to see if Carey or some of the others showed up.

"Hart was sure Smith and Lewis would rat us out. Heard's farm and Smith's house would be searched. If Carey didn't return before sunup, we needed to split."

"As time passed, Hart became anxious. He said we would be safer on the streets."

O'Conor asked, "What happened next?"

"At two o'clock in the morning," Keller resumes, "we grabbed a loaf of bread, some canned food, and several jars filled with water and left Carey's house. Keeping to the alleyways south of Gough Street and the narrow spaces between houses, we hiked nine blocks (west) to Patterson Park. We spent most of the day (August 19th) in a pump house near the lake."

"Jack felt funny in a place that would be hard to escape from if we were discovered. He wanted to relocate to a more secluded spot. Jack has connections in Washington and New York. Getting there was the hitch. Jack was nervous that isolated in the pump house there was no way of knowing what was going on and no way to find out."

"Noisy told Jack that 'Shorts,' I mean Virginia's parents (Sara and Frank Williams), lived on East Bond Street. Frank Williams was a stone mason. He worked for a company that built internment vaults in churchyards and cemeteries. Virginia told Noisy about an abandoned crypt located in Sweet Home Cemetery, a half mile northeast of Patterson Park where the railroad goes underground. Noisy wanted to look inside. One night, Noisy said, he talked Virginia into checking out the empty mausoleum. When they got there, Virginia was too scared to go inside."

"Jack wanted to know how isolated the vault was, where it was, and what was nearby. Noisy said the cemetery was a spooky place on the north side of the tracks. The entrance was at the end of Chase Street, about a half hour walk from where we were. As soon as it was dark, we left the pump house and walked north on Luzerne Avenue to Chase Street. The cemetery entrance is three blocks east."

"The crypt was easy to spot and just as Noisy said, the two bronze doors were cracked open. Jack thought it was perfect. Until I went to the Southern District on August 23rd, Jack sent me out to get cigarettes, newspapers, and groceries."

"It was easy to evade the police. No one said anything about the hunt for Jack and Noisy. No one seemed to recognize me at all. I was careful to avoid the police and only returned after dark."

Leach asks, "How do Chicago and Boston fit into this?"

Keller answers, "Through the newspapers, Jack learned that all the members of our gang, except for him, Noisy, and me were locked up in the Maryland Penitentiary. Jack was fixated on who he called the turncoats who were blaming him for the robbery and murder. He especially wanted to get his hands on Stinky Allers."

"From newspapers," Keller continues, "we learned about the nationwide manhunt. Realizing that remaining in the stifling hot mausoleum would result in being discovered, Jack began to frame an escape plan."

"Late on the night of August 23rd, while we were playing cards, Hart came up with the idea of a diversion that might mislead the police and give him and Noisy an extra day or two to get out of Baltimore."

"Jack wanted to get back at Stinky and create suspicion about whatever he was telling the police. One way or another, Jack swore that he would get Allers, the worst of the traitors, and the two dummies, Benny Lewis and Wiggles Smith, for getting themselves arrested in Essex."

Keller explains, "That's when Jack conceived the gangsters Chicago and Boston. Jack said he would frame Allers as Chicago and Carey as Boston. Since the police didn't seem to be looking for me, Jack came up with the idea of Chicago and Boston kidnapping me outside of Smith's house and dumping the cashbox and plates into the harbor. Jack still had the cash box that Lewis and Smith left in the Mercer, the license plate from his car and an old New York plate he had saved."

"Jack bragged that Chicago and Boston would be identified as Allers and Carey. They would be blamed for the robbery. Jack was excited that Allers would be pinned as Chicago, Norris' killer. How to get the story out, Jack said, was the question."

"Jack knew that Captain Leverton was close to Mr. Wolf, and that Wolf had to be worried about hiding Socolow and me from Detective Hammersla on August 18th."

"Wolf," Jack said, "had to help even if he didn't want too."

Hart knew that through Mr. Wolf, I had met Captain Leverton. I would take streetcars to the Southern Police District, find Leverton, and tell him the story about being kidnapped."

"Jack told me to tell Leverton that I needed to get in touch with Wolf because I knew where the gangsters that robbed the payroll and killed the businessman were hiding. I was to tell Mr. Wolf that Jack and Noisy were not the murders. The real killers were out of town gangsters named Chicago and Boston."

"Jack was sure the police captain, looking out for his friend, would contact Mr. Wolf with my message about Chicago and Boston before doing anything else. Mr. Wolf had to understand his predicament. Jack was certain Mr. Wolf would want to meet me to find out what he was facing. The question was when and how." Jack said, "We'll start with the cop."

"On the morning of Wednesday, August 23rd," Keller continues, "traveling on electric cars and walking the last several blocks, I got to the Southern District. Captain Leverton was parking his machine in the lot behind the station. As I approached, Leverton pulled his pistol and arrested me. He herded me into the station.

Southern District Police Building, circa 1922

When I told Leverton I had a message from Hart and Socolow for Harry Wolf, Leverton whisks me into his office and closed the door."

"Once in Leverton's office, I told Leverton about Chicago and Boston. Leverton placed a telephone call to Mr. Wolf. After the call ended, Leverton informed me that Harry looks forward to seeing me, He wants to help. As soon as he finishes with some paperwork, Leverton told me, he would drive me to Wolf's office."

"Before we left the station, Leverton was back on the telephone with Wolf. He made me sit outside his office, cuffed to a chair during the second call. Afterward, he told me that we wouldn't be going to Wolf's office until the next morning. For my protection, I would be spending the night in a holding cell. While in the cell, I was to keep my mouth shut and everything would work out for Jack, Noisy, and me."

Keller recounts, "Leverton was gone most of the day. He made sure the jailer supplied me with cigarettes, lunch, and dinner. He told the guard that I was being held as a witness in the Norris killing. At seven o'clock Thursday morning, August 24th, Captain Leverton returned. I already had breakfast and was able to clean up. He told me we were heading to see Mr. Wolf."

Keller said, "Mr. Wolf was unhappy to see me and angered by what I had to say. Wolf said he should never have let Noisy and me into his house."

"Despite being angry," Keller said, "Wolf agreed to advance Hart's story about Chicago and Boston. He wouldn't do it himself. Captain Leverton would take me to the courthouse to meet with you. It was up to me—not him—to make Jack's story believable."

"Mr. Wolf wasn't sure you would see us. The only way to know, he said, was to go to the courthouse and find out. I would be the anonymous informant Leverton had told Commissioner Gaither about the day before. Mr. Wolf said that should get Mr. Leach's attention."

"Wolf made it clear he didn't represent me. He would deny that he had anything to do with Walter and me and that I should stick to the Chicago-Boston story. If this was going to work, Wolf insisted, it had to come from me. Leach would never fall for it if it came from him."

Leach thanked Keller for revealing the details of Wolf's involvement and where Hart and Socolow had been hiding, telling

Keller, "You will stand trial for your participation in the robbery but, as a states' witness, you will be given consideration for your testimony. This will include limited prison time in a juvenile facility. Meanwhile, you will be held at City Jail, away from the members of Harts gang. While you're there, Warden Sweezey will look out for you. You will be called as a witness in each trial."

With that, the guard escorted Keller out of the room.

Assessment of Keller's Confession

Leach, Jenifer, O'Conor, Burns, and Murphy remain in the interrogation room to review what they had just learned. Wolf, Leach was certain, would never have trusted Squeaky Keller or Noisy Socolow not to implicate him. They agree that Wolf could argue that nothing Keller said was true.

Leach continues, "There is no way of knowing what Harry Wolf was thinking when Keller nattered out his far-fetched account. Wolf obviously knew none of it was true. After all, Socolow and Keller were in his house the night of the crime and admitted being part of it. Socolow confessed to the killing."

"Captain Leverton," Jenifer speculates, "will verify that the first time Wolf met Keller about the robbery and murder of Norris was the morning of August 24th when he brought Keller to Wolf's office. Leverton might not even admit he went to Wolf's office first."

O'Conor adds, "Captain Leverton's meeting with Commissioner Gaither on August 23rd was a ploy to separate Wolf from Socolow, Keller, and Hart. If the Chicago-Boston ploy was to give Socolow and Hart time to get out of Baltimore—it worked."

Jenifer adds, "There will never be verifiable proof that Wolf covered for Socolow and Keller the night of the crime. Detective Hammersla did not go into Wolf's house. Wolf appeared to be feeling sick and alone. If Hammersla thought differently, he would have returned or called for backup. But he didn't."

Leach predicts, "It will come down to Wolf's word against theirs. Hart and Socolow are well known criminals. Keller is a small-time crook. Who will believe these three gangsters over Harry Wolf who, although suspected of being corrupt, has never been arrested or charged with anything. And remember, Wolf has powerful friends like Frank Kelly,[7] who will testify to his good character."

O'Conor points out, "Leverton could say that he arrested Keller on the morning of August 23rd and interrogated him as being a known member of Hart's gang. He could say that he then delivered Keller to the courthouse and [our] office for all the reasons he conveyed to Commissioner Gaither on August 23rd. After all, "we were the ones who let Leverton stay on the case and told him, through Commissioner Gaither, to find out the anonymous informant's identity. Leverton, was just doing what Gaither told him to do."

Jenifer adds, "There is no question that Keller lied about being kidnapped by Chicago and Boston until he was coerced, out of fear of being hanged, to change his story. Why wouldn't what Keller told us not be interpreted by a jury as a lie too. The only reason for us to believe Keller is that he led Captain Burns and his men to the mausoleum."

Leach, O'Conor, and Jenifer know that Keller's confession doesn't get them any closer to capturing Jack Hart or Walter Socolow.

The best outcome is that Keller's admissions support Frank Allers as a states' witness. All conclude that Hart and Socolow have split up and are no longer in Baltimore.

---

7   "Boss" John S. (Frank) Kelly, the leader of the West Baltimore Democratic Club, controlled many of the politicians in and around Baltimore City during the late 19th and early 20th centuries. Leach suspected Kelly of using his connections to protect associates and mobsters like Jim D'Urso.

Despite hundreds of leads and reported sightings, from as far away as Saint Louis, they decide to focus on Washington, D.C. and New York City. As a precaution, they will ask Commissioner Gaither to continue extra police presence at bus and train terminals and for patrolman to keep a sharp eye out for Socolow and Hart who may be traveling separately.

Leach reminds Burns: "It is time to bring in Katherine Connelly."

Battle Monument Square

Originally known as "Courthouse Square," Monument Square was the site of Baltimore's first public buildings—a courthouse and jail, built in 1768. In 1805, the city erected a more substantial, brick courthouse on the site of the current courthouse (built 1894–1900). By the turn of the nineteenth century the square was firmly established as the center of civic life.

The construction of the Battle Monument in 1815–25 to commemorate the soldiers who had died in the Battle of North Point during the War of 1812 underscored the square's importance as a symbol of civic identity and pride. The Battle Monument, together with the Washington Monument in nearby Mount Vernon Place, prompted President John Quincy Adams to refer to Baltimore, in 1827, as "the monumental city."[8]

In 1922, the offices of the Baltimore State's Attorney were on the second floor of the courthouse shown to the left of the Battle Monument. The courthouse is now named in honor of Clarance M. Mitchell, Jr., a prominent civil rights leader.

---

8   From the Maryland State Archives.

18

KATHERINE KAVANAUGH CONNELLY

The following morning, Saturday, August 26th, O'Conor receives a call from Detective Charles Burns. Detectives Kahler and Comen are bringing in Katherine Kavanaugh Connelly for questioning. She was not coming willingly. Kahler had to threaten her with arrest. O'Conor tells Burns to bring her directly to Leach's office. He will meet them there. When they arrive at ten o'clock, Detective Comen excuses himself. He promised to take his kids swimming.

Except for Captain Burns, Lieutenant Kahler, Kitty Connelly, and Herbert O'Conor, Leach's office is empty. Kitty is escorted to a conference room with large casement windows that overlook Lexington Street to the north and Calvert Street to the east. Several windows are open. Wall fans circulate the humid air.

After greeting Mrs. Connelly, O'Conor, wearing a business suit, removes his coat and hangs it over the back of a leather armchair at the head of the conference table. As Detectives Burns and Kahler remove their coats, Burns offers Kitty a cigarette and asks if she would like coffee, ice water, or a Coca Cola.

Kitty replies, "I would love a cigarette and I'll take a Coke."

While Detective Kahler lights her smoke, Burns fetches a Coca Cola from the office refectory and brings it back with a glass of chipped ice.

To make Mrs. Connelly feel more at ease, O'Conor thanks her again for coming. He pulls out a chair next to him and directly across from Burns, holding it until Katherine settles in. Kahler grabs a chair to the right of Burns. Burns and Kahler light cigarettes.

O'Conor, sipping ice water, begins by asking: "Are you comfortable Mrs. Connelly? Would you like anything else?"

Kitty replies, "I'm fine."

O'Conor, looking at Kitty says, "You aren't in any trouble Mrs. Connelly. We just need to know more about your husband, James Connelly, and his motorcar."

Kitty becomes anxious.

Katherine "Kitty" Kavanaugh Connelly is a petite 21-year-old with auburn hair, blue-green Irish eyes, and a sharp tongue. She is visibly annoyed that she has been dragged downtown on a Saturday under threat of being arrested. She should be at work. Kitty tells O'Conor: "I already told your officers that I have no idea why Jimmy registered his car in my name. I don't drive and I haven't seen Jimmy, or his car, in months."

To break the ice and persuade Kitty to be more forthcoming, O'Conor says, "I'm sorry your day has been disrupted. If you would like, when we are finished here, Detective Kahler can drive you home or directly to your job."

Kitty responds, "No, thanks. He can take me home."

Instead of jumping in with questions about her husband, O'Conor, recognizing that Kitty has an Irish legacy, tells her about his grandparents who immigrated from Ireland and his grandfather finding work in the Texas quarry.

He tells her, "I was a choirboy at St. Paul's Parochial School on Caroline Street, not too far from where you grew up."

Then getting to the point, O'Conor says, "We brought you here, Mrs. Connelly, because we need to understand a little more about you, your husband, and his motorcar."

Kitty, less distrustful, begins, "I was raised in Highlandtown in the same house where I was born. I live there with my mother, my brother, and sister. My father died when I was 12."

O'Conor asks, "What is your mother's name?"

Kitty answers, "Mary. My little sister's name is Rachel and my brother Martin is named after my father. My older sister, Anna, is married. She lives with her husband, Sean Quinn, who works at the Broadway Market. I went to Catholic school too, Our Lady of Pompeii Church School on Conklin Street in Highlandtown," then adds, "I work at Epstein's Department Store on Eastern Avenue. I sell cosmetics and toiletries."

"Mr. Epstein," Katherine continues, "offered me a job when I graduated. I've been working at Epstein's ever since. I can't imagine what Mr. Epstein will think if he learns I was picked up by the police. He doesn't know I work nights at Eddie's Supper Club. I might get sacked."

"There is no reason," O'Conor assures Kitty, "to tell Mr. Epstein you were here. If he asks, you were helping us out."

O'Conor asks, "Tell me why your husband's motorcar is registered in your name."

Ignoring the question, Kitty pauses as Detective Kahler helps her light another cigarette, then begins to talk about her life with James Connelly.

"I met Jimmy at Eddie's Supper Club. I serve tables two nights a week – sometimes more if they need me. He was very attentive, a big tipper, and a sharp dresser. We started dating before New Year's—1918. I'm not sure of the exact day, but from the first day we met, Jimmy couldn't keep his eyes off me. When he came to the Club, Jimmy sat at one of my tables until closing. He brought me presents I couldn't afford. He asked me out a hundred times before I said yes."

Kitty reached for a gold cross attached to a delicate gold chain she was wearing as a necklace, then adds, "When he came to the Club, Jimmy showed up with a lot of cash. He was a bighearted spender who made sure all of the girls got some extra dough."

O'Conor asks, "When were you married?"

"We ran off to a Justice of the Piece in Dundalk, the Wednesday before Easter."

O'Conor questions, "1921?"

Kitty answers, "Yes. We moved into Jimmy's two-bedroom apartment at 1732 Fleet Street—near the Broadway Market. I like shopping there. You can buy just about anything. Jimmy loves crab meat. It's always fresh at the market. If his boss isn't around, Sean will cut the price."

O'Conor asks, "Why did you move back home?"

"Not long after we were married," Kitty answers, "Jimmy spent days away from our apartment. When he did come home, it was like before, we went out dancing and partying. I kept my job at the Club. Jimmy kinda liked that. After we were living together, I learned that it was feast or famine. Jimmy had dough, or he didn't.

When he was out of cash, it wasn't fun. I decided to move back home because I didn't like spending so much time alone and I was closer to Epstein's. Jimmy promised that we would move to Washington, where he had business connections. He was there a lot. But we never moved."

"After I returned to my mother's house, I saw more of Jimmy then before. He just (kinda) moved in. He would often be there for breakfast and dinner. But he still came and went as he pleased. My mother didn't mind as long as he kept leaving us money."

Kahler interrupted, saying that "your brother told us that he left you last Christmas."

Kitty answers, "Like I said, he came and went when he pleased. He stopped by the Club a lot. He would tell everyone we were married. Jimmy became jealous if someone paid too much attention to me. One time he punched a guy. I just didn't tell Martin every time I saw Jimmy."

O'Conor asks, "What kind of motorcar does your husband drive?"

Realizing she can no longer duck O'Conor's question, Kitty replies, "It's a sporty yellow coupé."

O'Conor asks, "What year?"

"I don't know." Kitty tells O'Conor, "Jimmy had that car when we met."

O'Conor asks, "Why is your husband's Mercer registered in your maiden name?"

"I don't know. I told your detectives, I don't drive. I never learned."

After taking another drink of water, O'Conor reaches for a file from a valise next to his chair and puts it in front of his place at the table. He opens a folder and pulls out several photographs and slides them over in front of Kitty.

Taking a lingering draw from her cigarette, Kitty becomes unsettled. She looks intently at each picture, even picks one up to examine the photograph more closely but says nothing.

O'Conor asks, "Do you know that man?"

Kitty doesn't look up. She sets the picture back on the table. Mulling over what to say next, she inhales another draw from her cigarette. Then after taking a sip of Coca-Cola, Kitty looks up at O'Conor and admits. "It looks like Jimmy."

O'Conor replies, "No, Mrs. Connelly, it's a man named Jack Hart. You must have seen this picture before. It's been in all the newspapers."

Kitty, becoming uneasy, acknowledges, "Yes, I have seen this picture, but I didn't believe it was Jimmy, just a lookalike."

"Well," O'Conor responds, "It's Jack Hart. Are Jack Hart and your husband, the same man?"

Kitty answers, "They're not the same! I am Mrs. James Connelly, not Mrs. Jack Hart!"

O'Conor, not letting up, questions, "Are you and James Connelly really married?"

Kitty responds, "I am Mrs. James Connelly. I have a marriage license to prove it. You can ask the judge who married us."

Then Kitty asks, "Am I going to be arrested?"

"No," O'Conor responds, "you are not going to be arrested. I believe you about being married to James Connelly. The question is—is your husband Jack Hart. Not knowing what your husband looked like and finding no record of him anywhere, I suspected that Jack Hart and James Connelly were friends or associates or possibly the same person. The car—the Mercer," O'Conor clarifies, "is the link."

Kitty doesn't reply.

O'Conor asks, "Do you know where the Mercer is?"

Kitty says, "I don't."

"When was the last time you saw your husband."

Kitty responds, "He came by the Club three weeks ago and handed me fifty dollars. That was the last time."

O'Conor asks, "Do you have any idea where he is?"

Kitty answers, "I don't. When Jimmy disappeared for days, I never knew where he went. He never said. He loves to talk about his friends in Washington and New York. Maybe he's there, Washington or New York. One of his best friends, a big guy named 'Buck,' lives in Washington. Maybe he's with Buck."

O'Conor asks, "What is Buck's full name?"

Kitty answers, "I can't remember. I only know him as Buck. He has a wife named Dorothy. Buck calls her Dede. They sometimes come to Baltimore to have dinner with Jimmy and me at Anthony's Restaurant in Little Italy. I think Buck and Jimmy are in business together, but I don't know."

O'Conor asks, "Do you know where Buck and Dorothy live in Washington?"

Kitty answers, "I don't."

Although her body language says differently, O'Conor, Burns, and Kahler realize Katherine Connelly is not going to admit her husband is Jack Hart. Without saying it, all three make the connection. Having heard enough, O'Conor ends the interview.

He tells Kitty, "You are free to go," adding, "We may have other questions."

Kitty replies, "I'm not going anywhere."

O'Conor [again] offers to have Detective Kahler drive her home or to Epstein's, whichever she prefers.

Putting out her cigarette in a glass ashtray and anxious to leave, Kitty responds, "Just take me home!"

As Kahler and Kitty depart, O'Conor reminds her, "If you see your husband or his car, let us know."

Kitty nods her head (implying she will).

O'Conor doubts he will hear back from Kitty. "Frankly," O'Conor tells Burns after Kahler and Kitty left, "I'm sure she knows exactly who her husband is and always has. She is probably still in touch with him."

Burns agrees.

"For now," O'Conor tells Burns, "There is no point in arresting Mrs. Connelly. It's unlikely she knows where her husband is. Keep an eye on her. She may lead us to Hart."

"More likely," Burns suggests, "he'll come looking for her."

O'Conor asks Burns to see if Connelly or Hart still rent the 1732 Fleet Street apartment. He also tells Burns to investigate her brother Martin Kavanaugh.

"I think he knows more about Hart then he revealed to your detectives. It sounds like the Kavanaughs are protecting someone. It might be Hart, or it might be Kitty."

Bernard "Buck" Livingston

As Burns and O'Conor leave the courthouse, Burns informs O'Conor that he is sure Buck is Bernard "Buck" Livingston, a thug from D.C. who bootlegs D'Urso's booze in the Capital and to soldiers at Camp Meade. Burns reminds O'Conor that there is a warrant out for his arrest, adding, "The Metropolitan Police are also after Livingston for selling whiskey in the Capital. Mr. Cox[9] is in charge of the case here in Baltimore."

"Now that we know Jack Hart is James Connelly or vice versa," O'Conor instructs Burns, "contact your friend in the New York police department and find out if they have anything on James Connelly. I think you told me his name was Gegan."

Burns responds, "Good memory. It's Lieutenant James Gegan. I'll give Jim a call."

O'Conor tells Burns, "Check out Anthony's Restaurant and the Joseph Kavanaugh Company. Try to track down Socolow's girlfriend, Virginia Williams."

Burns answers, "Kahler and Comen have already been to Virginia William's parents' house. Her parents haven't seen her for several days."

Burns tells O'Conor that he will have his detectives drop in on Anthony's Restaurant and the Joseph Kavanaugh Company first thing next week.

---

9   Fleet W. Cox, Deputy Baltimore City State's Attorney. Fleet W. Cox is the number two prosecutor in the Baltimore State's Attorney's office. Robert Leach appointed Cox, who was an Assistant United States Attorney, his Deputy when he assumed the office of State's Attorney for Baltimore City in 1920. Because of the workload, Cox is overseeing the prosecution of eleven other criminal cases. He has indicted Livingston for bootlegging and robbery in Baltimore. The police have been looking for Livingston for several weeks. Neither the Baltimore or Metropolitan police have been able to locate him and had no idea that Livingston and Hart were connected.

19

REMEMBRANCE

It has been a long ten days since William Norris was murdered. Public outrage hasn't subsided. In fact, it has amplified, and the hundreds of calls to the police have been time consuming. Not a single lead has panned out. Governor Ritchie and Baltimore Mayor Broening have been calling for updates. Leach would like to tell them something encouraging, but there hasn't been much to disclose. The good news is that everyone in Hart's gang, except for Hart and Socolow, is in custody. Charles Country Carey and John Wiggles Smith are about to be tried for murder. But the police are no closer to finding Hart and Socolow then they were on August 19th.

O'Conor decides to take the rest of the day off to be with his wife, Mary Eugenia. Their first child, Herbert Jr., was born on June 19th. For the past three months, O'Conor has hardly laid eyes on his son nor been helpful to Eugenia with Herbie's care. Eugenia, his biggest supporter, never complains about the hours he puts in. The rest of today and all tomorrow are reserved for them.

He received a letter from Sister Mary Romula, who is about to celebrate her sixty-fifth birthday. In 1915, her superiors sent her to a school in Philadelphia. Sister Mary Romula will be visiting her Baltimore cloister at the end of September and hopes her favorite pupil will find time to stop by. O'Conor is looking forward to introducing Eugenia and Herbie to the teacher who had such an impact on his life.

On the drive home, O'Conor's thoughts drift back to Monday, August 21, 1922, four days after Bill Norris was murdered. He, Robert Leach, Commissioner Gaither, Mayor Broening, and Secretary Stuart Janney, Governor Ritchie's chief cabinet member, attended William B. Norris' funeral held at the Norris' home at 508 Beaumont Avenue in Govans. It was a tearful standing room only ceremony. Amidst a plethora of fresh flowers, Bill Norris' mahogany casket was set up in front of the living room fireplace.

At eleven o'clock, the Norris' oldest son, 16-year-old William, Jr., spoke emotionally about his father's life. Pastor Horris Bowen, of the nearby Govans Presbyterian Church, the Norris' church, delivered the eulogy.

A disconsolate Mable Norris, dressed in black, thanked everyone for coming. She didn't expect so many people. She tells Bill's friends and associates that every morning their Labrador Retriever, Gracie, waits for Bill at the front door. She said, "Bills death has been especially tough on their eleven-year-old son Edward."

Bill Norris was buried, later that afternoon, in Woodlawn Cemetery on Woodlawn Drive in Baltimore County. Uniformed members of Knights Templers (Corinthian Lodge Number 98) where Norris was a member, served as pallbearers. Fifty-two members of the Boumi Temple Commandry escorted the flag draped coffin to the cemetery. O'Conor remembers a weeping Mable Norris placing flowers on her husband's casket.

Mayor Borening, Commissioner Gaither, and Robert Leach knew Bob Hicks and Ed Tate. The three officials plus Herbert O'Conor spent some time updating Norris' partners about what had taken place since the crime.

Both the Mayor and Commissioner expressed their condolences. Secretary Janney had been a Colonel in the Army during the recent Great War. In September 1918, Janney distinguished himself in the month-and-a-half-long Battle of the Argon Forest that was fought along the Western Front. Before Governor Ritchie was elected, Colonel Janney was his law partner. One of Janney's undertakings is to strengthen law enforcement throughout

Maryland. Janney was there to represent Governor Ritchie who was committed to a meeting in Washington, D.C. O'Conor was impressed by the plain-spoken stately Colonel that he met for the first time.

Leach took a few minutes to let Bob Hicks and Ed Tate know that there is a nationwide dragnet out for Socolow and Hart. "We haven't caught them yet," Leach admitted with the Mayor and Commissioner looking on, "but be assured we will."

Leach explained that they plan to go ahead and try John Smith and Charles Carey saying, "They have been indicted for murder. Their trials will be expedited—either in Baltimore City or Towson. It hasn't been decided."

O'Conor thought about the austere looking Mr. Hicks confessing that he couldn't get over Bill being murdered, and that poor Fred Kuethe was almost killed. Hicks broke down lamenting that he could never have imagined such a thing. He and Ed Tate thanked Broening, Gaither, Leach, and O'Conor for pursuing the killers with such zeal. Leach reiterated, "Jack Hart and Walter Socolow will be caught, tried for murder, and convicted."

Before parting, Ed Tate told O'Conor that he had learned from the company's receptionist that a brick mason employed by Hicks Tate and Norris until recently, named Johnny Jubb, had become friends with the Fulton Laundry truckdriver who had been arrested.

O'Conor told Tate, "We will have the police locate and question Mr. Jubb."

20

NEXT STEPS

On Monday, August 28, seven days after William Norris was laid to rest and two days following O'Conor's interview with Kitty Connelly, Captain of Detectives Charles Burns meets with the policemen most responsible for tracking down Hart's gang, Sergeant Bill Murphy, Lieutenant Charles Kahler, Detective James Comen, and most recently, Detective William Hammersla. The purpose of the meeting is to review and act on the information gained during Saturday's interview with Katherine "Kitty" Connelly.

Police Commissioner Gaither removed Police Captain John Leverton from the case last Friday afternoon, August 25, the day O'Conor had Murphy arrest John Keller.

Leach assigned his deputy, Fleet W. Cox, to investigate the relationship between Leverton and Harry Wolf. Leach, Cox, and O'Conor are certain that Leverton and Wolf colluded to throw the pursuit of Socolow and Hart off track.

Burns informs his detectives, "Katherine 'Kitty' Kavanaugh identified herself as Mrs. Katherine Connelly and reluctantly admitted (more accurately didn't deny) that her estranged husband is Jack Hart. She claims that she did not suspect this before meeting with Mr. O'Conor, Charles[10] and me at the courthouse."

Burns tells his unit, "We believe Mrs. Connelly is covering for her husband. There is no proof. Mrs. Connelly denies she knows the whereabouts of her husband or his Mercer."

"Despite what she says, I think she still has strong feelings for her husband. She disclosed that he continues to give her money.

---

10 Baltimore City Police Lieutenant Charles Kahler.

The whole family claims that when they saw pictures of Hart in newspapers, they didn't recognize Hart was Connelly. "If," Burns sarcastically adds, "you can believe that whopper!"

Burns tells Detectives Kahler and Comen, "Check out Anthony's Restaurant in Little Italy. Mrs. Connelly revealed that she and her husband had dinner there with our old friend Bernard Buck Livingston and his wife. She remembered Buck's wife's name is Dorothy and that Buck calls her Dede."

"Mrs. Connelly," Burns adds, "couldn't remember that Buck's last name is Livingston. O'Conor didn't tell Mrs. Connelly that the man she identified as Buck is the gangster we know as Bernard Livingston."

Turning to Sergeant Murphy, "Bill—you will be our liaison with the Metropolitan Police. There's a good chance Hart has hooked up with Buck Livingston somewhere in the Capital."

Burns further instructs Murphy: "You and I will visit the Joseph Kavanaugh Company. Joe Kavanaugh, the owner, is Katherine Kavanaugh's uncle. Her brother, Martin, said James Connelly sometimes parks his Merser there. We need to find out if it's there now. I want to talk to Joe Kavanaugh about any business he might be doing with Hart."

"The Joseph Kavanaugh Company," Burns continues, "is a metal fabrication business. I can't imagine what Hart would need from them, but we'll find out."

Speaking to Detective Hammersla, Burns says: "Check out James and Kitty Connelly's 1732 Fleet Street apartment and locate Virginia "Shorts" Williams. Begin by revisiting her parents."

Burns adds, "Track down Johnny Jubb who recently quit his job as a bricklayer at Hicks Tate and Norris. The company payroll department has Jubb's address listed at 5 North Curley Street.

Evidently Jubb and Buddy Blades are tight."

Burns tells Hammersla, "Fleet Cox wants you to stop by his office."

Hammersla asks, "Why?"

"Cox is interested in learning more about your visit to Harry Wolf's house on August 18th.

Hammersla replies, "I'll head there after the meeting."

Burns, addressing his squad, says "Last Saturday (August 26th), following the interview with Mrs. Connelly, I called New York Police Detective Lieutenant James Gegan. I've known Jim for years. I asked him to see what he could find out about James Connelly. I explained we are sure James Connelly is Jack Hart."

"Jim said that he would get on it and added that since he started looking for Jack Hart, the New York police have uncovered no less than 54 previously arrested criminals using the last name of Hart. I'm anticipating a call from Gegan today or tomorrow."

Murphy speaks up, saying, "New York has had pictures and descriptions of Hart and Socolow since August 19th. If Connelly has a record in New York, wouldn't they have already surmised that Hart and Connelly are one in the same."

Burns responds, "A lot of people in Baltimore know Connelly. He was out in the open and a big spender. He is married to Kitty Kavanaugh. Obviously the two of them weren't hiding. Mrs. Kavanaugh admitted they spent time in Little Italy where they joined Buck Livingston and his wife for dinner. No one identified either Hart or Livingston or, if they did, was willing to come forward. This might be the case in New York."

Burns adds, "All of you keep an eye on Eddie's Hylandtown Supper Club, the speakeasy where Kitty Connelly works on Wednesday and Friday nights. When you do, keep a low profile. If Hart wants to see his wife, he might try to catch up with her there."

Most of Burns' squad agree that Hart and Socolow are no longer in Baltimore. Their best guess is Washington D.C. or New York City.

With that, Burns tells his unit: "Let's hit the streets!"

Eddie's Hylandtown Supper Club, a basement backstreet speakeasy off Eaton Street in southeast Baltimore, circa 1922, is where Kitty Kavanaugh, working as a hostess on Wednesday and Friday nights, met James Connelly (aka Jack Hart) shortly before New Year's Eve, 1918. Speakeasies like Eddie's Supper Club depended on mobsters like "Boss" Vincenzo "Jim" D'Urso or freelancers like Jack Hart and Buck Livingston for their supply of beer and whiskey. Hart and Livingston would always make sure D'Urso got a hefty cut. As long as freelancers like Hart and Livingston stuck to bootlegging, gambling and prostitution (and were straight with D'Urso and his Baltimore Crew) they could count on Boss Jim's protection. The robbery and murder of a business-man, the stature of William Norris, was another matter.

21

ANTHONY'S ITALIAN RESTAURANT

*Detective James Comen (left) and
Detective Lieutenant Charles Kahler (right)*

By 10:00 a.m., Detectives Kahler and Comen are knocking on the door of Anthony's Italian Restaurant, located on High Street in little Italy. Mia Borrelli, Anthony Borrelli's short, full-bodied wife, invites them in. Anthony and Mia Borrelli are the proprietors. Anthony, locally famous for his Italian cuisine, spends most of his time in the kitchen. The effervescent Mia is the restaurant's indispensable hostess.

The Borrelli's and their staff of ten are getting ready for the lunch rush. Mia leads the two detectives into the restaurant's main dining room. Within minutes, Kahler, Comen, Anthony, and Mia are sitting at one of the tables in the converted rowhouse living room. Three of the staff, who Mia identifies as their daughter and two nephews, are scurrying about attending tables. Mia asks the detectives if they would like a glass of wine. Kahler and Comen decline, but would appreciate some ice water and ask would she mind if they smoked? Mia invites the detectives to light up and sends her daughter to fetch a pitcher of cold water.

Both Anthony and Mia are the children of Italian immigrants. Anthony's father is the restaurant's founder and although he has just turned 80, Papa Borrelli is there every night helping in the kitchen. By nine o'clock, he runs out of steam and retires to the house next door, where he and his wife Mirabella have lived for 40 years.

Until they passed away two years before, only weeks apart, Mia's parents had lived in Little Italy too. Anthony and Mia moved into her parent's home, located a block south on Exeter Street. Kahler and Comen soon learn that the Borrelli's know everybody in Little Italy and apparently just about everyone in Baltimore.

Mia lets Kahler and Comen know she can't help but remember Buck Livingston and Jim Connelly. They are regulars. Pointing to a table near a window overlooking High Street, Mia tells the detectives, "Mr. Buck and Mr. Jim insist on that table."

Kahler knows that the wine (individuals or restaurants, like Anthony's, stowed away prior to prohibition) is legal to consume until pre-prohibition stockpiles are depleted. But three years later, Anthony's still offers a tolerable Chianti. If questioned why the wine never runs out, Anthony's answer would be the same as for any of the restaurants in Little Italy. They were lucky to have a good supply left over. Kahler doesn't ask but understands that wine is available on the black market. Buck Livingston, before going into hiding, might have been Anthony's supplier.

The Borrelli's won't admit this even if it's true. Compared to the abysmal crime that festers throughout the city, because of mobsters settling scores, wine consumption in Little Italy is a minor transgression.

No matter how many questions Kahler and Comen put to Anthony and Mia about Buck Livingston and James Connelly, the Borrelli's answers are always the same. Other than being loyal *clientele*, the Borrelli's insist that they don't know much about Livingston's or Connelly's personal lives. The two good tippers simply enjoy spending time and money at Anthony's. Sometimes they bring friends, every once in a while, their wives.

Anthony and Mia hardly remember Kitty Connelly. Mia says, "She is an attractive young woman who has only been here two or three times. Buck's wife, Dede, is here more often. Sometimes she comes without Mr. Buck. When she does, Mrs. Livingston is accompanied by a pretty, well-dressed woman about the same age." But Mia Borrelli can't recall the name of Mrs. Livingston's friend.

Without asking anything more, Kahler and Comen thanked the Borrelli's for their time. Comen hands Mia a card saying, "Please give us a call if Mr. Livingston or Mr. Connelly return. We would appreciate knowing if Mrs. Livingston or her friend return. They may want to talk to us."

Mia smiling says, "Both of you are welcome to drop in anytime for dinner. Bring your wives and children. You will get *un prezzo molto speciale*."

When Comen asked what that means, Mia says, "For you, a special price," then adds, "Our tagliatelle with Bolognese sauce is the best in town."

Thanking Mia for her invitation, the two detectives head back to their car. On the way to Fayette Street, to catch up with Murphy and Burns, Comen looks over at Kahler and quips, "Looks like Mrs. Livingston isn't all that happy with Big Buck."

Kahler wisecracks, "Who would be?"

Kahler reminds Comen, "Last Saturday, in Leach's office, Kitty Connelly told O'Conor, Burns, and me that Dede was the name of Buck's wife."

Detectives Kahler and Comen will keep in touch with Anthony and Mia Borrelli. Maybe Dede Livingston will show up.

Besides, Kahler and Comen love Italian food.

On a Hunch

Detective William Hammersla catches up with Deputy Baltimore City State's Attorney, Fleet W. Cox, in Cox's courthouse office at ten o'clock. Hammersla has already been briefed about John Keller's conflicting statements during his August 24th and 25th interrogations. He wasn't surprised by anything he heard. Hammersla has known Harry Wolf for years. He has arrested some of the racketeers Wolf represents.

After greeting one another, Cox asks Detective Hammersla, "What was your reason for visiting Harry Wolf, at his home, the night of the crime on August 18th?"

Hammersla answers, "There was no way Wolf could know that Lewis and Smith had been arrested in Essex earlier in the day. I wanted to see Wolf's reaction when he found out that several of his former clients were suspects in the robbery and murder. I went to Wolf's house 'on a hunch.'"

"What did Mr. Wolf tell you?"

Hammersla explains, "despite being on opposite sides of the law, Wolf always treats me as if we were friends. It's part of his disingenuous charm. After Wolf opened the door and greeted me like an old pal," Hammersla tells Cox, "I advised him about the arrest of Benny Lewis and John Smith. Wolf said that he wasn't surprised. I asked him if he still represented Jack Hart or Walter Socolow. Wolf said he didn't. He was adamant that he didn't know anything about the robbery and couldn't imagine who would be so brazen or stupid to pull off such a crime. If he learned anything, he said he would call. He told me he was sick and needed to go to bed. After he went back inside, I left."

Cox brings up what Hammersla already knows: During his interrogation at City Jail, Keller divulged that Wolf had hidden him and Socolow in his kitchen pantry. "Did you suspect anyone was in the house other than Mr. Wolf?"

Hammersla answers, "I had no way of knowing that. I never suspected Socolow was in the house and wouldn't have given any thought to Keller."

Cox asks, "Do you know anything about the relationship between Captain Leverton and Mr. Wolf?"

Hammersla responds, "I know Captain Leverton and Harry Wolf have been close for years—since Wolf ran for office. I keep my distance from both of them."

Cox asks why.

"Captain Leverton and I are different kinds of cops and except for feeling him out on August 18th, I had no other reason to call on Wolf."

Cox says, "I understand." In a cordial ending to their meeting, Cox, expressing congratulations, reveals that he has heard Hammersla is about to be promoted to Lieutenant of Detectives. "Bill - it's well deserved."

Hammersla thanks Cox for his support but cautions, "I'm still waiting to hear from the Commissioner. Captain Burns has me busy following up on leads. The $10,000 reward," Hammersla jests, "seems to have turned half the country into private eyes."

Cox thanks Hammersla for stopping by, "Please keep in touch."

Hammersla answers, "I will," then shakes Cox's hand and heads back to the police building.

22
FIND ONE – FIND THE OTHER

The following day, Tuesday, August 29, at 8:00 a.m., Burns' squad gathers again in Captain Burns' office. Detectives Kahler, Comen, Murphy, and Hammersla share what they uncovered the day before. Given the exposed relationship between Buck Livingston and James Connelly (a.k.a. Jack Hart), Burns wants to double down on efforts to locate Buck Livingston. Both he and Murphy have been in communication with the Washington, D.C. Metropolitan police to let them know that Livingston and Hart know one another and appear to be cohorts in the distribution of illegal whiskey.

"There is a good chance," Murphy adds, "that either Hart or Socolow or both are holed-up in the Capital."

Murphy arranged a call between Commissioner Gaither, Burns and Metropolitan Police Chief, Henry G. Pratt. Burns said he told Chief Pratt the same thing he told Detective Murphy. "If we find Livingston, there is a good chance we'll find Jack Hart."

Pratt assured Commissioner Gaither that Baltimore would get his department's full cooperation.

Commissioner Gaither and Captain Burns assigned Murphy to go to the Capital and meet with Chief Pratt to synchronize their collaboration in tracking down Hart, Socolow, and Livingston. Gaither conveyed to Chief Pratt that there is a good chance all three are in the District.

"It's also an opportunity," Murphy tells his colleagues, "to catch up with Detective Lieutenant Richard 'Dick' Mansfield, who has been working with [us] to apprehend Hart and Socolow." Murphy has known Detective Mansfield since 1914.

Henry G. Pratt
Chief of Metropolitan Police

New York City Police Lieutenant James Gegan

Burns informs his squad that New York Police Lieutenant James Gegan got back to him about James Connelly.

"Connelly and Hart, Gegan confirmed, are the same man. In fact, Gegan told me, James Connelly is Hart's real name. Connelly has also gone under the names of Jack Holt and George A. Stewart."

"Connelly's criminal history began when he was 16 and sentenced to a reformatory for gang activities that included running errands for the mob, theft, and assault. He was released when he turned 18 and returned to New York's criminal underworld. Gegan said Connelly was thought to be one of the most notorious killers in their files. But added, it's hard to prove."

"Twelve years after being released and steadily rising in New York's gangland hierarchy, Connelly began to work with a notorious hit man Gegan said was known to the police as 'Jumbo' Wells."

"Connelly began a relationship with Well's girlfriend, a gin joint dancer named Peggy. When Wells found out, he went after Connelly. During a heated altercation, Jumbo pulled his gun and opened fired. He missed. Connelly shot back. The bullet from

Connelly's gun struck Wells in the chest. Wells bled out, choking on his own blood, on the seedy hallway floor of Peggy's Bronx apartment building."

"Connelly," Burns continues' "was arrested and charged with second degree murder. Because of the circumstances, mobster against mobster and witnesses confirming Wells fired first, Connelly was only convicted of manslaughter. He was sentenced to two years in Sing-Sing. When Connelly was let out in 1917, he vanished. Since there was no outstanding warrant for his arrest," Gegan said, "Connelly slipped through the cracks."

"Connelly's mother died in 1916 and wasn't married. He has an older brother named Thomas who is married and lives in Trenton, New Jersey. Gegan had a Trenton associate, Detective Sergeant Edward Fox, drop in on Thomas Connelly. Fox reported that Thomas works for the Trenton Iron Company and has not seen or spoken to his brother in years, not since he was imprisoned for killing Jumbo Wells."

"Their father, according to Thomas, abandoned the family when he and James were boys. From then on, getting by was a struggle for the Connellys. When he was 14, Thomas told Fox, James began hanging around with a bad crowd out of the Fort Greene neighborhood in Brooklyn. James was arrested when he was sixteen and imprisoned. After James was released, he returned to the mob. Worrying about James, Thomas believes, led to their mother's demise."

"Gegan doesn't believe Connelly will show up at his brother's house. Nevertheless, Sergeant Fox will keep an eye out. One more thing, when Connelly was in Sing-Sing his two front teeth were reported chipped during a prison-yard scuffle."

"This makes sense," Burns, then reading from Hart's arrest profile continues, "According to this report, Jack Hart was first arrested in Baltimore on June 24, 1917, along with some of Jimmy

D'Urso's heavies. His arrest profile lists Hart as *five-foot eight and one-quarter inches tall, 157 lbs., light chestnut to reddish hair, eyes – Azure blue, nose – medium, arms – freckled, forehead – high with a receding hair line and two upper front gold capped incisors on either side of his front teeth that were chipped."*

"According to Lieutenant Gegan, this was an accurate description of Connelly, minus the two gold teeth. Connelly was released from Sing-Sing on March 15, 1917."

Detective Keller asks, "Should we make Katherine Connelly aware of her husband's criminal record in New York?"

Burns answers, "I have already discussed this with Mr. Leach. Leach thinks she probably already knows. His office must prove that Hart and Connelly are the same person. For now, we are looking for Jack Hart. Leach's office will deal with his identity after he's caught."

The Baltimore City Police Building (circa 1922) was located at 600 East Fayette Street, near City Hall and the Courthouse. This view is of the building's east façade with its attached parking platform.

Charles "Country" Carey and Benny Louis were brought here from the Essex Jail and turned over to Baltimore Police Captain of Detectives, Charles Burns on August 18, 1922. They were transported to the Baltimore City Jail, located at 400 East Madison Street.

The building was demolished in 1984 and replaced.

113

23

THE CALL

On Thursday August 31st, a Baltimore Police Headquarters switchboard officer fields a call about Jack Hart. It was one of a dozen calls that morning transferred to Burns, Murphy or Kahler. Detective Murphy took the call.

A woman identifying herself as (Dorothy) wanted to know if the $10,000 reward for the apprehension of Jack Hart and Walter Socolow was still being offered. Murphy replied that it was if both fugitives were captured. Before Murphy could say anything more, the woman hung up.

Remembering that Mrs. Connelly revealed that Dorothy was the name of Buck Livingston's wife and that Mia Borrelli later disclosed that Buck Livingston called his wife Dede, Murphy knew this wasn't another dead-end call. This Dorothy had something to say but for whatever reason hung up.

Murphy called back to the switchboard to see if the line could be reconnected. The operator's reply was that she could not reconnect the call. Murphy asked if the caller left a name (possibly Dede or Livingston) or a contact number. Again, the answer was no.

After Murphy reported the call to Burns and Kahler, Burns let O'Conor know that Detective Murphy had received a call from a woman named Dorothy asking about the reward.

Burns told O'Conor, "The lady hung up without divulging her last name or address. I think it's unlikely she will call back."

O'Conor wasn't so sure. "We may still hear from this Dorothy."

24

MAKING THE CONNECTIONS

New York City Police Detective James Gegan

NYPD Bomb Squad Detective Lieutenant James Gegan
led the search for Hart and Socolow in New York City

On Friday, September 1, 1922, Captain of Detectives Burns boards a train to New York to meet with New York City Police Lieutenant James Gegan and detectives Christopher Kelly and Cornelius Browne.

"There is a good chance," Burns tells the New York detectives, "Jack Hart and Walter Socolow are in New York City. When we entered the Sweet Home Cemetery mausoleum, we found train and bus schedules with District of Columbia and New York departure times circled."

Burns updates the three New York detectives on the progress of the case and tells them about John Squeaky Keller's implausible fiction about Chicago and Boston. "Unfortunately, our main witness is a convicted thief and bootlegger named Frank Allers."

"We think Hart and Socolow," Burns discloses, "are no longer in Baltimore. Hart must still have friends in New York. It makes sense that he and Socolow would come here."

Gegan responds, "If they're here, we'll find them."

Gegan assures Burns, "All of New York's patrolmen are on the lookout and detectives are pressing their sources. It's unlikely either Hart or Socolow have traveled too far, especially out west where they don't know anybody. If they have any sense, they've separated; but either way, I'll bet both are somewhere between Baltimore and New York City."

Washington, D.C. – September 2, 1922

Commissioner Gaither and Detective Murphy have a similar get-together with Metropolitan Police Chief, Henry G. Pratt, Detective Richard "Dick" Mansfield, Lieutenant Frank McCatheran, and other Metropolitan Police officers assigned to the case. The difference being that in addition to Hart and Socolow, in the Capital, they are looking for Buck Livingston and his wife.

Virginia Williams

Virginia Williams

Detective Bill Hammersla located Virginia "Shorts" Williams. She had returned to her parents' house on East Bond Street. After

116

questioning Virginia, Hammersla reported that she is a frightened and introverted girl.

Hammersla said, "Shorts is well named. She isn't five feet tall. She has neck length light brown curly hair and brown eyes."

"Her mother persuaded Virginia to sit with me on their porch. I let her know that she wasn't in any trouble." Hammersla told his fellow detectives, "I was only at the Williams' house for a half hour. Virginia Williams was helpful when it came to the time she spent with Walter Socolow on August 17th, the day before the robbery. Williams confirmed that she, Keller, and Socolow went to a picture show and afterward returned to Smith's Broadway House. But this is where her recollection of events differs from Keller's. She said she became frightened when she found herself surrounded by Walter's friends, who were smoking, drinking, and carrying on. She left Smith's house as soon as she could get away and walked four blocks east to a former classmate's house on Washington Street. Her classmate, Margaret McCarthy, and Williams were friends who she said often spent the night at each other's homes."

"Virginia said she had no idea what happened after that. She didn't hear from Socolow the next day and did not learn that he had been involved in the robbery and murder until Mrs. McCarthy showed her the evening edition of the Baltimore News American. The headline was about the search for Jack Hart and Walter Socolow."

"After that, she was afraid Socolow would come looking for her. She was fearful people would think she had something to do with the robbery. If Socolow was on the run, she didn't want him dragging her along."

"Williams confessed that she regrets worrying her parents but thought Socolow might try to find her at her parents' house. She had no idea Socolow was hiding in Sweet Home Cemetery until it was reported in the paper. She admitted that she and Socolow had been at the cemetery to look inside mausoleums. She said that Walter's pranks often frightened her, but they had a lot of fun together when he wasn't with his friends trying to be a big shot."

"I told Virginia and her mother that it was unlikely Walter would risk coming to their house. He would know the police were watching."

Hammersla continued, "I visited and talk to Mrs. McCarthy to verify William's story. Mrs. McCarthy confirmed that what Virginia Williams said was true. When she read about the manhunt for Socolow and Hart in the newspaper, she thought it was a good idea for Virginia to stay for a few days."

Jack Hart's Fleet Street Apartment

Hammersla reported that his visit to the apartment building, at 1732 Fleet Street, was a dead end. "In 1919, the apartment was rented to James Connelly. The manager said Connelly moved out in March 1922, at the end of his lease. All he knew was that Connelly left after he was married. He paid his rent in cash. The apartment is now rented to a Hopkins doctor."

Johnny Jubb

Johnny Jubb

Hammersla informed Burns and the members of his squad that he visited Johnny Jubb's house at 5 North Curley Street on Thursday, August 31ˢᵗ. The small (12-foot wide) inside rowhouse was unoccupied. The next-door neighbor told Hammersla that Jubb and his family (wife and two children) had not been home for days.

"The neighbor told me that the Jubbs have lived on the street for four years and that Johnny has had more jobs than you can count. He was unaware that Jubb had worked for Hicks Tate and Norris."

"Later in the day, I located Johnny Jubb, his wife Edna, and their two children at 2406 East Fayette Street. The house belongs to Raymond Jubb, Sr. and his wife Ellen, Johnny Jubb's parents."

"Jubb told me that he had worked for Hicks Tate and Norris as a mason. He had also helped at Madison Street where building materials are stored on the first floor and in the basement."

"Jubb admitted that he was friends with Buddy Blades and acknowledged bouncing from job to job. He is losing his house on Curley Street because he is behind on payments. He quit his job at Hicks Tate and Norris, anyway, telling me, 'It was time to move on.'"

"I knew from speaking with Ed Tate at Mr. Norris' funeral, Jubb had quit. I wanted to know why he walked out the day after the robbery."

"Jubb said that after learning Buddy Blades had been arrested, he didn't want his friendship with Blades to link him to the robbery. He revealed that Buddy asked a lot of questions about the company. Blades introduced him to Benny Lewis, George Heard, and John Carey at the Belle Grove Inn."

Everyone on Burns' squad was familiar with the Belle Grove Inn. The police considered it a seedy hangout for rabblerousers. On July 11ᵗʰ, a fight broke out inside the Belle Grove that spilled out onto Annapolis Boulevard. One gangster was killed. Three others were too badly injured to flee before the police arrived.

"I asked Jubb," Hammersla continued, "if he knew about the gun fight at the Bell Grove Inn. Was he involved? Jubb said, he wasn't. After he heard about the shootout, he never went back."

"Jubb swore he didn't set up Mr. Norris. He said Mr. Norris always treated him well. He complained that Buddy took advantage of their friendship. Jubb said, he would never be involved in a robbery, much less, where he worked."

"I came away believing that Jubb was either duped by Blades or purposefully told Blades about Norris' Friday morning visits to Commonwealth Bank. But because we arrested Blades the day after the crime," Hammersla speculates, "he never had a chance to pay Jubb off. One way or another Jubb set up Mr. Norris."

25

THE JOSEPH KAVANAUGH COMPANY

On Friday September 7th, Burns and Murphy drive to the Joseph Kavanaugh Company located on Lynhurst Road in Sparrows Point. Joe Kavanaugh, an average size balding man about 60 years of age, with a thick mustache, is dressed in coveralls. When Kavanaugh realized Burns and Murphy were Baltimore City Police detectives, he whisks them into his small unkempt office with interior windows that looked out over the shop.

Joe Kavanaugh tells Burns and Murphy that they are coppersmiths. "We manufacture kettles for the candy, can food, and beverage industries, any company that cooks something. Prior to Prohibition, we did a lot of work for distilleries and breweries. We still have plenty of business. I employ 15 metalworkers including my four sons. You can see for yourselves how busy we are."

Burns asks, "Are you related to Katherine Kavanaugh Connelly?"

Joe responds, "Mary Kavanaugh is my sister-in-law and Kitty is my goddaughter. I am very fond of my brother's family. My brother died years ago. I do my best to help out. My nephew, Martin, makes deliveries and helps with installations."

Murphy asks, "Has Katherine's husband ever worked for or purchased something from your company?"

Joe answers, "No—I don't know Jimmy that well. He would stop by with Kitty or Martin. He hasn't been here for quite a while. We never did anything for him. I have no idea what he does for a living." "Epstein's, where Kitty works," Kavanaugh continues, "sells our copper cooking pots. Jimmy and Kitty would deliver our copper wares there. But that's about it."

Burns presses, "Your nephew Martin told our detectives that Jim Connelly sometimes parks his Mercer Raceabout here and that you may have worked together on something. Is this true?"

Joe responds, "I don't know where he got that idea. Jimmy left his car here a few times before he and Kitty split up, but we've never worked together. He's my niece's husband. That's it. He delivered a few pots. Is that a crime?"

Burns keeping up the pressure shows Kavanaugh a picture of Jack Hart. "Mr. Kavanaugh, have you ever seen this man before?"

Noticeably anxious, Kavanaugh answers, "No!"

Burns continues. "It's a picture of Jack Hart. Ever heard of him?"

Kavanaugh answers, "Everyone's heard of Jack Hart, but that's not Jimmy."

"I didn't say it was, but it sounds like you think it might be."

Edgy and on the defensive, Joe Kavanaugh snaps back. "I never met Jack Hart. He was never here. If I knew where he was, I would ask for the reward. But I don't!"

Realizing old Joe knew a lot more about Hart than he was saying and, in fear of being arrested, was about to wet his pants, Burns insists that Kavanaugh show him and Detective Murphy around his company. "We'd like to see what you do and talk to a few of your employees, including your sons. Is that okay?"

Pausing for a moment, a break from near hysteria, Joe realized he didn't have a choice. If he said no, Burns would return with a warrant.

Joseph Kavanaugh Company operates out of a brick and clapboard, wood framed one-story building (with an elevated storage loft) located in the middle of an industrial neighborhood on Baltimore's east side near Gunther Brewery and Bethlehem Steel.

It's a wide-open workplace with a large central manufacturing floor. Murphy estimates between 12,000 and 15,000 square feet. There are several furnaces and mechanical hammers needed to shape copper kettles and pots, even copper plates for the bottom of ships.

Murphy notices a partially concealed metal door and asks, "Where does this go?"

Joe answers, "The building has a basement that is only used for storage."

Burns replies, "Let's take a look."

Joe Kavanaugh leads Burns and Murphy down a wooden stairway into a dark humid (basement) chamber that reeks with the strong aroma of whiskey. Empty whiskey barrels are stacked against a stone wall next to a large coal furnace. A sizeable wooden coal bin on the south side of the furnace is connected to a shoot that opens to the street above. Fragments of disassembled copper pots and tubes, that looked to Murphy and Burns like still components, are piled up.

Murphy asks, "What are these?"

Joe Kavanaugh explains, "We did a lot of distillery work before Prohibition. The barrels, copper cuts and whiskey smell are remnants of that. We manufactured metal bands for the whiskey barrels we assembled. The barrels are leftover."

Murphy comments, "I'm surprised such a strong whiskey smell would linger for three years."

Joe explains, "In this enclosed area with no windows, it certainly would."

Burns asked, "Were you producing whiskey for James Connelly?"

Kavanaugh, noticeably agitated, replies, "Absolutely not! I told you we have more legal business then we can handle."

Interrupting, Burns asks, "Did you know, Mr. Kavanaugh, [that] Hart was selling bootleg whiskey?"

Joe fires back, "Well he didn't get it from here! I don't know how many times I can say it. I never met Jack Hart!"

Burns didn't respond. Pointing to the stairway he says, "We're done here. Let's head up."

Back in the shop, Burns and Murphy ask all four of Joe's sons if they were in the whiskey business with James Connelly or knew Jack Hart. The responses were the same. Kavanaughs never produced whiskey. It's illegal. Yes, they know James Connelly, their cousin Kitty's husband. They don't know what he does for a living. Like everyone in Baltimore, they have read about Jack Hart. But that's as far as it goes.

Burns tells Kavanaugh, "We've seen enough. If you hear from James Connelly, we expect you to give us a call."

Kavanaugh answers, "I don't expect to hear from Jimmy."

As Murphy hands Kavanaugh a contact card, he says, "I don't suppose you will."

Driving back to Fayette Street, Burns, and Murphy agree that the link between Joseph Kavanaugh Company and James Connelly is whiskey. It was being distilled in the basement.

Burns and Murphy believe Kitty Connelly, her mother, brother, and sisters all know about James Connelly's illicit sideline. More than that, they know he is Jack Hart. Except for the lingering whiskey smell, Joe and his crew did a good job of eliminating the evidence. But Burns and Murphy have raided the same kind of backroom distillery before.

They have learned enough to believe Jack Hart and Joe Kavanaugh were business partners. At the same time, they are sure that Joe and his sons have no idea where Hart is. They can deal with the Kavanaughs down the road. What happens to them is up to Mr. Leach.

Joe Kavanaugh (far right) with family and friends (circa 1922)

26

ROUNDING THE BASES

Monday, September 11 – So far there are no breakthroughs in the search for Jack Hart and Walter Socolow. There have been hundreds of false sightings and leads that Burns' detectives have arduously run down. There was no call back from a woman named Dorothy. The Burns unit, as well as uniformed police assigned to Burns, have kept an eye on Kitty Connelly's mother's Glover Street house, Epstein's Department Store on Eastern Avenue, Eddies Highlandtown Supper Club off South Eaton Street, Virginia Williams' parents' house, Johnny Jubb, the Belle Grove Inn, and the Joseph Kavanaugh Company to no avail.

Detectives Kahler and Comen have stopped by Anthony's Restaurant to speak with Mia Borrelli who had nothing more to add other than to ask them when they were coming to dinner. And although everyone in the police department has been searching for it, Hart's yellow Mercer is still missing.

Burns' detectives, along with Baltimore City and Baltimore County police officers including Captain Andrew Coppin along with Sergeant Walter and Officer Tom Hagerty, who arrested Benny Lewis and Wiggles Smith in Essex, have been to George Heard's farm.

The neglected shingled and gabled farmhouse, barn and several outbuildings were searched for evidence. The first floor of the house had been occupied and left unattended. The kitchen was a mess. Dirty dishes were piled up. Wastebaskets overflowed with discarded refuse. A horde of houseflies were buzzing about, feasting on a smorgasbord of garbage.

The four small rooms on the first floor were unkempt. Empty bottles, cans and plates, ashtrays full of cigarette buts, newspapers, clothing, and boxes full of magazines and plain junk were scattered about.

Ashes in the living room fireplace contained bits of scorched currency bands. As the house was uncomfortably hot, the fire was a clear attempt to destroy anything connected to Commonwealth Bank.

Wooden boxes of illegal whiskey were hidden under a pile of straw in the farm's dilapidated barn along with a rusted Frick Company tractor and thrasher, a wobbly dust-covered horse-drawn wagon, moldy horse tack and half-filled burlap sacks of rotting grain. It was apparent, other than as a hiding place for whiskey, the barn hadn't been used in years. There were no clues that might lead to the apprehension of Jack Hart or Walter Socolow. The county police destroyed the whiskey and padlocked the buildings.

Baltimore City police were regularly checking Smith's rented Broadway House and, after Keller identified it, Charles Country Carey's Durham Street rowhouse.

Kahler and Comen were also tailing Captain Leverton who seemed to be aware that he was under suspicion. Avoiding Harry Wolf, his routine was reduced to traveling from his house in Arbutus to the Southern District and back.

Harry Wolf was also being watched. On Tuesday, September 4th, Wolf asked to visit John Keller at the Penitentiary. Because he insisted that he didn't represent Keller, the visit was denied by Warden Sweezey. When Wolf's request to visit Keller was reported to Leach and O'Conor, the consensus was that Wolf was getting nervous about what Keller might have revealed. No one from Leach's office made any effort to contact Wolf. Leach told O'Conor, "Best to keep him guessing."

While Robert Leach, Courtenay Jenifer, and Herbert O'Conor were following police efforts to ferret out Hart and Socolow, they were also preparing the case against Charles Carey and John Smith.

Carey's and Smith's attorneys had tried to get their clients out on bail, but at Leach's request, bail and writ of *habeas corpus* petitions were denied. None of the others arrested had retained attorneys or had been able to make bail.

Frank Allers and John Keller are separately isolated from each other and the members of Hart's gang. Both Allers and Keller have been interviewed, multiple times, by Leach, Jenifer, and their assistant prosecutors (O'Conor, Wells, and Andrews).

On Thursday, September 7th, O'Conor returned the portion of the payroll that had been recouped to Fred Kuethe, who had recovered enough to return to work.

Kuethe was still unable to remember much about the robbery. He thought he recognized Charles Carey but wasn't sure. He was unable to identify Jack Hart or Walter Socolow as his attackers, saying "It happened too fast."

Burns was in regular contact with New York Detective Lieutenant James Gegan.

Captain Burns, Commissioner Gaither, and Sergeant Murphy were back and forth with Metropolitan Police Chief Henry Pratt and Detective Lieutenant Richard Mansfield.

The Metropolitan Police Raid Buck Livingston's Apartment

A call to Murphy from Mansfield on September 7th, was the first promising lead to the whereabouts of Buck Livingston, his wife, and possibly Jack Hart.

The day before, on September 6th, Mansfield informed Murphy that his taskforce raided a small upscale apartment building located on East Capital Street, two blocks west of Lincoln Park. Mansfield had received a tip that Buck Livingston lived there.

When Mansfield and his heavily armed squad arrived early that

Wednesday morning, they found the apartment unoccupied. Mrs. Iris Millman, an attractive young widow who acquired ownership of the building following the death of her husband, showed Mansfield a lease that had been signed by Thomas Brown. She confirmed that the Browns moved out at the end of August.

Iris Millman had gotten to know Mrs. Brown, whose first name was Dorothy. Her husband called her Dede. Dede Brown and Iris Millman were the same age and often spent time together. Mrs. Millman's description of Thomas Brown matched that of Buck Livingston. There was no forwarding address and Mrs. Millman couldn't provide any information as to why or where the Brown's moved. She had read newspaper accounts about the ongoing manhunt for Jack Hart and Walter Socolow. Mrs. Millman asked Mansfield if Thomas Brown was Jack Hart.

Mansfield assured Millman that Brown was not Hart. He reported to Murphy that he wasn't persuaded that everything Mrs. Millman, who seemed sympathetic and guarded about Mrs. Brown, told him was truthful. Mansfield believes Brown is Livingston. If so, Buck and his wife are still somewhere in the Capital. Does Mrs. Millman know where they are. Mansfield isn't sure. He intends to keep Millman and her apartment building under surveillance.

27

IRIS AND DEDE
SEPTEMBER 15, 1922

At 9:00 a.m. on Friday, September 15th, Detective James Comen received a call through the police switchboard. Comen was out with Detective Lieutenant Charles Kahler. The message is from Mia Borrelli. She has information about Jack Hart and Buck Livingston.

At eleven o'clock, Detectives Comen and Kahler return to headquarters. As soon as Comen reads Mrs. Borrelli's message, he and Kahler race down the hall to Burns' office. Burns, displaying the first upbeat excitement in two weeks, jumps up and says, "Let's go."

Kahler and Comen, with Captain of Detectives Burns in the back seat, head to High Street and Anthony's Italian Restaurant. The three detectives arrive at 11:45. Anthony's lunch rush is underway. Mia Borrelli is standing at the reception desk welcoming patrons. When she spots the three detectives, Mia ask her daughter to take over. She thanks Comen and Kahler for coming so quickly. Explaining that Burns is their boss, Comen introduces Captain Burns to Mia. Mia asks them to follow her upstairs.

The second floor of Anthony's is divided into additional dining space and two adjoining rooms used for private events. In the room at the High Street end of the building, an attractive well-dressed young woman is sitting at a red and white checkered cloth covered table. When the detectives, led by Mia Borrelli, enter, the stylish woman, with a modern-day flapper hairstyle, puts out her cigarette and stands up. Mia introduces Burns, Kahler, and Comen as the Baltimore detectives she had talked about.

Burns introduces himself as Captain of Detectives, Charles

Burns. Gesturing toward his colleagues, Burns presents Detective Lieutenant Charles Keller and Detective James Comen then inquires, "May I ask who you are?"

Looking directly at Burns, the woman responds, "My name is Iris Millman."

Mrs. Iris Millman

Before anyone can say anything more, Mia chimes in affirming that Iris is the lady who has been here for lunch with Mrs. Livingston. Glancing over at Iris, Mia explains, "Miss Iris came in this morning asking if I had spoken to any policemen about Jack Hart." Looking at Detective Comen, Mia adds, "I told her you were easy to talk to and that you wanted to meet her or Dede."

Burns asks Mia Borrelli if she would mind if they met with Mrs. Millman alone.

Mia says, "Take all the time you need. I'll be downstairs."

As Mia heads downstairs to deal with Anthony's lunchtime regulars, Burns, Keller, Comen, and Mrs. Millman sit down. Burns and his detectives already know that Iris Millman owns the boutique apartment building that was raided on September 6th (nine days ago) by Metropolitan Police Detective Mansfield's criminal taskforce. At the time, even though she must have known (or at least suspected) Thomas Brown was Buck Livingston, Mrs. Millman misled Mansfield by asking if Thomas Brown was Jack Hart.

The reason for this is Burns' first question.

Iris answers, "I had no reason to believe Thomas Brown was Buck Livingston or his friend, James Connelly was Jack Hart. Mr. Brown was often away on business. When he was home, he kept to his apartment."

Iris continues, "I was aware of the hunt for Jack Hart and Walter Socolow, but I had no reason to associate either of them with Thomas Brown. The Browns were good tenants who paid their rent."

"The truth is," Iris explains, "I didn't know Thomas Brown was Buck Livingston, for sure, until Detective Mansfield told me when he came to my building with a search warrant."

"I have become very fond of Dede Brown. She was often alone and seemed unhappy. When Thomas was away, Dede and I began to do things together. We would join each other for lunch, sometimes dinner in each other's apartments. We enjoyed visiting the Washington, D.C. sights like the Capital, Washington Monument and the Japanese Cherry Trees planted along the Potomac River—things like that."

My husband purchased our Chevrolet shortly before he died. We loved to take driving trips—especially after he became ill. We often traveled to Baltimore where we purchased seafood at the city docks or dined in neighborhood restaurants."

"Dede told me that her husband had business partners in Baltimore. Anthony's was a restaurant where Dede's husband met friends. It was because of Dede Brown, I mean Livingston, that I first came to Anthony's."

Iris tells the detectives, "Driving to Baltimore can be an adventure.

It's great to have company. After my husband passed, Dede became my traveling companion. We would drive out Rhode Island Avenue to the Washington and Baltimore Turnpike. A trip to Baltimore takes a little over an hour. There are a million things to see along the way."

"We love browsing through the Broadway Market. We would take steamboat excursions from the Fells Point docks. Because Dede had been to Anthony's with her husband, she brought me here for lunch. We've been back a number of times."

"During our trips together, I got the impression that Dede was unhappily married. There were things about her husband Dede didn't want to talk about. I came to think Dede was afraid of Thomas or Buck—whatever he calls himself."

The three detectives patiently listen to Iris Millman's story without interruption. Then, Burns askes, "Why are you here, Mrs. Millman?"

Iris answers, "The police pursuit of Buck Livingston has been in all the newspapers. After Detective Mansfield's raid, I realized Thomas Brown was Buck Livingston. But I held back from saying this to Lieutenant Mansfield for fear of adding to Dede's troubles."

"The day after Mansfield's unit went through the Brown's apartment, Dede showed up visibly distressed. I invited her in. I told her what took place the day before. Dede already knew. For the first time, Dede disclosed that Livingston was her real name and the fugitive, Jack Hart, was hunkered down (hiding) in their new apartment.

"Nervous and frightened, Dede confided to me that (alone in the apartment) she called the Baltimore police on Thursday, August 31st, to see if the $10,000 reward for the capture of Hart and Socolow was still being offered. She was informed that it was, but hung up when she heard her husband and Hart returning."

"Dede said she wanted to leave Buck. They were married in Washington when she was only 18. Dede confessed that she was miserable and fearful of what might happen to her. She said she first met Jack Hart when he called himself Jim Connelly. Dede told me Jim Connelly and Buck Livingston were often together, either in Washington or Baltimore."

Iris explains that "Dede and Buck moved out at the end of August soon after Connelly showed up with a disheveled young companion. Both were unkept and wearing work clothes. This was particularly true of Connelly. On previous visits, except for a mustache, she said Connelly was always clean shaven and dressed in pricey suits. And he didn't have his fancy car. They arrived on foot. Connelly and his friend were only there a few hours. By the end of the week, Dede and Buck disappeared."

"Dede said every day with Hart is a nightmare. He's a bully. Even her husband, a much bigger man, is intimidated by Jack. If she could turn Hart in without being arrested herself—or worse, shot by Hart—she would do it. She called the Baltimore police to see if she might be entitled to some of the reward. From Dede's point of view, turning Hart in was not only a way to get rid of him but also a chance to get away from Buck. Dede insists that she still cares for Buck but doesn't want to spend the rest of her life running from the police. The reward would enable her to start over."

"She did not go directly to the police out of fear of being arrested herself or putting her and her husband in danger. She told me that if Jack found out, he would kill her and Buck. He brags about being a soldier for the New York mob and said he knew what to do with snitches. That," Iris said, "is the reason I'm here."

"Mia Borelli knows a lot of people. Through her contacts, we believed Mia could arrange for me to meet someone from the Baltimore City Police Department. Dede and I were sure that if Jack Hart's name was mentioned, the Baltimore police would respond. It's a chance we took." Warmly smiling, Iris proclaims,

"And here you are."

Burns tells Iris, "We could detain you as an accessory, complicit in covering for Livingston and Hart."

Iris asks, "What good would that do?"

Backing off, Burns explains, "I understand your friend's predicament, but my job is to arrest Jack Hart. Are you here to tell us where he is?"

Iris answers, "Dede Livingston wants to come in and talk to someone who can protect her from Hart and her husband. She can tell you about Hart herself."

"What I am asking you, Mrs. Millman, is do you know where Jack Hart is?"

Iris answers, "I don't. Dede hasn't told me her new address. She is anxious about Hart and Buck learning that we are still getting together. Hart told her if he found out she was talking to anyone, even me, it would be her last conversation."

"Dede is willing to let you know where Hart is but wants assurances that she will be safe."

Burns asks, "What does Mrs. Livingston want?"

"She doesn't want to be arrested or charged with protecting Hart or her husband. She would like to be somewhere else when you arrest Jack and Buck. She is hoping to share in the reward for Hart's capture. And for reasons I don't understand, she wants you to go easy on her husband."

Burns says, "Granting these requests is not in my power. It's up to Mr. Leach—the District Attorney. I promise that if Mrs. Livingston is willing to meet with Mr. Leach, on her own, she will be protected. Can you bring her to Baltimore?"

Iris answers, "I need to check with Dede."

Burns gives Iris his card telling her, "I will get back to Mr. Leach this afternoon. Can I call tonight?"

Iris answers "Yes," and gives Burns her telephone number.

Burns asks, "When do you plan to drive back to D.C.?"

Iris responds, "As soon as you let me."

Burns says, "I will call at six o' clock with an answer from Mr. Leach."

Iris replies, "I'll be home."

Burns asks, "Can you get in touch with Mrs. Livingston without her husband knowing?"

Iris says, "I can."

Stopping briefly to thank Mia for setting things up, Burns, Kahler, Comen, and Iris Millman leave Anthony's together. Burns makes it clear to Mia Borrelli that she must not say anything about this to anyone. As Mia gives Iris a kiss on the cheek, she nods to Burns saying, "*Va bene.*"

The three detectives walk Iris to her Chevrolet cruiser parked behind Anthony's. After Iris is out of sight, Burns, and his two detectives, head for Leach's courthouse office. They arrive at 2:45.

Leach and O'Conor are in a conference. Mrs. Fitzpatrick lets them know Captain Burns wants to see them. "He has information about Jack Hart."

Burns invites the three detectives into his office. Kahler and Comen explain how they got in touch with Mia Borelli in the first place. Burns explains the details of his conversation with Iris Millman.

Leach asks, "Why did you let her go?"

Burns answers, "I believe things will work out better if we follow along."

Leach and O'Conor, think about it for a moment, then agree.

O'Conor wants to know how fast they can get to Hart.

Burns replies, "Once we locate where he is in the Capital, we can be there within a few hours. We will coordinate things with the Metropolitan Police."

Leach and O'Conor agree with Burns that there is no point in arresting or prosecuting Dorothy Livingston. Leach calls in Fleet Cox to see where thing stand in the case against Buck Livingston.

"Livingston," Cox clarifies, "has been indicted in the District for selling illegal spirits to the military at Camp Meade. Although Livingston is associated with D'Urso's Baltimore Crew, he hasn't been tied to any killings."

Leach changes the subject to the reward. All agree that both Dorothy Livingston and Iris Millman are entitled to at least half of the reward if Jack Hart is captured. How they share it is up to them. Leach also makes it clear that his office is willing to protect Dorothy Livingston's and Iris Millman's identities.

"If we catch Hart," Leach directs, "the official statement from this office, or the police, will be that an anonymous tip led to the capture of Jack Hart."

Burns asks Leach and Cox, "How much immunity can we grant Livingston?"

Leach defers to Cox. "From what Detective Burns has told us," Cox questions, "I would think Mrs. Livingston will want to be protected from her husband. But if she leads us to Hart, there is no reason we can't work something out. I'm not sure about what we can do in the District?"

Leach asks Burns, "When can we meet Mrs. Livingston?"

Burns replies, "I told Mrs. Millman I will call her at six o'clock tonight."

Leach asks, "Can you get Mrs. Livingston here tomorrow?"

Burns replies, "I'll try."

Leach instructs Burns to get his unit ready: "Coordinate the operation with the Metropolitan Police."

Burns replies, "Everything is set with the Metropolitan police. Chief Pratt says we will have his cooperation."

Then, Leach has a change of mind.

He tells Burns, "It doesn't make sense to bring Mrs. Livingston to Baltimore. Let's keep this in the District. If we get an address," Leach instructs Burns, "don't wait. If Mrs. Livingston gives us Hart, make your move (immediately) with the Metropolitan police. There is no reason to have Mrs. Livingston come here first."

Everyone agrees with Leach.

As the meeting breaks up, Leach tells everyone, "I will wait to notify Mayor Broening and Governor Ritchie until we're sure it's a go. With any luck, Jack Hart will be in custody tomorrow."

Metropolitan Police Chief, Henry G. Pratt

Back at Police Headquarters, Commissioner Gaither's first call, with Detectives Burns and Murphy present, is to Metropolitan Police Chief, Henry G. Pratt, to let him know what has been discussed, at least in Baltimore. Chief Pratt lets Gaither know that when they learn Hart's location, he will have a unit, commanded by Detective Mansfield, meet Burns when his men enter the District. Pratt further explains that if they pick up Livingston, he will hold Livingston there. "He's wanted in the District."

With Gaither's permission, Burns tells Pratt that Mrs. Livingston is hoping that if we arrest her husband, Leach will drop the charges against him. Burns explains that granting this may be an incentive in getting Mrs. Livingston to turn Hart over.

Pratt responds, "That's for Mr. Leach to decide in Baltimore, but in the District, the decision is up to Payton Gordon, the U.S. Attorney for the District of Columbia. Pratt recommends Leach call Gordon. "When and if we arrest Livingston," Pratt tells Gaither and Burns, "We'll hold him here until the prosecutors decide."

"Jack Hart," Pratt assures Gaither and Burns, "is yours."

Gaither and Burns have no choice but to agree with Pratt. Burns tells the Chief, "As soon as I hear from Mrs. Millman, I will call you back."

Iris Millman

A few minutes before six o'clock (Friday, September 15th), Burns calls Iris Millman. Commissioner Gaither along with Detectives Murphy, Kahler, Comen and Hammersla are in the room.

Burns asks, "Did you have any trouble getting back home?"

Iris responds, "I didn't."

Burns asks, "Have you spoken to Mrs. Livingston?"

Iris says, "I haven't. I know she will call as soon as she can."

Burns, disappointed, nevertheless goes on to tell Iris what Mr. Leach has agreed to. "Both you and Mrs. Livingston will be protected. Your identities will be kept confidential. Mrs. Livingston will not be arrested. You and Mrs. Livingston are entitled to one half of the reward when Jack Hart is arrested."

Burns says nothing about how they plan to deal with Buck Livingston and Iris doesn't ask.

Iris says, "I don't want any of the money."

Burns replies, "That's up to you."

Burns says, "If everything goes well with Mrs. Livingston, my men will drive to Washington and meet up with a unit of the Metropolitan police. We will make sure you and Mrs. Livingston are safe before we raid her residence."

Burns continues, "If Mrs. Livingston can come to your apartment, Detective Mansfield can arrange for officers to stay with both of you until it's over.

Iris responds, "As soon as I hear from Dede, I will call back. If I don't hear from her by one o' clock tomorrow afternoon, I will call you anyway."

Iris reminds Burns, "I don't know Dede's address or telephone number. She is terrified to tell anyone – even me. She is sure Hart will kill her if he finds out. Dede won't want to be anywhere near Hart when you arrest him. I'm certain she will cooperate."

Burns reminds Iris, "Hart is looking to get out of Washington. He wants to get to New York where he has friends. It's important you understand, time is of the essence. Please be sure, if you don't hear from her by one o'clock tomorrow, you will call me anyway. I need to know you're okay. Don't forget, one o'clock – even if you haven't heard from Mrs. Livingston."

Iris replies, "One o'clock, no matter what."

28

THE WAIT

The first call Gaither and Burns make after talking to Iris Millman is to Robert Leach's office. They get ahold of Herbert O'Conor, who tells them "Good work"; he will let Leach, Jenifer, and Cox know. O'Conor asks if they have spoken to Chief Pratt. Gaither answers, "We are about to call him."

During Gaither's and Burns' call to Metropolitan Police Headquarters, Chief Pratt agrees that it is a good plan and re-assures Commissioner Gaither that the Baltimore police will have his support. Pratt appreciates that this unanticipated windfall from a frightened and unhappy wife offers the best chance to catch Jack Hart.

To save time, Pratt recommends that Burns and his unit come to Washington and wait for Mrs. Millman's call from his office. Burns responds that he doesn't want to call Iris Millman back and alter their plan. He reminds Chief Pratt that when (or even if) she calls back is an unknown. "It depends on Mrs. Livingston being able to leave her apartment."

Commissioner Gaither agrees with Burns. "With your authorization," he suggests to Chief Pratt, "When Detective Burns receives the call from Mrs. Millman, his unit, accompanied by six of my uniformed officers, will drive directly to the Metropolitan Police building or meet Detective Mansfield at the location he thinks best."

Chief Pratt replies, "I'm okay with this approach. I will tee things up on this end with Lieutenant Mansfield. In the interim," he tells Gaither and Burns, "I will have an undercover car positioned near Mrs. Millman's apartment building."

Gaither and Burns respond that they are grateful for this and will call back with updates.

Now, it's just a matter of waiting.

The night of September 15th is much cooler than usual, a welcome break from August's oppressive heat. Detectives Burns and Murphy are camped out in Burn's office waiting for Iris Millman's call. They catch up on paperwork, read newspapers and play checkers. Even so, as hours pass, it's an anxious time.

Detective Kahler drops by at 7:30 p.m. He doesn't show up empty handed. He has stopped by Sussman & Lev's Delicatessen on Baltimore Street and purchased four of Sussman's legendary corn beef sandwiches and four of the biggest dill pickles on the planet, a favorite at police headquarters.

Gaither calls at 8:30, 9:30, and 10:30 p.m. Leach checks in at 9:00 and 11:00 p.m. O'Conor dials in at 10:00 and 11:30. The answer remains the same: "No news from Mrs. Millman."

The Baltimore City Police headquarters building is far from empty. Patrolmen are changing shifts. Citizens are registering grievances. Arrests are being made. Suspects are being booked, and the switchboard is open.

Outside, it is a typically busy Friday night in downtown Baltimore. Gaps of stillness are interrupted by an amalgam of familiar sounds and clatters. Steam-powered switch locomotives from Camden Yards, traversing rails imbedded in the city's cobblestone streets, deliver freight and retrieve empty cars throughout the night. Horse-drawn wagons and motor trucks are loading produce from clipper ships lined up along Fells Point and Pratt Street docks. Electric cars run on their rails 24-hours a day.

Saturday, September 16, 1922

When the clock on the top of Emerson's Bromo-Selzer tower, the tallest building in Baltimore, strikes midnight, Kahler volunteers to stick around so Murphy and Burns can get some rest. It's not likely Mrs. Millman will call before sunup. The three detectives do the only thing they can— hunker down and continue to wait. Everyone tries, unsuccessfully, to get a little sleep. Murphy keeps the coffee going.

Commissioner Gaither calls at 6:15 a.m. He will be there by 7:30. O'Conor calls and informs Burns that he will be working today at his courthouse office. Leach will be coming in around noon. Chief Pratt and Detective Mansfield check in for an update at 7:30.

By eleven o'clock the wait is becoming intolerable. Burn's unit (Murphy, Kahler, Comen, and Hammersla) are scattered about his office looking out over Fayette Street, slouching in chairs, draining the water cooler, drinking coffee and smoking cigarettes. Nothing cuts the tension.

As the morning drags on, downtown Baltimore comes to life. Clipper ships moored at the docks along the Broadway and Pratt Street piers sell fruits and vegetables from Maryland's Eastern Shore to an ever-increasing crowd of shoppers. From other boats, Eastern Shoremen are vending blue crabs, oysters, flounder, and rockfish. Two-hundred-foot-long wooden paddlewheel excursion ships are loading passengers. They will be setting out for the sandy beaches along Solomons Island or Chesapeake Bay towns including Annapolis, Cambridge, Easton, and St. Michaels.

Grain, lumber, fabrics, oils, tobacco, cotton, canned goods and other essentials are being loaded and unloaded from steamships lining Light Street's warehouse piers. Hundreds of picnickers, taking advantage of the good weather, gather on Federal Hill, a 125-foot-high five-acre prominence overlooking the harbor's inner basin.

Saturday morning editions of Maryland newspapers editorialize the story of the decade: Where are Jack Hart and Walter Socolow? Some articles are critical of the police. After all, it's been a month. No matter what people are doing, they don't want to miss an update about the seemingly interminable search for Hart and Socolow.

On an update call with Chief Pratt, Burns tells Pratt that he has heard nothing yet but has been assured, by Mrs. Millman, that she will call by one o'clock. Pratt again suggests that Gaither and Burns send a unit to Washington in anticipation of Mrs. Millman's call. "Doing this," he emphasizes, "will give us a head start when we find out where Hart and Livingston are staying."

Pratt tells Burns, "I can send Detective Mansfield and Lieutenant Frank McCatheran to the intersection of Rhode Island Avenue and Eastern Avenue North East. There is a Capital Gas Station on the southwest corner where Otis Street empties into the intersection from the southeast. You can't miss it. Coin telephones are in the station and an attached grocery and hardware. It's up to you."

Gaither doesn't disagree but Burns argues, "If part of my unit goes to the Capital in advance, it will be hard to keep in touch. Once we are separated, there is no way to communicate. It's imperative to keep my unit together." He repeats, "Iris Millman promised to call me by one o'clock or earlier. By then she will have hopefully spoken to Mrs. Livingston. Once we hear from Mrs. Millman," Burns stresses, "we can move from here immediately to join Detectives Mansfield and McCatheran at the District line."

As an afterthought Burns adds, "If Mrs. Millman hasn't heard from Mrs. Livingston by one o'clock, we can modify our strategy. Either way, the Capital Gas Station sounds like a good place to hook up. I'm just asking to wait for Iris Millman's call."

Gaither and Pratt agree to wait.

Gaither returns to his office to update Leach and O'Conor.

Burns gets ahold of Sergeant Patrick Oberon to let him know that he and the three officers, assigned to the Burns Squad, need to remain on standby, ready to drive to Washington at a moment's notice.

Baltimore City Police Sergeant Patrick Oberon

Oberon responds, "My men have been ready since four o'clock this morning."

After checking in with Oberon, Burns turns to Murphy saying, "We've bought an hour. I hope it's enough?"

At 11:50 a.m., thinking everyone in Burns' office must be famished, Sergeant Oberon, wanting an update, shows up with sandwiches. Burns tells Oberon, "When Mrs. Millman calls, we'll be out of here in minutes," then asks, "Do you know the Capital Gas Station at the intersection of Rhode Island and Eastern Avenues just inside the D.C. line?"

Oberon answers, "Of course, It's at the entrance to the turnpike. There's a grocery there too. Easy to spot."

Burns replies, "That's where we'll meet the Metropolitan police."

As Oberon heads back downstairs, he tells Burns, "We can be at the Capital Gas Station in less than an hour. It's a good place to meet."

Burns, Murphy, Kahler, Comen, and Hammersla, ravenous from the stress of uncertainty, devour the sandwiches Oberon delivered. Comen is brewing another pot of coffee, the sixth pot since midnight. Hammersla and Murphy are having a smoke by an open window watching the traffic pass by on Fayette Street. Kahler is standing by Burns' desk where Burns, trying to locate Otis Street, is scrutinizing a map of the District.

A telephone ring pierces the silence. It's 12:35 p.m. on Saturday, September 16, 1922. Suddenly, everyone is focused on Burns as he unhooks the receiver. The switchboard officer relays that she is transferring a call from a Mrs. Iris Millman.

Sounding out of breath, Iris tells Burns that she has just heard from Dede Livingston—"She called from her apartment asking if (you) were able to talk to the District Attorney. I told her that you had and it went well. Can you come quickly?"

Burns answers, "as soon as you're off the telephone."

Without asking any more questions, Iris resumes, "Dede wanted to know if she can come to my apartment. I told her yes. She said she will be here between 2:00 and 2:30 p.m. I said I would be waiting." Iris then tells Burns, "Before I could say anything more, Dede hung up. Are you coming now?"

Burns answers, "Yes."

He assures Iris, "We will arrive at your building by 2:30, maybe earlier. What is your apartment number?"

Iris replies, "East Capital and 9th Street, Apartment 101, on the first floor."

Even before the call ends, Keller, Comen, and Murphy set off, racing downstairs, to where Sergeant Oberon and his squad are waiting. Three unmarked police cars, motors running, are lined up on the police building's east side parking platform. Officer George Cummings and his partner Thomas Baker, dressed in plain clothes, are in the first car.

Burns makes two calls. The first is to Chief Pratt confirming that they will connect with the Metropolitan Police at the Capital Gas Station. "We should arrive by two o'clock."

Pratt says, "Detective Mansfield and his men will be there."

Burns' second call is to the top floor office of Commissioner Gaither to let him know that they have heard from Iris Millman and are on their way to Washington. "I am taking three of my detectives and six officers. Detective Hammersla will stay behind to keep you informed."

Gaither tells Burns, "Good luck. I'll let Mr. Leach know."

Burns hangs up and sprints to join his men waiting in the three-car caravan. George Cumming's patrol car, the only machine equipped with a siren, leads the way.

Burns' unit reaches the D.C. line at Otis Street and pulls onto the Capital Gas Station lot at 1:50 p.m. Detective Mansfield and Precinct Lieutenant McCatheran are standing by two Metropolitan patrol cars along with six officers. Burns and Murphy jump out to greet Mansfield and McCatheran. Minutes later they are back in their cruisers.

Mansfield leads the combined force to Mrs. Millman's apartment building. It's a 20-minute drive along South Carolina Avenue, then southwest on the Bladensburg Pike to Tennessee Avenue to Lincoln Park and East Capital Street. Millman's apartment building is located four blocks west. When they arrive, two young women are standing outside the building's entrance with Metropolitan officers Charles Moss and Stan Arnold.

Iris Millman recognizes Captain Burns, Detectives Kahler, and Comen and D.C. Detective Richard Mansfield. She introduces them to a distraught Dorothy Livingston. Burns assures Livingston that she is safe. He asks Iris, "Can we go into your apartment to coordinate our next move?"

Iris, nodding her head in agreement, turns and takes hold of Dede's hand, then guides Burns, Murphy, Kahler, Comen, Mansfield and McCatheran up the granite steps into the four-story baroque sandstone building.

Dorothy "Dede" Livingston

Millman's apartment is spacious. From a large entry foyer, an expansive living room and equally roomy dining area are visible. Iris invites the detectives into her living room and offers everyone a seat. Iris and Dede sit next to one another on a Victorian settee perpendicular to an ornate fireplace. Burns and Mansfield settle in on a similar couch facing Iris and Dede, separated by a rectangular mahogany coffee table. Kahler, Comen, and McCatheran remain standing.

The Auburn Apartments

Looking at Burns, then back to Dede, Iris tells Burns that she told Dede about last night's conversation. Still holding Iris' hand, Dede nervously speaks up. "I just need to know I can stay someplace safe."

Burns assures Dede Livingston that they have already made sure of that. "You won't be charged with any crime and if you want, we can arrange for you to stay in Baltimore at the Southern Hotel.

Anxious to get going, Burns asks Mrs. Livingston, "Where is your apartment located?"

Dede replies, "The Auburn Apartments. The address is 2006 Pennsylvania Avenue – North West, at the corner of 22nd Street. "My apartment number is 2006-2B, on the second floor."

Lieutenant McCatheran speaks up saying, "That's about three miles northwest of here, maybe a fifteen-minute drive."

Dede nods her head in agreement adding, "It's not far."

Burns wants to know how her apartment is laid out.

Dede answers, "I can draw a diagram."

Iris retrieves a pad of writing paper and a pencil from her desk.

Laying several sheets of paper on the coffee table, Dede sketches the layout of 2B, explaining that "there are two separate entrances from Pennsylvania Avenue, each with a mailing address."

"Both entrances (2004 and 2006) front Pennsylvania Avenue. There are three floors. Each level leads to eight apartments, four to the right and four to the left. We are the first apartment to the right (east) on the second floor of 2006's lobby. The entrance to our apartment," Dede, referring to her diagram, "opens into the living room. The kitchen and dining area are to the left. The bedrooms and bathroom are down a hallway to the right. Jack has been using the second bedroom but when he's not sleeping, he is usually in the living room. That's where he and Buck hang out. And that's where you will probably find him today." Then Dede adds, "Jack always has his revolver."

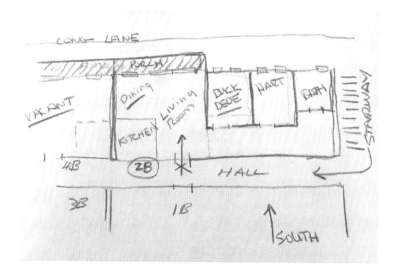

Murphy breaks in asking, "Does your husband have a gun?"

Dede replies, "He does. There are other handguns and a shotgun in the apartment."

Detective Mansfield asks, "Doesn't your building have balconies on the upper floors?"

Dede answers, "Yes. Out porch extends south—off the living room."

Mansfield asks, "Do all the second-floor apartments have balconies?"

Dede answers, "Yes," then adds, "the apartment next door (4B) is vacant."

Burns wants to know if a manager lives in the building.

Dede answers, "Ben and Bertha Garner live in unit 2004-1A at the corner of 22nd Street and Pennsylvania Avenue. It's on the first floor. Mr. Garner manages things. Hank, our maintenance man, has a basement apartment below the Garners."

Burns asks, "Do the Garners or Hank have keys."

Dede replies, "I think so."

Burns asks, "How were you able to get out today?"

Dede answers, "Both Buck and Jack drink a lot, usually late into the night. They sleep until ten or eleven o'clock. When they wake up, both want breakfast. I can't do anything until they're finished. Sometimes I can get out to buy groceries. But Buck and Jack want to know where I am every second. I have to be careful. It's never easy to get away."

Burns asks, "Do they stay in the apartment all day?"

Dede says, "They don't. Buck and Jack get bored. They slip out to hook up with Buck's friends. They left the apartment after lunch. When I was sure it was safe, I hailed a taxi and came here. I'm not going back."

Burns asks, "Do you know where they are?"

Dede says, "I don't. They will be back around four thirty."

Burns responds, "How do you know that?"

"Because I promised them a steak dinner with baked potatoes, cooked carrots and spinach, everything Jack loves. You can be sure they won't miss supper. I told them it will be on the table at five-thirty—then adds, "Friday and Saturday nights are when the police raid the nightspots. They'll be there."

Burns thanks Mrs. Livingston for her cooperation, but realizes what she has just revealed means a change in plans.

Iris invites them to use her library, a comfortable oak paneled chamber on the west side of the apartment with a large casement window that overlooks a garden west of the building. As she escorts them into the library, Iris tells the detectives that this had been her husband's office. The finely appointed room keeps a sitting area surrounding a decorative marble hearth, rich mahogany desk, and floor to ceiling bookshelves on the wall opposite the window.

Learning that Livingston and Hart are not in the apartment, Burns and Mansfield have no choice but to accept Mrs. Livingston's assertion that Hart and her husband, lured by the promise of dinner, will return between four and five o'clock. But what if they are already there?

Detectives Mansfield and Lieutenant McCatheran are familiar with the neighborhood and the Auburn Apartment Building that was constructed in the mid-1800s. They agree that the building can be surrounded. Mansfield recommends staging their motorcars on Pennsylvania Avenue and 22nd Street.

McCatheran adds, "There is a narrow alleyway called Long Lane separating the building from garages and stables on the south side. Some of our officers can find cover there. The first step is knowing if Hart and Livingston are in the apartment."

Kahler suggests that he and Comen can find out by entering the adjacent vacant apartment (4B). McCatheran quickly approves of this. He points out that Keller and Comen can cross over the balcony from 4B to Livingston's apartment to get a look inside saying, "If they are there or not, either way, Keller and Comen will be in position to back up Burns, Murphy, and Mansfield when they break through the front door."

Burns leaves the library to ask Mrs. Livingston if the balconies between apartments connect.

Dede answers, "They do. There is a door and two double windows. The window-shades are up but when my husband comes home, he'll pull them down."

Iris picks up Dede's apartment drawing from the table and hands it to Burns. Burns heads back to the library.

The detectives decide that McCatheran, Kahler, Comen and Ray Marshall, a D.C. Police officer, will park on 22nd Street, locate the Garners and reveal what is about to take place—hopefully get a key to the vacant apartment.

Mansfield says, "If the Garners or Hank can't be located, Lieutenant McCatheran can manipulate the lock and enter 4B anyway. Officer Marshall will stay with the Garners. Kahler and Comen will head to the vacant apartment and wait for McCatheran to arrive with the key. From 4B, Kahler, Comen, and McCatheran can use the porch to check out Livingston's apartment."

Burns agrees that this is a good idea adding, "Sergeant Oberon's squad will park east of the building on 21st Street and find concealed positions on Long Lane. Cummings and Baker will park on 22nd Street south of Long Lane."

Burns and Mansfield decide they will take up positions on Pennsylvania Avenue across from the Auburn Apartments. Burns and Murphy, with two officers, will park one-half block east. Mansfield will park one-half block west.

"From these positions and with Sergeant Oberon's unit concealed on Long Lane," Mansfield says, "all entrances are covered."

Burns agrees, "If Livingston and Hart are there, Kahler, Comen, and McCatheran will remain on the balcony ready to support us when we break in. If the apartment is unoccupied, they will return to 4B and wait."

"Before doing either," Burns adds, "Kahler will signal Sergeant Oberon on Long Lane. Thumbs up if Hart and Livingston are there. Thumbs down if they are not. It will be up to Sergeant Oberon to notify me and Mansfield on Pennsylvania Avenue and Commings and Baker on 22nd that Hart and Livingston are there or not."

It is decided that if Hart and Livingston are there, Burns, Murphy and Mansfield will immediately storm the apartment.

If Hart and Livingston are not there, everyone will maintain their positions until Livingston and Hart show up. Burns and Mansfield will give Hart and Livingston time to enter the apartment before they move in. Cummings and Baker, positioned on 22nd Street, are back-up. They will follow and support Burns, Murphy, and Mansfield.

Dede also reveals that Buck has a 1917 Ford Model T that he keeps in a former stable on the south side of Long Lane near 22nd Street. Dede doesn't know if Hart and Livingston took Buck's Ford or walked wherever they went. "It could be either."

Sergeant Oberon is assigned the task of looking out for Hart and Livingston entering the building from Long Lane.

"Even if they used Livingston's Ford," Mansfield points out, "there are only two entrances to 2006 Pennsylvania Avenue and the Long Lane service entrance. Both will be covered."

"If there not there," Kahler asks, "how will we know when to break through the porch door when we are in the adjacent apartment?"

Burns answers, "Before Mansfield, Murphy, and I break through the hallway door, Sergeant Murphy will tap on the door of apartment 4B alerting you that you need to take positions on the balcony outside Livingston's unit."

"Two minutes after the signal," Burns continues, "we will smash open the front door and hopefully surprise Hart and Livingston. At the same time, the three of you will break through the balcony door. Hart and Livingston won't have time to react."

Mansfield says, "Officers Moss and Arnold will remain here with Mrs. Millman and Mrs. Livingston."

"If we fail to apprehend Hart and Livingston, Mrs. Millman and Mrs. Livingston will receive police protection. I think they would be safest at the Southern Hotel until Hart and Livingston are tracked down."

The general feeling is that if Hart and Livingston are in the apartment or show up later, they will be taken.

At 3:20, the combined Baltimore-Metropolitan police taskforce, with the exception of the two officers remaining with Iris and Dede, head for the Auburn Apartments.

Pennsylvania Avenue NW, 1922

29

SETTING THE TRAP

At 3:55, Lieutenant McCatheran and DC patrol officer Raymond Marshall knock on the door of Apartment 2004 -1A. Bertha Garner answers. McCatheran identifies himself and Officer Marshall and explains why they are there. In less than five minutes, McCatheran is racing up the stairway to apartment 2006-4B (the vacant apartment) to join Kahler and Comen. By 4:10 the three detectives are inside. Comen tells McCatheran that they had listened for conversation coming from 2B. They heard nothing.

The detectives make their way onto the balcony and advance to a position where they can look inside 2B. The Livingston's shades are up. A single light is dimly radiating from the kitchen. Jack Hart and Buck Livingston are not there. As the three detectives return to 4B, McCatheran signals "thumbs down" to Sergeant Oberon.

Oberon dispatches Police Corporal Mike Hastings to let Cummings and Baker (on 22nd Street) and Burns and Mansfield (on Pennsylvania Avenue) know the Livingston apartment is unoccupied.

Hastings returns to his concealed position on Long Lane. An hour and thirty minutes slip by with no sign of Hart or Livingston. For the ten officers from Baltimore and the six from the District, the question becomes, will Hart and Livingston show?

It was becoming overcast, but the sun wouldn't set for another 90 minutes. From their perch two stories up in Apartment 4B, Kahler, Comen, and McCatheran can see Sergeant Oberon peering over a hedgerow adjacent to a clapboard garage, gazing up and down Long Lane. The streets on all sides of the Auburn Apartments are humming with Washingtonians enjoying the day.

It is a typically hectic, mild Saturday afternoon. The White House is one-half mile southeast. Ten blocks south, the National Mall connects the newly-completed Lincoln Memorial to the west with the United States Capital to the east. Motor cars, no longer novelties for the wealthy, are omnipresent. They rumble along Washington's boulevards competing for the right-of-way with horse-drawn buggies and wagons.

Except for Oberon's squad trying to be invisible on Long Lane, the heavy volume of street and foot traffic make it easier for Burns' and Mansfield's taskforce to go unnoticed.

Lincoln Memorial Dedication Ceremony – May 30, 1922

30

SPRINGING THE TRAP

Suddenly, Oberon hears a car shifting into a lower gear as it slows and turns west onto Long Lane from 21st Street. It's a black Ford sedan. As he steps back behind the shrubbery, Oberon checks his watch. It's 6:20.

The Ford accelerates as it passes Oberon's hiding place. There is no time to identify the occupants. About 50 yards further on, the Ford stops short of 22nd Street. Oberon chances a peak. An average size man wearing a suit and brimmed hat jumps out of the passenger side of the car and scans Long Lane. Oberon ducks out of sight.

Seeing nothing out of place, the man walks 15 feet to a stable on the south side of the lane. Lugging open two hefty wooden doors, he motions the driver to pull in. Minutes later, the two men exit the stable, close the doors, and walk to 22nd Street.

Although Oberon can't identify either as Hart or Livingston, he nonetheless signals the "thumbs up" sign to Kahler, Comen, and McCatheran, watching from apartment 4B. Oberon is sure Officer Hastings, who is camouflaged close to the stable, will get a better look. And if not Hastings, Tom Baker and George Cummings positioned on 22nd Street, have police mug-shots of Hart and Livingston.

After the two men are out of sight, Hastings leaves his concealed position and heads toward Oberon.

Hastings tells his boss, "It's them!"

Oberon swings around and looks up at Apartment 4B. Raising his right hand, he vigorously signals "thumbs up." Kahler, concealed on the balcony, gestures he understands.

Sergeant Oberon's instinct is to notify Burns and Mansfield on Pennsylvania Avenue, but he doesn't. He can only hope that they will recognize Hart and Livingston. Instead, Oberon motions to Hastings and the other two members of his squad to assume concealed positions opposite Livingston's apartment, across from the service entrance on Long Lane.

Oberon can see Kahler and McCatheran, revolvers drawn, shifting into position, along the balcony. As he begins to position his men, Oberon spots George Cummings and Thomas Baker crossing Long Lane. They waited for Livingston and Hart to turn the corner at Pennsylvania Avenue. Cummings, looking at Oberon, gestures they are following the right outlaws. Oberon returns the thumbs up sign.

Both Burns, parked a half-block east, and Mansfield, a half-block west, recognize the wiry five foot eight, 157-pound Hart and the stout six-foot two-inch, 225-pound Livingston as they turned the corner at 22nd Street and casually walk east on Pennsylvania Avenue. Ironically, like Bill Norris and Fred Kuethe who were oblivious to being stalked by Hart's gang as they were returning to their office on Madison Street, Hart and Livingston, smoking and chatting away, are unaware of the combined police force about to pounce.

The distance from the corner of 22nd Street and Pennsylvania Avenue to the doorway of 2006 is 150 feet. Hart and Livingston climb the steps and enter the building's foyer at 6:45 p.m.

At 6:50, Burns and Murphy with two Baltimore police officers equipped with a ram, and Mansfield, with three additional Metropolitan officers, cross Pennsylvania Avenue to join Cummings and Baker.

Three officers remain outside. Burns and Mansfield lead Murphy, Cummings, Baker, and two officers (ram ready) into the building. They climb the stairway to the second floor, turn right and advance along the hallway to Apartment 2B.

Murphy walks the additional 25 feet to Apartment 4B. He looks back at Burns who is checking his watch. At 7:06, Burns signals the go-ahead. Murphy taps lightly on the door of 4B. Comen, who has remained inside waiting for the signal, taps back then heads for the balcony to join Kahler and McCatheran.

At 7:08, the two officers, smash open the door of apartment 2B. As the door crashes against the inside wall, Burns, Mansfield, and Murphy, guns drawn, flood into the room with Cummings and Baker close behind.

Hart, reclining in a lounge chair, smoking a cigarette, with his feet stretched out on a table, is caught unaware. He grabs his .38, springs to his feet, and pointing his revolver, rotates towards Burns, Murphy, and Mansfield. Simultaneously, Kahler, Comen, and McCatheran, weapons drawn, slam through the balcony door.

Hart, startled by the explosive entrance from behind, swivels back. As he does, his gun goes off. The bullet, zipping past Burns' head, strikes the wall above the door.

Not waiting for Hart to take better aim, Burns, Mansfield, and Kahler rush forward and tackle Hart, splintering the table as they slam the startled felon to the floor. With Hart face down, prostrate on the floor between the chair and the shattered table, Burns yanks the gun from his grasp as Mansfield and Kahler cuffs Hart's hands behind his back.

At the same moment Hart fired, Buck Livingston, wielding his pistol, emerged from the bathroom and raced down the hallway.

Murphy swung his revolver towards Livingston.

Livingston nose-dives to the floor.

Lying flat, face down, on the hallway runner, Livingston pleads:

"I surrender—Don't shoot—Please don't shoot!"

McCatheran kicks Livingston's gun to the side as he and Murphy fold Buck's arms behind his back and cuff his wrists together.

Both Hart and Livingston are yanked to their feet.

Burns takes a look at the cut over Hart's right eye—sustained when the table disintegrated. Comen retrieves a dish towel from the kitchen and wipes the blood from Hart's face. "For now," he tells a dumbfounded Hart, "you're better off than you should be. This will do until we reach Baltimore."

Wasting little time, Burns and Murphy grab Hart, hands secured behind his back, by both arms. Mansfield and McCatheran seize Livingston. The two suddenly-not-so-intimidating felons are ramrodded into the hallway, down the stairs, and out onto Pennsylvania Avenue where Sergeant Oberon and his squad with the Metropolitan police are waiting along with a crowd of onlookers.

Detective Comen has parked his patrol car directly in front of the entrance. Sergeant Marshall pulls up behind. As Hart is being stuffed into the back seat of Comen's car and Livingston into the car driven by Marshall, people in the crowd shout, "Is it Hart?" "Is that Jack Hart?"

With Comen driving, Burns in the front passenger seat, and Hart sandwiched between Murphy and Hastings in the back, they don't wait to answer. Comen steps on the gas and heads for Baltimore.

Seconds later, with Detective Mansfield in the front passenger seat and Livingston squeezed between two strapping Metropolitan police officers in the back, Ray Marshall activates his siren and takes off for Metropolitan Police headquarters.

Detective Kahler and Metropolitan Police Lieutenant McCatheran and the rest of the taskforce remain. They search the Livingston's apartment and retrieve several firearms, a shotgun, and $925 in cash.

Before heading back to either Baltimore or Metropolitan Police headquarters, Kahler and McCatheran catch up with Ben and Bertha Garner. McCatheran lets the Garners know that Mrs. Livingston is not under arrest and isn't guilty of any crime.

Ben Garner reveals that the apartment is not leased to anyone named Livingston. "It's leased to Mr. and Mrs. Thomas Hill."

McCatheran responds, "'Hill' is an alias."

Back at the Garner's apartment, Detective Kahler places a telephone call to Baltimore City Police headquarters and asked for Detective Hammersla. He reports that Hart and Livingston are in custody. He tells Hammersla, "Hart is injured and may need medical attention. I anticipate Burns will reach the courthouse in about an hour."

Kahler asks Hammersla to notify Commissioner Gaither.

McCatheran makes a similar call to Chief Pratt.

After reporting in, Kahler and McCatheran, in separate cars, with taskforce officers, return to Mrs. Millman's apartment. They let Dorothy Livingston and Iris Millman know that Jack Hart and Buck Livingston are in custody.

McCatheran tells Mrs. Livingston, "You need to deal with the apartment manager. The lease is not in your name."

Kahler tells Dede and Iris, "You are welcome to come to Baltimore and stay at the Southern Hotel."

Iris answers, "We are fine here. If Jack Hart and Buck are in jail, we're not worried."

Dede asks, "Why isn't my husband being taken to Baltimore?"

Kahler explains, "As you requested, Robert Leach has withdrawn charges, but your husband is wanted in the District."

McCatheran tells Mrs. Livingston, "Your husband will be booked and held in the Capital Jail under federal custody. The charges are not related to anything in Baltimore. You should speak with Payton Gordon. He is the United States Attorney for the District of Columbia."

Kahler reminds Iris and Dorothy, "You need to come to Baltimore to meet with Robert Leach about any agreement with his office including recovering the reward."

Iris replies, "I will drive Dede to Baltimore on Monday."

Officers Charles Moss and Stan Arnold, who have been staying with Iris and Dede, are leaving too.

Kahler and his men head back to Baltimore.

McCatheran and his unit return to the Metropolitan Police building.

31

BACK IN BALTIMORE

At 8:15 p.m. Saturday evening, September 16, 1922, Detective Comen stops his unmarked Chevrolet police cruiser in front of the Baltimore City Courthouse. Robert Leach, Herbert O'Conor, Fleet Cox, Commissioner Gaither, Mayor Broening, and Detective Hammersla, along with what seems to be everyone working in the police department and State's Attorney's Office are gathered on the courthouse steps.

The news of Jack Hart's capture has spread throughout Baltimore. Several thousand people fill the streets, hang out of windows, look down from rooftops, have climbed light posts and are standing on mailboxes to catch a glimpse of the infamous Jack Hart. It takes 20 police officers to keep the swarm of cheering bystanders away from Comen's car.

Hart is hustled up the courthouse steps between spectators who separate just far enough to enable Comen and Murphy, grasping tightly to their prisoner, to pass.

Leach, O'Conor, Commissioner Gaither, Mayor Broening, and Detective Hammersla do their best to stay close. Burns, wanting to give Comen and Murphy the honor of bringing in Jack Hart, switched places with Comen. Dodging pedestrians, he cautiously drives the squad car around the building to Calvert Street and parks in a reserved space. Burns enters the courthouse from Calvert Street and climbs the stairway to Leach's second floor office.

As Comen and Murphy usher Hart through the ornamental doors and into the imposing St. Paul's Street atrium, Mayor Broening pauses at the top of the steps then turns to address a disappointed crowd. In his most flamboyant political intonations, the mayor pleads for quiet. When there is a slight ebb in the hullabaloo, Broening tries to explain why they had to get Hart inside. "Please go back to your homes. We got him! We got Jack Hart! Please disperse!"

This at least draws some cheers. Others chant, "We want to see Jack Hart."

As if holding back the raucous tide, Broening raises his hands. The mayor tries one more time. "Jack Hart will suffer the full measure of the law. For now," the mayor again pleads, "we need you to disperse. Please go to your homes."

This nearly impossible to hear oration, along with the 20 police officers surrounding the courthouse stairs, is enough to dissipate the dissatisfied multitude, robbed of the chance to see the ill-famed felon up close. Within twenty minutes, most of the crowd wandered off.

Inside Leach's courthouse office, a doctor summoned from Baltimore City Hospital examines the cut over Hart's eye. He tells his peevish patient, "You're a lucky man." Hart's wound requires six stitches. After applying a dressing, the doctor leaves.

Leach orders Hart, with dried blood still on his face, shirt, and suit coat, to take a seat in the same chair that John Keller occupied back on August 23rd. Everyone else remains standing.

Burns reports, "On the way back Hart had plenty to say. He is not the leader of any gang and denies he robbed or shot anyone. According to Mr. Hart, Charles "Country" Carey, and Frank "Stinky" Allers are the scoundrels who planned the robbery and did the shooting."

Hart sneers, "That's about it. I didn't shoot nobody."

O'Conor, looking down at Hart, tells him "I guess you know Frank Allers is a state's witness. He will testify that you are responsible for Mr. Norris' death."

Hart responds, "What would you expect that fool to say! What would you expect any of them to say. They're trying to save their goddam hides!"

Pounding his fist on the arm of the chair, Hart repeats, "I didn't kill nobody. You can't prove I did. I can't wait to get my hands on that worthless sonofabitch. Stinky's a goddam liar!"

O'Conor askes Hart about his name. "Are you Jack Hart or James Connelly?"

Hart answers, "I guess I'm both."

"Your wife claims she's Mrs. Connelly."

"Hart snaps back, "Good for her!'"

"Just for the record," O'Conor asks again, "Are you married to Katherine Kavanaugh?"

Less hostile, Hart says, "Yes, I guess I am. If Kitty wants to be called Mrs. Connelly, that's fine with me."

Hart, realizing he's in a bad spot, looks at Leach.

"If you make me a deal, I'll give you Walter Socolow. I know where he is."

Leach dismissing Hart's offer replies, "Mr. Hart or Connelly or whatever your name is, we tracked you down, and we'll get Walter Socolow without your help."

Leach orders Captain Burns to lock Hart up.

Before Hart can say another word, Burns and Murphy muscle him out of his chair. With Hart yelling, "Watch it—you're hurting my goddam arm," the two detectives hustle him toward the office door.

Hart pulls back and blurts out, "He's in New York! Noisy's in New York!"

Leach, without looking up, answers, "I think we know that."

Hart hollers back. "I can tell you where he is! I know where he is! You'll never find him without me!"

Leach doesn't respond.

Ignoring Hart's rantings and with Comen cuffed to Hart's left wrist and Murphy holding onto his right arm, they follow Burns into the hallway and down the stairway to the Calvert Street entrance.

Detective Kahler, Sergeant Oberon and Officer Hastings, back from Washington, along with Detective Hammersla are waiting in the parking lot.

Hart is packed into the back seat between Comen and Murphy. Hammersla jumps in next to Burns who is driving. Kahler, Oberon and Hastings follow in a second car. It's a ten-block drive northwest to 400 East Madison Street, the entrance to City Jail.

By 9:30 p.m., Jack Hart, locked in an eight-by-ten-foot cell, still whining about the gash on his brow and the dried blood caked on his face and clothes, is bellowing...

"No jail can hold me!—You'll see—No jail can hold Jack Hart!"

32
"THEY'VE CAUGHT JACK HART"

The following morning Sunday, September 17, 1922, "THEY'VE CAUGHT JACK HART" is the front-page lead in the *Baltimore News American's* morning addition. Other newspapers open with a similar headline. By mid-day, the apprehension of Jack Hart is a national story.

A rehash of the crime and the apprehension of Hart is the main story in the Sunday additions of *The New York Times* and *The Washington Post*. Sunday morning radio broadcasters embellished the daring capture of the infamous Jack Hart in the nation's capital. The lead article in *The Washington Herald* reads "GUNFIRE BLAZES AS JACK HART IS TAKEN."

The night before, Robert Leach called Governor Ritchie, Colonel Janney, Baltimore County State's Attorney Courtenay Jenifer, Mrs. William Norris, Robert Hicks, and Ed Tate to let them know that Hart was off the streets.

He asked Courtenay Jenifer if their staffs could meet on Monday to discuss the prosecutions of John Smith, Charles Carey, Jack Hart, and the other members of Hart's gang.

Jenifer agreed.

Leach and Commissioner Gaither called Metropolitan Police Chief Pratt to thank him and the men of his department for their help in tracking down and arresting Hart.

Pratt, appreciative of being part of the largest manhunt in decades answered, "It couldn't have gone any better."

Pratt reports that Buck Livingston is locked up in the District of Columbia Jail. He will remain there until his trial. Payton Gordon is charging Livingston with the illegal sale of whiskey on federal property, robbery, and tax evasion. "He will be tried in federal court in the capital."

Leach and Gaither thank Pratt again for his assistance and letting them know what awaits Bernard "Buck" Livingston. Leach isn't the slightest bit sorry that the fate of Livingston is out of his hands.

Robert Leach called for a Sunday meeting, in his office, to review the circumstances surrounding the arrest of Jack Hart and what to do next about unearthing Walter Socolow.

He has already met privately with Courtenay Jenifer.

Allowing everyone time to attend church services, Leach requests that Fleet Cox, Herbert O'Conor, Police Commissioner Charles Gaither, Captain of Detectives Charles Burns, and Detectives Sergeant William L. Murphy be in his office by eleven o'clock.

All agree to attend.

33

September Bombshell

Sunday, September 17, 1922, is a perfect early fall day. The temperature is a balmy 74 degrees. Church bells are ringing across Baltimore. The American flag over Federal Hill oscillates in a gentle breeze. People, dressed in their Sunday best, are browsing through the Broadway, Lexington, and Cross Street markets. There is minimal motorcar, wagon, and buggy activity on city streets.

With the exception of a telephone switchboard operator and four security guards, no one is working in the courthouse when everyone gathers in Leach's office. At 10:50, amidst a relaxed and almost casual atmosphere, Leach opens the meeting at the same conference table where Katherine Kavanaugh Connelly was interviewed on Saturday, August 26th.

There is good reason for the relaxed mood. Jack Hart is sitting in a jail cell ten blocks away. And the feeling is that Walter Socolow, in New York or somewhere else, can't evade capture much longer. Then it will be about establishing the evidence that will put Hart and his accomplices behind bars. Leach passes around an agenda. He plans to seek the death penalty for Hart, Carey, Smith, and Socolow. The first topic is Hart's name.

Leach and Jenifer have decided that Jack Hart (a.k.a. Connelly, among others) will be prosecuted as Jack Hart. His married name, James Connelly, will be presented as one of his pseudonyms. Cox suggests that they list his aliases in the indictment to cover all the bases.

Item two is about Hart's proposal to be a state's witness. Even though the previous day Leach dismissed Hart's offer to locate Walter Socolow, he brings it up. The consensus is, what can Hart add?

O'Conor says, "He doesn't have anything to offer. Socolow is probably in New York. But wherever he is, he has learned, like everyone else in the country, that Hart is in Baltimore City Jail. Socolow will be on the move."

Cox says, "I can only imagine the public outrage if Hart is tried for anything less than first-degree murder."

Burns points out that he and Lieutenant James Gegan have been in constant contact since his trip to New York on September 1st. "Yesterday, I told him about Hart's arrest and that Hart was desperate to make a deal. He said Socolow was in New York City. Gegan told me his department has been acting on this assumption from the beginning."

The sentiment in the conference room is that there will be no deal for Jack Hart.

Item three is locking in the evidence. Leach points out, "Frank Allers is still a questionable witness. So is John Keller. Their testimonies will be questioned. Allers is a hardened criminal and Keller is a teenage want-to-be. Both have traded their confessions to avoid being charged with first-degree murder. The defense will make an issue of this. We need credible witnesses to support Allers' and Keller's testimony."

Everyone agrees. Securing a death penalty in Baltimore City is never easy.

Leach asks, "What do we do about Katherine Kavanaugh Connelly. Should she be charged as an accessory or subpoenaed as a witness?"

O'Conor advises, "If Katherine Kavanaugh is put on the stand, she will muddy the waters by insisting she is Mrs. James Connelly—not Mrs. Jack Hart. Little will be gained by either calling her as a witness or prosecuting her. She will come across as a sympathetic young woman who despite being taken advantage of by her husband, if she was taken advantage of, still cares for him."

"With Hart in jail and after Socolow is arrested and no longer a threat," Leach predicts, "the members of Katherine Kavanaugh's family - mother, sister, and brother - should be more forthcoming. I have no doubt that Joe Kavanaugh was in the whiskey business with Hart. Kavanaugh knows and always has known Jack Hart and James Connelly are the same man. I don't think Joe Kavanaugh will risk his company to protect Hart."

Cox says, "Joe Kavanaugh's testimony will be of little value. For now, I think we should keep Old Joe in the dark—unsure if he will be charged."

There is no opposition to this.

Addressing Commissioner Gaither, Leach says, "We need for the police to talk to everyone again, every person associated with this case, including Bernard Livingston and his wife. Dorothy Livingston is scheduled to meet us tomorrow. We can start with her."

Leach asks the Commissioner, "Can you have Captain Burns' unit contact every witness to affirm their statements?"

Gaither, gesturing toward Burns, responds, "Charles' men are already on this."

Burns responds, "We are."

Leach brings up Harry Wolf and Captain Leverton. "I want to prosecute Wolf for obstruction of justice."

He asks Gaither to have his detectives keep Wolf and Leverton under surveillance.

Gaither answers, "I will." Then adds, "I have decided to leave Leverton on duty—easier to keep track of him. When he learns of Wolf's indictment, my guess is he will be less inclined to protect him."

O'Conor adds, "There is no question but that Wolf and Leverton helped perpetuate the Boston-Chicago fiasco."

Cox interjects, "A case against Wolf will depend on the believability of John Keller. It might be a good idea to call Wolf as a witness when we prosecute Socolow. Wolf is a slick character—sometimes too slick. He won't let a little thing like perjury block his efforts to separate himself from Socolow and Keller. Wolf's best defense is to deny everything. He will argue that anything Keller or Socolow say to incriminate him is fabricated. Who can say otherwise?"

Leach reminds everyone, "Herb,[11] Courtnay,[12] the Commissioner,[13] and I have had this conversation and agree with Fleet.[14] Wolf will deny everything starting with inviting Socolow and Keller into his house on August 18th."

All concur that an indictment of Harry Wolf and possibly calling him as a witness when they try Socolow makes good sense. If nothing else, it will prevent Wolf from representing Socolow or Hart.

"It could very well lead," O'Conor interjects, "to Wolf's conviction and disbarment."

The consensus is Harry B. Wolf should be indicted.

The conversation continues until 11:55, when Leach adjourns the meeting so that Sunday won't be a total recreational loss to the individuals who have been on the job, nonstop, since August

11 Herbert O'Conor, Assistant Baltimore City States Attorney.

12 Courtnay Jenifer, Baltimore County State's Attorney.

13 Charles Gaither, Baltimore City Police Commissioner.

14 Fleet Cox, Deputy Baltimore City States Attorney.

18th. He thanks everyone for coming.

As the group collects their notes, stand up and begin to leave, Detective Lieutenant Charles Kahler bolts into the conference room. Everyone stops to hear what the out-of-breath detective has to say.

Kahler exclaims: "Socolow has been arrested in New York!"

Burns asks—"When?"

Kahler answers, "This morning about ten o'clock at a Manhattan newsstand."

"Lieutenant Gegan has the details and is waiting for you to call him back. He's at the Centre Street headquarters building. I have the number."

Gaither asks Leach, "Can Captain Burns call Lieutenant Gegan from here?"

Leach answers, "Yes! We can use the telephone in my office. It's coupled to an amplifier."

At 12:25, New York Detective Lieutenant James Gegan answers the telephone.[15]

Burns lets Gegan know who is present. New York Detective Lieutenant James Gegan begins to unwind the story that led to the arrest of Walter Socolow.

---

15 On the call: New York City Police Lieutenant, James Gegan, Baltimore City Police Captain of Detectives, Charles Burns; Baltimore City State's Attorney, Robert Leach; Deputy Baltimore City State's Attorney, Fleet Cox, Assistant Baltimore City State's Attorney, Herbert O'Conor; Baltimore City Police Commissioner, Charles Gaither, Baltimore City Police Detective Lieutenant, Charles Kahler.

34

THE REEMERGENCE OF NOISY

Walter "Noisy" Socolow

G egan begins: "Walter Socolow was spotted by detectives Christopher Kelley and Cornelius Browne at 9:15 this morning. Socolow was purchasing a *Baltimore Sun* newspaper at the corner of 6th Avenue and 42nd Street, at the north end of Bryant Park in Manhattan."

"According to Detectives Browne and Kelly, Socolow was disheveled and unshaven. They were certain; however, it was Noisy Socolow they were watching cross 42nd Street to the corner newsstand."

"The detectives had his description and picture. They had been on the lookout for Socolow since September 1st and had come close to capturing him yesterday."

"The previous afternoon (about the same time Burns and Mansfield were in Washington waiting for Jack Hart and Buck Livingston to return to the Auburn Apartments), Kelly, Browne and several uniformed officers raided the once opulent American

Hotel[16] in the town of Sag Harbor on Long Island, east of the City on Gardiner's Bay. Sag Harbor is a good place to blend in among those unlikely to ask questions."

"My unit missed capturing Socolow by a few hours. The desk clerk told them that the newcomer, who had been there since Monday, September 11th, was expecting a buddy who never checked in. The clerk informed Detective Kelly that the man, who identified himself as Bill Smith, looked to be about twenty years old."

"Smith had checked out less than three hours earlier. The clerk added that Smith, visibly frustrated that the person he was waiting for didn't show, asked about catching a train to Chicago. He told Smith – Grand Central Terminal at 42nd Street and Park Avenue in Midtown. Smith paid in cash and left."

"I moved to have the police swarm the 42nd Street Terminal. My men remained positioned throughout the terminal until 11:30 p.m. Socolow didn't appear. There were four patrolmen in the terminal throughout the night. I made certain each officer had Socolow's description."

"The first train to Chicago was scheduled to leave at 11:45 a.m. today, Sunday, September 17th. Beginning at 5:00 a.m., I had a sizable force, led by Browne and Kelly, stakeout the perimeter of the terminal (North-South from 40th to 43rd Streets and East-West from 3rd to 6th Avenues). By chance, Kelly and Browne were waiting in their patrol car at 41st Street and 6th Avenue, directly across from the western edge of Bryant Park, when they spotted Socolow."

---

16 The American Hotel, located in Sag Harbor, an incorporated village in Suffolk County, New York was built in 1846 at the height of the whaling industry. By 1922, with whaling in decline, the hotel and town fell into disrepair. Today, the American Hotel is a restored small luxury guesthouse sandwiched between the affluent townships of South Hampton and East Hampton (known as the Hamptons) overlooking Sag Harbor Bay (formally Gardner Bay). But in 1922, when Walter Socolow was on the run, Sag Harbor was a good place to blend in and avoid recognition.

"Socolow never saw them coming. He was still standing in front of the newsstand hurriedly paging through the *Baltimore Sun* when Browne and Kelly, guns drawn, approached from behind. As Browne and Kelly grabbed hold of the unsuspecting Socolow, Kelly gave him a good look at his drawn revolver and sarcastically asked, 'Do you see anything interesting in the paper—Noisy?'"

"Socolow began to resist but went submissively limp, expelling a slurred groan, when Brown delivered a hard punch to Noisy's ribs. Within seconds, Socolow was cuffed. Browne retrieved a snub nosed .38 from Noisy's coat pocket. There was only $26 left in Socolow's otherwise empty billfold. Detective Kelly noticed that the leather billfold was embossed with the initials WBN."

"As he was being hauled across 6th Avenue to Browne's and Kelly's patrol car, Socolow insisted his name was Bill Smith and protested that they were arresting the wrong man. Kelly pointed out that the name Bill Smith didn't match up with "WBN," the letters on his wallet. Paying no attention to Kelly's observation, Noisy moaned that he was in pain because of Browne's unwarranted blow. Browne recounted that Socolow said he was going to report him for beating up an innocent bystander. Browne and Kelly paid little attention as they hauled Socolow to their car and cuffed him to the frame of a seat."

"While Socolow droned on that Browne must have broken a rib, he continued to plead that his name was Bill Smith. He never heard 'of that other guy.' Kelly retrieved an FBI wanted poster picturing Socolow and showed it to Noisy. Undeterred, Socolow insisted that the picture wasn't him. Browne, having had enough of Noisy's incessant squawking, threatened another wallop if he didn't shut up."

"With Kelly driving and Browne directly behind Socolow, who was still cuffed to the seat, they headed for Department Headquarters where they turned Socolow over to me. By then Socolow had confessed his identity."

Gegan continued, "We have Socolow booked and locked in a detention cell. Kelly and Browne recounted that on the way to department headquarters, Socolow, hungry, tired, and smelly, began to talk"

"Realizing that the police were looking for them everywhere, Socolow and Hart left the cemetery (Sweet Home Cemetery in East Baltimore) and walked south to Pratt Street, where they were able to ditch their suits and procure nondescript clothes from the Salvation Army Mission. They spent two days sleeping in an abandoned tug. Despite their faces printed on wanted posters and in newspapers, no one seemed to recognize them. Unnoticed among the stevedores and shipwrights working in Fells Point, they even helped offload produce from Eastern Shore clippers."

"Socolow and Hart reached Buck Livingston's apartment by hitching a ride on an oyster schooner that dropped them off at Spa Creek, close to Annapolis. From Annapolis, they caught a bus to the Washington, D.C. terminal and walked to Livingston's apartment. Livingston's wife became upset when her husband invited them to stay. Through a Washington bootlegger, Phil Falesca, one of Livingston's cohorts, Socolow and Hart were able to get a room at the View Hotel."

"On Thursday, September 7th, Hart and Socolow split up. Despite his wife's protest, Buck Livingston agreed to let Hart stay at their apartment. Socolow made his way to Harrisburg, Allentown, Newark, and then New York City. Hart told Socolow to go to the American Hotel, at the east end of Long Island, where he had a contact that would help them relocate to Chicago. Hart would follow, in five or six days. He never showed up."

"On Saturday, September 16th, it took Socolow all afternoon to bum rides and walk from the American Hotel to Manhattan. By the time he reached Midtown, it was too late to catch a train to Chicago. He spent the night in the basement of Holy Cross

Church on 42nd Street, two blocks west of Bryant Park."

"Having no idea that Hart had been arrested or anything going on in Baltimore, Socolow stopped to buy a *Baltimore Sun* and a train schedule. He planned to lay low in Bryant Park until he could purchase a ticket to Chicago."

"While passing time waiting for Jack Hart at the American Hotel, Socolow met a Chicago mobster named Charlie "The Ox" Reiser, who worked for Dean O'Banion—the boss of Chicago's North Side Gang. O'Banion, according to Socolow, had sent Reiser to New York to recruit a few out-of-towners to join the North Side Gang to avoid local hoods who he suspected might be loyal to rivals."

"Three days before, Reiser set out for Chicago with two aspiring goons from Newark, but left an address, telling Noisy that O'Banion could give him something to do if he made it to Chicago."

Gegan then informs Burns, "We can't turn Socolow over without an extradition order—that should be easy enough."

Burns agrees and reminds Gegan, "Commissioner Gaither and Baltimore State's Attorney Robert Leach are listening in."

Leach tells Burns, "Let Lieutenant Gegan know—I will get Governor Ritchie to sign a fugitive warrant tomorrow."

"One more thing," Gegan adds, "I thought it was a revelation of foolish chutzpah that after smugly telling Browne and Kelly how he and Hart escaped apprehension, Socolow swore he was innocent of the crime for which he fled Baltimore."

"He told Kelly and Browne that he didn't shoot anyone. He was on the other side of town, asleep in bed with his girlfriend when Norris was shot. He blamed the Carey, Smith, Lewis Gang and Stinky Allers, for robbing and killing William Norris. Sounds crazy," Gegan tells Burns, "but that's what the dummy said."

Leach asks O'Conor to get the extradition papers ready for Governor Ritchie's signature. "I will call and update the Mayor and Governor."

Relieved that Socolow is no longer on the run, Commissioner Gaither, Captain Burns, and Detective Kahler walk back to the police building. Robert Leach, Fleet Cox, and Herbert O'Conor head home with a well-earned sense of relief. It's been 31 days since William Norris was gunned down on Madison Street. Today the last thug involved in the crime, the man who pulled the trigger, was behind bars in New York.

Despite the pervasive broadsheet criticisms of Leach's secrecy and Commissioner Gaither's failure to find Hart and Socolow fast enough, the arrest of Socolow is a triumph worth celebrating.

The lead story on Monday morning September 18, 1922, heralded:

SOCOLOW CAPTURED IN NEW YORK

....

SOON TO BE RETURNED TO BALTIMORE

It wouldn't be that easy.

1922 Postcard of the Baltimore Sun *Building. Completed in 1905, it was erected on the southwest corner of Charles and Baltimore Streets after the first Sun building was destroyed in the 1904 Baltimore Fire. In 1922, the* Baltimore Sun *was a premier national newspaper. It remains Baltimore's newspaper of record. It was founded in 1837 by Arunah Shepherdson Abell. At the time, the intersection of Charles and Baltimore Streets was considered Baltimore's central commercial intersection. In 1960, the building was raised to make way for the Lyric Theater, which was demolished in 2006 to make room for a residential building, which as of 2023, has not been built. The lot remains undeveloped. Although diminished in its national circulation because of new communication technologies, the* Baltimore Sun *remains Maryland's foremost newspaper. The* Sun *also circulates a daily internet edition. In 1922, the* Baltimore Sun *covered the Norris murder case and associated criminal trials of Charles Carey, John Smith, Walter Socolow, and Jack Hart. The* Baltimore Sun *provided, upon request, photographs, articles and transcripts germane to portions of* Murder on Madison Street.

35

EXTRADITION DELAYED

On Monday Morning at 10:00 a.m., Governor Albert Ritchie signed a Fugitive Warrant requesting the extradition of Walter Socolow from New York City to Baltimore, Maryland.

On Tuesday September 19th, Commissioner Gaither dispatched Detective Sergeant William Murphy and Detective Lieutenant Charles Kahler to Albany, New York, to deliver the extradition warrant to Governor Nathan L. Miller for his signature. After a seven-hour train ride, with delays in Wilmington and New York City, Murphy and Kahler finally pulled into Albany at 5:15 p.m. Governor Miller, who had been waiting, signed the extradition order 30 minutes later.

With the extradition order signed by both governors, Murphy and Kahler headed back to New York City. When the Western Express pulled into Pennsylvania Station at 8:50 p.m., Lieutenant Gegan and Detective Lieutenant George Gilbert, whose unit was instrumental in New York's hunt for Hart and Socolow, were waiting with luckless news.

Walter Socolow had agreed to return to Baltimore. As of today, Gegan and Gilbert apprised Kahler and Murphy, Socolow has an attorney who filed a writ of *habeas corpus* in his behalf. Detective Gilbert ask Murphy and Kahler, "Do you know a Baltimore attorney by the name of Harry Wolf?"

Kahler answers, "Yes—very well."

Gilbert goes on to explain, "Wolf called New York Police Commissioner Richard Edward Enright's office demanding to speak with Socolow on the premise that he was Socolow's attorney. When questioned, Socolow confirmed that Wolf represented him in Maryland. After conferring with New York City State's

Attorney Joseph Banton, Enright had no choice but to let Wolf speak to Socolow. Shortly after the call, a lawyer named Moses Polakoff met with Socolow. Polakoff then filed a writ of *habeas corpus* in New York's Supreme Court."

Murphy and Kahler understood the ramifications. Socolow will be brought before a judge to secure his immediate release on the grounds that he was being wrongly detained. New York City State's Attorney, Joseph Banton, must prove that there are lawful grounds for Socolow's continued detention. Extradition then becomes another issue. How long he is held in New York, or possibly released, is up to a judge. Socolow could be in New York for months. Lieutenant Kahler called Robert Leach.

As a precaution, Leach tells Kahler that he is sending Herbert O'Conor to New York tonight. "I want Mr. O'Conor in New York's Supreme Court tomorrow when Socolow's lawyer argues for his release. O'Conor can request immediate extradition after the judge rules on the writ. I'm confident the writ will be dismissed, and Socolow will be turned over to you, but you never know. Mr. O'Conor will be there just in case something unexpected happens."

Leach also tells Kahler that he will place calls to New York City State's Attorney Joseph Banton and William Hayward (United States Attorney for the Southern District of New York) to secure their advice and assistance. Leach explains, "Much depends on the judge, but I don't anticipate extradition will be delayed."

Herbert O'Conor arrives at New York's Pennsylvania Station at 10:55 p.m. Lieutenant Gegan has arranged lodging for O'Conor, Murphy and Kahler at the Grand Central Hotel, compliments of New York Police Commissioner, Richard Enright.

The Central Hotel is located on Broadway, only a few blocks from Police Department Headquarters and the New York County "Tweed" Courthouse next to City Hall. Lieutenant Gilbert, who had met Murphy when they were working together on another interstate investigation, offers to be their driver.

Even though it was past midnight, United States Attorney William Hayward calls O'Conor. Following up, after his telephone conference with Leach, Hayward offers his support telling O'Conor, "I can't imagine that the writ will be upheld. I believe Socolow will be handed over to your Baltimore detectives—tomorrow."

Hayward tells O'Conor that he will meet him in the Courthouse at 8:30 a.m. Hayward knows the nine Supreme Court Justices and if need be, will assist in arguing for the extradition of Socolow. "I anticipate the hearing will take place before noon; but the time and the presiding judge will not be posted until 8:00 a.m."

After Hayward's call, Kahler and Murphy join O'Conor in his suite to review Leach's and Hayward's assessments of what to expect tomorrow. Both are confident that Socolow will be turned over to Kahler and Murphy.

September 20, 1922 – Breakfast at the Grand Central Hotel

At 6:30 a.m. Detective Lieutenant Gilbert meets Kahler, Murphy, and O'Conor for breakfast in the Central Hotel's dining room, a stately chamber with 20-foot ceilings. O'Conor thanks Gilbert for his help while they are in New York.

Gilbert asks, "After the judge turns Socolow over to Kahler and Murphy, how are you returning to Baltimore?"

O'Conor answers, "I've booked tickets for a private compartment on the Capital Limited. It leaves Pennsylvania Station at four o'clock."

Gilbert says, "I'll stay at the courthouse and drive you to the station."

O'Conor replies, "That would be great—thanks!"

Gilbert adds, "I'll park my car in front of the courthouse. When the hearing is over, in afternoon traffic, it's about 30 minutes to Pennsylvania Station."

O'Conor says, "I hope it will be that easy to get Socolow back to Baltimore."

Over poached eggs, toast, mixed fruit, and coffee, the three detectives and one prosecutor swap stories about cases in New York and Baltimore. Kahler and Murphy detail the capture of Hart and the other members of his gang. Kahler boasts, "They are not the smartest lot of crooks. Except for Hart and Socolow, we swept them up in less than a week, six by the next day."

Gilbert is particularly fascinated by the Boston-Chicago kidnapping ruse. He imagines, with enthusiasm, how delightfully miserable it must have been for the cunning Mr. Hart and his fatuous buddy, Noisy Socolow, sweating in that unbearably hot, rubbish filled mausoleum.

Murphy recaps the apprehension of Hart and Livingston at the Auburn Apartments. "The two tough guys," Murphy tells Gilbert, "didn't put up much of a fight. I couldn't believe the size of the crowd when we showed up at the courthouse. It looked like everyone in Baltimore was there. I suppose it will be the same when we haul in Socolow."

There was no mention of Iris Millman or Dorothy Livingston. When asked whose tip led to Hart's capture, O'Conor tells Gilbert, "Mr. Leach has ordered us not to disclose the name of the informant." Gilbert didn't press the issue. He understands the importance of anonymous sources whose names are too often leaked. In New York. Once outed, anonymous sources can disappear.

Revealing to Lieutenant Gilbert that they believed Harry Wolf hid Socolow and John Keller in his kitchen the night of the crime, Kahler tells Gilbert, "We were surprised to learn that Wolf called New York Police Commissioner Enright claiming he was Socolow's attorney."

Gilbert answers, "Polakoff is a criminal attorney who has represented members of the D'Aquila crime family. James Connelly, your Jack Hart, was a soldier for Salvatore "Toto" D'Aquila before leaving New York after he was released from Sing-Sing for killing Jumbo Wells."

O'Conor isn't surprised that Wolf is representing Socolow. Inwardly, O'Conor thinks it's a smart move. As Socolow's attorney, Wolf will have influence over what Socolow might or might not say during his trial. It could prevent Wolf from being named as a witness for the prosecution. He can reframe his involvement. O'Conor explains, "It is all the more reason to prosecute Wolf for obstruction of justice."

At 7:50 a.m., Lieutenant Gilbert drops O'Conor, Murphy, and Kahler off at the New York County Courthouse's imposing 52 Chambers Street entrance.

Forever under construction, the cornerstone of the Italianate style edifice was laid in 1861. Its original design was based on the United States Capitol. A 40-step granite stairway leads to the first mezzanine portico entrance buttressed by four three-story-high Corinthian columns.

The courthouse basement is above ground with huge casement windows at street level. The first and second Romanesque marble-faced mezzanine floors are where the court chambers, with ornamental ceilings, are situated around a massive central rotunda.[17]

United States Attorney for New York's Southern District, William Hayward, and New York City State's Attorney Joseph Banton were waiting for O'Conor and Detectives Murphy and Kahler when they entered the main lobby.

New York City District Attorney Joseph "Joab" Banton has some more disheartening news. "The Socolow hearing," he tells O'Conor, "will be held in courtroom 202 on the second mezzanine level. The presiding judge is a Tammany Hall Democrat—Francis W. Martin. Before becoming a Supreme Court justice in 1921, Justice Martin was openly critical of and vehemently opposed to Governor Miller. Believe me," Banton tells O'Conor, "there is no love lost between the two of them."

---

17 Located just south of City Hall, The New York County Courthouse, the second oldest government building in New York City, was soon dubbed the Tweed Courthouse after William M. Tweed, a Tammany Hall politician known as "Boss Tweed." The building wasn't called the Tweed Courthouse out of veneration for Boss Tweed. Rather the twelve-year construction project became infamous as one of New York City's greatest financial boondoggles.

Over the years of construction, Tweed, who ran Tammany Hall and was a New City Senator and Aldermen, embezzled between twenty and thirty-million dollars for himself and his Tammany Hall accomplices. No one has ever been able to tabulate the exact amount.

In 1873, under Federal indictment, Tweed was convicted of forgery, larceny, and other crimes. He was sentenced to fifteen years in jail. He managed to escape, with inside help, in 1875. Having stashed millions of dollars in the United States and overseas, Tweed fled to Miami where he bribed a boat captain to take him to Cuba. From Cuba, Tweed boarded a steamship to Spain. In 1876. Two years later, Tweed was recognized, arrested by Spanish police, extradited back to the United States, and returned to prison. On April 12, 1878, William M. "Boss" Tweed died of pneumonia in the Ludlow Street Jail, the federal penitentiary in Manhattan.

Justice Martin was born in the poorest section of the Bronx in 1878 and never left Bronx County. By the time he graduated from New York Law School in 1902, he was an ascending star in the Bronx County Democratic Party. Martin prides himself on rising from modest circumstances to becoming the first Bronx County District Attorney in 1913. It was with the support of Tammany Hall Boss, Charles Francis Murphy, that he ran for Bronx County District Attorney and was elected. With the backing of Mayor John Hylan, another Tammany Hall Democrat, Martin was appointed a Justice of the New York Supreme Court in 1921.

Martin had little use for and was often critical of Governor Miller, who is tight with Andrew Carnegie, the founder of United States Steel Corporation, and a staunch conservative Republican. Miller had unseated Al Smith, Martin's Tammany Hall friend and patron, in 1920. Governor Miller views Tammany Hall as a corrupt political machine that he has promised to defuse.

Joab Banton tells O'Conor, "Justice Martin requested to rule on Walter Socolow's petition. Even though the extradition warrant to return Socolow to Maryland is a fugitive warrant, signed by both governors, Martin is not likely to make it a *fait accompli.*"

"Judge Martin opposes Governor Miller's efforts to appoint conservative Republican judges and his—in Martin's view—unwarranted investigations into Tammany Hall's influence over state court proceedings. Even if he has little choice," Banton tells O'Conor, "Martin will extract his pound of legal flesh, beginning with the time of your hearing. Socolow's petition is scheduled to be the last item on today's docket."

Although not a federal matter, Bill Hayward tells O'Conor, "Justice Martin has no options. He will have to dismiss the writ. The question is will he honor the extradition warrant immediately or string things out."

O'Conor responds, "Justice Martin or any Judge can't block

Socolow's extradition. Article IV, Section II, Clause 2 of the Constitution is well-defined. It requires criminals like Walter Socolow to be delivered, upon demand, to the State having jurisdiction. He should dismiss the writ and turn Socolow over to Murphy and Kahler."

Banton quips, "The founding fathers didn't know Justice Martin. It's impossible to predict what he will do. He may dismiss the writ but delay extradition. Anyway, the hearing won't take place until after lunch, as late as three o'clock."

O'Conor realizes that even if Martin dismisses the writ and turns Socolow over to Murphy and Kahler, there is no chance they will make a four o'clock train to Baltimore. O'Conor accompanies Banton to the office of a courthouse clerk to place a call to Robert Leach—telling Banton and Hayward, "Mr. Leach won't be pleased with what I have to say."

Hayward excuses himself. He promises to return before the hearing, telling O'Conor, "My support might be helpful."

Hayward, a 20-year veteran prosecutor recognizes that O'Conor is a young State's Attorney who has no experience with the workings of the New York judicial system, not to mention the unpredictable temperament of Justice Martin.

New York police Lieutenants Gegan and Gilbert show up at 9:30 a.m. Murphy and Kahler explain the situation. Gegan tells his Baltimore counterparts, "Judge Martin can be tough, but I can't believe he will delay extradition." The four detectives return to New York police headquarters. Gegan and Gilbert want to show Murphy and Kahler how things are done in the biggest city in America. They let O'Conor know that they will return after lunch.

Courtroom 202 – Wednesday Afternoon, September 20, 1922

At 2:45 p.m., the Bench Clerk calls for the hearing in the case of Walter Socolow. Socolow has been brought to the courtroom from a ground-floor holding cell. He is clean shaven. His hair is slicked down and he is outfitted in a light grey suit. A sheriff escorts Socolow to his seat next to Moses Polakoff. Before Socolow sits down, the sheriff removes his handcuffs .

O'Conor, Bill Hayward, and Joseph Banton take seats at a table to the right of Socolow, who can't help staring at his antagonists. Banton, as New York City State's Attorney, will represent the defendants named in the writ of *habeas corpus* (Mayor John F. Hylan and Police Commissioner Richard E. Enright). Neither Hylan nor Enright will attend the hearing.

Hayward knows Martin. He collaborated with the judge on several cases when Martin was the Bronx County District Attorney. Hayward and Martin maintain a cordial relationship. Hayward (when and if asked by Justice Martin) will offer his legal opinion favoring extradition. But arguments for and against the writ come first.

Detectives Kahler, Murphy, Gilbert and Gegan take seats in the gallery directly behind Banton and O'Conor. A court stenographer assumes her place next to the bench clerk. A seemingly humorless bailiff, in charge of courtroom discipline, stands quietly by the bench watching over the gallery that is filling up.

Everyone wants to get a look at the man charged with killing William Norris. Journalists flood in. Kahler and Murphy wave to George Dorsch, the *Baltimore Sun* crime-beat reporter who nods back. The *Baltimore News American* sent Richard "Dick" Erwin, its top crime reporter. Since August 19th, anything involving the whereabouts of Jack Hart and Walter Socolow has solicited national coverage.

At 2:55 p.m., Justice Martin enters the courtroom from a door leading to the bench from his private chambers and assumes his seat. Martin, without reacting to anyone, takes a few minutes to review Socolow's (writ) petition. At three o'clock, he gestures to the bailiff, who awakens from his self-induced coma and calls for everyone to stand—a superfluous command, as from the moment Judge Martin entered the courtroom, everyone was standing. In a booming voice the bailiff announces: "The Supreme Court of New York is in session—the Honorable Justice Francis W. Martin Jr. presiding. Please be seated."

Justice Martin doesn't waste any time. "We're here today to uphold or deny the request of Mr. Walter Socolow to be released for unlawful arrest as stated in the plaintiff's petition. It is any individual's right, should they be detained, to be brought before the court seeking recourse for unlawful arrest." Judge Martin concludes, "We are here this afternoon to determine whether or not the plaintiff, Mr. Walter Socolow, should be released or continue to be detained in New York."

Justice Martin adds that there is a secondary issue. "The State of Maryland is requesting that Mr. Socolow, in accordance with the extradition agreement between Maryland and New York, be returned to Baltimore, Maryland, to stand trial for an alleged crime he is accused of having committed there."

Then looking at Polakoff, Martin inquires: "Does your client understand these two separate issues."

Polakoff replies. "Your Honor, the reasons for Mr. Socolow's release, as presented to the court, are fully understood by my client."

Noisy nods his head in agreement.

Polakoff continues, "We believe, Your Honor, extradition is a separate matter for another day."

Martin answers, "Duly noted."

Shifting to the Defendant's side of the bench, speaking directly to New York City State's Attorney Joseph Banton, Martin wants to know if Banton is prepared to defend against the Grounds for

Relief cited in Mr. Socolow's petition.

Banton answers, "Yes, Your Honor"—then adds, "I am representing the defendants, Mayor of New York, and Commissioner of Police. They will not be appearing in court today. We believe Mr. Socolow's petition is an effort by the plaintiff to avoid extradition."

Turning toward O'Conor, Banton formally introduces Herbert R. O'Conor as an Assistant State's Attorney for Baltimore City, here representing Baltimore City State's Attorney Robert Leach.

Justice Martin, addressing O'Conor, asks, "Mr. O'Conor, do you have anything to add?"

O'Conor restates his name and position then clarifies that he is ready to answer questions related to Mr. Socolow's petition and the reasons for his extradition. "I am respectfully requesting," O'Conor continues, "Mr. Socolow be turned over as soon as possible in accordance with the warrant signed by both Governor Albert Ritchie of Maryland and Governor Nathan Miller of New York."

Martin questions, "If extradition is so important to Maryland, Mr. O'Conor, why isn't your boss, Robert Leach, here?"

O'Conor, somewhat taken back, replies, "Mr. Leach appointed me associate prosecutor for the Norris case. Learning that a petition for a writ of *habeas corpus* was filed in New York, Mr. Leach thought I might be needed to assist the detectives dispatch to bring Mr. Socolow back to Baltimore."

Looking at Joseph Banton, Martin questions, "Mr. O'Conor says he's here to assist his detectives. I assume you are also here to assist Mr. O'Conor?"

Banton standing, replies, "Yes, Your Honor." Then adds, "Assuming the writ is dismissed, I have offered to support Mr. O'Conor during the extradition hearing that will follow."

"Are you assuming," Martin responds, "I will routinely dismiss Mr. Socolow's petition?"

"No, Your Honor," Banton answers, "I would not be so presumptuous."

Martin pauses for a moment but doesn't respond, then turns to William Hayward, who is also standing. "Good to see you, Mr. Hayward. I trust you've been well." Then adds, "I didn't know this was a matter for the U.S. Attorney."

Hayward, who has known Judge Martin for years replies, "Thank you, Judge. I am doing very well indeed. It's good to see you also." Then Hayward explains, "Mr. O'Conor has not argued in a New York court. I'm here, as a friend of the court, and if asked, to assist Mr. O'Conor."

"With your and Mr. Banton's help," Martin, looking at Hayward, says, "young Mr. O'Conor seems well advised."

Martin addressing Polakoff, who quickly stands, asks: "As the plaintiff's attorney, Mr. Polakoff, why don't you begin."

Glancing at the petition (of which Justice Martin, Banton, O'Conor, and Hayward have copies) Polakoff begins to recite his "Grounds for Relief" explaining why Walter Socolow should be released from City Jail, known as the Tombs.

"Mr. Socolow is not guilty of any crime in New York City or the State of New York. He was snatched off the street by two police brutes who beat him up and booked him without cause. He was subsequently transferred from a holding cell in the police building to City Jail where he has been incarcerated since his arrest on September 17th."

"My client is accused of a crime, in Baltimore City, [that] he did not commit. Mr. Socolow was, in fact, asleep in bed at the time, more than a mile away from the scene of the crime. There are witnesses in Baltimore that will testify to this."

"The only witness against my client in Baltimore is a convicted criminal named Frank Allers, who did take part in the crime, and lied about Mr. Socolow to avoid being charged with murder."

Judge Martin interrupts: "Why did Mr. Socolow flee Maryland?"

Polakoff continues, "Mr. Socolow was convicted in the newspapers and by the police before he had a chance to turn himself in, which he was willing to do. He had an associate, a friend, named John Keller, go to the police for this very reason. The police arrested Mr. Keller. He is presently in custody, isolated in the Maryland Penitentiary, for the purpose of preventing him from exonerating my client. Mr. Socolow believed he was being railroaded and needed to get as far away from Baltimore as possible. This, of course, was an error in judgement, but my client is just a frightened young man who acted impulsively."

"But as I said, Your Honor, this petition is not about an alleged crime in Baltimore. It's about being falsely accused, arrested, and illegally imprisoned here in New York. My client is a victim of adversely aroused public sentiment inflamed by the fallacious assertions by the Baltimore Police and State's Attorney to newspapers across the country. Mr. Socolow should be released at once."

"Mr. Polakoff," Martin questions, "if Mr. Socolow fled Baltimore as a fugitive to avoid arrest, why then was his arrest in New York unlawful?"

Polakoff has a ready answer. "Your Honor, there was no extradition order in place when my client was arrested. He has not been indicted in Baltimore by a grand jury. As far as my client is concerned, he was guilty of nothing in Baltimore or New York, and was therefore arrested without cause, brutally palpitated by the police, and wrongly imprisoned. Extradition is not the purpose of this hearing and should not now be considered."

Martin calmly replies, "Please leave it to me—what should be considered."

Polakoff backing off—says, "I meant no offense.

Justice Martin acknowledging Mr. Polakoff's argument then turns to Banton, "Your turn, Mr. Banton."

State's Attorney Joseph Banton begins, "On August 19, 1922, Your Honor, a Bench Warrant was issued by Judge Carol T. Bond of the Supreme Bench of Baltimore City. I am told by Mr. O'Conor that the pending charge is murder in the first degree of William B. Norris on August 18, 1922, on Madison Street in Baltimore City. The arrest warrant, signed by Judge Bond, is sufficient to validate Mr. Socolow's extradition."

Justice Martin responds, "So noted."

Then Banton recites Article IV, Section II, Clause 2 of the Constitution, adding: "The return of Walter Socolow to Maryland is precisely what the United States Constitution and the Extradition Agreement between New York and Maryland requires by law. This, supported by Judge Bond's arrest warrant, is the lawful reason the plaintiff was arrested in Bryant Park."

"Yes," Banton continues, "It's true that no extradition warrant was issued when Mr. Socolow was arrested in New York City, but it is certainly enforceable regardless of timing. By any extradition warrant's denotation, its execution can only occur after a fugitive has fled the issuing jurisdiction."

"Finally, Your Honor, everyone in the United States, perhaps much of the world, is aware of the crime committed in Baltimore and the subsequent search for Jack Hart and Walter Socolow. It has been widely publicized as far back as August 19, 1922, the date Judge Bond's warrants were issued for the arrest of Mr. Socolow, and Jack Hart, who is in custody, and others involved in the robbery and murder. Whether or not an extradition warrant was signed before Mr. Socolow's arrest is immaterial."

"The City of New York, on behalf of the Mayor and Commissioner, is not here arguing that the Plaintiff should or should not be extradited; that is explicitly elucidated in the extradition warrant signed by Maryland Governor Ritchie on September 18th and New York Governor Miller the following day. Rather, given the August 19th warrant for the arrest of Mr. Socolow and his pending trial in Baltimore City, Mr. Socolow's petition should be denied on the grounds that he is a known fugitive on the run and should accordingly be held here in New York until he is remanded to the State of Maryland. Mr. Socolow is a dangerous criminal who will surely flee if released."

Banton thanks Justice Martin for his attention and takes his seat.

Martin then asks, "Mr. O'Conor do you have anything to add?"

O'Conor stands and replies, "I have nothing to add beyond what Mr. Banton has presented to the court. I request, Your Honor, if you rule to dismiss the writ, that you order Walter Socolow to be turned over to Baltimore City detectives Kahler and Murphy forthwith."

Martin responds, "Not so fast, Mr. O'Conor."

Martin, addressing the court, announces, "I will consider the arguments so stipulated in Mr. Socolow's petition, Mr. Polakoff's remarks, and Mr. Banton's argument against the petition and rule (on the writ - only) tomorrow, Thursday, September 21, 1922, at four o'clock."

Martin, addressing O'Conor, asks, "Do you have proof that Mr. Socolow was in Baltimore on August 18, 1922? Are there witnesses that can, without equivocation, place Mr. Socolow at the scene of the crime?"

Before answering, O'Conor looks quizzically at Banton as if to say, "What's the Judge talking about?"

Shrugging his shoulders, Banton gestures back to O'Conor with his hands implying: tell the Judge there are witnesses.

O'Conor, regaining his composure, looks at Martin who is waiting for an answer and responds. "Yes, Your Honor, there are witnesses."

Martin then informs O'Conor and Banton, "If I dismiss Mr. Socolow's petition" (emphasizing the word if) "The State of Maryland, 'that means you, Mr. O'Conor,' will need to produce, before this court, one or more witnesses that can substantiate that Mr. Socolow was in Baltimore, at the scene of the crime, on August 18, 1922. You must produce such a witness before I will rule on extradition."

O'Conor, thrown off kilter by what Justice Martin just said, tries to respond, but Martin cuts him off and orders Socolow returned to City Jail. As Justice Martin stands and retires to his chambers, the previously noiseless courtroom swells with the lurid natter of reporters buzzing about trying to speak to Polakoff, Banton, O'Conor, and Hayward. Others are racing out of the courthouse to file their stories in time for evening additions.

O'Conor's reaction is one of astonishment. He asks Banton, "What objections can the Judge possibly have to extraditing Socolow?" And in frustration he adds, "It's clear cut. The writ should have been dismissed and Socolow released to our custody."

Banton reassures O'Conor, "I am sure Socolow's petition will be denied and the extradition warrant upheld. Justice Martin has his own timeline, and it isn't yours. Be patient—everything will work out. I recommend that you call Mr. Leach and arrange to have a witness in court tomorrow."

Hayward, who has been listening, tells O'Conor and Banton: "I may not make it to court tomorrow. I'm expected in Washington for a meeting." Speaking to O'Conor directly, Hayward says, "I will drop in on Justice Martin this afternoon before he leaves the courthouse and recommend that he dismiss the writ and order the immediate extradition of Socolow without the need for a witness."

Hayward adds, "That doesn't mean Judge Martin will follow my recommendation. He has a bug in his bonnet when it comes to anything involving Governor Miller and considers you an inexperienced rookie. He wants you to remember you were here."

O'Conor, calling from a telephone in a clerk's office, informs Leach that Justice Martin has postponed ruling on Socolow's writ. "He will not consider extradition until a witness is produced who can verify that Socolow participated in the robbery and murder of Mr. Norris."

Leach replies that he has already heard this. When O'Conor asked how, Leach responds, "There were 50 reporters in the courtroom. The important thing," Leach reminds O'Conor, "is to get Socolow back to Baltimore."

Leach adds, "If absolutely necessary, I will have Detective Hammersla produce Allers and possibly Keller." Leach tells O'Conor, "Neither witness can be in New York by tomorrow. The writ must be dismissed first. Hopefully, Mr. Hayward can work his magic with Justice Martin."

Leach, like Hayward and Banton, believes that Justice Martin cannot block extradition, and this means he is bound to deny Socolow's petition. He predicts Martin will drop the need for a witness, dismiss the writ and turn Socolow over to Kahler and Murphy, if not tomorrow then Friday.

Back at the Grand Central Hotel, Murphy and Kahler pull Lieutenant Gilbert aside. Murphy asks Gilbert if he and Gegan would join them and Mr. O'Conor for dinner. Gilbert accepts and says he will ask Gegan.

That night, at six o'clock, Detectives Murphy, Kahler, Gilbert, Gegan, and Assistant State's Attorney Herbert O'Conor gather in the Central Hotel's well-appointed dining room. Many out-of-town reporters recognize O'Conor and ask him to comment on today's proceedings. O'Conor declines to answer.

Gegan makes it clear to the broadsheet inquisitors that they are having dinner and would appreciate being left alone. The five men request a table away from the correspondents. A formally dressed Maître D' escorts them to a sequestered corner and introduces their waiter.

Throughout dinner, despite Leach's encouragement, O'Conor remains flummoxed over Judge Martin's treatment of him in open court. A routine hearing that should have been over today is still lingering indecisively on.

The four detectives listen patiently. They aren't prosecutors. They're cops who often find the aims of district attorneys and the rulings of judges difficult to comprehend. Their job is to track down and arrest the bad guys. Even so, they sympathize with O'Conor. Socolow should be on his way back to Baltimore.

Unbeknownst to O'Conor, the detectives have something up their sleeve (or in this case—sleeves). They're not ready to tell O'Conor. They just listen to the youthful district attorney's lamentations as they munch through one of the finest meals available in an élite New York hotel, a rare gratuity for four civil servants.

Later that night in Kahler's suite, the four veteran cops will nail down what they have in mind, After they have worked out the minutiae, the detectives plan to spring their scheme on O'Conor tomorrow morning at breakfast.

What are the chances O'Conor will go along?

36

COURTROOM 202
SEPTEMBER 21, 1922

Present for breakfast at eight o'clock: Herbert R. O'Conor; Baltimore City Police Detectives, Charles Kahler and Bill Murphy; New York City Police Detectives George Gilbert and James Gegan.

It was a cloudless Indian summer day in New York City. The complimentary morning additions of *The New York Times* and the *New York Tribune* had been distributed throughout the hotel before sunup.

"NO DECISION ABOUT THE EXTRADITION OF WALTER SOCOLOW" is one of the headlines.

"JUSTICE WAITS FOR WALTER SOCOLOW" is the headline in the *Baltimore News American.*

No one is more apprehensive about the outcome of today's proceedings than Herbert O'Conor as he joins Detectives Kahler, Murphy, and Gilbert for breakfast at 8:30 a.m. It will be another long day of waiting before they hear Justice Martin's ruling on Socolow's writ of *habeas corpus.* And if Martin does deny Socolow's petition, will he release Socolow to Kahler and Murphy?

At 9:40 a.m., Detective Gegan joins them in the Central Hotel's dining room. Holding back until the waiter pours him a cup of coffee and walks away to attend another table, Gegan tells O'Conor he has heard, through a source at the courthouse, that in anticipation of today's ruling, Moses Polakoff is prepared to immediately serve a second writ of *habeas corpus.*

O'Conor asks, "How long will this take?"

Gegan has no idea. "Serving a second writ is the real stumbling block. It holds everything up."

Murphy asks, "What if Justice Martin upholds Socolow's petition?"

Gegan responds, "It is unlikely, but either way, you are in the same place. Socolow isn't going back to Baltimore today."

Recognizing O'Conor's frustration, the four detectives exchange glances, questioning among themselves, "Should we tell him?" Detective Murphy breaks the silence. Over the next 45 minutes, Murphy, Kahler, Gilbert, and Gegan let O'Conor in on their scheme.

At first O'Conor is against the idea. The four determined investigators continue to drive home their rationale. A skeptical O'Conor emphasizes, "Have you considered everything that can go wrong?"

Gesturing that they have, Gegan says, "we can do this."

O'Conor asks, "Have you discussed this with anyone else?"

Gegan says, "No."

O'Conor asks, "What about Mr. Banton?"

Gegan answers, "Of course not. No one knows but us."

O'Conor, against his better judgement, agrees to consider what these four veteran law enforcement officers are suggesting. He warns, "If things go wrong, you have a lot to lose."

The detectives again insist they thought this through and understand the pitfalls. O'Conor, partially acquiescing, says, "I'll let you know before the hearing."

Assistant New York State's Attorney, Michael Driscoll

As breakfast is breaking up, Assistant New York State's Attorney Michael Driscoll shows up. Driscoll and O'Conor, both assistant state's attorneys, are about the same age. The two prosecutors have corresponded by telegraph, relative to the search for Jack Hart and Walter Socolow, but have never met.

Although Hayward is the U.S. Attorney and Driscoll is an Assistant New York State's Attorney, they have become professional friends. Hayward has asked Driscoll to join his office. Driscoll was with Hayward when Hayward met with Justice Martin yesterday afternoon. Hayward asked Driscoll to update O'Conor.

Driscoll, and detective Lieutenants Gegan and Gilbert, know each other from working together on investigations. After everyone greets one another, the four police officers excuse themselves. All agree to meet at the Courthouse at three o 'clock.

Now alone, Driscoll updates O'Conor on Bill Hayward's meeting with Justice Martin.

"The Judge," Driscoll tells O'Conor, "didn't have much to say. From Justice Martin's perspective, it has become both political and personal. Martin doesn't believe your trip to New York was necessary. Mr. Hayward's interpretation is that your presence is a message to Martin, from your boss, that he cannot interpret the law."

Dirscoll adds, "Mr. Hayward argued that the fugitive warrant signed by both governors is reason enough not to require Maryland to produce an eyewitness. Martin said he would think about it but would rule on the writ of habeas corpus first. Extradition will require another day."

O'Conor responds, "It was never Mr. Leach's intent to question a New York judge. He didn't want two Baltimore police detectives in a New York court without legal backup."

Driscoll answers, "Tell that to Justice Martin."

O'Conor asks, "Is it possible the bad blood between Governor Miller and Judge Martin is the reason for this nonsense."

Driscoll replies, "Maybe. But ill feelings should not derail Martin from eventually making the right ruling."

"Are you sure about that, Mike?"

Driscoll answers, "Pretty sure, but I wouldn't anticipate an easy time of it this afternoon. Judge Martin wants to drive home that it's his courtroom and his decision, not Governor Miller's, yours, Mr. Leach's, or Governor Ritchie's."

Driscoll offers to drive O'Conor to his Manhattan office telling O'Conor, "You might find what we are working on interesting. I am leading the investigation of Giuseppe 'Joe the Boss' Masseria, for extortion and racketeering in New York's garment district. How about joining me and the detectives working on the case, for lunch?" Then he adds, "Bill Hayward told me he will try to make it back to the hearing."

While at the New York State's Attorney's office, O'Conor makes one more call to Robert Leach to let him know that Justice Martin has delayed the ruling on Socolow's writ petition until four o'clock. "According to Bill Hayward," O'Conor tells Leach, "Justice Martin will not sign off on the Governors' extradition order today. When Hayward argued against requiring an eyewitness, Martin only agreed to think about it."

Leach tells O'Conor, "Getting Frank Allers or another witness on a train today isn't going to happen. Justice Martin's ruling on Socolow's petition needs to come first. An eyewitness is not a legal requirement for a judge to execute a fugitive warrant. It's a preposterous demand. Despite what he says," Leach continues,

"I suspect Justice Martin will change his mind and turn Socolow over to Kahler and Murphy. Do your best to make it happen."

O'Conor ends the conversation by telling his boss that he intends to read up on the law relative to extradition. He doesn't tell Leach what Kahler, Murphy, Gegan, and Gilbert have proposed.

3:00 p.m. – Thursday, September 21, 1922

Police Lieutenant George P. Gilbert pulls up to the courthouse's Chambers Street entrance. Baltimore Police Detective Sergeant William Murphy and Lieutenant Charles Kahler exit Gilbert's car and begin the long climb up the courthouse steps.

Even though Walter Socolow's hearing is scheduled to begin at four o'clock, reporters, from dozens of newspapers, are already in the imposing edifice or ascending the steps toward the main rotunda lobby. Rumor and speculation abound. The broadsheet reporters are hoping for a great story. It is obvious, like yesterday, Courtroom 202 will be standing room only.

NYPD Lt. George P. Gilbert

At 3:10 p.m., O'Conor and New York District Attorney Joab Banton, hook up with Murphy, Kahler, and Gegan in an anti-room off the first-floor lobby (the floor above the ground level basement).

Banton, who has spoken to Martin's clerk in the Rotunda, informs O'Conor that "Socolow's hearing has been delayed until 4:30. Polakoff is prepared to file a second writ," adding, "Socolow is in a holding cell on the ground floor."

O'Conor (gesturing toward Lieutenant Gegan) tells Banton, "Lieutenant Gegan told me that earlier this morning."

Looking at Banton, Gegan says, "That's right, I heard it from a clerk working for Justice Strong."

Banton responds, "Are you sure?"

Gegan answers, "He could be wrong, but that's what the man said."

Speaking to O'Conor, Banton says, "Whoever is paying Polakoff's fee is doing their best to keep Socolow in New York."

O'Conor replies, "Harry Wolf."

Banton asks, "Why Wolf?"

O'Conor answers, "Wolf helped Socolow and Hart flee Baltimore."

Banton replies, "Reason enough," then adds, "Justice Martin heard arguments in a civil case most of the morning. He adjourned court at 11:30, had lunch with the mayor, and returned around 3:30. Nothing is on his docket until he rules on Socolow's petition."

O'Conor reminds Banton, "I have reserved a private compartment on the Capital Express that leaves New York's Pennsylvania Station at 7:15. If Socolow's extradition is delayed beyond a day, there is no point in hanging around."

Banton excuses himself. He is needed in courtroom 100 for another hearing. He tells O'Conor, "I will be in 202 by four o'clock."

Shortly after Banton leaves the room, Detective Gilbert enters telling everyone, "My car is parked (facing Chambers Street) at the southwest end of the courthouse just inside the carriageway."

He asks Detectives Murphy and Kahler if they would like a tour of the landmark courthouse before the hearing. "Because of the delay, we have more than an hour to look around."

Murphy and Kahler answer that they are eager to look the place over. Gegan says, "I'll join you," then asks O'Coner, "Care to come with us, Counselor?"

O'Conor answers, "Thanks—no. I want to look over the notes I compiled at Banton's office. I'll be fine here." He reminds everyone to be in the courtroom no later than four o'clock.

As the four detectives leave the first-floor anti-room, O'Conor stops them. Without looking up, in a low-key voice, he says: "I'm in."

O'Conor enters courtroom 202 at 3:50 p.m.

Except for the bailiff, the large ceremonial chamber is empty. The bailiff, the same burly seemingly ill-disposed character of yesterday, is insisting, except for O'Conor, everyone remain outside the courtroom in the stuffy hallway.

Courtroom 202 was designed for momentous occasions. The Rococo gallery can accommodate more than one-hundred spectators. From O'Conor's perspective, this legal festival is anything but momentous. The circus should have been over yesterday.

O'Conor's viewpoint certainly doesn't balance with the consensus of the dozens of reporters packed in the suffocating corridor waiting to grab a seat. The nationwide pursuit of Jack Hart and Walter Socolow is, after all, the biggest crime story of the decade. And here, in a New York courtroom, the manhunt for the last member of Jack Hart's gang is playing out. All the better that

Justice Martin is making things thorny. What courtroom journalist could hope for more? Readership is up.

4:00 p.m. – Thursday, September 21, 1922
Justice Martin's Courtroom

Detectives Murphy, Kahler, Gegan, and Gilbert enter the courtroom. The bailiff, on guard for pretrial intruders, waves them back into the hallway. Gegan, pointing to O'Conor, signals (we) are with him. The bailiff gestures – okay.

As O'Conor and the detectives gather at the defense table, New York City State's Attorney Banton enters the courtroom from a side door. Banton lets the assemblage know that if Martin dismisses the writ, he now knows for sure, Polakoff will serve the court with a second writ. Despite O'Conor's earlier explanation, Banton says, "I can't believe all this fuss is over a second-rate hood from Baltimore."

O'Conor explains, "Anything that delays Socolow's return to Baltimore keeps Wolf off the stage. It's the reason for his call to New York Police Commissioner Enright. Why would Polakoff agreed to represent Socolow when Socolow is a small-time bandit who doesn't have a dime. Wolf is worried about what Socolow will say."

At 4:05, Moses Polakoff enters the courtroom and takes his place at the plaintiff's table. About the same time, a handcuffed Socolow is brought in. As he is escorted to his place next to Polakoff, Noisy can't help but eyeballing O'Conor, Banton, and the four detectives gazing grimly back. Before Socolow takes a seat next to Polakoff, the guard removes his handcuffs. Noisy, still looking awkwardly at his tormentors, rubs his wrists. It's understandable. The four detectives are imposing figures. In their view, Socolow should already be in Baltimore.

Just after Socolow is brought in, the bailiff unhurriedly treads down the aisle and pushes open the two immense oak doors. As the waiting host of reporters, broadcasters, and just plain curious flood in to grab seats, he orders them to walk. Few pay attention.

Murphy and Kahler take seats directly behind Polakoff and Socolow. Gegan sits down behind Banton and O'Conor. U.S. Attorney Bill Hayward, who made it back from Washington, enters from the detainees' doorway. He grabs a first-row seat, next to Gegan and behind O'Conor. As he sits down, Hayward taps O'Conor on the shoulder letting O'Conor, engrossed in conversation with Banton, know he is there. O'Conor turns and says, "Thanks for coming," then resumes his conversation with Banton.

Detective George Gilbert commandeers a back-row aisle seat a few feet from the hallway. After latecomers squeeze into the courtroom, the doors are closed.

At 4:29, emerging from his chambers, Justice Martin, noticeably put off by the pandemonium, pauses and glares sternly at the packed courtroom where spectators, despite the bailiff's order to be quiet, are still embroiled in conversation.

The bailiff, responding to Justice Martin's discontent, pops to life and orders silence.

Waiting a minute for Martin to take his seat and the gallery to settle down, he announces: "The Supreme Court of New York is in session, Justice Francis W. Martin, Jr., presiding."

Just to make sure everybody crammed into his courtroom gets the message, Justice Martin, pounding his gavel, orders everyone who has a seat to sit down and stop talking.

As if echoing Martin's pronouncement, the bailiff, standing by the Bench, bobbles his head in agreement.

At 4:35, without explaining the purpose of today's hearing (he did that yesterday) Justice Martin declares that he is prepared to rule on the petition for writ of *habeas corpus* filed on behalf of Walter Socolow.

Then, addressing Moses Polakoff, Martin asks, "Is the plaintiff ready or do you have something more to say before I rule?"

Polakoff responds, "I have nothing more to add, Your Honor."

Turning to Mr. Banton, Martin makes the same solicitation. Banton responds, "The Defense is ready."

Speaking to both Polakoff and Barton, Justice Martin asks them to approach the bench. Polakoff jesters to Socolow that he should follow. Banton, representing Mayor Hylan and Commissioner Enright, leaves his place behind the defense table to join Polakoff and Socolow.

No one notices Detective Gilbert slip out of the courtroom.

There will be two parts to Justice Martin's ruling. First, upholding or denying Socolow's petition. If denied, Socolow will be remanded and transported back to the Toombs. If upheld Socolow is free to go. What comes next will be an opportunity to ask questions or submit additional filings.

Martin, waiting for Polakoff, Socolow and Barton to gather in front of the Bench, glances down at his brief then looks up and removes his spectacles. The courtroom is suspensefully quiet. Justice Martin, staring directly at a fidgeting Walter Socolow—in a resolute voice—declares

"The Writ is dismissed. The prisoner is remmm.......!!!"

Before Martin's words are fully out of his mouth, Detectives Kahler and Murphy spring from their seats, sprint toward the Bench, shove the astounded bailiff aside and grab Socolow by both arms.

Justice Martin, momentarily stunned, suddenly jumps to his feet and begins hammering his gavel, at the same time yelling:

"What are you doing? Stop! Come back here!"

Paying no attention to Martin, and (literally) carrying a dumb-struck Noisy Socolow toward the courtroom doors, Kahler and Murphy push aside equally flabbergasted spectators. They reach the entrance in seconds.

O'Conor who simultaneously sprung to his feet when Kahler and Murphy seized Socolow, helps shove Socolow and the two Baltimore detectives through the portal and into the hallway. He turns and slides a wooden police baton, left by Gilbert, through the brass door handles, momentarily trapping the baffled herd of reporters inside courtroom 202, which was becoming a cauldron of vocal mayhem.

Justice Martin's imperious voice continues to explode over the bedlam: "Stop them! Stop them! Bring those men back!"

Then, looking straight at Detective Gegan, he bellows, "Didn't you hear me Lieutenant? Arrest those men. Bring them back here—now!"

Gegan, in halfhearted compliance, flashes his badge as he maneuvers his way through the bemused assemblage and pushes against the big oak posterns. "They seem to be stuck," was his understated rejoinder to those close enough to hear.

Gegan begins to direct the ensnared bystanders to the detainee's entrance where Socolow was brought into the courtroom. It leads to a back stairway, elevator, and ancillary passageway to the Rotunda that is suddenly brimming with curious spectators, emerging from everywhere to find out what was causing all the brouhaha.

Martin, still bugling his commands to arrest the kidnappers, looks directly at his chunky bailiff, ordering, "Get off your damned ass and go after them. Don't let them out of the building!"

Martin whirls back to his chambers to call Police Commissioner Enright. When Enright answers, Martin yells into the receiver, "They've kidnapped the prisoner!"

Enright responds, "What prisoner?"

Martin barks back, "Walter Socolow! I demand you track them down—now. I want (that) upstart junior Baltimore attorney and the officers with him arrested. If they break out of the courthouse, they will head for Pennsylvania Station. Don't let them board a train! I don't care how you get them. Just bring them back!"

While all this is going on, Joseph Banton and Bill Hayward impassively survey the anarchy from their front row seats. Until the courtroom clears, the two prosecutors take it all in with entertaining incredulity.

The Rotunda

37

THE GREAT ESCAPE

As soon as Murphy and Kahler muscle a befuddled Noisy Socolow from Justice Martin's courtroom and O'Conor bars the doors, it was a matter of escaping Tweed's Taj Mahal.

As they begin to race down the Rotunda's marble staircase, dragging a whimpering Socolow, they come face to face with *Baltimore Sun* reporter George Dorsch, who is determined to be complicit in the getaway. With no time to shake Dorsch loose, they continue down to the first level only to confront a gaggle of bailiffs emerging from other chambers moving to cut them off.

Kahler's and Murphy's earlier reconnaissance with Gegan and Gilbert, at least for the moment, pays off. They twirl around and lug Noisy back up the staircase and sprint down an auxiliary hallway that Gegan and Gilbert pointed to as seldom used. It leads to the north end of the courthouse overlooking City Hall Park.

At the end of the passage, after whirling through a narrow doorway, the band of Baltimore escapees reach a little used (fire) stairwell that spirals to the ground floor. Once in the basement, with Murphy on one side, Kahler on the other, and O'Conor and Dorsch shoving from behind, Socolow is whisked back south and into a utility room beneath the west side of the Chamber's Street staircase.

An ordinarily locked access door leading to Chambers Street has been unbolted. Kahler and Murphy, lugging Socolow reluctantly along, race to the southwest corner of the courthouse and the unmarked New York City patrol car where Detective Gilbert is waiting.

Bailiffs and police officers, along with a throng of meddlesome spectators, spill out onto the courthouse's Chambers Street portico. Spotting their quarry fleeing west on Chambers, the court-house posse hurtles down the Chambers Street steps in pursuit.

With no time to spare, Kahler, Murphy, and Dorsch jam Socolow into the back seat. O'Conor jumps in next to Gilbert, who is having difficulty firing up the engine. The starter is whining but not engaging. With Kahler and Murphy yelling "Let's Go—Let's Go" and the posse closing in, Gilbert's machine suddenly ignites. He releases the clutch and steps on the gas.

With their footbound trackers losing ground, the black Ford takes off onto Chambers Street. In two-hundred feet, Gilbert swings north onto Centre Street then circles eastward around City Hall where Centre intersects Broadway. Gilbert accelerates south on Broadway. Four blocks further on, he veers right onto Liberty Street. The Central Railroad's Liberty Street Ferry Terminal is a quarter mile west.

Before fleeing the courthouse, and even though they had publicized their tickets on the Pennsylvania Railroad's Capitol Express, Gilbert and O'Conor had ruled out trying to reach Pennsylvania Station. Penn Station, located at 8th Avenue and 31st Street, is over three miles north through Solo. In afternoon traffic, it would take 30 minutes to get there. O'Conor had no doubt New York's finest would be waiting. A ferry across the Hudson, to Jersey City, was a better bet.

At 5:05, Gilbert arrives at West Street and the Central Railroad of New Jersey's Pier 9 Terminal. The 250-foot double-decker ferry, *Elizabeth*, is completing its loading for the 1.4 mile, eight-minute, voyage across the Hudson River to the Central Railroad's Jersey City Communipaw Terminal.

The Communipaw Terminal is also used by the Baltimore and Ohio Railroad that runs its Washington Express (nicknamed the Marylander) from Jersey City to Baltimore's Mt. Royal Station before continuing to Washington, D.C.

Busses, cars, and horse drawn wagons are still loading. Those disembarking are crowding the terminal on their way to West Street and into Manhattan. Gilbert stops directly in front of the Terminal entrance. The *Elizabeth* is scheduled to shove off at 5:10.

Gilbert and O'Conor vault out of the front seat. Murphy and Kahler yank a now handcuffed Noisy from the back seat. Dorsch, more in the way than anything else, is trying to assist from behind. With Gilbert in the lead, followed by a reluctant Noisy being propelled along by both arms, it's a race to the ticket booth. The clerk, taken back by five men in suits holding onto a kid in handcuffs, informs Gilbert that the *Elizabeth* is sold out. "It's too late anyway." Undeterred, Gilbert, displaying his New York City detective's shield, tells the clerk, "It's a police matter." Not waiting for a response, Gilbert, O'Conor, Murphy, Kahler, Dorsch and a shackled Noisy bolt through the turnstile and sprint to the dock.

The *Elizabeth's* crew is loading the last vehicles and checking tickets. Without stopping to request permission to board, Gilbert and his Baltimore band leap onto the deck and ascend the crew gangway to the pilot house. The Captain is making notes in his logbook when O'Conor and his entourage pile into the bridge. Without waiting for the startled Captain to respond to this sudden intrusion, Gilbert again flashes his badge.

More ordering than asking Gilbert tells the captain, "This is a police emergency. These detectives are taking this felon back to Baltimore. There is no time to spare, we are being pursued." Gilbert doesn't say by whom. "You need to castoff. Get these men to New Jersey"! Adding, "You are in danger too."

The captain doesn't think of asking what danger. He orders boarding halted, lines pulled-in and rotates the helm's Engine Room Telegraph ahead one-third. By the time Gilbert jumps back onto the pier, the *Elizabeth* is under way.

Within minutes, eight uniformed New York City police officers burst out of the terminal and dash to where Lieutenant Gilbert is standing at water's edge. A burley sergeant named Sullivan tells Gilbert that they made a beeline here when the Baltimore detectives didn't show at Pennsylvania Station. "A ferry to New Jersey," Sullivan tells Gilbert, "seemed the logical alternative. Other squads are converging on all of Manhattan's ferry terminals. If there're on that boat, Lieutenant, we need to get them off."

Gilbert, appearing suitably perplexed asks, "What's going on Sergeant?"

Sullivan explains, "The attorney you were driving and his two detectives kidnapped a prisoner out of a New York courtroom. The Judge is pissed as hell. He wants them arrested and brought back."

Gilbert, acting surprised responds, "So that's why they told me to bring them here."

The Sergeant answers, "There's no way you could have known, but we need to stop that ferry."

Gilbert, pointing towards the *Elizabeth* steaming north, 400 yards out, answers; "I don't think that's possible."

The Sergeant, looking out at the *Elizabeth*, its props churning the choppy Hudson into an ensuing foam, frustratingly responds, "I guess you're right" and instructs his men to return to the Precinct.

Gilbert momentarily stays behind, pausing to watch the *Elizabeth*, trailing a dense plume of murky smoke, steam northward into the Hudson's busy main channel. The ferry steamer *Anna*, returning from Jersey City, is plowing into view. One last look, then Gilbert heads to his car.

Out in the Hudson, the sprawling Communipaw Terminal is easy to spot. O'Conor knows he is not out of the woods. By now the New York authorities have had time to contact Jersey City's terminal police. The Communipaw Terminal might be as far as they get before being detained and unceremoniously hauled back to New York to face a fuming Francis Martin.

Central Railroad of New Jersey's steam ferry, Elizabeth

5:20 p.m. - Jersey City, New Jersey

With the *Elizabeth* securely moored, passengers, motorized vehicles, and horse drawn drays are disembarking. Commuters stream down from the upper passenger decks. Recognizing that the captain is happy to get rid of his uninvited stowaways, O'Conor thanks the old ferryboat veteran for his aid.

Making their way off the *Elizabeth* and into the congested Communipaw terminal, all the while clutching their handcuffed recidivist, draws the questioning gawks from just about everyone, including two Jersey City terminal cops.

Kahler and Murphy don't wait for the two officers to open the conversation. They jump in explaining that they are returning Walter Socolow to Baltimore to be tried for murder.

Like everyone else in the country, the patrolmen know all about the nationwide hunt for Jack Hart and Walter Socolow. It is the highlight of their day to meet the infamous Noisy Socolow. "He doesn't look all that tough."

MURDER ON MADISON STREET

Kahler responds, "He's not."

To the relief of O'Conor, his detectives, and their inhouse *Baltimore Sun* reporter, the two terminal officers—who appear to know nothing about today's courtroom kidnapping—offer their assistance.

O'Conor asks, "We need to catch the B&O's Washington Express that goes directly to Baltimore's Mt. Royal Station."

One of the officers answers: "You just missed it." Then adds, "If you can get to Philadelphia, you can transfer to Baltimore from there. The New Jersey Central's Crusader is arriving on Track 11. It's scheduled to leave here at 5:25 for the Reading Railroad's Market Street Station, in center city Philadelphia."

O'Conor says, "There isn't time to purchase tickets." The two Jersey City officers are confident the Crusader's conductor will find them seats. They escort the Baltimore contingent to Track 11.

The Crusader, powered by its 5,800-horsepower Olive Drab Baldwin Steam Locomotive, trailing its fleet of Pullman cars, roars into the terminal like a massive iron dragon and screeches to a stop. The first to swing-down onto the platform is the Crusader's conductor, impeccably dressed in his dark blue CNJ uniform.

The two Jersey City patrolman approach and introduce the no nonsense conductor to O'Conor who, in turn, introduces Murphy, Kahler, and Dorsch. O'Conor explains, "We just arrived on the *Elizabeth* and have no time to purchase tickets. It's imperative we get to Baltimore tonight. Can you help us?"

The Conductor matter-of factly responds, "This train will only get you as far as Philadelphia. You might be able to catch the Congressional. It leaves Pennsylvania Railroad's Broad Street

Station about a quarter hour after we arrive. "Broad Street," he says, is a three-block walk. We should arrive in Philadelphia around seven o'clock."

One of the Jersey cops chimes in, announcing: "The kid in cuffs is Walter Socolow."

The conductor, displaying no reaction upon learning the skinny adolescent is none other than the notorious Noisy Socolow, pauses to introduce himself. His name is John Heintz.

Heintz began his 22 year career with the New Jersey Central Railroad Company as a switchman. He has been the senior conductor of the Crusader since 1916. Heintz has read all about the pursuit of Walter "Noisy" Socolow. He is familiar with the capture of Jack Hart in Washington and Socolow's arrest in Manhattan. That was yesterday.

In his characteristic lowkey demeanor, Heintz tells O'Conor, "I have an open reserve compartment on the second Pullman. It's yours!" As Chief Operating Officer of the Crusader, Heintz tells O'Conor, "Your trip to Philadelphia will be complements of the CNJ."

Looking at Noisy, Heintz asks, "So this is the famous Walter Socolow."

O'Conor replies, "It is."

Then talking directly to Socolow, Heintz jibes, "Welcome to New Jersey Mr. Socolow. We will get you to Philadelphia safe and sound."

Noisy, still confused by the events of the day, at least from his prospective, and now forced to face this tough austere railroad man, is uncharacteristically at a loss for words. He looks down at his feet to avoid eye contact.

Because it only requires ten minutes for the Crusader to unload and load passengers and baggage, there is no time to call Leach or Burns.

No doubt, Detective Gegan or Detective Driscoll have called Burns. They would relay that O'Conor made it across the Hudson to New Jersey but have no way of knowing O'Conor and his detectives missed the Marylander. And if they make it to Philadelphia on the Crusader, they will need to get to Pennsylvania Railroad's Broad Street Station to catch the Congressional, which arrives at Union Station in Baltimore—not the B&O's Mt. Royal Station.

O'Conor asks the New Jersey terminal officers, who introduced him to Heintz, if they would send telegrams to both Robert Leach's office and police headquarters in Baltimore. The New Jersey patrolmen respond, they will.

Before boarding, O'Conor jots down a message.

It's short and to the point:

Socolow in custody – Stop.
Returning on Pennsylvania Railroad – Not B&O
ETA – Baltimore Union Station 9:30 – On Congressional - Stop
O'Conor

The Crusader

The compartment Heintz assigns O'Conor is a well-appointed reserve coach. It provides seating for six including two berths that fold down. A second smaller compartment contains a lavatory. Socolow, still handcuffed, sits next to Detective Kahler. O'Conor, Murphy, and Dorsch take places on the opposing lounge.

After the Crusader is underway, Heintz drops in telling his Baltimore passengers, "The dining car opens in fifteen minutes. We should arrive in Philadelphia at 7:05."

O'Conor, first thanking Heintz for getting them to Philadelphia, says, "I think its best that we remain in the compartment for the duration. Can we get some snacks or sandwiches—something to drink? We haven't had anything to eat since noon." Heintz responds, "I'll see to it."

O'Conor remains apprehensive. There is still the chance they will be detained when they reach Philadelphia. He hasn't conveyed his trepidations to Kahler or Murphy. They have enough to worry about. George Dorsch, who Kahler teasingly deputized when they were crossing the Hudson, is already busy writing tomorrow's byline.

Noisy suddenly finds his voice. He asks Kahler, sitting next to him, and Murphy directly across, "What is going to happen to me when we reach Baltimore?" Back to his old tale of woe, Socolow complains, "I shouldn't have been arrested in New York. You had no right to snatched me out of that courtroom. I'm innocent. I didn't shoot anybody."

In this version, Jack Hart did it.

With O'Conor quietly listening and Dorsch mentally searching for the right words for tomorrow's column, Kahler and Murphy display little patience with the boy crook's whining. Socolow pleads to have his handcuffs removed. Kahler responds, "The handcuffs stay."

Murphy, tuning Noisy out, leans against the window side bulkhead and closes his eyes. It's been a tiring day. O'Conor hopes Leach or Burns, or both, received his telegrams and will be waiting at Union Station—that is, if they make it past Philadelphia.

Inwardly, O'Conor regrets he was unable to speak to his boss. By now the word must be out. How did Leach take the news? A by-the-book prosecutor, Leach wasn't likely to endorse a courtroom kidnapping regardless of the reasons.

What would Governor Ritchie do? At some point, Ritchie will need to set things right with Governor Miller. Ritchie could send Socolow back to New York with the stroke of a pen.

Will Commissioner Gaither, a strict law and order man and former army general, sack Murphy and Kahler?

What will happen to Lieutenants Gegan and Gilbert? Can they conceal their involvement? O'Conor thinks probably not.

What about Joseph Banton, Michael Driscoll, and Bill Hayward? They stood by him in Justice Martin's courtroom unaware of the plot to kidnap Socolow.

It was an absolute given that Judge Martin, left with a good bit of egg on his face, wasn't going to let this drop.

On the way to Philadelphia, the Crusader stops at Boundbrook, Bellemead, and West Trenton, New Jersey before entering Pennsylvania. After briefly stopping at Jenkintown and Elkins Park, they pull into Wayne Junction, on the northern outskirts of Philadelphia, at 7:04.

The Crusader is eight minutes behind schedule. The lights of Philadelphia are beginning to reflect against a darkening September sky. O'Conor can't help but think about what will be waiting for them in the City of Brotherly Love.

O'Conor, his detectives, and Dorsch begin to straighten up the compartment. They don't have much to collect. In the rush to escape Tweed's courthouse, they left their suitcases in the first-floor room where they had gathered before the hearing. Kahler and Murphy enjoy last draws on their cigarettes before crushing them out in ashtrays. Socolow, who had consumed a ham and cheese on rye within seconds then gulped down a Coca-Cola without lowering the bottle, was still babbling about being mistreated.

Heintz enters the cabin to let them know that they will be passing

Pennsylvania Railroad's Broad Street Station momentarily. "We should arrive at Market Street in a few minutes."

Heintz tells O'Conor, "Because we were held up at Elkins Park, you won't be able to get to Broad Street station in time to catch the 7:14 Congressional unless it's running late."

O'Conor asks, "If we miss the Congressional, is there another train?"

Heintz responds, "Maybe. We'll know when we pull in. You may still be able to connect."

Triple blasts of the locomotive's air trumpet, mounted on the smokebox, forewarn the station master and waiting passengers of the Crusader's arrival. The panting locomotive lets loose hormonic discharges of surplus steam as it slows to a jolting stop on Track 6.

O'Conor scans the station for those coming and going. Heintz emerges on the platform inspecting his train, directing baggage handlers, and welcoming passengers. Two Philadelphia police officers approach Heintz. O'Conor thinks, this might be as far as we get. To his relief, the two patrolmen return to the terminal. Will they come back with reinforcements? It's a possibility.

By now the New York, New Jersey, and Pennsylvania authorities must know they boarded the Crusader at Communipaw Terminal. The New York police could have caught an express out of Pennsylvania Station. If so, they reached Philadelphia a half-hour earlier. If they did, will the Philadelphia police cooperate? If they aren't intercepted here at the Reading terminal, will they be detained at the Broad Street station? Why rush to Broad Street if the police are waiting for them. O'Conor checks his watch. It's 7:10. If the Congressional is on time, they'll never make it.

The B & O has a terminal, next to the Schuylkill River on 24th Street, 14 blocks west. Would going there be a better choice?

The immediate question is—will the Congressional be late? And if it is, can they get to Broad Street in time to catch it; and if they do get to Broad Street in time, will they be arrested?

As O'Conor's party steps down onto the platform (Kahler and Murphy holding tightly to Socolow with Dorsch looking for a newspaper while stuffing his note pad into his coat pocket) Heintz approaches. "The Congressional," he tells O'Conor, "is five minutes behind schedule. By the time you walk to the Broad Street station, unless there is another delay, you won't make it."

Heintz then explains, "Reading's Train #441 is about to depart for Scranton. It makes its first stop at the Fairmont Station where Market Street ends at the Schuylkill River before it crosses the river heading west. The Congressional stops there too before turning south to Wilmington. The Scranton Express will reach the Schuylkill before the Congressional. You can catch the Congressional there if you leave now."

O'Conor doesn't have to think about it twice.

Heintz directs O'Conor to Track 2 and introduces him to the Scranton Express' conductor, a man named Atwell. There are no private compartments on #441, but Atwell finds seats at the front of the first car behind the tender. O'Conor and his troop hardly have time to settle in when the locomotive begins to chug west toward Fairmont and the Susquehanna River Connecting Bridge 69.

Fairmont Station

O'Conor, his posse, and a still handcuffed Noisy Socolow step down on the station platform at 7:16. The station master informs O'Conor that the Congressional is six minutes out. It may or may not stop depending on passengers. Just in case, he activates the stop signal.

Minutes later the Pennsylvania Railroad's Washington D.C. bound Congressional, gushing murky smoke mixed with explosions of vented steam, begins to slow as it comes to a screeching stop alongside the platform. A robust PRR Conductor jumps onto the platform before the Congressional comes to a complete stop. O'Conor moves to meet him and explains his predicament. The conductor introduces himself. His name is John Hollis.

Hollis, who lives in Washington, knows all about the courtroom hijacking, getaway across the Hudson, and flight south on the Crusader. He tells O'Conor, "Everyone [knows]. The telegraph lines are humming with accounts about Socolow being snatched from a courtroom. You gentlemen are famous."

Hollis is enthusiastic about being part of, as he coins it, the Great Escape. "I have an open compartment on the third Pullman, one coach back. It's all yours."

Even before Hollis could hustle his celebrated passengers off the platform and into Coach #3, the gigantic Baldwin locomotive was building a head of steam. With repetitive blasts of the trumpet, steam discharging from both sides of the boiler and black smoke blistering from the firebox, the Congressional crosses the Schuylkill River and turns south. Next stop—Wilmington Delaware—twenty-five miles and twenty minutes out.

O'Conor, thankful they dodged a bullet in Philadelphia, hopes they dodge another in Wilmington. They hardly have time to settle in when Hollis stops by to let O'Conor know they will be arriving at the Pennsylvania Railroad's Wilmington Station in ten minutes. "It should be a quick stop. By the way," Hollis adds, "you gentleman have made quite a stir in New York. Many of the passengers on this train have read about the kidnapping and are asking if your prisoner is Walter Socolow."

"I hope," O'Conor responds, "you haven't been giving us away."

"No, I haven't," Hollis answers, "but it's not hard to figure out who you are."

Kahler, unable to restrain himself, retorts: "We didn't kidnap anybody! We're bringing a murderer back to stand trial."

Hollis calmly replies, "I'm sure that's true," adding, "We'll only be in Wilmington for five minutes."

The Express rolls into the Pennsylvania Railroad's South French Street Wilmington Station at 7:38 p.m. With the exception of passengers coming and going, nothing appears unusual. There are no police, only baggage handlers and railroad personal scrambling to facilitate arrivals and departures.

O'Conor, Murphy, and Kahler keep an eye on the station building and platform until the Congressional begins to amble southwest, following the sharp bend in the Christiana River before the engineer unchecks the throttle. Next stop—Baltimore. O'Conor looks at his watch. It's 7:45.

Pennsylvania Railroad's Union Station is sixty-five miles from Wilmington. The 200 ton, 122-foot-long Baldwin locomotive can generate 8,000 horsepower and reach speeds of 80 miles per hour. Along the way, the ravenous boiler will consume five tons of coal and 10,000 gallons of water. Blasting its steam trumpet before every crossing and spewing a half mile spoor of exhausted coal and steam, the Congressional is a marvel of railroad technology. As it flies through the open countryside, even for those who watch the Brunswick Green leviathan roar through every day, the eight-coach streamliner is a compelling sight.

Not long after the Congressional is up to speed, Conductor Hollis returns. He tells O'Conor, "We are scheduled to arrive at Baltimore's Union Station at 9:25." Then asks, "Would anyone like something to eat or drink." Kahler, Murphy, and Dorsch, if possible, would like coffee. Hollis good-humoredly responds,

"Everything is available on my train. You just need to ask. I will have the Steward bring a pot with extra cream and sugar. Oh yes—and some of the chef's sugar cookies. They're the best."

O'Conor, who is content with water, asks, "Any chance we can get a soft drink for our prisoner?" Hollis answers, "How about a Coca-Cola."

O'Conor says, "A Coke will be fine."

Hollis responds, "I'll have it delivered. We will be crossing the Susquehanna River and the town of Havre de Grace in twenty-six minutes."

As he turns to leave, Hollis retrieves a folded telegram from his uniform pocket. It was sent to both the Philadelphia and Wilmington stations. The French Street station clerk delivered it to Hollis on the platform. It's addressed to Detective Lieutenant Charles Kahler.

After Hollis leaves, Kahler unfolds the telegram and reads it aloud. It's from Captain of Detectives, Charles Burns.

Meet you at PRR Union Station – Stop

Gaither and Leach will join – Stop

Burns

Murphy responds, "Is that it?"

O'Conor answers, "At least we know Captain Burns, and probably Bob Leach, received my telegrams from Jersey City."

As he lights a smoke and flops down on the couch, Murphy says,

"Meet us with what?"

Unlike local commuters, the Congressional makes few stops—New York, Philadelphia, Fairmont, Wilmington, Baltimore, and Washington D.C. The Express crosses the Susquehanna River Bridge and bypasses the Havre de Grace station at a speed of seventy-two miles per hour (106 feet per second). With the exception of dissipating smoke, for the citizens of Havre de Grace, the fastmoving Express is a thirty-second memory .

Fifty-five Minutes to Baltimore

O'Conor, silently rationalizing the day's events, can't help but ponder if kidnaping Socolow was a good idea. It was one of those decisions that once put into action has no negotiable middle ground with a big potential downside. For a young, ambitious lawyer, the abduction of Socolow in front of a New York Superior Court Judge may not have been the best way to advance his career.

Mike Driscoll was probably right when he said Justice Martin wouldn't be rushed, but in the end, had to dismiss the writ and honor the extradition warrant. It's difficult to believe all this is about ill feelings between a Democratic judge and a Republican governor. Anyway, Robert Leach said bring Socolow back to Baltimore. He was certainly doing that.

O'Conor predicts that when the Congressional pulls into Union

Station, they will be besieged by thousands of onlookers eager to catch a glimpse of Noisy Socolow.

After Havre de Grace, the townships of Aberdeen, Perryman, Riverside, Middle River, and Rosedale quickly came and went. When the Congressional approached the eastern boundary of Baltimore near Erdman Avenue, it slowed and curved northwest to Edison Boulevard skirting the southern edge of Sweet Home Cemetery. The engineer reduced speed as the Express continued westward to the entrance of Union Tunnel at Bond Street. From the Bond Street entrance, the tracks extend 3,410 feet underground, emerging 200 yards from Pennsylvania Railroad's Union Station.

Union Station is situated between Charles and St. Paul Streets, Baltimore's two main center-city north-south thoroughfares. The tracks are 30 feet below street level. O'Conor isn't sure what to expect, but presumes Burns will have assembled a contingent of police to prevent a recurrence of the crush of onlookers that showed up to greet Jack Hart. He checks his watch. It's 9:25.

As the Congressional clears Union Tunnel, everyone looks out of the coach windows to see who might be waiting on the platform. Murphy begins to straighten the compartment. Kahler offers Socolow one more chance to have a bathroom break. Socolow, noticeably ill at ease says, "I don't need to go."

There is one more blast of the engine's trumpet as the Congressional rolls to a stop along the station platform. Passengers waiting to go to Washington are held back from the tracks by a host of uniformed police.

O'Conor spots Robert Leach, Fleet Cox, Commissioner Gaither, and Captain of Detectives Burns looking at each Pullman as O'Conor's car (the third in line behind the locomotive's tender) slowly passes them before coming to a stop.

Conductor Hollis stops by.

Despite the Pennsylvania Railroad, like the Reading Railroad, picking up the tab for their trip, Hollis tells O'Conor, "Great having you aboard."

O'Conor says, "Thanks. It's appreciated."

Hollis replies, "I wouldn't have missed this for the world—good luck!" Hollis accompanies O'Conor to the Pullman's rear entrance—then moves on to assist other passengers.

By now, Leach and the others with him had been told that Socolow is on the third Pullman and have walked southward toward the engine to greet O'Conor and his fellow conspirators, not to mention the man of the hour, Walter "Noisy" Socolow.

O'Conor, expecting the worse when he came face to face with his boss, was surprised when neither Leach nor Cox had much to say other than to express relief that O'Conor made it to Baltimore without being arrested.

Gaither, with Burns by his side, reached out to shake both Kahler's and Murphy's hands. "Glad you made it boys," was the extent of Gaither's greeting.

Burns, on the other hand, tells both detectives, "We will review what took place in Justice Martin's courtroom tomorrow morning 7:30 "sharp" in my office."

Given the hullabaloo that came with Jack Hart's return to the courthouse, a considerable effort had been made not to advertise that Socolow would be returning to Baltimore by way of Philadelphia courtesy of the Pennsylvania Railroad instead of the B & O. There was of course plenty of speculation. But other than the passengers traversing the station platforms and 100 or so onlookers who guessed right, few had gathered at Union Station to greet Noisy.

A police motor-wagon is on hand to transport Socolow straight to City Jail. There will be a bail hearing in front of Judge Offutt tomorrow morning at nine o'clock.

Burns tells Kahler and Murphy, "New York Police Commissioner Enright has been in touch with Commissioner Gaither. Judge Martin is on a rampage over what happened in his courtroom. Sergeant Oberon will drive you to your cars at police headquarters. Charlie and Bill[18] will escort Socolow to City Jail. We will deal with all this tomorrow morning."

Baltimore Sun reporter George Dorsch, with his story scribbled on a notepad, hails a taxicab to the *Baltimore Sun* building located downtown, at the intersection of Charles and Baltimore Streets.

Robert Leach drives Cox and O'Conor to the courthouse. On the way, Leach tells O'Conor, "I have spoken to Banton. Justice Martin is insisting that Banton form a grand jury to indict you, Kahler, and Murphy for interfering with court proceedings. Martin also wants Banton to investigate Gegan and Gilbert to determine if either of them had a hand in the kidnapping. Justice Martin signed Socolow's second writ of *habeas corpus* and is demanding Socolow be returned to New York."

---

18 Baltimore City Police Detectives Charles Comen and William Hammersla.

38

BROADSHEETS AND JUSTICE MARTIN

Newspapers went wild with a story far better than they could have hoped for.

SOCOLOW KIDNAPPED
FROM A NEW YORK COURTROOM
JUDGE ENRAGED – DEMANDS REPRISALS

There are two versions of the kidnapping editorializing who was right or who was wrong. Newspapers with Democratic affinities, like the *Evening World*, condemn O'Conor for his lack of regard for the law, headlining:

"The kidnapping is nothing less than an affront to the State of New York."

The *New York Herald*, disposed to Republican causes, drew editorial enjoyment from what it called, *"Justice Martin's discomfiture."*

George Dorsch wrote: *Assistant Baltimore City District Attorney Herbert O'Conor with Baltimore police officers Lieutenant Charles Kahler and Sergeant William Murphy had every right, legal and moral, to remove Walter Socolow from Justice Martin's courtroom. Outwitting a determined New York pursuit, they brought Walter Socolow back to Baltimore.*

A *News American* op-ed concludes, *Thanks to the Baltimore Police and Assistant Baltimore State's Attorney, Herbert O'Conor, every one of the scoundrels who took part in the robbery and murder of William Norris is behind bars.*

A *Sun* editorial, expounding on the "Kidnapping," was less complementary:

The method by which Herbert O'Conor felt called upon to use smacks so strongly of the frontier. Had such an event occurred in one of the so-called unenlightened areas of the world it would have been quite understandable.

We can only hope that the nation will not consider the occurrence an expression of mob spirit, which superficially it might appear to be and construe it as the somewhat headstrong tactics of an earnest and anxious young man beset on all sides by cunning men plotting to forestall the course of justice.

National news articles and commentary reflect a mix of opinions. The general sentiment is Walter Socolow belongs in Baltimore. The wild west show in New York, the all-out pursuit through the streets of Manhattan and across the Hudson, leading to an escape with only seconds to spare, is the stuff of folklore—ingredients editors can't wait to bake into editorials. Everyone in America is riveted on the particulars highlighting the hero or villain of the journalistic feast—Baltimore's young Assistant State's Attorney, Herbert R. O'Conor.

Everyone in America does not include Justice Francis W. Martin, Jr.

Shortly after realizing O'Conor had escaped to Baltimore, Justice Martin, in an open letter to Joseph Banton, made his indignation public. Newspapers across the country printed his frustration word for word.

Mr. District Attorney,

I direct (you) to prepare papers to punish, for contempt, the police officers of this city who in any way acted with the Baltimore police in disturbing the orderly proceedings of the Supreme Court yesterday afternoon. There is not the slightest doubt, in my mind, that the police planned to do just what they did. I do not know all of them; and it may have been the hope of receiving part of the reward or unheard of enthusiasm to perform their duty that caused that outbreak. Before I'm through they will learn to respect this court. Accordingly, I direct (you) the District Attorney to place before the grand jury for indictments the names of the police officers (and others) from this city or from Baltimore.

I also direct you to notify the Governor of Maryland to return (that) prisoner in order that justice may be carried out in an orderly manner.

I believe the whole thing was engineered by the police of this city and Baltimore; but it will be the last time they will try anything of that kind in my court.

Justice Francis W. Martin, Jr. (circa 1940)

39
POLICE HEADQUARTERS BUILDING
7:30 A.M., FRIDAY, SEPTEMBER 22, 1922

Office of Captain of Detectives
Present:
Chief of Detectives, George J. Henry
Captain of Detectives, Charles Burns
Lieutenant Charles Kahler
Lieutenant William Hammersla
Detective Sergeant William Murphy
Detective James Comen

While O'Conor and Detectives Kahler and Murphy were in New York, Chief of Detectives George J. Henry, after an extended illness that included two weeks in the hospital because of cellulitis, a painfully serious life-threatening bacterial infection, returned from a month leave of absence. During his medical sabbatical, Henry followed the unfolding events of the Norris case. He remained in regular contact with Commissioner Gaither and his temporary stand-in, Captain Burns. Despite debilitating pain, Henry was itching to get back to work.

Henry, who answers only to Commissioner Gaither, oversees all Baltimore City Detective units. Were it not for his sudden illness, Henry would have run the Norris investigation. Back on the job, Henry, a former military man and stickler for process, has no intention of taking over. Captain of Detectives, Charles Burns, remains in charge of the Norris inquiry (at least what's left of it). Chief Henry, however, will be present at staff meetings.

At 7:30 on the morning of September 22nd, Burns' unit (Lieutenant Kahler, Sergeant Murphy, newly promoted Detective Lieutenant Hammersla, and Detective Comen) along with Chief Henry gather in Captain Burns' Fayette Street office. With Henry back, Commissioner Gaither does not attend but expects a follow up report by ten o'clock.

The main topic is: "What happened in New York?"

Kahler, who was the senior officer, did not hesitate to give his version of the episode. Despite Murphy's insistence that it was his decision, as much as Kahler's, to kidnap Socolow, Kahler assumes full responsibility. He tells Henry and Burns, "We had a fugitive warrant signed by Governor Ritchie and Governor Miller. That should have been enough for Justice Martin to turn Socolow over on Tuesday evening, certainly by Wednesday morning."

"Socolow," Kahler continues, "wasn't being sought in New York for any crime. It was a Maryland (in fact a Baltimore) matter. Justice Martin knew this as well as us. We had had it, along with Detectives Gegan and Gilbert, with the political baloney blocking the extradition of Socolow. When we learned that Harry Wolf was involved, we were determined to bring Socolow back. As far as we knew, Justice Martin could have held Socolow in New York for months. Socolow might have even been released. This was not going to happen. I thought it was worth the risk to yank him out of the courtroom and hope we could escape. When the Judge said, 'Writ Dismissed,' Walter Socolow was our man. We were not about to let him go."

Henry wants to know how O'Conor fits into this. "He's a state's attorney—not a cop."

Murphy answers, "We talked Mr. O'Conor into hijacking Socolow at the eleventh hour. He went along."

Both Kahler and Murphy knew this was anything but true. O'Conor was very much a part of the plot to kidnap Socolow. Without O'Conor, they couldn't have pulled it off. And once they whisked Socolow out of Martin's courtroom, O'Conor was a full partner in the getaway. O'Conor wanted Socolow back in Baltimore as much as they did. Kahler and Murphy, however, were not going to implicate O'Conor, even to Burns and Henry, definitely not Commissioner Gaither. They view O'Conor as an advocate, a prosecutor who listened to and went along with a couple of cops, even if their remedy was a bit nuts.

"No," Kahler tells Henry and Burns, "Mr. O'Conor did not help in the planning. But he didn't stop us. Given the chance to do things differently, we wouldn't change a thing. Let the chips fall where they may."

Henry interjects, "The chips will probably include the New York City State's Attorney seeking indictments for both of your arrests for interfering with Supreme Court proceedings. The Judge will want to go after Mr. O'Conor too. According to Commissioner Gaither, who has been in touch with Commissioner Enright, Justice Martin is adamant to have the three of you back in New York to face charges. He is insisting that Socolow be returned. Whatever happens from here on, depends on Governor Ritchie and Robert Leach. It's out of our hands."

Updating George J. Henry

For the next two hours, beginning with Fred Kuethe, Burns has his detectives fill Henry in on the progress of their investigations.

Fred Kuethe

Recovering from his injuries, Fred Kuethe began to remember more about being robbed and assaulted. After Hart was captured, Burns escorted him to City Jail to have a close look at the members of Hart's gang. He thought John Smith was the man who attacked him but remains unsure about Hart and Socolow. He never saw the Hudson.

Dr. Clarence Grieves

Dr. Grieves came in to sign an affidavit. Grieves is the only person who witnessed the entire crime beginning with noticing the Hudson parked across the street from the church. He is positive Allers was the driver. He identified Charles Carey as being in the Hudson and Jack Hart as one of the men who jumped out of the Hudson and attacked Norris and Kuethe. Grieves remains unsure about Socolow. Nevertheless, he can place Hart, Carey, and Allers in the Hudson.

Sergeant Charles S. Orem

Sergeant Orem spotted the Hudson heading east shortly after the crime. At the time, he recognized Walter Socolow. After seeing Frank Allers and John Wiggles Smith, at City Jail, he identified both as being in the Hudson.

Sadie Egnatz and Loula Riley

When first interviewed, Mrs. Egnatz and Miss Riley were reluctant to disclose what they saw. They didn't remember anything. During a second interview, after Jack Hart was captured, Mrs. Egnatz remained unwilling to talk. Miss Riley, however, told Burns that Hart was the man who pointed his pistol at her. Feeling less exposed to reprisal, her memory returned. Any reward that might come her way, Miss Riley hinted, would be appreciated.

Robert Johnson

Mr. Johnson followed Norris and Kuethe out of Commonwealth Bank. He was a half block away when he saw three men jump out of a machine and attack Norris and Kuethe; Johnson still says he was too far away to identify anyone.

Albert Conley

Albert Conley, the insurance salesman, initially denied he saw anything. After Hart's gang was locked up, Conley admitted he could identify John Smith and Walter Socolow as two of the men who jumped back into the Hudson after attacking Norris and Kuethe. He said, Socolow almost didn't make it. He leaped onto the machine's running board and dove in at the last minute.

Johnny Jubb and Buddy Blades

After Burns and Hammersla interviewed Johnny Jubb a second time, there was little doubt that Jubb had set Norris up with Buddy Blades. When interrogated at City Jail, Blades confessed that he knew Jubb before he worked at Hicks Tate and Norris. During an interview with John E. Jenkins, proprietor of the Belle Grove Inn, Hammersla learned Jubb had been a regular at the Belle Grove where the Saperstein-Lewis-Carey Gang hung out before Saperstein was shot dead.

Blades was still professing his innocence. According to Blades, he wasn't anywhere near Madison Street when Norris was murdered. His story is that he was just picking up and delivering laundry when the police yanked him out of his truck and arrested him. Despite being caught with what was thought to be payroll money in his pocket, Blades swears he had nothing to do with the robbery.

Blades would not admit that he intended to pay off Jubb. Jubb similarly wasn't going to confess that he sold his boss down the river for a few bucks. Because Blades was arrested before he had time to meet up with Jubb, no money was exchanged. Just the same," Burns tells Henry, "Johnny Jubb is the man who started the ball rolling."

Virginia Williams

Hammersla brought in Virginia "Shorts" Williams for a second interview. Her father came along. Virginia was clear about what took place on August 17th at John Smith's 909 Broadway row-house. She did not spend the night. Terrified of Walter's friends, Virginia left Smith's place as soon as she could slip out unnoticed. She spent the night with Margaret McCarthy, a high school girl-friend. What Virginia does remember is that in addition to Keller, Socolow and herself, Country Carey, Wiggles Smith, Stinky Allers, Fatty Novack, Benny Lewis, George Heard, Buddy Blades, and Jack Hart were there the night of the 17th.

Katherine Kavanaugh "Kitty" Connelly

Two days after Jack Hart was arrested, his wife Katherine Kavanaugh Connelly showed up at City Jail to visit her husband. She insisted Hart's name was Connelly and she was Mrs. Connelly. Kitty demanded to see her husband. After checking with Leach, Warden Sweezey arranged for her to meet across a table from Hart in the penitentiary's visitor's room.

Kitty visited her husband on three consecutive days beginning the day after Socolow was arrested by Detectives Kelly and Browne outside Bryant Park on Sunday, September 17th.

It became apparent that Kitty was not as estranged from her husband as she had led O'Conor and the police to believe. For one thing, they held hands across the table. Kitty complained that the dressing covering her husband's head wound (inflicted when he crashed through the table in Buck Livingston's apartment) needed to be changed. She requested permission to bring him home made treats like peach cake and fudge. Although Hart acted indifferently when Leach questioned him about Kitty, insisting he didn't care what she called herself, he was affectionate towards her when they were together.

Jack Hart, Vincenzo "Jim" D'Urso, and the Baltimore Crew

When Courtenay Jenifer, Robert Leach, and Herbert O'Conor (with Detective Burns present) interrogated Hart at City Jail on Monday, September 18th, the day after Socolow's arrest, Hart realized that any chance of making a deal with prosecutors by outing Socolow had evaporated. If there was a bargain to be made, it had to be something else.

Hart wanted to get out in front of Socolow, who was placing blame for the murder of William Norris on him. So, in the same City Jail room where John Keller was interrogated, Hart played his last card. He told Leach and Jenifer where he stashed his Mercer Raceabout and outed Vincenzo "Jim" D'Urso as boss of the Baltimore Crew.

Still fuming that D'Urso's boys wouldn't lend him a car, Hart was ready to finger Jimmy D'Urso. "Anyone who didn't work for the Baltimore Crew," Hart told Leach, Jenifer, and O'Conor, "paid D'Urso a hefty share of the take. Trying to sidestep D'Urso, usually meant a one-way trip to the harbor."

From the first day he was elected Baltimore City State's Attorney, Leach had his eyes on D'Urso. He wasn't about to turn down any helpful information. Leach's response to Hart was, "Tell us where your motorcar is, and I'll think about what [we] can do for you."

Hart informed Leach the building where he stashed his Raceabout was 1130 East Lombard Street. The building (garage and warehouse) is situated on the south side of East Lombard close to its intersection with Central Avenue. There are entrances on East Lombard and Gramby Street, the next east-west street south.

Hart revealed that his Mercer, hidden among cars and trucks, is parked in the Lombard Street end of the building. Further south is a second attached building where D'Urso stores whiskey. Four or five of D'Urso's heavies watch the place. That afternoon Burns, Comen, and Hammersla (with 20 uniformed officers) surrounded the warehouse.

The squad led by Burns smashed through the Lombard Street entrance startling eight men inside who were working on machines. When Burns demanded everyone "stay where they were," the shocked mechanics dropped their tools and raised their hands.

At the same time Burns' unit stormed in from Lombard Street, the unit commanded by Hammersla smashed through the building's Gramby Street entrance only to find themselves in an empty chamber. Sprinting 50 yards north, they slid open two large wooden (garage type) doors that separated the south side of the structure from the north where Burns' men (guns still at the ready) were wondering what to do with eight unarmed motorcar mechanics.

After an uncomfortable pause, Burns asked who was in charge. A middle-aged man dressed in work clothes and noticeably shaken by the unexpected intrusion stepped forward. He told Burns his name was Chester Jenkins and that this was his repair shop. He moved in at the end of August.

Jenkins told Burns that he started his company in 1919 right after the war. He needed a bigger place where he could sell gasoline. The building came up for rent and he moved in. Jenkins only rents the front 4,000 square feet. The 12,000 square foot warehouse, from which Hammersla's and Comen's unit emerged, was empty. Jenkins told Burns that the space was unoccupied when he moved in.

Burns asked, "Do you know who owns the property?"

Jenkins answered, "A lawyer named Harry Wolf."

Burns told Jenkins that he and his staff could relax. He was looking for a 1917 Yellow Mercer Raceabout.

Jenkins' response was that "there were no cars in the building when he moved in. The building was empty."

Apologizing for scaring the wits out of Jenkins' employees, Burns told his men to stand down. Outside on East Lombard Street, Burns suggested to Comen and Hammersla that Hart's car was probably at the bottom of the harbor. When Comen brought up Harry Wolf, Burns answered, "Wolf is fronting for D'Urso."

Joseph Kavanaugh

"The following day," Burns tells Henry, "Detective Comen and Sergeant Oberon paid another visit to the Joseph Kavanaugh Company on Lynhurst Road in Sparrows Point. This time, Joe

Kavanaugh admitted that he and Hart (who he continued to refer to as Jimmy Connelly) had been in cahoots. He had been distilling whiskey in the basement."

"Joe Kavanaugh," Burns continued, "admitted Connelly and his friend, Buck Livingston, along with their associates, picked up and delivered what he produced in the basement. After the Norris killing and Connelly disappeared, Kavanaugh said he broke down the distillation equipment and disposed of the left-over booze."

"Kavanaugh acknowledged that his niece Kitty knew that he was distilling whiskey for her husband. I informed Kavanaugh that he must have known, when he hooked up with Hart, that he was breaking the law. It was his choice to embroil his family in an illegal enterprise." Burns said, "I didn't arrest Joe Kavanaugh. What happens to him is up to Robert Leach."

Chief of Detectives George Henry

After Burns and his detectives finished updating Chief Henry, Henry filled in Captain Burns and his detectives on yesterday's meeting with Commissioner Gaither.

Henry informed Burns, "Commissioner Gaither has been in touch with Chief Pratt to see if a date can be set to interview Buck Livingston. Pratt said anytime was fine with him, but such a meeting should be arranged through Payton Gordon.[19] Pratt added that Livingston was not being cooperative. He claims that Hart, who he knew as James Connelly, was only staying with him and his wife for a few days. Livingston told Gordon that he had no idea Connelly was Hart. According to Livingston, James Connelly, was a house guest."

"Mr. Leach," Henry adds, "called Mr. Gordon. Gordon confirmed that Livingston refused to admit James Connelly was Jack Hart.

---

19 Payton Gordon, U.S. Attorney for the District of Columbia.

Gordon is indicting Livingston for selling whiskey on military bases, conspiracy to defraud the government and tax evasion. He told Mr. Leach that he was welcome to interview Livingston but thought it would be a waste of time. Livingston even refuses to see his wife."

Chief Henry continues, "Mr. Leach told Gordon that his office has enough evidence to convict Hart, Socolow, Carey, and Smith for murder and put the other members of Hart's gang in jail for years. He informed Gordon that his office has verified that Hart and Livingston were associates in a bootlegging ring on the east side of Baltimore. A lot of Hart's and Livingston's whiskey ended up at Camp Meade. Gordon said he would welcome any evidence that might help convict Livingston. Please work with Mr. O'Conor to provide Mr. Gordon with whatever he needs."

Burns replies, "Understood."

Henry then reveals, "Mr. Gordon asked if Mrs. Livingston was to receive any of the reward. Mr. Leach told him that she was. Anything leftover will be donated to the Norris' church."

"Gentlemen," Henry then addressing Burn's unit, "It is the policy of the State's Attorney and the Baltimore City Police Department that Mrs. Livingston's and Mrs. Millman's names will not be released to anyone—not to friends and family—not to any members of the press. Officially, an unnamed informant led to the capture of Jack Hart. Both Chief Pratt and Mr. Gordon concur."

As the meeting in Burns' office winds down, the questions are:

Will Joseph Banton indict Kahler and Murphy?

What about Herbert O'Conor?

Is there a chance Governor Ritchie will send Socolow back to New York?

Chief Henry tells his detectives, "There is no way of knowing and nothing we can do about it anyway. For now, finalize your investigations and get ready for the Norris Case prosecutions. Mr. Leach has asked that we reinterview witnesses. We need to make certain all bases are covered. Jury selection for the Carey-Smith trial begins in nine days."

40

OFFICE OF ROBERT F. LEACH, JR.
7:50 A.M., SEPTEMBER 22ND
BALTIMORE CITY COURTHOUSE

Robert Leach, Baltimore City State's Attorney
Fleet Cox, Deputy Baltimore City State's Attorney
H. Courtenay Jenifer, Baltimore County State's Attorney
Herbert O'Conor, Assistant Baltimore City State's Attorney
Baltimore Mayor, William F. Broening
Governor Ritchie's Cabinet Secretary, Stuart Janney
Mrs. Martha Fitzpatrick, Assistant to the State's Attorney
and Office Manager

Herbert O'Conor pulled into his Calvert Street parking spot about the same time Burns' taskforce was beginning their meeting with Chief of Detectives, George Henry.

Yesterday afternoon, after Leach and Cox let O'Conor off at his car in the courthouse parking lot, Leach told O'Conor to be in his office at eight o'clock. He didn't say what the meeting was about—but it didn't take a genius to figure it out.

The Socolow kidnapping saga was beginning its final chapter. O'Conor isn't sure what to expect. The only thing he knows for sure is that yesterday, during the drive back from Union Station, Leach let him know that Joseph Banton was being pressured by Justice Martin to form a grand jury to indict him, Kahler and Murphy, maybe New York Detectives James Gegan and George Gilbert for obstruction of justice. O'Conor has read Justice Martin's inflammatory remarks. The obvious leverage for Banton to forgo seeking indictments is for Maryland to return Socolow to New York, if in fact, that would be enough to satisfy Martin.

O'Conor thinks it isn't. He can't help but imagine that after to-day's meeting with his boss, Socolow will be New York bound.

Then again, it could be worse. Was he going to be sacked? Cleaning out his desk after a year on the job would (put) the brakes on a political career. It was going to be difficult to justify what happened in New York. With his and Eugenia's first child almost four months old, would he be able to find another job. What law firm would hire a discredited Irish Catholic kidnapper?

As O'Conor was finishing a cup of coffee, getting ready to face Leach and anticipating the worst, the whole damned mess suddenly became more troublesome. Secretary Stuart Janney, the former Army Colonel, Governor Ritchie's law partner and closest confidant appeared in the lobby. Janney spoke briefly with the office manager, Martha Fitzpatrick, who escorted the colonel to Robert Leach's office.

Minutes later, a noticeably disgruntled Mayor William F. Broening showed up. Broening avoided speaking to O'Conor when the two men came awkwardly together, along with Fleet Cox, as they trail Janney into Leach's office.

Leach invited everyone to take seats around an oval mahogany table adjacent to a huge casement window on the Lexington Street side of the richly paneled (uncomfortably quiet) conference room. It's eight o'clock.

Leach opens the conversation requesting that everything said remains confidential, "As of this morning, there have been no further communications from Mr. Banton or Governor Miller insisting that Socolow be returned or threatening to indict Herbert. Justice Martin, however, is still on the warpath. We will probably hear something from Banton or Governor Miller or both later today or early next week."

Leach continues, "The newspapers and radio commentators

are having a marketing bonanza opining on the kidnapping of Walter Socolow. It seems that everyone in the New York County Courthouse, in particular those who were momentarily imprisoned in courtroom 202, have something to say. I have learned from experience that if what we talk about today gets out, it will be second-guessed or incorrectly reported by a cavalcade of newsprint conjecture."

"One observer," Leach points out, "is certain he saw the Baltimore cops carrying Socolow down the rotunda stairway high over their heads. Another witnessed the getaway car speeding through City Hall Park, dodging trees, and pedestrians, as the machine, jumped the curb, heading north at breakneck speed. Another pundit agrees with Justice Martin. It had to be an inside conspiracy. Someone was paid off. There is nothing gained in [us] fueling the flames."

"The main issue is—we have Walter Socolow and New York doesn't. Justice Martin is demanding his return. Do we send him back?"

The tension is briefly interrupted when Courtenay Jenifer enters the room apologizing for being late. He was held up in traffic. "It gets worse every year. Too many machines on the roads."

Jenifer takes a seat between Fleet Cox and Colonel Janney.

Mayor Broening is quick to regenerate the atmospheric discomfort. The mayor of the eighth largest city in America isn't the least bit pleased with what he refers to as Mr. O'Conor's antics in New York. Looking at O'Conor, Broening questions, "Why would you do such a thing?"

But before O'Conor can respond, the mayor keeps going: "I have received a telephone call from New York Mayor John Hylan who is as outraged about Socolow being swiped out of his city as Justice Martin. According to Hylan, New York extended every courtesy to Baltimore only to be blindsided by two rogue cops and a duplicitous junior district attorney." Broening unfolds a copy of *The New York Times* and begins to read the front-page article that quotes Justice Martin.

"The whole affair is a disgrace to my court. I never saw anything like it in my life, in a Supreme Court." Broening looks up saying, "Justice Martin told the *Times* reporter, and anyone else within ear shot, the first thing he did was sign the second writ of *habeas corpus* and demand that Socolow be returned to New York."

Referring back to the *Times*, Broening reads, *"Unless that man is in my court chambers by 2 o'clock today, someone is going to prison."*

As he indifferently flings the *Times* onto the table, Broening confronts O'Conor: "That someone is you, Mr. O'Conor, along with the two Baltimore City officers who helped you do it. The three of you must have been out of your ever-loving minds."

Broening, who had been elected Baltimore City State's Attorney twice (1911 and 1915) before becoming mayor, has no intention of demanding that O'Conor be dismissed. Firing O'Conor isn't up to Broening. He is enough of a politician not to suggest it. O'Conor works for Leach, and like Broening, Leach was elected by the citizenry of Baltimore.

Even though their allegiances are to opposing parties (Broening a Republican and Leach a Democrat) Broening has endorsed Leach's tough stance against organized crime. Leach has similarly been responsive to Broening's crime initiatives. Mayor Broening considers the robbery and murder of William Norris as reprehensible as the other four men at the table. But insulting a New York Supreme Court judge and offending New York's mayor, all on the same day, grates on Broening's touchy temperament.

"Removing you," Broening tells O'Conor, "is Mr. Leach's choice, but I can do something about Lieutenant of Detectives Kahler and Sergeant Murphy. They work for Commissioner Gaither and Commissioner Gaither works for me!"

In his agitation, Broening seemed to forget that selecting the Baltimore City Police Commissioner is the Governor's prerogative. Even though the mayor has technical authority over the Department, Ritchie appointed Gaither, not Broening. This oversight didn't seem to matter to Mayor Broening. Colonel Janney, recognizing that there was nothing gained by correcting the mayor, lets Broening's version of the chain of command pass.

Infuriated, in his view, by O'Conor's recklessness, Broening points out, "The day Martin is talking about producing Socolow in his court happens to be today." The mayor sits back in his chair, crosses his arms and waits to hear what others have to say.

As long as Broening broached the subject, Leach asks O'Conor, "Would you mind explaining what happened in New York? Was there a good reason for kidnapping Socolow or did it boil down to misplaced judgment? It seems to me, if you had been a little more patient, Justice Martin would have dismissed the writ and sign off on Socolow's extradition. Why wasn't waiting an option?"

Before answering Leach, O'Conor addresses the mayor—he wants to dissuade Mayor Broening from going after Kahler and Murphy.

"What took place in New York," O'Conor explains, "was my responsibility. Once Bob sent me to New York, I assumed, like Kahler and Murphy, that they were answerable to me. All of us were determined to bring Socolow back to Baltimore. That is precisely what we did. Lieutenant Kahler and Sergeant Murphy were acting at my direction."

Broening, straightening up and leaning assertively forward, "Even if I were to believe that—Mr. O'Conor, why in the name of Christ would you do such a thing? Why didn't you wait?" Gesturing toward Leach, Broening asks, "Why didn't you discuss your idiotic plan with Mr. Leach, who, the last time I checked, is your boss!"

O'Conor, not backing down, replied, "There is precedent, Mr. Mayor."

"What precedent," Broening snaps back.

With Broening opening the door, O'Conor has a ready answer.

"In August 1919, when you were still Baltimore City State's Attorney, Detective Richard Freeman was dispatched to Louisville, at your request, to bring [a one] Albert Mackay back to Baltimore. The Governor of Kentucky, Edwin P. Morrow, had already, no different than Governor Miller of New York, signed the extradition warrant that had previously been issued by Maryland Governor, Emerson Harrington. Immediately upon the judge's dismissal of the writ, while Mackay's attorneys were, at that very moment, in the courtroom, in front of the judge, attempting to serve a second writ, Freeman grabbed Mackay and fled the jurisdiction. Mackay was returned to Baltimore where you prosecuted and convicted him for grand larceny and other crimes."

Broening, a little less belligerent, "Where did you learn all this?"

O'Conor answers, "Actually Mr. Mayor, Thursday when I was at Joab Banton's office in Manhattan before the hearing. Assistant State's Attorney Mike Driscoll invited me to visit and meet some of his colleagues working on another investigation. While I was there, I read up on the law relative to extradition and came across Albert Mackay."

Caught off guard, Broening responds, "That was a different situation altogether. The judge never signed the second writ or threatened Detective Freeman with arrest. The police didn't chase Freeman back to Baltimore."

"With all due respect, Mr. Mayor," O'Conor counters, "Detective Freeman couldn't have known that at the time."

O'Conor, speaking to everyone at the table, continues. "For whatever reason, maybe because he is at odds with Governor Miller, it became clear that Justice Martin wanted to make an issue of Socolow's extradition. He used the writ to do it. When he dismissed Socolow's petition," O'Conor, looking at Broening and quoting Detective Kahler, "Socolow was, at that moment, our prisoner. We grabbed him and brought him back, no different than Detective Freeman."

Taking a little steam out of the air, Leach chimes in, "You certainly did that Herbert, no question about it." Then Leach more seriously adds, "Do we send Socolow back or stand our ground?"

Jenifer argues, "Why send him back to New York? However, it happened, he is in Baltimore waiting to be tried for a murder he committed here—not New York. Judge Martin is playing politics."

"Why in the world," Cox questions, "would the Judge demand that we produce a witness to prove what everybody already knows. Socolow should have been on a train back to Baltimore the same day Governor Miller signed the extradition warrant. I say he stays where he is."

"What are the chances," Leach asked Cox, "Judge Martin will force Banton to call a grand jury to charge Herbert and Detectives Kahler and Murphy with obstruction?"

Cox answers, "He can demand it, but that doesn't mean Banton will do it," then adds, "Martin can certainly hold Herbert, Kahler, and Murphy in contempt. However, Martin is a judge not a prosecutor. If Martin is bent on trying Herbert and our detectives for obstruction of justice, or anything else, he will need Banton to do it."

"If Banton cooperates," Cox turning to O'Conor, "and you are indicted then Martin, on his own, cannot force you to return to New York or insist that he be the presiding judge. The irony (Cox now addressing everyone) is that Banton would need to go to Governor Miller and have him sign a fugitive warrant to extradite Herbert and our detectives back to New York. And even if Miller did sign a warrant, it would have to be cosigned by Governor Ritchie."

Sitting back in his chair, Cox speculates, "If I were Governor Miller, I would like to be done with this embarrassing legal mess. If Justice Martin had any sense, he would be done with it too. Martin can make ultimatums, but now that Socolow is in Maryland, he has no means to enforce a court order to return him to New York and no power, on his own, to prosecute Herbert or Detectives Kahler and Murphy. An indictment, in my view, will go nowhere."

Speaking directly to O'Conor, Cox says, "Had it been me, I would have waited for Martin to deny the petition and execute the warrant. If Martin insisted on hearing a collaborating witness, even though unprecedented, I would have complied."

Leach interrupts, "Are you sure Judge Martin would have demanded we produce a witness before releasing Socolow. Do you think he was doing anything but his damndest to annoy Governor Miller and stick it to Herbert."

Cox answers, "I'm not sure. I wasn't there. Herbert was and what's done is done. I'm satisfied Socolow is in Baltimore. The issue is how he got here."

Leach interjects, "I have had two telephone conversations with Mr. Banton. Both times, although hospitable, Banton insisted that Socolow be returned to New York to Justice Martin's court to finalize proceedings on the first petition and rule on the second. He thinks that might be the end of it."

"Banton was firm," Leach tells everyone, "If Socolow isn't returned, he will accommodate Justice Martin and call for a grand jury to indict Herbert and Detectives Kahler and Murphy for interfering in New York Supreme Court proceedings. If compelled to do this," Leach adds, "New York officers Gegan and Gilbert will likely be charged. Commissioner Enright, at Martin's request, has begun an internal investigation to uncover their involvement."

Leach, suddenly more animated, said "If you boil it down to politics, Justice Martin and Mayor Hylan are beholden to Tammany Hall. There is little chance they will do anything to accommodate Governor Miller. What reason would Miller have," Leach questions, "to insist that Socolow be returned to New York just to satisfy his political antagonists? Miller knows as well as [we] that the fugitive warrant he signed was the legal authority to extradite Socolow."

Colonel Janney, who had been sitting back in his chair patiently absorbing the essential elements of the exchange, abruptly straightens and leans forward.

"Gentlemen—On behalf of the Governor, I thank each of you for solving this horrifying crime so expeditiously. All of the suspects are in custody awaiting trial, including Walter Socolow. How he got here is another matter. My request is that you keep the Governor informed. You can call him or me anytime."

Janney, speaking directly to Mayor Broening, said "In the absence of Chief Henry, and despite all the other burdens placed on Baltimore police because of gangster related crime, tremendous weight was exerted on Commissioner Gaither, Captain of Detectives Charles Burns, and his men to solve the Norris case. No one has been more insistent than Governor Ritchie. Because of their efforts that include the contributions of Detectives Kahler and Murphy, Jack Hart and his gang are in jail."

"Bill," Janney suggests to the mayor, "It's up to you; but I would go easy on the police officers who have upheld your own law and order position."

"Governor Ritchie anticipates receiving a formal request from Governor Miller to return Walter Socolow to New York. He suspects Bob[20] will receive some form of correspondence, veiled in the threat of pending indictments, from New York City's district attorney. As to Mr. Banton's or Judge Martin's options, I am inclined to agree with Mr. Cox."

Janney reaffirms his request to keep him and Governor Ritchie informed. Thanking everyone for their time, Janney heads back to Annapolis.

Realizing this hasn't been his finest hour, Mayor Broening returns to City Hall.

In the foyer, before Janney departs, he talks privately with O'Conor. "Young men," he tells O'Conor, "every now and then, make rash decisions that appear foolhardy to older men like Mayor Broening and, quite frankly, me. Sometimes the consequences of such spontaneous choices work out and can lead to accolades, even heroism. I was witness to this when I commanded a brigade during the Argonne Offensive along the Western Front. Spontaneity can also end in disaster. Either way, the outcome is usually different than anticipated."

As Colonel Janney reaches out to shake O'Conor's hand, he smiles and adds, "I think, Mr. O'Conor, public opinion is on your side."

Lunch Break at the Belvedere Hotel

Attending:
Robert Leach
Courtenay Jenifer

---

20 Robert F. "Bob" Leach, Jr., Baltimore City State's Attorney.

MURDER ON MADISON STREET

Fleet Cox

Herbert O'Conor

J. Bernard Wells, Assistant Baltimore City State's Attorney

Timothy Andrews, Assistant Baltimore County State's Attorney

Mrs. Martha Fitzpatrick, Assistant to Robert Leach and Office
Manager

Following the tense morning conference, Leach invites
everyone to join him for lunch at the Belvedere Hotel,[21] before
the afternoon session, to talk about Norris case prosecutions.

Jay Bernard Wells, who was hired by Robert Leach a month after
Herbert O'Conor and has been assisting O'Conor in compiling
pre-trial discovery, will be joining them. Timothy Andrews, one
of Jenifer's young assistants (Well's counterpart in the county office), will meet them at the Belvedere.

The afternoon meeting is to review the upcoming prosecutions
of Jack Hart's gang beginning with the combined trial of Charles
Carey and John Smith. Whether Socolow is or is not returned to
New York is, for the most part, out of their hands. But for now,
Leach and Jenifer will proceed as if Socolow is here to stay.

---

21 Built in 1902–1903, The Belvedere Hotel was (and remains) a Baltimore
landmark. It is located in the city's fashionable Mount Royal neighborhood at the
southeast corner of North Charles Street and East Chase Street. The hotel takes
its named from the former "Belvidere Estate" of American Revolutionary War
hero Colonel John Eager Howard (1752–1827), who commanded the famous
"Maryland Line Regiment" of the Continental Army. He received the equivalent
of the Medal of Honor for his victory over the British at Cowpens, South
Carolina that led to the British surrender at Yorktown, Virginia on September 19,
1781. Howard was a member of the Continental Congress, new United States
Congress, Senator, and Governor of Maryland. Howard County, Howard, Eager,
and John Streets in Baltimore City, are named in his honor. Colonel Howard
is venerated by a statue (on horseback) on historic Mount Vernon Square.
The Belvedere was Baltimore City's premier hotel. Its restaurants (one on the
top floor) were considered exclusive epicurean gems. They were continually
occupied by prominent patrons. Both restaurants, although less exclusive, are
still open.

It was always Leach's and Jenifer's intent to prosecute John Smith and Charles Carey first. The trial will be held in the Baltimore City Courthouse beginning on Monday, September 25, 1922. Both Smith and Carey are charged with armed robbery, assault, and murder in the first degree.

Smith's attorney, John A. Meyer, had been unable to talk Judge Bond into releasing his client on bail. Carey's lawyer, E. Milton Altfeld, struck out too. Unable to secure bail, Meyer and Altfeld filed writs of *habeas corpus* to have their clients released on grounds of unwarranted imprisonment—no different than the writ Moses Polakoff filed in New York on behalf of Socolow. Both writs were denied by Judge Bond. Petition for a change of venue and to have Smith's trial separated from Carey's were also denied. In a final move to avoid first degree murder charges, Meyer and Altfeld approached Leach and Jenifer, proposing that Smith and Carey would be valuable state's witnesses.

Leach rejected this, pointing out that both John Smith and Charles Carey claim they had nothing to do with the robbery and murder of Mr. Norris. Both have insisted that they don't know Jack Hart or Walter Socolow. "If this is true," Leach responded, "what can your clients possibly offer?"

Meyer and Altfeld recognized that Leach and Jenifer had no intention of offering Carey or Smith a deal. The high-profile courtroom dramas that will play out over the next several months, possibly into 1923, begin with the Carey-Smith prosecution.

Even though finalizing the details of the Carey-Smith trial was the topic of today's afternoon discussion, it was difficult (during lunch at the Belvedere) not to think about the elephant in the room.

Will Joseph Banton form a grand jury? If so, will indictments be forthcoming? There is little question about Justice Martin holding O'Conor in contempt. Will New York Detectives Gegan's and

Gilbert's part in the plot be uncovered during Commissioner Enright's investigation? If so, what happens to them?

Despite Colonel Janney's encouragement, how will Governor Ritchie respond to a demand from Governor Miller to return Socolow to New York? More than anyone else, Socolow being shipped back to New York is up to the Governor.

In spite of Leach and Jenifer wanting lunch to be a pause from the work at hand, these questions pervaded lunchtime conversations. When they weren't talking about the possibility of Socolow being returned to New York or the Smith-Carey trial, Bernie Wells and Tim Andrews were curious about the particulars of the kidnapping.

When did O'Conor decide to commandeer Socolow? How did he get out of the building? Who helped? How did O'Conor know what ferry to take?

O'Conor did his utmost to be vague without being discourteous. He downplayed the involvement of Baltimore and New York police detectives.

Hardly taking a bite of lunch, O'Conor was relieved to get back to the office.

1:45 p.m. Afternoon Staff Meeting – Robert Leach's Office

Leach begins the discussion by letting everyone know that he and Courtenay will be the lead prosecutors for the Carey-Smith trial. "Herbert," he adds, "will assist with cross examinations and closing arguments. Bernie and Tim will be support."[22]

Cox begins: "Socolow's attorney, Gus Grason, has filed for a

---

22 Courtenay Jenifer, Baltimore County State's Attorney; Herbert R. O'Conor, Assistant Baltimore City State's Attorney; Bernard "Bernie" Wells, Assistant Baltimore City State's Attorney; Timothy "Tim" Andrews, Assistant Baltimore County State's Attorney; Fleet W. Cox, Deputy Baltimore City State's Attorney.

change of venue with Judge Bond. There is a chance his trial will be held in Towson. If so, Courtenay, I assume, will lead the prosecution."

Leach answers that Courtenay will head up any trials in Towson; "Either way, we won't schedule Socolow's trial until after Carey and Smith are sentenced."

"Hart's trial date," Leach adds, "is uncertain. In a meeting with Courtenay, Fleet, Herbert, and me, last Tuesday, Hart's attorney, Oscar Bermau, proposed Hart—who now insist he is James Connelly—will forgo a trial and enter a guilty plea if the death penalty is taken off the table. Bermau said that in exchange for this, 'Jack, will tell everything on the witness stand.'"

"We told Bermau we were confident of a conviction and that he must be too or wouldn't be trying to save Hart's life before his trial begins. We implied that we were not willing to make Hart a deal. The reality is that the death penalty is rarely the unanimous decision of a twelve-member jury. Hart was the ringleader—not the killer. If called as a witness, he can verify the testimony of Frank Allers and John Keller. He can confirm that Socolow and Keller told him that Harry Wolf hid them in his kitchen pantry on August 18th. And foregoing a jury trial, prevents disclosing Dorothy Livingston as our anonymous source."

Leach then asks, "Do we want to make a deal with Hart? Is it the best application of justice. We know if Hart pleads guilty to first degree murder, he will likely spend the rest of his life in prison. Courtenay and I want everyone to think about this and submit your comments on Monday."

"Another unknown," Leach brings up, "Is the believability of Frank Allers. He is our lead state's witness. How well he comes across in the Carey-Smith trial will be an indication of his influence going forward. Unless we accept Hart's guilty plea in exchange for life in prison, there will be three separate trials. Each trial will have different defense attorneys, juries, and possibly judges. How Allers comes across in the first trial will impact the others."

O'Conor adds, "Bernie, Tim, and I have spent hours with Allers and Keller going over the essentials each should highlight and what to expect from the defense. I don't think we need to worry about Allers. He's prepared."

"It's rumored," Jenifer adds, "In addition to Meyer, John Smith may be represented by New York criminal defense attorney Joseph T. Higgins. Higgins has been effective in getting high pro-file gangsters off the hook. I'm curious why he would be coming all this way to represent a petty crook like Wiggles Smith."

Courtenay Jenifer turns to Bernie Wells, "I don't think Higgins can make much of a difference but find out what you can about him."

Wells responds, "Will do."

Wells brings up John Keller: "Keller," he says, "will come across as a gullible juvenile hoodlum. Bob and Courtenay scared the pants off him about being hanged but during interviews with Herbert and I, he talks incessantly and is inconsistent. Who knows what he'll say on cross."

O'Conor adds, "We should limit Keller's testimony to the night of the crime at Harry Wolf's house and his part in the Boston-Chicago ruse. Too much of Keller will confuse the jury. Allers, on the other hand, was in on the robbery from the start and drove the Hudson. He doesn't mince words about what took place, and his recollections never change."

"The downside," Wells resumes, "is that Allers has been convicted of and served time for armed robbery. His nickname isn't 'Stinky' for nothing. His estranged sister-in-law, Ester, will testify that he is a habitual thief and liar. Meyer and Altfeld and Higgins, if he's retained, will rely on Ester Allers to impugn her brother-in-law."

Leach brings up Katherine Connelly. "Mrs. Connelly was not forthcoming about her relationship with her husband when she was interviewed by Herbert on August 26th. She knew then that her husband and Hart were the same man. Warden Sweezey has reported that Hart has remained in close contact with his wife. She visits him regularly."

"The reason Hart moved out of Mary Kavanaugh's house," Leach suggests, "is he was being sought for other crimes including the Glennbrook Whiskey heist. Living with the Kavanaughs, he was too exposed—easy to find."

O'Conor adds, "During follow up interviews, Burns and Murphy reported that they are positive Katherine Connelly knew all about the deal between her husband and her uncle to produce whiskey."

"On the stand," O'Conor predicts, Katherine Connelly will revert to the trusting wife. She told us she is willing to testify that Walter Socolow shot Mr. Norris, not her husband. But she wasn't there. Her testimony will be a distraction. She will do her best to tug at the jury's heartstrings. There is nothing to be gained, by calling Mrs. Connelly."

All express their agreement in not charging Katherine Connelly or calling her as a witness.

Leach brings up Harry Wolf. "I have decided to charge Harry Wolf with obstruction of justice for hiding Socolow and Keller in his home the night of the crime and lying about it to Lieutenant Hammersla. I will have a warrant issued for Wolf's arrest as soon as we are sure Socolow is in Baltimore to stay. When Courtenay and I learned that Wolf had contacted New York Police Commissioner Richard Enright and informed him that [he] was Socolow's attorney, we decided not to wait."

Cox interjects, "Wolf will never admit Socolow and Keller were in his house. He will argue that he told Detective Hammersla the truth when he showed up on his doorstep on August 18th."

Leach responds, "Wolf can claim whatever he wants, but we know he told Hammersla that he did not represent Socolow and Hart. He prevented the arrest of Socolow, who was in his house with John Keller at the time. He is complicit in helping Socolow and Hart get out of Baltimore. Let him deny that!"

Cox answers, "It will be hard to prove."

Cox lets everyone know, "Captain Leverton resigned on Tuesday, September 20th following the weekend arrests of Jack Hart in Washington and Walter Socolow in New York. During Hammersla's investigation, he uncovered that Leverton had acted improperly with other criminal prosecutions. This was certainly the case when he showed up at our office, with John Keller, insisting that Keller was Wolf's unnamed source."

"Unfortunately," Leach interjects, "other than Keller, Socolow and Wolf, Leverton is the only person with firsthand knowledge that Socolow and Keller were in Wolf's house."

Cox replies, "It's difficult to imagine that the testimony of either Socolow or Keller will bode well against the rebuttal of a slick lawyer like Wolf. Leverton knows that Wolf was hiding Socolow and Keller, but I doubt he will ever admit it."

"Nevertheless," Leach counters, "We have a solid circumstantial case against Wolf for obstruction of justice. If he is indicted, we will schedule his trial following Socolow's."

"There is a good chance," O'Conor adds, "when Socolow takes the stand, he will incriminate himself and Wolf."

Around the table everyone agrees the benefit of indicting Wolf earlier than planned is to keep him from representing any of the men being tried for murder and shield himself from incrimination.

"As of last Saturday," Leach resumes, "Socolow is maintaining his innocence. He now claims that he told Detectives Browne and Kelly what they wanted to hear to keep from being pummeled. He didn't mean a word of it. He was under duress, fearful of being beaten again by Detective Browne who he says, threatened him. Socolow told the New York cops what they wanted to hear to prevent further thrashing. He is back to his old alibi that he was asleep in bed with his girlfriend at John Smith's house when William Norris was gunned down. He claims Jack Hart shot Norris, and that he never told Harry Wolf otherwise."

"This coming Monday," Leach adds, "We are scheduled to interview Socolow at City Jail. By then he may change his story again. We'll find out."

Cox adds, "Socolow's attorney is C. Gus Grason, not Harry Wolf. Grason will be there Monday. Grason is a smart attorney, not tainted with the stink of corruption we suspect of Wolf. He is a formidable lawyer."

Cox continues, "I don't believe our interview with Socolow, if Grason is present, will uncover what we don't already know. Grason will do his best to keep Socolow quiet. Warden Sweezey reports that Socolow has been acting up and arguing he is being framed by Hart. If we are successful in convicting Socolow of first-degree murder, Grason will argue that Socolow is still a kid, only 19 years of age. Jack Hart, Grason will tell the jury, is responsible for the death of Mr. Norris. Socolow was doing what Hart told him to do. He will argue that minus Hart's influence over the members of his gang, Mr. Norris would still be alive."

It is decided to schedule Socolow's trial for mid-October, hopefully no later than October 15th, after Smith and Carey are sentenced.

The subject reverts to the other members of Hart's gang who did not participate in the robbery. Leach and Jenifer will not indict them for first or second-degree murder [accessory before the fact is the more likely charge]. Leach and Jenifer explain that if John Smith and Charles Carey are convicted of murder and sentenced to life and possibly death by hanging, it will entice the others not involved in the robbery to plead guilty to the lesser charge avoiding costly and time-consuming trials where murder convictions are unlikely.

Such a prosecutorial balance of jury trials, plea deals, limited immunity agreements, and sentencing recommendations, Leach and Jenifer agree, is an achievable approach within a reasonable timeline. Leach and Jenifer want the Norris case prosecutions concluded by the end of the year. Both Robert Leach's and Courtenay Jenifer's first terms as Baltimore City and Baltimore County State's Attorneys end on January 1, 1924. The date of the election is November 6, 1923.

Leach and Jenifer aim to reserve 1923 to focus on their commitments to prosecute gang-related crime. Leach's and Jenifer's offices are working jointly on a number of prosecutions, including uncovering political boss Frank Kelly's link to organized crime. Leach makes no secret about building a case against D'Urso and his Baltimore Crew.

At 4:30, as the meeting is winding down, Martha Fitzpatrick enters the room. The conversation abruptly ends as everyone stands. Fitzpatrick, who has been working in the State's Attorney's office for twelve years, responds, "No need to stand gentlemen. I'm an old fixture around here." She hands Leach a telegram. It's from New York City State's Attorney Joseph Banton. The telegram is addressed to Robert F. Leach, Jr., Baltimore City State's Attorney.

Leach reads it aloud.

Dear Mr. Leach,

This is to advise you that, by the directive of Justice Francis W. Martin of the New York Supreme Bench, this office has assembled a grand jury to consider the indictments of Mr. Herbert R. O'Conor of your office and Baltimore City Police Detective Lieutenant Charles Kahler and Detective Sergeant William Murphy who interfered with Supreme Court Proceedings on September 21, 1922, in Justice Martin's courtroom.

Banton's telegram further requests, *The prisoner, Walter Socolow, removed from Justice Martin's courtroom, be returned to New York forthwith.*

Banton expects that his grand jury will hand down indictments no later than Friday, September 29, 1922.

O'Conor is noticeably shaken by Banton's telegram.

Leach, gesturing towards Fleet Cox, reminds O'Conor what Fleet said at the morning meeting relative to the legal and political roadblocks Banton will face even if his grand jury returns indictments against him, Kahler and Murphy. "After all," Leach reminds O'Conor, "Judge Martin dismissed the writ. Banton knows this as well as us. And unless the Governor decides otherwise, we are not sending Socolow back."

Leach assures O'Conor that he will respond to Mr. Banton this afternoon before leaving the office. He decides to end the meeting early saying, "It's been a long week—time to head home and enjoy the weekend."

Leach tells O'Conor, "Forget about this for now. Focus on Monday's interview with Walter Socolow and Gus Grason. Everything will work out. If it wasn't for the doggedness of Judge Martin, Banton would not be indicting anyone."

Robert Leach's response to Joseph Banton

At 5:30, before leaving the office, Leach hands Mrs. Fitzpatrick the texts of his telegram to Joseph Banton.

Mrs. Fitzpatrick reads it back.

September 22, 1922

TO: Joseph Banton, Esq., State's Attorney for New York City
FROM: Robert Leach, Esq., State's Attorney for Baltimore City

Dear Mr. Banton,

Mr. O'Conor, of this office, and the Baltimore Police acted in good faith free of intention to proceed otherwise than regularly, except of course, intense desire to circumvent further trifling action by Socolow's attorneys.

Regarding your request for the return of Walter Socolow, there is no reason to return Mr. Socolow to New York as the writ had been dismissed and the prisoner remanded to the proper authorities.

Maryland intended no slight to you, the state of New York, or its courts, but what has been done is justifiable both legally and morally.

Baltimore City Police Commissioner, Charles Gaither

As Leach leaves the courthouse, Commissioner Gaither meets up with him in the Calvert Street parking lot. Before meeting with the mayor, he wants to talk to Leach about a telegram he received from New York Police Commissioner Enright, two hours earlier.

"Enright," he tells Leach, "is requesting information uncovered during the debriefing of Detectives Kahler and Murphy, which could shed light on the involvement of his detectives in removing Walter Socolow from Justice Martin's courtroom. When I respond, we should be on the same page."

Leach tells Gaither about the telegram he received from Joseph Banton and his response to it.

"I wrote Mr. Banton that Mr. O'Conor and your officers acted in good faith. The judge dismissed the writ, and we took legal custody of Socolow. I implied we are not sending him back."

Gaither asks, "Given your telegram to Banton, what do you believe is an appropriate reply to Commissioner Enright?"

"In your telegram to Commissioner Enright," Leach responds, "you might emphasize there was no intent to embarrass his department. It is likely when we try Socolow, we will call Detectives Gegan, Browne, and Kelly as witnesses relative to how Socolow was apprehended and what he said after he was arrested. Hopefully, we can minimize any opposition to this from the officers or their superiors. There is the possibility," Leach suggests, "Commissioner Enright would like to be done with this as much as us."

Leach tells Commissioner Gaither, "Governor Ritchie is anticipating correspondence from Governor Miller requesting Socolow's return to New York. In my telegram, I did not want to undercut anything the Governor might communicate."

Gaither thanks Leach and heads back to his office on Fayette Street. Upon his return, Gaither dictates a telegram to Commissioner Enright.[23] In the telegram, like Leach, he expresses regret for any misunderstanding, writing:

---

23 Richard Edward Enright (August 30, 1871–September 4, 1953) was the first man to rise from the rank-and-file to assume command of the New York City Police Department. He was extremely loyal to the men and women of his department and was popular among them. Enright served as Commissioner from 1918 through 1925.

During his eight-year tenure as commissioner, he and Mayor John F. Hylan, a Tammany Hall Democrat, were frequently at odds—mostly over Hylan's ongoing efforts to control the NYPD. Finally, having had enough of Hylan's criticism of the NYPD and ongoing insinuations that he was dishonest, Enright resigned.

Enright's accomplishments were eventually recognized as valued contributions to the NYPD (and welfare of New York City) that spanned 30 years of service on the police force.

It was never the intention of my officers to act in a way that might impugn the good standing of your department.

After speaking with my Chief of Detectives, George J. Henry, his men thought when Justice Martin said, "writ dismissed," the proceedings were over, and that Socolow was turned over to them.

With Gegan[24] and Gilbert[25] in mind, Gaither closes,

Responsibility is entirely on Baltimore's representatives.

Richard Edward Enright,
New York City Police Commissioner

---

24 James Gegan, New York City Police Lieutenant in charge of tracking down Jack Hart and Walter Socolow in New York City.

25 George P. Gilbert, New York City Police Detective Lieutenant, drove O'Conor, Kahler, and Murphy while they were in New York. Gilbert drove O'Conor, Kahler, Murphy, Walter Socolow, and newspaper reporter George Dorsch to the Central Railroad's West Street Ferry Terminal. Gegan and Gilbert were the New York Police Officers most responsible for the kidnapping of Walter Socolow from Justice Francis Martin's courtroom.

<u>41</u>

Annapolis, Maryland
Monday –8:00 a.m., September 25, 1922
Governor's Office
Maryland Statehouse

Albert Ritchie, Governor of Maryland
Stuart Janney, Cabinet Secretary
Alexander Armstrong, Maryland Attorney General

Albert Cabell Ritchie was elected Maryland's 49th Governor in November 1919 and assumed office on January 14, 1920. He was born in Richmond, Virginia, into a prominent old-line Virginia family on August 29, 1876. His mother, Elizabeth Caskie Cabell, was a descendant of Joseph Cabell, a close friend and associate of Thomas Jefferson. Her bloodline included William H. Cabell, the 14th Governor of Virginia. His father Albert, a law professor and judge, was a delegate for the Maryland Constitutional Convention in 1867.

In 1896, Ritchie graduated from Johns Hopkins University and, in 1898, the University of Maryland School of Law, where he met his future law partner and close friend Stuart Janney. In 1920, the year he assumed the Governorship of Maryland, Ritchie received his Doctor of Law Degree from St. Johns College and the University of Maryland through a shared doctoral program.

Ritchie was a no-nonsense erudite student of the law. He might have remained a law professor or become a judge were it not for his strong political beliefs and his ability to sway people to his point of view. Previously elected Maryland's Attorney General, passage of the 18th Amendment (as much as anything) was the catalyst that compelled him to seek the Governorship.

Ritchie, a staunch conservative Democrat, was a supporter of states' rights. He opposed the 18th Amendment (that banned the manufacture, sale, and transportation of alcoholic beverages in the United States and its possessions), viewing it as an unconstitutional intrusion by the federal government upon the states. Ritchie was equally opposed to the Volstead Act, which was passed to enable enforcement of Prohibition.

He predicted that Prohibition, coupled with the Volstead Act, would create a violent criminal element that would step in to provide illegal spirits to a population that, in the main, was against the 18th Amendment. This, in turn, Ritchie believed, would foster crime and corruption, inflicting an adverse impact on the country greater than the availability of alcohol.

During his 1919 campaign to become Governor, Ritchie championed states' rights over an invasive federal authority. Beyond this, he promised to improve public education, and expand and rebuild Maryland's roadways, bridges, and highways. His persuasively calm, almost patrician character enabled him to squeak by in the election against his popular Republican opponent, Harry Nice.

Because they were conservative Democrats who championed states' rights, opposed prohibition, and were committed to combat crime and corruption, Ritchie was aligned with and supportive of Robert Leach and Courtenay Jenifer. Ritchie considered the robbery and murder of William Norris a cruel manifestation of the lawlessness spawned by the rise of the gangster class baptized by the 18th Amendment and its enforcer, the Volstead Act.

This morning—first on the Governor's agenda, is a meeting with Stuart Janney and Alexander Armstrong to review a correspondence received late last Friday from New York Governor Nathan L. Miller.

8:30 p.m. – September 22, 1922
110 State Street, Albany, New York – Office of the Governor
From: Governor Nathan L. Miller of New York
To: Governor Albert C. Ritchie of Maryland

My Dear Governor,

Requesting to Cause (To Be Returned) to this State, Walter Socolow, who was kidnapped from Justice Francis W. Martin's Courtroom in New York City on (September 21, 1922) and taken to Baltimore where he is wanted for Murder.

Miller's measured telegraph is, in the collective opinion of Ritchie, Armstrong, and Janney, a dry, impersonal, halfhearted appeal to have Walter Socolow returned to Martin's jurisdiction.

Ritchie and Miller could not have been more opposite in their political understandings—not just because Ritchie was a Democrat and Miller was a Republican, but because Ritchie was a States' Rights advocate and Miller was, at heart, a Federalist. Miller was a strong supporter of the 18th Amendment and the enforcement of it.

Ritchie appreciates that whatever he writes to Miller will be quoted nationwide in newspapers and through radio commentary. He doesn't want to insult or demean Miller. On the other hand, he, Janney, and Armstrong believe Justice Martin had been way out of line in using his judicial authority to delay Socolow's return to Baltimore and in doing so, created the present dilemma.

Miller, who could have been more influential in a pre-kidnapping resolution, had until now said nothing. They agreed that Miller's silence had much to do with his upcoming reelection, in which his opponent will be the man he defeated in 1920, New York's most influential Tammany Hall Democrat, Al Smith. It's no secret that the 1922 New York Governor's race will be a nasty contest. New York Mayor John Hylan and Justice Francis Martin will be behind Al Smith. Ritchie and Janney concur that Miller would not be pressing for the return of Socolow except to avoid giving Al Smith political ammunition to use against him.

With the advice of Alex Armstrong and the concurrence of Stuart Janney, Ritchie sent his reply.

10:00 a.m. – September 25, 1922
TO: Governor Nathan L. Miller
FROM: Governor Albert C. Ritchie

Dear Governor:

It is regrettable that this misunderstanding over the disposition of the fugitive, Walter Socolow, has become such a high-profile and discordant issue. After consideration, however, it is my determination that Walter Socolow is in Maryland and will stay in Maryland until he is tried.

Socolow has committed no crime in New York and therefore cannot be extradited to New York.

As to whether the Baltimore police acted with propriety in bringing Socolow to Baltimore City, that is another matter. But Socolow is here now and here he will stay.

For Governor Miller, Mayor Hylan, New York State's Attorney Banton, and even the still vehement Justice Francis W. Martin, like it or not, this was the end of it as far as returning Walter Socolow to New York.

It was further the belief of Ritchie, Armstrong, and Janney that a charge against O'Conor could at best be one of "technical contempt"—unlikely to go anywhere and ultimately dismissed. They felt similarly about Detectives Kahler and Murphy.

If Justice Martin had something else in mind, he should not have been so quick to dismiss the writ. It is their consensus that although the kidnapping of Socolow was creative, no laws were broken.

42

AFTERMATH

Herbert, R. O'Conor, Assistant Baltimore City State's Attorney, Charles Kahler, Baltimore City Police Detective Lieutenant, William Murphy, Baltimore City Police Detective Sergeant, James Gegan, New York City Police Detective Lieutenant, and George Gilbert, New York City Detective Lieutenant, were indicted for interfering with New York Supreme Court Proceedings.

Neither New York State's Attorney Joseph Banton nor New York Police Commissioner Richard Enright were wholeheartedly in favor of the indictments handed down against O'Conor, Kahler, Murphy, Gegan, and Gilbert. Without the relentless pressure applied by Justice Martin, Joseph Banton[26] (as Fleet Cox and Robert Leach predicted) would not have charged O'Conor or the four police officers.

Like Fleet Cox, Banton concluded that once Justice Martin dismissed the writ, there was no ensuing crime. Banton explained this to Martin. If he did secure indictments, charges against the Baltimoreans would be limited to "technical contempt of court or interfering with court proceedings." Martin, however, was unbending.

The charges came down to interfering with Supreme Court proceedings and contempt of court for the way Socolow was spirited away. Despite Governor Ritchie's telegram to Governor Miller stating, *"Socolow is here now and here he will stay,"* Martin demanded that Socolow be returned to New York.

The reality that Martin didn't seem to grasp was that without the cooperation of Governor Ritchie, there was no way to compel

---

26 Joseph "Joab" Banton, New York City State's Attorney.

the return of Socolow, much less O'Conor, Kahler, or Murphy to New York. Added to this, public opinion throughout the country was that Martin was wrong and O'Conor was right.

"What people think has no legal precedent," Martin repeatedly emphasized, but the seemingly endless newspaper editorials and articles that romanticized the hijacking and favored Socolow's return to Baltimore generally portrayed Martin unfavorably. The New York Supreme Court was getting bad press. Even Martin's fellow justices recommended he let the matter drop.

It didn't take long for Banton to realize that he wasn't about to get much help from Commissioner Enright, or the officers Enright impowered to investigate Gegan, Gilbert, Browne, and Kelly.

It was clear, from the get-go, that after Browne and Kelly arrested Socolow outside Bryant Park and turned him over to Gegan, their involvement ended. Browne and Kelly, as it turned out, like everyone on the force, had nothing to say. A plurality of New York police officers privately expressed no little delight at the success of the 'coup' bantering, *"It takes Baltimore to come up here and give us a real sensation."*

Enright was more direct: *"In any court where the writ of habeas corpus was dismissed, and the prisoner remanded, he belonged to the persons holding extradition papers for him."*

When Lieutenant James Gegan was summoned (by Banton's grand jury) to explain himself, he showed up with two attorneys, Alexander L. Rorke and Robert F. Kane. Rorke and Kane presented a statement for the record that began: *"No New York policeman assisted in the spiriting away of Socolow."*

It was Lieutenant Gegan's unit, they emphasized, that was responsible for apprehending Socolow, not for monetary reward but because they were doing their duty. Gegan was instructed to assist the Baltimore officers and that's precisely what he did.

When Socolow was whisked away, to the surprise of everyone, Lieutenant Gegan obeyed Justice Martin's order to help prevent the escape. He and many other officers, sent to Pennsylvania Station and Manhattan's ferry terminals, despite every effort, were unable to prevent the Baltimore contingent from reaching New Jersey. "Whose fault is this," Kane asked the members of the grand jury. "Nobody's," he said, "certainly no one from the New York Police Department who did their upmost to prevent the Baltimoreans from fleeing the city."

In their statement, Rorke and Kane argue that Lieutenant George Gilbert, who drove Baltimore City State's Attorney O'Conor to the Central Railroad's Liberty Street Ferry Terminal, had no way of knowing that Justice Martin's court proceedings had been interrupted. He was not in the courtroom. Gilbert was assigned to both assist and drive O'Conor, Kahler, and Murphy while they were in New York. This is exactly what he did.

Police Sergeant Conor Sullivan was called to testify. Sullivan was the first to join Lieutenant Gilbert on the Liberty Street dock soon after the ferryboat *Elizabeth* left the pier. Sullivan confirmed Gilbert was unaware of the kidnapping.

On October 2, 1922, Joseph Banton withdrew the charges against Assistant Baltimore City State's Attorney Herbert R. O'Conor, Detective Lieutenant Charles Kahler and Sergeant William Murphy.

On October 5th, Banton made the decision not to go forward with charges against Lieutenants Gegan and Gilbert.

Even Justice Martin came to realize the futility of his determination to punish those involved in, as he termed it, "*The Socolow Affair*." Martin issued no further public statements. He reconciled himself to follow the advice of his associate justices and let it drop.

On Monday morning, September 25, 1922, the broadsheet world was fixated on the Smith-Carey murder trial that began at nine o'clock in the Baltimore City courthouse. The brouhaha that took place in Justice Martin's courtroom the week before was old news. Newspaper reporters and broadcasters from across the country flocked to Baltimore to report on the trials of the men who robbed and murdered William B. Norris—beginning with the Smith-Carey Trial.

John L. "Wiggles" Smith   *Charles P. "Country" Carey*

43

SMITH-CAREY MURDER TRIAL
TUESDAY, SEPTEMBER 26, 1922

Present in the Courtroom:
Chief Judge (Supreme Bench), James Polk Gorter
Circuit Court Judge, Hugh L. Bond, Jr.
Circuit Court Judge, Edward Duffy
Joseph Quinn, Bailiff
Edward McCauley, Elected Jury Forman

For the Prosecution: Robert Leach, Baltimore City State's
Attorney
Herbert R. O'Conor, Assistant Baltimore City State's Attorney
Bernard Wells, Assistant Baltimore City State's Attorney
Courtenay Jenifer, Baltimore County States Attorney

For the Defense: Attorneys Joseph T. Higgins of New York and
John A. Meyer of Baltimore representing John L. Smith.
Attorney E. Milton Altfeld representing Charles P. Carey

Chief Judge James Polk Gorter – Jury's Trust – 9:00 a.m.

All of Tuesday, September 26, 1922, was spent selecting the
jury. At 4:30 in the afternoon, Chief Judge Gorter[27] swore

---

27 In 1922, the Baltimore City Courthouse, formally the Baltimore County Courthouse when the city was part of the county, consisted of five separate courts. All
came under the Supreme Bench of Baltimore City. In 1922, James Polk Gorter
was Chief Judge of the Supreme Bench, and therefore, oversaw all of Baltimore
City courts that included the Superior Court, two Circuit Courts and the Court
of Common Pleas. The Carey-Smith trial was held in courtroom 600, the ceremonial chamber—reserved for the Supreme Bench. There were three judges:
Chief Judge Gorter, and Superior Court Judges Bond and Duffy. Unlike today,
all three judges could break into testimony and ask questions of a witness. Judge
Gorter was the final arbitrator of rulings but would confer with Judges Bond and
Duffy.

in the twelve jurymen. Acknowledging the elected jury foreman, Judge Gorter asks, "Mr. McCauley do you accept, without prejudice, your election as foreman of this jury?"

McCauley answers, "I do, Your Honor."

All twelve jurymen live and work in Baltimore. They make up a cross section of occupations—businessmen, factory workers, longshoremen, a trolley conductor, construction superintendent, firefighter, an accountant, and two retirees. Judge Gorter, taking his time explaining what is expected of them, adds:

> "You gentlemen are not to discuss anything related to this trial with anyone, including your fellow jurors, until closing arguments are concluded. Keep in mind the defendants, Charles Carey and John Smith, are charged with murder in the first degree. You will consider five possible verdicts.
>
> *First, guilty of murder in the first degree leaving it to the direction of this Court to impose the supreme penalty—hanging or sentence them to the Penitentiary for their natural lives.*
>
> *Second, murder in the first degree without capital punishment— meaning imprisonment in the Penitentiary for life.*
>
> *Third, murder in the second degree with a sentence not to exceed eighteen years also in the Penitentiary.*
>
> *Fourth, manslaughter, carrying a punishment not to exceed ten years in the Penitentiary or jail.*
>
> *Fifth, a verdict of not guilty.*
>
> Listen to the arguments presented by both the prosecution and the defense. Do not be influenced by what you might have heard or read or what you will hear or read outside of this courtroom. If you have questions direct them to the bench through Mr. McCauley."

Addressing all twelve jurymen, Judge Gorter asks, "Do you gentlemen understand the charges against the two defendants and what is expected of you in determining their guilt or innocence?"

Edward McCauley, looking at his fellow jurymen, who collectively nod in agreement, turns back to Judge Gorter and responds, "We do, Your Honor."

"Then," Gorter, addressing everyone in the courtroom: "We will adjourn for the day. Court will reconvene at nine o' clock tomorrow morning."

Joseph Quinn, the Bailiff, asks everyone to rise as the three judges retired to Judge Gorter's chambers. Quinn then restates that the Superior Court of Baltimore City is adjourned until tomorrow (Wednesday, September 27, 2022) at nine o' clock.

The courtroom quickly empties as reporters rushed to file their stories. There wasn't much to write about other than the prosecution and defense question thirty-four potential jurors before agreeing on the twelve men who will decide the fate of Charles Country Carey and John Wiggles Smith.

Carey and Smith, it was reported, sat passively during the first day of the trial that would determine their fate—guilt or innocence—possibly life in the state penitentiary or death by hanging.

Stuart Olivier, Editor of the *Evening News* wrote: ...*both men appeared disinterested in the goings on. The two defendants, separated by their attorneys, E. Milton Altfeld representing Carey and Joseph T. Higgins and John A. Meyer representing Smith, avoided looking at one another and only spoke when addressed by one of the judges or their attorneys. The one time Carey and Smith had a good look at the jam of spectators was when the courtroom was clearing and they were led away in handcuffs.*

Opening Arguments – 9:00 a.m.,
Wednesday, September 27, 1922

By nine o' clock when the three judges assumed their places behind the bench, courtroom 600 was standing room only. Bailiff Joseph Quinn announced, "The Superior Court of Baltimore City is now in session."

Addressing the prosecution, Judge Gorter asks, "Mr. Leach, is the prosecution ready to proceed?"

Leach responds, "Your Honor we are."

Judge Gorter, "Please begin."

Robert Leach spends the next hour presenting the government's case beginning with the planning of the crime in John Smith's 909 Broadway house on the night of August 17, 1922. He details how Robert Norris and Fred Kuethe were ambushed on Madison Street as they return to Hicks Tate and Norris Construction Company from the Commonwealth Bank. As Leach names each member of the Hart, Carey, Smith, and Lewis gang (the newspapers are calling the Broadway Gang), he summarizes their criminal history.

"There will be other trials," Leach tells the jury, pointing toward Carey and Smith, "but these two defendants, Charles Carey and John Smith, are as guilty of murdering Robert Norris and almost killing Frederick Kuethe as the other three men who were in the murder car that day. They never gave Mr. Norris or Mr. Kuethe a chance."

"Mr. Kuethe barely survived. Bob Norris, the father of three young sons—one of them in this courtroom today—did not. He was gunned down in cold blood. Afterward these two bandits, along with the others, fled the scene, believing they were free and clear, without an ounce of remorse for the gruesome crime they had just committed. "For what," Leach asks the jurymen—then answering his own question, "For a little more than seven thousand dollars. Not much money in exchange for a man's life. Yes, to be absolutely clear, Charles Carey and John Smith did this. We will prove to you, beyond a doubt, that they did."

After Leach concludes his opening, Judge Gorter addressing the three defense counselors, asks, "Which of you gentlemen will speak first for the defendants?"

Joseph Higgins, already standing, answers, "Your Honor, it is agreed that I will open for my client, John Smith."

Judge Gorter, "Please proceed."

Higgins, walking toward the jury begins, "Gentlemen of the jury—I intend to prove that John Smith (Higgins turns to look at Smith) was nowhere near Madison Street when Mr. Norris was shot."

"It is a tragedy, of course, that a man died—but John Smith did not shoot anybody. At the time of the robbery, Mr. Smith was in Essex with his friend Benny Lewis. It may speak ill of their condition, but both men were inebriated. They were too drunk to drive a machine much less rob anyone. They were arguing over starting a motorcar, a Mercer Raceabout that belonged to a friend, when they were arrested by the county police."

"This motorcar," Higgins resumes, "is missing. It was left on the side of Eastern Avenue. After Mr. Smith and Mr. Lewis were arrested, the Mercer vanished. A yellow Raceabout is not an easy motorcar to hide. So where is it?"

"Mr. Smith and Mr. Lewis, unfortunately for them, befriended Jack Hart, a man with a record from New York City. Mr. Hart now insists his name is James Connelly. Maybe his name is Connelly. Maybe it's Hart. Whatever his name is, he lent my client and his friend his Raceabout for the weekend. And because my client and Mr. Lewis were arrested in Jack Hart's motorcar, miles from the crime, well—Mr. Leach assumes they took part in the robbery. And now that yellow Mercer, the proof that Mr. Smith was in Essex at the very time of the crime, is missing. How convenient!"

Higgins pauses—looks at the jury—then shift his gaze toward Frank Allers, who is sitting next to Captain Burns directly behind Herbert O'Conor, and then turns back to the jurymen. "There's the real criminal, Frank Allers, sitting right there. He's the man who helped plan and carry out the robbery and murder. Mr. Allers even drove the murder car, as the State's Attorney likes to call it."

"To save himself," Higgins stresses, "Mr. Allers is now the State's main witness against my client, John Smith, and Mr. Altfeld's client, Charles Carey. For his fictional testimony, the State's Attorney is letting him off the hook. Mr. Allers is getting a pretty sweet deal. He won't be hanged —and I bet not much jail time.

"Then, of course, the newspapers have had a field day linking my client to Jack Hart—or is it James Connelly? Who knows? But one thing I do know, there is no trial date for Jack Hart or James Connelly. Looks like another deal in the works." Turning to the jury, Higgins asks, "What does it look like to you men of the jury? I suggest to you, my client's only guilt is guilt by association."

Higgins continues, "My co-council, John A. Meyer, and I will prove, although John Smith has his faults, drinks too much, was arrested in a borrowed motorcar, the police can't seem to find, he is not a murderer." Pointing toward his client, Higgins finishes, "Gentlemen of the jury, John L. Smith is a family man. He has a regular job, like you, at the steel plant in Sparrows Point. He had nothing to do with the robbery of William Norris and Frederick Kuethe."

Following Mr. Higgins' opening remarks, Judge Gorter announces that the court will break for lunch. He asks everyone to remain until the jury and the defendants leave the courtroom. After the jury exits, the judges retire to Gorter's chambers. Joseph Quinn announces that the Superior Court of Baltimore City is in recess until two o'clock.

Although it's September 27th, the air in the crowded courtroom is clammy. It was unseasonably warm and had been drizzling all morning. Spectators were anxious to get some fresh air. Battle Monument Square became congested with people leaving the courthouse and mingling with the throng of pedestrians outside, waiting to learn what was going on. Like yesterday, there wasn't much to tell other than Robert Leach gave an impassioned oration about the vicious mugging of Fred Kuethe and the heartless killing of Robert Norris. Joe Higgins said his client didn't do it. Even so, reporters race to submit their stories for afternoon additions.

Attorney E. Milton Altfeld, Representing Charles P. Carey

When Milton Altfeld approached the jury at 2:00, he began: "I can't disagree with anything Mr. Higgins said. And everything he said holds true for my client, Charles Carey. Mr. Carey did not take part in the robbery. He was outside the Acme Lunchroom playing cards with his friend, Boris Falasea,[28] waiting to be picked up by Mr. Smith and Mr. Lewis. But as Mr. Higgins explained, Mr. Smith and Mr. Lewis never showed up. They were arrested on Eastern Avenue, very much intoxicated, when the motorcar they were driving broke down."

"Mr. Falasea will testify that when Mr. Smith and Mr. Lewis didn't show, he drove my client" (pointing to Charles Carey) "back to his Durham Street house. Mr. Carey could not have been at Madison Street the morning of August 18th—unless, that is, he was at two different places, miles apart, at the same time."

---

28 Boris Falasea was initially a suspect in the Norris Case but Burns' squad could not link him to the crime. The Acme Lunchroom was a favorite hangout of Vincenzo "Jimmy" D'Urso's Baltimore Crew. Charles Carey, Benny Lewis, Wiggles Smith, Noisy Socolow, Fats Novack, Frank Aller, and big Buck Livingston were known to the police as Acme Lunchroom regulars.

"Truth is—Mr. Carey wasn't anywhere near the Commonwealth Bank or Hicks Tate and Norris Construction Company at the time of the crime—or for that matter, any time. He was with a friend, playing cards, waiting for Smith and Lewis."

Altfeld, pointing at Frank Allers, continues, "Everything the prosecution will tell you about Mr. Carey depends on Frank Allers, that man, sitting behind the States Attorney, Mr. Leach, and his assistant, Mr. O'Conor. As Mr. Higgins so rightly pointed out, he is the man who took part in the crime. He drove the murder car. But Mr. Allers is not charged with murder. Why—because he made a deal. Good for him." Then looking directly at the jury, Altfeld declares, "If you have any doubt, any doubt at all, about the yarn he will blather, in exchange for his hide, you must not convict Mr. Carey."

Altfeld, lowering his arms, thanks the jurymen for their attention then returns to the defense table.

Judge Gorter announces that the court will recess for 30 minutes, at which time the State will begin to present its case. The judges rose and returned to Judge Gorter's chambers. After the jury retired, Carey and Smith were removed and Mr. Quinn announced a 30-minute recess. The courtroom became abuzz with conversation. This time few left the unventilated chamber.

3:10 p.m., Wednesday, September 27, 1922
Herbert O'Conor

The first witness called is Dr. Clarance J. Grieves. O'Conor asks Dr. Grieves to describe what he witnessed at the corner of Park Avenue and Madison Streets on Tuesday morning, August 22, 1922.

Dr. Grieves begins, "I noticed a large blue motorcar parked near the corner of Park and Madison. Five hoodlums were just sitting there."

Higgins objects to the word hoodlums.

Dr. Grieves, "Well sir, that's exactly what they were."

Judge Gorter asks Dr. Grieves to refrain from expletives and just respond to questions.

O'Conor asks: "Where were you when you spotted the blue Hudson with its five suspicious looking passengers?"

Dr. Grieves replies: "I was about to go into the Presbyterian Church—directly across the street. I thought, what are these scoundrels up to. So, I kept an eye on them."

O'Conor: "What happened then?"

Dr. Grieves: "Three men jumped out of the motorcar and attacked two men walking east on the south side of Madison Street, from behind. The two men who were ambushed, were about to cross Park Avenue. There was a scuffle and four of five gunshots. I saw both men drop to the ground."

O' Conor: "You mean Mr. Norris and Mr. Kuethe?"

Dr. Grieves: "That's right. I thought both of them had been shot."

O'Conor: "Then what happened?"

Dr. Grieves: "The Hudson lurched forward to where Mr. Norris and Mr. Kuethe were lying on the sidewalk. I heard the gang yelling at one another to get into the car."

O'Conor: "Were you able to identify any of the three men who attacked Mr. Norris and Mr. Kuethe?"

Dr. Grieves: "Only Jack Hart. I recognized him from a newspaper photograph the following day. He was the one waving his pistol at two women trying to cross Park Avenue. I couldn't identify the other two. It happened too fast. When the Hudson pulled up to where Mr. Norris and Mr. Kuethe had fallen, my view was blocked."

O'Conor: "Can you identify anyone who was in the Hudson?

Dr. Grieves, pointing to Charles Carey: "Yes, that man—the defendant, Charles Carey. He was in the back seat looking straight at me when he fired his revolver at the church."

O'Conor: "To be clear, are you certain you saw Charles Carey in the Hudson?"

Dr. Grieves, "Yes—I'm sure. When I saw him again at City Jail, I knew he was the same man."

O'Conor: "Anyone else?"

Dr. Grieves (pointing toward Frank Allers, sitting in the gallery next to Captain Burns, behind Robert Leach): "I recognized that man as the driver of the Hudson when I visited City Jail."

O'Conor: "Let the record show that Dr. Grieves has identified Frank Allers as the driver of the Hudson." O'Conor, turning back to Dr. Grieves, asks: "What happened then?"

Dr. Grieves: "They took off, at high speed, heading east on Madison."

O'Conor: "What did you do after the Hudson sped off?"

Dr. Grieves: "I hurried across the street to see if I could help the two men on the ground."

O'Conor: "Please describe the scene."

Dr. Grieves: "A crowd had gathered. There was blood all over the sidewalk. Mr. Norris was dead. He had been shot through the chest. There was nothing I could do. Mr. Kuethe was unconscious and bleeding badly from the head. I did what I could for him until the police arrived about 30 minutes later. I explained what I saw to the police. One ambulance crew removed Mr. Norris' body. The second transported Mr. Kuethe to Women's Hospital on Eutaw Street where I'm on the staff. I checked in on Mr. Kuethe, from time to time, until he was released.

O'Conor: "Thank you Dr. Grieves. No more questions at this time."

E. Milton Altfeld Cross-examines Dr. Grieves

"Dr. Grieves," Mr. Altfeld begins, "Do you wear glasses?"

Dr. Grieves: "Yes."

Altfeld: "Didn't you tell the police that you could not identify the men in the Hudson because you dropped your glasses when you tripped on the steps trying to enter the church?"

Dr. Grieves: "Yes, I think I did."

Altfeld: "Then how could you identify my client, Charles Carey as being in the Hudson?"

Dr. Grieves: "I saw him in the Hudson before the robbery—same as Mr. Allers. I recognized him again at City Jail."

Altfeld: "You said you noticed the motorcar parked across the street before the robbery. You didn't say you studied who was in the Hudson—one hundred feet away."

Dr. Grieves: "Before the gunfire, I was wearing my glasses. I saw Mr. Carey and Mr. Allers in the motorcar."

Altfeld: "Isn't the truth more like—you think Mr. Carey was in the Hudson after you saw him days later, at City Jail, when Mr. O'Conor pointed him out?"

Dr. Grieves: "No sir—that's not what happened."

Altfeld: "Isn't it?"

As Altfeld returns to the defendants table, he says, "Your Honor, I have no more questions of this witness."

O'Conor Calls Police Sergeant Charles S. Orem

After Sergeant Orem is sworn in, O'Conor begins: "Where were you a little before ten o' clock on the morning of August 22, 1922?"

Sergeant Orem: "I was at Eager Street and Patterson Park Avenue."

O'Conor: "Please describe to the jury what you saw."

Orem: "A dark-blue Hudson, full of questionable characters and dodging motor cars came roaring through the intersection."

O'Conor: "Did you recognize any of the passengers?"

Orem: "I recognized Noisy Socolow carrying on in the rear seat."

O'Conor: "How do you know it was Walter Socolow?"

Orem: "He's a local troublemaker. I took him in once for starting a fight and threatening customers in Cooper's Grocery on Orleans Street. At the time, he was carrying a .38 revolver. When Socolow saw me, he ducked down behind the seat—tried to hide his face. I know Noisy Socolow when I see him."

O'Conor: "What did you do next?"

Orem: "When Socolow spotted me, they sped up—weaving through traffic. I got a good look at the license plate—85-065. First chance I got; I called it in. Turns out, the Hudson was stolen."

O'Conor: "Did you recognize anyone else?"

Orem: "I got a good look at the driver, Frank Allers, and the defendant, John Smith. He was sitting next to Mr. Socolow. When

Socolow ducked, I saw Smith, looking back at me, plain as day."

O'Conor: "Thank you Sergeant—no more questions."

Joseph Higgins Cross-examines Sergeant Orem

Higgins: "Sergeant, you testified that the car that passed you at high speed on Patterson Park Avenue was a dark-blue Hudson—is that correct?"

Orem: "Yes, that's correct."

Higgins: "If it was going so fast, how did you have time to recognize my client and take down the license number? You reported recognizing Mr. Socolow not my client."

Orem: "I recognized Socolow because I arrested him before. I identified Mr. Smith the following day at City Jail when I saw him in a lineup with Mr. Lewis."

Higgins: "How do you know it was the same man."

Orem: "As I told Mr. O'Conor, when Socolow tried to hide his face and ducked down, Mr. Smith was looking right at me. He's the same man. I have no doubt about that."

Higgins: "What about Mr. Lewis. Did you recognize him in the Hudson or at City Jail the following day?"

Orem: "No—I didn't see Mr. Lewis in the Hudson and I didn't recognize him at City Jail."

Higgins: "If Mr. Smith and Mr. Lewis were together, in Mr. Hart's Mercer, when they were arrested in Essex, why weren't they together in the Hudson?"

Orem: "I didn't say they weren't together in the Hudson. I said I recognized Walter Socolow when the Hudson sped passed me on Patterson Park Avenue. The next day, at City Jail, I recognized Mr.

Smith as a passenger."

Higgins: "Isn't it possible that Mr. Smith wasn't in the Hudson? You only had seconds to identify anyone."

Orem: "Smith was looking right at me."

Higgins: "How could Mr. Smith be in the Hudson at the same time, or about the same time, he was arrested in the Mercer with Mr. Lewis?"

O'Conor objects: "Sergeant Orem already testified that he did not see Mr. Lewis in the Hudson."

Judge Gorter, speaking to Higgins: "Sergeant Orem answered the question. Please continue."

Higgins: "Sergeant, a lot was going on when the Hudson flew past you. In those few seconds, you say you wrote down the license number and recognized one of the passengers, Mr. Socolow. The next day, you say you recognized my client as being in the car when he was in Essex with Mr. Louis. Couldn't you be mistaken?"

Orem heatedly responds: "Mr. Smith was in the Hudson!"

Higgins: "I don't believe he was. I don't believe Mr. Smith could have been in the Hudson when he was in Essex. I have no more questions of this witness."

O'Conor asks to redirect.

O'Conor: "Sergeant to be clear, are you certain, beyond a doubt, that you recognized the defendant, John Smith, as a passenger in the Hudson when it passed you on Patterson Park Avenue the morning of August 22, 1922?"

Orem: "I am certain."

O'Conor: "Thank you Sergeant."

Herbert O'Conor Calls Baltimore County
Police Sergeant Wade Walter

After Sergeant Walter is sworn in, O'Conor begins: "Sergeant please describe the arrest of the defendant, John Smith, and his companion, Mr. Lewis, at approximately 1:15 on the afternoon of August 18, 1922."

Sergeant Walter: "Officer Hagerty and I had just left the Essex station. We were driving our cruiser west on Eastern Avenue when we spotted the defendant and Mr. Lewis in the street fighting with one another. They were next to a yellow Mercer that appeared to be broken down. The engine cover was up. We pulled up about twenty-five yards behind. Smith and Lewis were still throwing punches when we approached."

O'Conor: "What did Smith and Lewis do when they saw you and Officer Hagerty?"

Walter: "They didn't do anything. They were yelling at one another and were surprised when we pulled them apart. I don't think either of them saw us approaching."

O'Conor: "What was their condition?"

Walter: "They were drunk and banged up."

O'Conor: "What do you mean by banged up?"

Walter: "They had gotten into it pretty good. There was blood coming from Lewis' nose. Smith's knuckles were bleeding. Their jackets were torn. There was some money scattered about. We pulled them apart and told them they were under arrest."

O'Conor: "Were they armed?"

Walter: "Yes, both of them were carrying revolvers. We disarmed and handcuffed them at gun point. They were intoxicated and incoherent."

O'Conor: "Tell us about the money."

Walter: "There was about one-hundred dollars, in new bills, scattered on the roadway. When we searched them, we confiscated a lot more."

O'Conor: "How much more?"

Walter: "When we took them in, we counted nine-hundred-ninety dollars between them—all new bills."

O'Conor: "Beside the fight was there another reason you approached the defendant, Mr. Smith and his companion, Mr. Lewis, with your firearms drawn?"

Walters: "Before we left the station, we received a teletype warning us to lookout for a blue Hudson that was connected to a robbery and murder that took place on Madison Street, in the city, earlier that morning."

O'Conor: "What made you suspicious of Smith and Lewis? They were in a yellow Mercer."

Walter: "Socolow was reported as being in the Hudson. I arrested Benny Lewis six months earlier for selling illegal whiskey in Essex. My partner, Tom Hagerty, recognized Smith. We knew Smith and Lewis hung out with John Novack, George Heard, Walter Socolow, and a kid named Keller. That was enough for us to be cautious."

O'Conor: "How do you know Keller, Heard, and Novack?"

Walter: "We didn't know Keller, but everyone in Essex knows George Heard. Before they died, Mr. and Mrs. Heard worked a farm on the north side of Back River. George took the place over after his parents died. He and his friend, Fats Novack, were always in some kind of trouble."

O'Conor: "Have you ever been to the Heard Farm?'

Walter: "Yes, a number of times - before and after Mr. and Mrs. Heard passed away."

O'Conor: "What was the farm like?"

Walter: "It was well cared for before Mr. and Mrs. Heard passed. George let the place go."

O'Conor: "Have you been there within the past several months?"

Walter: "Yes. My partner, Tom Hagerty, our precinct commander, Captain Coppin, Captain Burns, and Sergeant Murphy of the Baltimore Police Department and I went there after we learned that's where the payroll was split up."

O'Conor: "What did you find?"

Walter: "The farmhouse was a mess. Trash was everywhere. It was obvious the house had been recently occupied."

O'Conor: "What was in the house?"

Walter: "We found remnants of Commonwealth Bank currency bands in the fireplace."

O'Conor: "Did you find anything else?"

Walter, "Not in the house, but when we searched the barn, we found fifty-four cases of bootleg whiskey hidden under a mound of straw."

O'Conor: "What did you do with that?"

Walter: "We destroyed it. Then we padlocked the buildings."

O'Conor: "One more question, Sergeant. What time of the day did you arrest Smith and Lewis."

Walter: "A little after one o'clock."

O'Conor: "The robbery and murder occurred around nine o'clock that morning—about four hours before you arrested Smith and Lewis?"

Walter: "That's about right."

O'Conor: "Sergeant - doesn't that leave plenty of time to drive the Hudson to Heard's Farm and back to the Highlandtown garage to exchange it with Jack Hart's Mercer."

Higgins objects: "That's speculation – The Sergeant wasn't driving the Hudson. His answer is at best a guess, and therefore, not the least bit relevant!"

Judge Gorter tells the jury to disregard Mr. O'Conor's question to Sergeant Walter.

O'Conor: "I have no more questions of the witness." Then turning to Walter: "Thank you Sergeant."

Higgins on Cross

Higgins: "Sergeant Walter, the truth is you have no proof my client, Mr. Smith, or Mr. Altfeld's client, Mr. Carey or for that matter Mr. Lewis were ever at George Heard's farm. Isn't that correct?

Sergeant Walter: "Yes. That's correct."

Higgins: "You have no proof whatsoever that Mr. Smith or Mr. Lewis were in the Hudson. Correct?

Walter: "Yes."

Higgins: "You have no proof that the money you found on Mr. Smith and Mr. Lewis came from Commonwealth bank. Correct?"

Walter: "The bills were new."

Higgins: "That isn't what I asked. Were you able to identify that the bills you seized from my client, or Mr. Lewis, came from Commonwealth Bank?"

Walter: "No."

Higgins: "No more questions."

O'Conor on Redirect

O'Conor: "Sergeant Walter, were there two-dollar bills mixed in with the money you confiscated from Mr. Smith and Mr. Lewis?"

Walter: "Yes."

O'Conor: "Your Honor, I have no more questions of Sergeant Walter, but I would like to call Mr. Alex Baker, the Manager of the Commonwealth Bank."

As Sergeant Walter leaves the witness stand, Alex Baker takes his place and is sworn in.

O'Conor: "Mr. Baker, were you in the bank when Mr. Norris and Mr. Kuethe withdrew the Hicks Tate and Norris Company payroll on the morning of August 22nd?"

Baker: "I was."

O'Conor: "Were you present when Mr. Norris and Mr. Kuethe were handed the Hicks Company payroll?"

Baker: "I was. Mr. Kuethe needed to sign some papers."

O'Conor: "Did you speak to either Mr. Norris or Mr. Kuethe?"

Baker: "Yes, I went over the documents with Mr. Kuethe, and I thanked Mr. Norris for being a long-standing customer."

O'Conor: "Did you see Mr. Norris and Mr. Kuethe leave with the payroll?"

Baker: "Before they left, I when back to my office, but Mr. Norris always put the weekly payroll in his briefcase. I was there when our teller was handing him the currency bundles."

O'Conor: "I have here Exhibit 1C—an envelope with ten two-dollar Federal Reserve notes that Sergeant Walter and Officer Hagerty confiscated from Mr. Smith and Mr. Lewis."

Higgins interrupts: "Can I see those bills?"

O'Conor pauses to show the ten two-dollar notes to Higgins, then returns to Baker: "Mr. Baker, can you identify these two-dollar notes as being issued by Commonwealth Bank?"

Baker: "Yes."

O'Conor: "Please explain."

Baker: "We generally distribute two-dollar notes with payroll. Customers like Hicks Tate and Norris use two-dollar bills when they fill their pay envelopes. Employees often request two-dollar notes. Anyway, we keep a list of the serial numbers of two dollar notes to help us identify which customer withdrew a given payroll. These two-dollar bills were part of the payroll we assembled for Hicks Tate and Norris Company on August 22, 1922."

O'Conor: "Thank you Mr. Baker—no more questions."

Judge Gorter tells Mr. Baker that he can step down then addresses both the defense and the prosecution: "Gentlemen, its five o'clock. We will adjourn for the day."

Judge Gorter dismisses the jury—reminding them, once again, not to talk to anyone about the trial. After the jurymen leave the courtroom, Carey and Smith are removed, and Judges Gorter, Bond, and Duffy retire to Gorter's chambers. Bailiff Quinn announces: "Court is adjourned until nine o'clock tomorrow morning, Thursday, September 28th."

Chatter builds throughout the courtroom. Reporters race to file their stories. What transpired today will be broadcast across the country. Some editorials headline that the prosecution has a strong case against John Smith and Charles Carey. Although attorneys for the defense have not presented their cases, it will be difficult to refute today's testimony. The State's main witness, Frank Allers, has not taken the stand. That will probably be tomorrow. What Allers reveals, one reporter wrote, may tighten the rope around the necks of John Wiggles Smith and Charles Country Carey.

Thursday, September 28, 1922 – Superior Court of Baltimore City Robert Leach Calls Frank Allers to the Witness Stand

Newspapers reported—*At precisely nine o'clock, Frank Allers, the State's Ace in the Hole, in the prosecution of those accused in the William B. Norris murder case, was called to the witness stand in the trial of John Smith and Charles Carey. Robert F. Leach, Jr., State's Attorney, took up direct examination. Mr. Leach proceeded to bring to light every detail of the story Allers told in his confession a few days after the murder.*

Mr. Leach begins: "What is your name?"

Allers, standing in the witness box with his arms crossed, answers: "Frank Allers."

Leach: "What is your home address?"

Allers: "1007 St. Paul's Street."

Leach: "How old are you?"

Allers: "Twenty-six."

Leach: "Married or single?"

Allers: "Single."

Leach: "What has been your occupation or trade or profession?"

Allers: "Accountant."

Leach: "Do you know John L. Smith—otherwise known as Wiggles Smith?"

Allers: "Yes."

Leach: "How long have you known him?"

Allers: "About a year and a half."

Leach: "Do you know Charles P. Carey—otherwise known as Country Carey?"

Allers: "Yes."

Leach: "How long have you known Carey?"

Allers: "About two years."

Leach: "Do you know Walter Socolow—otherwise known as Noisy Socolow?"

Allers: "Yes."

Leach: "How long?"

Allers: "About a year."

Leach: "Do you know Jack Hart—who is also known as James Connelly?"

Allers: "Yes."

Leach: "How long have you known him?"

Allers: "About two years."

Leach: "Where did John Smith live on or about the eighteenth day of August 1922?"

Allers: "909 Broadway."

Leach: "How do you know that? Did you ever visit him there?"

Allers: "Yes."

Leach: "More than once?"

Allers: "Yes."

Leach: "How long had he lived there by August 18th?"

Allers: "At least six months—probably longer."

Leach: "Where was Walter Socolow living the week of August 18, 1922?"

Allers: "909 Broadway."

Leach: "The same place as Mr. Smith?"

Allers: "Yes, he was often there."

Leach: "Where did Jack Hart live during the same time?"

Allers: "Jack is married and lived several places in Baltimore, but he was at Smith's place a lot."

Leach: "909 Broadway?"

Allers: "Yes."

Leach: "How about a man named George Heard?"

Allers: "George lives on his parents' farm but was there too."

Leach: "How long have you known George Heard?"

Allers: "More than a year."

Leach: "Do you know a man named John Novack—otherwise known as Fatty Novack or Fats?"

Allers: "I know him—yes."

Leach: "Was he ever at 909 Broadway?"

Allers: "He was often there."

Leach: "Do you know a man named Allen N. Buddy Blades?"

Allers: "Yes."

Leach: "How do you know him?"

Allers: "I met him at the Belle Grove Inn about a year ago. He drives a truck for the Fulton Laundry Company."

Leach: "Was Blades ever at 909 Broadway?"

Allers: "Yes—he was there."

Leach: "Do you know a man named Benny Lewis?"

Allers: "Yes."

Leach: "How do you know him?"

Allers: "He is a good friend of Wiggles Smith and Country Carey."

Leach: "Was Lewis ever at 909 Broadway?"

Allers: "All the time."

Leach: "Do you know a boy named John Keller—otherwise known as Squeaky Keller or Kelly?"

Allers: "Yes."

Leach: "How long have you known Keller?"

Allers: "I'm not sure. Not long."

Leach: "Where does he live?"

Allers: "I'm not sure. Right now, he's at City Jail."

Leach: "Was he ever at 909 Broadway?"

Allers: "All the time. He ran errands for Hart, Smith, and Carey."

Leach: "Were you with these men on August 17th at 909 Broadway."

Allers: "Yes."

Leach: "Prior to the week of August 22, had you seen these men with any degree of frequency, or did you merely have what might be called a casual acquaintance with them?"

Allers: "Well—I saw them quite often."

Leach: "So that I understand you correctly, if you wanted to get in touch with any of the men you have identified, it would be at 909 Broadway—John Smith's house?"

Allers: "Yes—but we sometimes met at the Belle Grove Inn or Brady's Place?"

Leach: "Where is the Belle Grove Inn?"

Allers: "South of the city on Annapolis Road."

Leach: "Were you and these men often at the Bell Grove Inn?"

Allers: "Yes, we were there a lot."

Leach: "Where's Brady's Place?"

Allers: "6 North Wolf Street. It's a saloon and pool room. Brady is the owner. We were there almost every day."

Leach: "Where you there the day before the robbery—August 17th?"

Allers: "Yes, most of the morning."

Leach: "Were John Smith and Charles Carey there—at Brady's saloon?"

Allers: "Yes—they were there."

Leach: "Did you talk about robbing the Hicks Tate and Norris payroll when you were at Brady's?"

Allers: "Not much. We decided to wait. We planned the robbery at Smith's house."

Leach: "909 Broadway?"

Allers: "Yes."

Leach: "Did you ever get together at George Heard's farm?"

Allers: "Yes."

Leach: "For what reason?"

Allers: "It was a place to hang out. Hart, Carey, and Smith stored whiskey there—in the barn."

Leach: "Is that where the men you identified, including the defendants, divided-up the Hicks payroll after you returned from the robbery on August 18th?"

Allers: "Except for Buddy Blades—yes—that's where we split up the money."

Higgins objects: "Who split up the money is hearsay, and the question is leading the witness."

Leach: "I'm not leading the witness, but I'll rephrase. Were the defendants, Charles Carey and John Smith, with you in the Hudson on August 18th when you returned to Heard's farmhouse after you robbed Mr. Norris and Fred Kuethe?"

Allers: "Yes. Carey and Smith were in the Hudson when we returned to Heard's farm. Walter Socolow and Jack Hart were in the Hudson too."

Leach: "Who was waiting, in the farmhouse, for you to arrive?"

Allers: "George Heard, Squeaky Keller, Benny Lewis, and Fats Novack."

Leach: "For what reason?"

Allers: "To split up the payroll."

Leach: "Do you know anything about any woman who lived on the first floor of 909 Broadway no matter what her relationship with Smith might have been?"

Mr. Higgins objects to this question as leading, asking: "Where is Mr. Leach going with this?"

Mr. Leach: "I'll rephrase. Do you know whether anybody else lived on the first floor—male or female?"

Allers: "I know that a woman lived there."

Leach: "What was her name?"

Allers: "Edna—I think."

Leach: "Was her name Edna Dorsch?"

Allers: "I think so."

Leach: "Are Smith and Edna Dorsch married?"

Allers: "I don't know. She was just there. Wiggles sometimes called himself John Dorsch."

Leach: "Was Edna Dorsch there the night of August 17th?"

Allers: "No—just us. Noisy's girlfriend was there, but she left."

Leach: "Do you know her name—Noisy Socolow's girlfriend?"

Allers: "We call her Shorts."

Leach: "Her real name is Virginia Williams, correct?"

Allers: "Yes, Virginia Williams."

Leach: "When did Virginia Williams leave 909 Broadway on August 17th?"

Allers: "I don't know."

Leach: "Did Virginia Williams hear you talking about the robbery?"

Allers: "I don't know. I don't know when she left."

Leach: "So, when you said, 'just us,' you mean the men you identified as knowing?"

Allers: "Yes."

Leach: "To be clear, was everyone I have named and you have identified, with the exception of Edna Dorsch and Virginia Williams, together at 909 Broadway on August 17, 1922."

Allers: "Yes. We were all there."

Leach: "Did the defendants—John Smith and Charles Carey—help plan the robbery of the Hicks Tate and Norris Company payroll the night of August 17th at 909 Broadway?"

Allers: "Yes. All of us planned the robbery."

Leach: "Whose idea was it to rob the payroll?"

Allers: "Buddy Blades. He picked up and delivered laundry from Hicks Tate and Norris. He found out when Mr. Norris picked up the payroll from the bank."

Leach: "Commonwealth Bank located at the corner of Howard and Madison Streets?"

Allers: "Yes."

Leach: "What day was that?"

Allers: "Every Friday morning at nine o' clock."

Leach: "On Thursday, August 17th, at 909 Broadway, you, and the men you have identified, including the defendants, Charles Carey and John Smith, plotted to rob Mr. Norris the following day—Friday, August 18th. Is that correct?"

Allers: "Yes."

Leach: "Did you ride with them?"

Allers: "Yes."

Leach: "Before the robbery, did you ride with any of the men you identified in your machine and in their machines?"

Allers: "Yes—often."

Leach: "Did you use any of their motorcars to check out the Hicks Tate and Norris Company and the Commonwealth Bank on Madison Street?"

Allers: "Yes. After Jack decided to pull off the robbery, Wiggles and I drove Jack's car to Madison Street to check things out."

Leach: "By Jack you are referring to Jack Hart and by Wiggles you mean one of the defendants—John Smith?"

Allers: "Yes."

Leach: "When did you and Smith check out the Hicks Tate and Norris Construction Company and The Commonwealth Bank, in Jack Hart's machine?"

Allers: "Right after we met on August 17th."

Leach: "What kind of machine did Hart have?"

Allers: "A yellow Mercer."

Leach: "Do you know where Hart's Mercer is now?"

Allers: "I don't."

Leach: "I take it that you and Mr. Smith picked the location where you, he, John Carey, Walter Socolow, and Jack Hart attacked Mr. Norris and his accountant, Mr. Kuethe?"

Allers: "Yes—across the street from the church."

Leach: "That would be the southwest corner of Madison Street and Park Avenue—across from the First Presbyterian Church?"

Allers: "Yes—like I said, across from the church."

Leach: "Your part in the robbery was driving the murder car?"

"Objection"—Higgins objects to the use of the phrase "murder car."

Leach: "I called it the murder car before—so did Mr. Higgins."

Higgins, addressing the court: "That was during his opening."

Leach: "I'll rephrase. "Did you drive the stolen Hudson to Madison Street the morning of August 18th?"

Allers: "Yes."

Leach: "Why did you need the Hudson?"

Allers: "No one could tie us to the Hudson."

Leach: "Where did you get the Hudson?"

Allers: "I don't know. Jack found it."

Leach: "Who attacked Mr. Norris and Mr. Kuethe?"

Allers: "Jack Hart, Noisy Socolow, and the defendant - Wiggles Smith."

Leach: "Where was the defendant, Charles Carey?"

Allers: "He stayed in the car."

Leach: "Did you have weapons?"

Allers: "We had pistols."

Leach: "Were you prepared to use them?"

Allers: "No one was supposed to be shot."

Leach: "I asked if the five of you were prepared to use the handguns you were carrying?"

Allers: "I guess we were."

Leach: "Isn't it true that shots were fired?"

Allers: "Yes. Country Carey and Walter fired their guns."

Leach: "Who attacked Mr. Kuethe?"

Allers: "Wiggles Smith."

Leach pointing to Smith: "The defendant John Smith?"

Allers: "Yes."

Leach: "Who shot and killed Mr. Norris?"

Allers: "Noisy – Noisy Socolow shot Mr. Norris."

Leach: "What did Jack Hart do?"

Allers: "He chased off anyone nearby."

Leach: "With his revolver?"

Allers: "Yes."

Leach: "What about the defendant, Charles Carey?"

Allers: "Country pointed his gun at people across Madison Street in front of the church - to scare them off."

Leach: "Did Charles Carey (pointing to Carey) fire his pistol at people in front of the church?"

Allers: "Yes—once or twice. I can't remember. "

Leach: "Once or twice at the people across the street like Dr. Grieves?"

Allers: "I guess."

Leach: What does 'I guess' mean? Mr. Allers, did the defendant, Charles Carey, fire his .38 at pedestrians across Madison Street – Yes or No."

Higgins interrupts: "Your Honor, Mr. Leach is badgering his own witness."

Leach: "Is the defense council objecting to something? If so I didn't hear it."

Judge Gorter: "Mr. Leach – That will be enough sarcasm."

Leach: "My apologies, Your Honor." Then turning back to Mr.

Allers asks: "Mr. Allers was the defendant aiming his pistol at the people across the street when he fired?"

Allers: "Country fired at the church. I'm not sure he was aiming at anyone."

Leach: "They were lucky Country Carey isn't a very good shot."

Higgins: "Your Honor!"

Judge Gorter: Mr. Leach…" before Judge Gorter finishes his sentence Leach says:

"Sorry, Your Honor – won't happen again."

Judge Gorter: "Please continue."

Leach: "Mr. Allers, tell the jury what happened after Mr. Norris was shot dead and Mr. Kuethe was knocked unconscious."

Allers: "I pulled forward to the intersection, revved the engine, and yelled at Jack, Wiggles, and Noisy to get back in the Hudson. Once they were in, we drove off."

Leach: "With the payroll money?"

Allers: "Yes."

Leach: "Where did you go?"

Allers: "George's farm."

Leach: "George Heard's farm?"

Allers: "Yes."

Leach, again pointing toward Carey and Smith: "And these two defendants, Charles Country Carey and John Wiggles Smith were in the Hudson with you, Walter Socolow, and Jack Hart. Is that correct?"

Allers: "Yes. Country and Wiggles were in the Hudson."

Leach: "To be clear, after Mr. Kuethe was knocked senseless and Mr. Norris was murdered, all five of you drove off with the payroll money?"

Allers: "Yes, as fast as we could."

There was some laughter in the courtroom. Judge Gorter ordered quiet, saying: "Anyone causing interruptions will be removed."

Leach continues: "What did you do when you reached Heard's farm?"

Allers: "We split up the money."

Leach: "All of the payroll money?"

Allers: "No. We took Buddy's share back to Wiggles' house. George, Fatty, Noisy, Squeaky, Country, and I drove back to Wiggles' house on Broadway, in Fatty's machine."

Leach: "So the jury understands exactly who you were with— George Heard, John Novack, Walter Socolow, John Keller, Charles Carey, and you returned to 909 Broadway after you split up the payroll."

Allers: "Yes. In Fatty Novack's Ford."

Leach: "What about Jack Hart, the defendant, John Smith, and Benny Lewis?"

Allers: "They stayed behind."

Leach: "Why?"

Allers: "Jack had to get the Hudson back to where he found it. We were to meet up later at Wiggles' —I mean Smith's house."

Leach: "Did Hart, Smith, and Lewis show up the night of the murder at 909 Broadway."

Allers: "No."

Leach: "Do you know why?"

Allers: "They just didn't show. The next day we learned Wiggles and Benny were arrested. Jack disappeared."

Leach: "What about Buddy Blades?"

Allers: "He was already at Smith's when we got there."

Leach: "The day of the murder—August 18th?"

Allers: "Yes—around one o'clock."

Leach: "When Smith, Lewis and Hart didn't show, what did you do?"

Allers: "We split up."

Leach: "Where did you go?"

Allers: "I went to my apartment on St. Paul's Street."

Leach: "Where did the others go?"

Allers: "I'm not sure. Keller and Socolow took off before me. Carey, Blades, Heard, and Novack were still there."

Leach: "Was that the last time you were together?

Allers: "Yes—that was the last time."

Leach: "So there is no misunderstanding, the men you just identified, including yourself, planned the robbery of the Hicks Tate and Norris Construction Company on August 17, 1922, in John Smith's 909 Broadway house—correct?"

Allers: "Yes."

Leach: "The next day, Friday morning—August 18th, the two defendants (Leach pointing to Smith and Carey) John Smith and Charles Carey were in the Hudson with you, Jack Hart and Walter Socolow for the purpose of stealing the Hicks Tate and Norris Company payroll. Is that correct?"

Allers: "Yes."

Leach: "And during the holdup, Mr. Norris was murdered—shot three times in the chest—and Mr. Kuethe was almost killed. Is that correct?"

Allers: "Yes."

Leach: "So all five of you, including the defendants, are responsible for the murder of Mr. Norris and seriously injuring Mr. Kuethe?"

Higgins objects: Mr. Leach is leading the witness."

Judge Gorter: "Sustained. Mr. Leach - ask a question ."

Leach: Mr. Allers, in your view, are all five of you – Charles Carey, John Smith, Jack Hart, Walter Socolow and yourself equally responsible for the murder of Mr. Norris on August 18th?"

Allers: "I guess you could say that. All of us were there."

Leach: "And each one of you, including the defendants, took a share of the payroll money?"

Allers: "Yes, after we got back to Heard's farm."

Leach: "Tell me Mr. Allers, did any of you feel the slightest regret about killing Mr. Norris and almost killing Mr. Kuethe? The fact is - for all you knew, Mr. Kuethe was dead too. Isn't that correct ?"

Allers: "At the time, we didn't think about it."

Leach: "By that, you mean—no?"

Allers doesn't answer.

Judge Gorter breaks in: "Mr. Leach, do you have many more questions for the witness?"

Leach: "Yes, Your Honor. The prosecution would like the witness to reveal what took place leading up to the robbery, during the attack on Mr. Kuethe and Mr. Norris, the murder of Mr. Norris and what the defendants and their accomplices did following the crime."

"In that case," Judge Gorter continues, "The court will adjourn for lunch."

After the defendants are removed from the courtroom, the jury is dismissed, and the Judges retire, Bailiff Quinn announces: "Court is adjourned until one o'clock."

The courtroom overflows with conversation as the gallery disperses for the lunchtime break.

At 1:15, Frank Allers steps back onto the witness stand. Assistant State's Attorney Herbert O'Conor takes over where Robert Leach left off. Over the next two hours, with numerous objections from defense attorneys Joseph Higgins, John Meyer, and Milton Altfeld, O'Conor focuses on the details of Allers' earlier testimony, asking questions including:

- How long has Hart's gang been together?
- How did they plan the robbery?
- What route did they take to and from Madison Street?
- Who was armed and with what?

- Describe in detail the robbery that led to the death of William Norris.

- Why did they go to Heard's farm?

- How did they divide the payroll?

- When did they return to 909 Broadway?

- Why did Smith and Lewis drive the Hudson back to the Highlandtown garage instead of Hart?

- Why was the Mercer left on the side of the road?

- Where were Charles Carey and John Smith before, during and after the robbery and murder?

Finally, O'Conor asked Allers: "Tell the jury the reason the defendants, Charles Country Carey and John Wiggles Smith, were in the Hudson, with you, Jack Hart, and Walter Socolow on August 18th."

Allers, looking directly at Carey and Smith, answers: "Because they wanted their share of the money."

O'Conor asks: "How did they react after Mr. Kuethe was down and Mr. Norris was shot dead?"

Higgins and Altfeld separately object. "Mr. O'Conor's question is leading the witness. How can the witness know how our clients reacted?"

Judge Gorter responds: "Mr. O'Coner didn't ask what Mr. Smith and Mr. Carey were thinking, he asked how they reacted. I'll allow the question." Judge Gorter tells Allers: "Answer the question."

O'Conor repeats: "How did Carey and Smith react when Mr. Norris was shot?"

Allers: "They didn't react."

O'Conor: "Did you realize Mr. Norris was dead?"

Allers: "I don't think there were any doubts about that. We just wanted to get out of there."

O'Conor, addressing the three judges, says: "I have no more questions of Mr. Allers."

As O'Conor returns to the prosecution councils' table, Judge Gorter nods to the defense.

Joseph Higgins stands and approaches Allers.

Defense Attorneys Joseph Higgins and Milton Altfeld on Cross

Looking at Allers, Higgins points toward Smith and Carey, then asks: "Isn't it true, Mr. Allers, that if the defendants took part in the murder of Mr. Norris, you, who admit driving the murder car, as Mr. Leach likes to refer to it, are just as guilty of the crime?"

Allers answers: "I guess."

Higgins: "I think you are."

Leach objects: "Is there a question?"

Judge Gorter orders the jury to disregard Mr. Higgins last statement.

Higgins continues: "You are not being tried for murder—are you?"

Allers: "No!"

Higgins: "Fact is, you're getting off pretty easy for turning on your friends. Isn't that true?"

Allers: "I'm going to prison."

Higgins: "But not for murder—not for life—and not for very long."

O'Conor interrupts: "Where is the question?"

Higgins, addressing the court: "I don't believe my client was in the Hudson, Your Honor. He was in Essex. The witness will say what he must to avoid a murder charge. This is the gist of my defense."

Judge Gorter: "I'll allow your question."

Higgins, turning back to Allers, continues: "Mr. Allers did the State's Attorney offer you limited immunity if you accused my client and Mr. Carey of being in on the robbery?

Allers: "I didn't accuse anybody. I told the truth."

Higgins: "It's pretty clear that's exactly what you did—accused Mr. Smith and Mr. Carey of being complicit in the robbery and murder, by your own admission, you were a part of."

O'Conor objects: "Your Honor..."

Before O'Conor finishes explaining his objection, Judge Gorter tells Higgins to save his suppositions for his summation.

Then Higgins asks Allers: "Have you ever been in prison?"

Allers: "Yes."

Higgins: "For what?"

Allers: "What do you mean?"

Higgins: "It's a simple question Mr. Allers. Have you been convicted and sentenced to prison for another crime?"

O'Conor objects: "Whether Mr. Allers served time in prison for another crime is not relevant."

Higgins: "It goes to character, Your Honor."

Judge Gorter responds: "Overruled. Answer the question."

Allers answers: "I have been in the penitentiary."

Higgins: "For armed robbery and selling illicit whiskey?"

Allers: "Yes."

Higgins: "How long were you in prison?"

Allers: "Two years."

Higgins: "Tell me, Mr. Allers, why should this jury believe anything you say?

Allers: "Because it's the truth."

Higgins: "When the truth suits you—right, Mr. Allers?"

Leach objects: "Mr. Higgins is leading the witness."

Judge Gorter rules: "Sustained. The witness admits he has been in prison. It's up to the jury to determine the truth."

For the next hour and a half, Joe Higgins and Milton Alfred did their best to punch holes in Allers' story. At 4:30, Higgins, Meyer, and Altfeld conclude their cross examination of Frank Allers.

Judge Gorter excuses Allers from the witness stand.

Following Allers, O'Conor called both John Keller and Virginia Williams to the witness stand to confirm that the two defendants, John Smith and Charles Carey, were present at 909 Broadway on August 17th. Keller further testified that Smith and Carey took part in the planning of the robbery, were in the Hudson along with Allers, Hart, and Socolow, and took their share of the payroll after returning to George Heard's farmhouse.

Higgins and Altfeld objected to Virginia Williams testimony arguing that she was at 909 Broadway for a brief time and could not have known if the defendants were part of a plan to rob the Hicks Tate and Norris payroll. They objected to several of the questions O'Conor put to John Keller, but both Higgins and Altfeld declined to cross examine Keller.

After Keller stepped down from the witness stand, Robert Leach announced that the prosecution rests its case.

Judge Gorter, speaking to defense counsel, asks, "I assume you gentlemen are prepared to present the defense?"

Higgins, Meyer, and Altfeld collectively assert that they are.

Judge Gorter answers: "You can begin tomorrow at nine o'clock. Court will adjourn until then."

Following the third day of the trial, Bailiff Quinn announces that the Supreme Court of Baltimore City is adjourned until tomorrow morning, nine o'clock, Friday, September 29, 1922.

Much of Allers' testimony is transcribed, word for word, in broadsheets throughout America. Radio broadcasts and editorials speculate that it looks grim for Charles Country Carey and John Wiggles Smith. After almost two days on the witness stand, Frank Allers was reported to be composed and believable. Through hard questioning by State's Attorney Robert Leach and Assistant State's Attorney Herbert O'Conor, Frank Allers exposed the cruel realities of the crime.

Defense attorneys, Joseph T. Higgins, John A. Meyer, and E. Milton Altfeld had little success in refuting what Frank Allers had to say. If Charles Carey and John Smith have any chance of dodging the hangman, many conclude, it must happen tomorrow when the defense attorneys present their case.

Friday, September 29, 1922 – Attorney E. Milton Alfred,
Representing Charles "Country" Carey, and Attorneys Joseph T.
Higgins and John A. Meyer, Representing John "Wiggles" Smith
Present the Defense

Defense counsel called a series of character witnesses, including:

Miss Antoinette Smith, who appeared very nervous, testifying
that her brother (John Wiggles Smith) "has never been anything
but the best boy possible and the best brother a sister could ask
for. When we were young, we lived next to a professor who took
a liking to us. He called me Waggles and John Wiggles. Everyone
in the neighborhood was fond of John. He cut grass and helped
people load their coal bins in the winter. I believe John when he
says he was in Essex. I've seen him get pretty drunk. There is no
way he committed the robbery."

Smith's other sister, Bessie Smith, was even more nervous than
her sister Antoinette when she took the stand. Higgins asked her
about her brother's personality. Bessie said her brother would
never be involved in a robbery and murder. "He has been a very
good brother to all of us."

Higgins called Edna Dorsch. Edna testified that she owned 909
Broadway and that she lived there with John Smith, who she met
at the Bell Grove Inn. Edna said that Smith was fond of spirits
and often had too much to drink. "He can't help himself." She
testified that during the week of August 18th, when Mr. Norris
was shot, John was too drunk to rob anybody. "John's drinking,"
Edna testified, "is the reason I often stay with my friend Mary
Kisling. When Mr. Norris was killed, John and his friend Benny
Lewis were off on a binge. He wasn't at Madison Street during the
robbery. He was in Essex."

During his cross examination, O'Conor asked Edna Dorsch if she
and John Smith were married. Her answer was "we live like that
but no. We have been living together on and off for years. I know

him as well as anyone."

O'Conor asked: "Were you at 909 Broadway on August 17th?"

Edna answered: "No—but if you're asking if John killed Mr. Norris, I know he didn't. He may drink too much, but he is not a murderer."

John Smith, against Joe Higgins and John Meyer's, advice took the stand to testify in his own behalf. He claimed that he had been drunk all week beginning Tuesday August 15th, three days before the holdup. "I couldn't have robbed anyone," was his answer when Higgins asked him if he was involved in the robbery of the Hicks Tate and Norris Company payroll. When Higgins asked him if he remembered being in the Hudson with Carey, Socolow, Allers, and Hart, Smith answered: "I wasn't there. I wasn't with them."

On cross, O'Conor asked: "Do you reside at 909 Broadway?"

Smith: "Yes—with Edna Dorsch."

O'Conor: "And were you not at 909 Broadway the night of August 17th when your codefendant, Charles Carey, and the other members of Jack Hart's gang planned the robbery of the Hicks Tate and Norris Company payroll?"

Smith: "I don't remember. I was drunk. I don't think I was there."

O'Conor: "Mr. Allers testified that you were."

Smith: "What does he know? I wasn't there."

O'Conor: "Do you remember being arrested in Essex with Benny Lewis in Jack Hart's Mercer?"

Smith: "No. I don't remember being arrested in Essex or fighting with Benny or being transferred to Baltimore City Jail. All I remember is that I woke up in jail on August 19th and was accused of being in on a robbery and murder. I didn't know what the police were talking about."

O'Conor: "Baltimore Police Sergeant Orem identified you as being in the Hudson on the morning of August 18th."

Before O'Conor could finish his question, Smith snapped back: "I wasn't in the Hudson."

O'Conor: "Sergeant Orem testified that you were."

Again, before O'Conor could finish his question, Smith interrupted barking: "He's wrong!"

O'Conor: "Seems like everyone is wrong but you, Mr. Smith. I have no more questions of this witness."

News reporter George Dorsch later reported that John Wiggles Smith should have taken his attorneys' advice and not testified. He did himself little good and much harm. Everything he said, Dorsch reported, made him and his codefendant, Charles Carey, appear guilty.

Charles Carey's alibi wasn't much better then John Smith's. E. Milton Altfeld called Boris Falasea, who was purported to be at the Acme Lunchroom playing Gin rummy with Carey at the time of the robbery. Falasea testified that, waiting for John Smith and Benny Lewis to pick up Carey the morning of the crime, he and Carey were playing cards and talking about baseball. "Wiggles and Lewis never showed up."

When O'Conor asked what time in the morning of Friday, August 18th, he and Carey were playing cards, Falasea wasn't sure. "Most of the morning" was his reply.

O'Conor: "And when the defendant John Smith and Benny Lewis did not show, you claim you drove Mr. Carey home. Is that correct Mr. Falasea—remember you are under oath."

Falasea: "Yeah, that's about right."

O'Conor: "Do you want to stick to that story Mr. Falasea. No one else interviewed at the lunchroom remembers seeing Mr. Carey on the morning of August 18th. Credible witnesses, we (and you) have heard, say otherwise. Here is your chance to tell the truth."

Falasea: "I don't remember the exact time, but Wiggles and I were playing Gin Rummy."

O'Conor: "I'm sure you were—just not on August 18th. I have no more questions of Mr. Falasea."

E. Milton Altfeld called several witnesses who collectively testified that Carey was a friend who wouldn't harm anyone. Richard Sticks, who worked with Carey at the Sparrows Point Steel Plant, testified that Charles was a hard and reliable worker. On cross examination, however, Sticks admitted that Carey had not worked at the steel mill for several months.

Altfeld did not call Charles Carey to the stand. Realizing John Smith's testimony made things worse for both of them, Carey declined to testify.

At 2:30, E. Milton Altfeld, on behalf of Charles Carey, and Joseph Higgins and John Meyer, on behalf of John Smith, rested the defense of Carey and Smith.

Summations

Judge Gorter ordered that court adjourn until three o'clock, at which time the prosecution and defense would present their summations to the jury.

Joseph Higgins and Milton Altfeld Speak for Smith and Carey

The three defense attorneys seemed resigned that their clients, John Smith and Charles Carey, would be convicted. They did not deny that Smith and Carey were part of Jack Hart's gang (or the

Broadway gang) or that they participated in the planning of the crime. Instead, Higgins and Meyer sought to convince the jury that neither Smith nor Carey were guilty enough of William Norris' murder to be hanged. "They did not shoot Mr. Norris" was the argument Higgins and Altfeld made to the jurymen.

Higgins called Mr. Leach's tactics outrageous to justice—that because one man pulled the trigger, his client John Smith and Mr. Altfeld's client Charles Carey are guilty of murder.

Higgins turned to where Frank Allers sat behind Leach and O'Conor and raised his voice: "If ever a brainy and more callous criminal lived, there's the man! Mr. Allers, the ex-convict, who has served a term for larceny—if the story he tells be true, Mr. Smith and Mr. Carey are no more guilty of murder than Mr. Allers. But Mr. Allers will go free. He has immunity. He will not suffer an extreme penalty, and neither should Mr. Smith or Mr. Carey. They are innocent of murder."

Robert Leach for the Prosecution

In his summation, Mr. Leach outlined the particulars of the crime. He summarized the testimony of each witness. Leach admitted that Frank Allers was a convicted criminal. "This," Leach said, "should make what he said all the more believable. Every man in that Hudson, Jack Hart, Walter Socolow, the defendants—Charles Carey and John Smith—even Frank Allers are equally guilty of robbery and murder. They are (all) responsible for pulling the trigger that took the life of Mr. Norris."

Leach paused—looked around the courtroom—then turned to Frank Allers—then shifted back to the jurymen and began: "Yes, it's true that Mr. Allers took part in the crime. Yes, it's true that he has a record. But it is also true that Mr. Allers came forward and admitted his guilt and provided the key evidence that insured the others who took part in this ugly killing—the murder of a prominent Baltimorean, for not very much money, were caught and no doubt will be convicted by you men of the jury. Will Allers get off free and clear as Mr. Higgins implies? The answer is no! He will serve many years in the Maryland Penitentiary for his part in the crime."

"Justice for Mr. Norris required someone in Hart's gang to tell the truth. Like him or not, Frank Allers did this. No other member of the gang, with the exception of John Keller, was willing to come forward until it was too late for their statements to make a difference. Was Frank Allers truthful? I think you men of the jury, like me, believe he was. And his testimony, combined with the other credible witnesses you have heard, prove without a doubt that John Wiggles Smith and Charles Country Carey are guilty of the heartless murder of William Norris."

Pointing toward the defendants, John Smith and Charles Carey, Leach concludes: "I ask you not only to convict John Smith and Charles Carey of murder in the first degree but to also impose upon them the extreme penalty—to be executed for the murder they so heartlessly committed."

Leach then thank the jury for hearing him out, saying: "You are on trial here along with these men. So am I. So is everybody in this community. Millions from around the United States, even Canada, want to know if the workings of our justice system still possesses ample vigor to convict a band of vicious criminals."

The Jury Is Addressed by Judge Gorter

Although it was past five o'clock when Robert Leach finished his summation, Judge Gorter told the jury that they would begin deliberations following their dinner break. He again charged the jury with being deliberate and to return a fair and just verdict. He reminded the jurymen of the five possible outcomes resulting from their deliberations: guilty of first-degree murder with a recommendation for the extreme penalty, murder in the first degree with a recommendation of without capital punishment, murder in the second degree, limiting prison time to eighteen years, manslaughter, limiting prison time to ten years, or a verdict of not guilty.

Judge Gorter then dismissed the jury. He notified the defense and prosecution that if the jury did not return a verdict by ten o'clock, they would be dismissed for the night. In such a case, the jury would return tomorrow, Saturday, September 30, at ten o'clock a.m., to renew deliberations.

Judge Gorter ordered the defendants remanded to a holding cell in the courthouse until a verdict is rendered. Court will adjourn until Richard McKindless, Clerk of the Court, notifies the Judges, defense, and prosecution counsels that a verdict has been reached.

Judges Gorter, Bond, and Duffy returned to Judge Gorter's chambers. Bailiff Joseph Quinn announces that the Supreme Court of Baltimore City is adjourned until further notice.

Courtroom 600 began to clear. Reporters rushed to file their stories. Word quickly spread that the jury was out, and a verdict could be returned by ten o'clock tonight. Hundreds of spectators did not venture far from the courthouse. Those who lived close by, including the three judges, waited in their homes. Others crowded restaurants and public places. Many gathered on Battle Monument Square. Courtroom 600 was emptied and the doors closed. People were permitted to linger in the first-floor lobby. The *News Post* editorialized that millions of followers across America were waiting for the verdicts. Would it be tonight? No one was going anywhere.

The Verdicts

At 8:45 p.m., Clerk of the Court Richard McKindless appeared out of breath when he encounters Joseph Quinn, smoking a cigarette while guarding the courtroom door from the press and other intruders. McKindless had just returned from telling Judge

Bond: "The jury has agreed." Judge Bond called Judges Gorter and Duffy. Gorter and Duffy were rushing to the courthouse from their homes.

After notifying Quinn, McKindless sprinted up the courthouse steps to the office of the Baltimore City State's Attorney to let Robert Leach, Courtenay Jenifer, and Herbert O'Conor know that the jury had reached a verdict. Then it was down the hallway to the room where Joseph Higgins, John Meyer, and Milton Altfeld were waiting. Hearing the news of an unanticipated early decision, the defense attorneys headed for the basement and the holding cell where John Smith and Charles Carey were finishing their dinners and complaining to the guards about the food.

By then, it seemed everyone in Baltimore had heard the jury had reached a verdict. Reporters and spectators rushed to courtroom 600 where Quinn had unlocked the doors.

At 9:10 p.m., the three judges assumed their places on the bench. The courtroom—which had reverberated with conversation as spectators jostled to claim seats—suddenly became still. As the twelve jurymen filed in and took their places, Bailiff Quinn announced that the Superior Court of Baltimore City was in session. Although he didn't have to, because of the silence, Judge Gorter tapped his gavel on the desk. As the attorneys took their places, Judge Gorter ordered Quinn to bring in the prisoners. It took a few minutes for the guards to escort Smith and Carey to their places at the defense counsel's table and remove their handcuffs. Smith and Carey appeared anxious. Smith's overconfidence had evaporated. Carey walked sluggishly with his head down.

Robert Leach invited William B. Norris, Jr. to have a seat at the prosecution counsel's table. Young Norris shook hands with Leach, O'Conor, Jenifer, and Captain of Detectives Burns, who was sitting directly behind. He did not acknowledge Frank Allers, who was standing next to Burns.

Looking out over the gallery, Judge Gorter began: "When the verdicts are read there must be no demonstration from anyone in this courtroom. You in the audience will remain as you are until court is adjourned—no exceptions." Gorter nodded to Richard McKindless, Clerk of the Court, who stood up holding two folded papers that contained the verdicts.

Turning toward the defense counsel's table, McKindless, looking directly at John Smith, ordered, "John L. Smith stand up!" Then turning toward the jury, he continued, "Gentlemen of the jury—look upon the prisoner!" Shifting back to Smith, he said, "Prisoner—look upon the jury!"

Smith, now standing, folded his arms across the breast of his blue suit coat and, showing no emotion, looked at the jury. McKindless, addressing the jurymen, said: "Gentlemen of the jury have you agreed upon a verdict?" Speaking for the jury, Edward Cauley, stood up and answered, "We have."

McKindless asked, "How say you—guilty or not guilty?"

In a voice strong enough to be heard throughout the courtroom, McCauley answered: "Guilty of murder in the first degree!"

Smith slumped back into his chair next to Joseph Higgins, who in an effort to console his client patted Smith on the back with his right hand.

McKindless turned to Charles Carey and ordered Carey to stand and face the jury. Milton Altfeld helped Carey stand up. Once Carey was standing, McKindless repeated the same formal procedure, asking jury foreman McCauley: "How say you—guilty or not guilty?"

McCauley answers: "Guilty of murder in the first degree!"

Carey wiped his brow with a handkerchief and dropped back into his chair.

McCauley took his seat in the jury box.

McKindless handed the verdict document to Judge Gorter, then sat at his desk next to the bench.

Judge Gorter ordered Quinn to have the prisoners removed. Guards handcuffed Carey and Smith. With one sheriff deputy on each arm of each prisoner, Carey and Smith were removed from the courtroom.

Addressing the jury, Gorter began: "Gentlemen of the jury, we thank you for your service here. You had a trying ordeal, and we appreciate your patience and attention. The bailiff will escort you to the clerk's office to be dismissed for tonight."

Judge Gorter, speaking to everyone still sitting motionless and silent, announced: "This court will adjourn until Monday morning at ten o'clock, at which time we will commence with the sentencing hearing for the prisoners, John L. Smith and Charles P. Carey." After the jury left the courtroom and the three judges retired to Judge Gorter's chambers, Quinn announced: "Court is adjourned until ten o'clock Monday morning [October 2, 1922]."

The crowd, silent as the grave until Quinn announced adjournment, rose in an explosion of conversation as they flooded out onto Battle Monument Square where newsboys were already shouting: "Extra—Extra—Guards seized the two convicted Norris bandits and handled them through the iron doors where the black wagon waited!"

Courtroom 600 - Monday Morning, October 2, 1922

The two prisoners were brought into the courtroom at 9:45 a.m. and ordered to take their seats at the defense councils' table. Last Friday, the jury found them guilty of murder in the first degree. These verdicts did not determine what the sentence would be for either defendant. Because the verdict for both Smith and Carey was murder in the first degree, the jury, and the three-judge panel, were left with two options. The jury could recommend either the extreme penalty (death by hanging) or life in prison.

The three judges could confirm or vacate the jury's sentencing verdict. During the sentencing hearing, the twelve men of the jury are charged to listen to arguments by prosecution and defense counsel for and against the extreme penalty. Edward McCauley remains jury foreman.

By ten o'clock, the courtroom overflowed with reporters and spectators. The police had to limit entry. Latecomers were turned away. Most of those denied access to the courtroom returned to Battle Monument Square, outside the courthouse's St. Paul Street entrance, where they mingled with the hundreds already there— waiting to hear if it would be life or death.

At 10:15 a.m., Herbert O'Conor stepped forward to argue in favor of capital punishment. O' Conor spent nearly an hour reviewing what he called "the awful facts that led to the murder of William Norris."

Gesturing to where Mable Norris and her oldest son, William, Jr., were sitting in the gallery, in the second row behind Captain Burns and the men of his taskforce, O'Conor declares: "There is a heartbroken wife and her three young sons, who will never see their husband and father again, awaiting justice."

Elevating his voice, O'Conor continued: "Don't feel sorry for the defendants, Charles Carey and John Smith. They knew exactly what they were doing. Were they not apprehended; these two convicted criminals would be planning their next crime." Turning and pointing directly toward Smith and Carey, O'Conor proclaims: "To those two villains, sitting right there, a man's life matters little!"

O'Conor, looking at each of the jurymen, resumes: "At the beginning of this trial, Judge Gorter spelled out five possible judgements. Of the five, you gentlemen chose murder in the first degree. And rightly so. John Smith and Charles Carey, along with those other cowardly schemers, set out on the morning of August 18th with one idea on their minds—to highjack the Hicks Tate and Norris Company payroll. In the heat of a vicious attack, they almost killed Fred Kuethe—and [they] murdered William Norris. Now I ask you to do the right thing and impose upon both John Smith and Charles Carey the extreme penalty—execution by hanging!"

Pausing for a moment and in a lower voice, O'Conor continues: "Don't let your humanities become your weakness. You should give to Baltimore and example of punishment and allow the citizens to know that the law will take care of such men as these. For Mr. Norris and for his widow and his children, and for the sake of justice, you men of the jury must set aside your compassions and render a verdict for the extreme penalty in the sentencing of these two convicted outlaws."

O'Conor thanked the jury and returned to the prosecution council's table where Robert Leach said, "Well done."

Joseph Higgins and E. Milton Altfeld Argue for Life in Prison

When Joe Higgins stepped forward to speak for John Smith, it was no longer a matter of "not guilty" or even the lesser verdict of manslaughter. For the next three quarters of an hour, Higgins tried to persuade the jury to save Smith's life. He called one character witness—John Smith's mother, Betsy Smith.

Betsy Smith said she was a widow and that since the death of her husband—an army veteran—John had been helping the family get by. He was a good boy who worked hard at his job at the Sparrows Point steel mill. "If my boy was involved in this crime," Betsy pleaded, "he must not have known what he was getting into. John would never intentionally kill anyone. Please spare my son."

After Betsy Smith stepped down, Higgins aimed his appeal for leniency directly at the twelve jurymen. "Mr. Leach's and Mr. O'Conor's tactics were shameful," Higgins argued. "They said my client, John Smith, attacked Mr. Kuethe, but Mr. Kuethe never identified Mr. Smith as his assailant. Mr. Leach tried to make the relationship between Mr. Smith and his girlfriend Edna Dorsch unholy—as if their natural and close relationship had anything to do with the crime."

Higgins turned and pointed toward Frank Allers, then raising his voice, continued: "Allers there, Mr. Allers, the ex-convict, the man who drove the murder car, should be the one climbing the gallows! Or for that matter, how about the man who pulled the trigger, Walter Socolow, or the leader of the pack, Jack Hart. What about them? Looks like Allers and Hart are getting a deal. The truth is Mr. Smith did not shoot anybody and therefore should not suffer a trip to the gallows. Save that for Jack Hart and Walter Socolow. If you value the meaning of justice, I challenge you gentlemen of the jury to do the right thing and return a sentencing verdict of first-degree murder without capital punishment. Mr. Smith will spend the rest of his life in prison. That is justice enough."

After Mr. Higgins concluded his remarks and returned to the chair next to John Smith, who sat passively through Higgins' summation, never once looking at the jury, Milton Altfeld rose in the cause of Charles Carey.

E. Milton Altfeld

Like Higgins, Milton Altfeld called one character witness—Charles Carey's sister, Miss Helen Carey. Helen Carey, who had lost an arm working at the Mount Vernon-Woodberry Cotton Mills, said that she was with her brother and Boris Falasea at the Acme Lunchroom on the morning of August 18th. "Charles," she pleaded, "did not rob Mr. Norris. He didn't shoot anyone. Since my accident, my brother has taken care of me. I don't know what

I will do without him."

Altfeld—also launching a bitter attack upon Frank Allers—questioned every word of Allers' testimony. "On the testimony Mr. Allers has offered, in this case, a yellow dog should not have been convicted much less sentenced to hang by the neck until dead. Frank Allers and John Keller," Altfeld continued, "are co-conspirators. What they had to say, convicted my client of murder in the first degree. So be it. I must respect your verdict. But you must agree, there is a difference between robbery and murder. Charles Carey did not murder anyone. Mr. Allers and Mr. Keller confirm this to be the truth. This should be enough for you gentlemen to take capital punishment off the table. I ask you; I implore you to return a sentencing verdict of first-degree murder without capital punishment."

As Milton Altfeld returned to the defense counsels' table, Judge Gorter asked Mr. Leach if he had any closing remarks. Leach replied, "We have sympathy for the families of the defendants. We understand why Charles Carey's sister committed perjury. But the defendants, Charles Carey and John Smith, were convicted by this jury of a terrible crime. William Norris was murdered. Above all else, we seek justice for him and his family.

The Sentencing of John Smith and Charles Carey

After Mr. Leach returned to his seat, Judge Gorter charged the jury to deliberate upon two possible sentencing recommendations—murder in the first degree with capital punishment, or murder in the first degree without capital punishment. As it was with Smith's and Carey's murder convictions, the jury's sentencing recommendations will be individually determined and must be endorsed by the three-judge panel. After the three judges retired to Judge Gorter's chambers, the Bailiff, Joseph Quinn, announced that the Supreme Court of Baltimore City was adjourned until further notice.

John Smith and Charles Carey were once again removed to a holding cell in the courthouse basement. Robert Leach, Courtenay Jenifer, and Herbert O'Conor retired to the second-floor offices of the State's Attorney. The defense lawyers, John Meyer, Joseph Higgins, and Milton Altfeld returned to the counselors' lounge. Captain of Detectives Charles Burns and Detective William Murphy escorted the state's witnesses, Frank Allers and John Keller, to a ground floor anteroom. Many reporters remained in the courtroom. Others gathered on Battle Monument Square or headed for a local eatery for lunch.

At two o'clock, Joseph Quinn was once again making the rounds notifying everyone that the jury had reach a unanimous agreement on sentencing verdicts. At 2:30 p.m., courtroom 600 was again brimming with speculative banter. The twelve jurymen, led by Ed McCauley, took their places in the jury box. John Smith and Charles Carey were escorted to the defense counsel's table. Their lawyers, Higgins, Meyer, and Altfeld were already there. Robert Leach, Courtnay Jenifer, and Herbert O'Conor assumed their places at the prosecution counsel's table. William Norris Jr. was again invited to sit with Leach, Jenifer, and O'Conor. As the three judges entered from Judge Gorter's chambers and took their places at the bench, Joseph Quinn, in a resonant voice, proclaimed: "Please rise—the Supreme Court of Baltimore City is now in session. Please be seated." Judge Gorter, wasting no time, asked Ed McCauley if the jury had reached sentencing verdicts.

McCauley answered: "We have."

Judge Gorter instructed Clerk of the Court, Richard McKindless, to retrieve the sentencing verdicts (two folded sheets of paper) from Mr. McCauley. McKindless then handed the documents to Judge Gorter.

The three judges (commenting quietly among themselves) reviewed the verdicts. Judge Gorter then announced that he, Judge Bond, and Judge Duffy would conference in his chambers with prosecution and defense counsels before making a final ruling in open court. The jury will remain in place, as will the defendants, John Smith and Charles Carey.

Judge Gorter informed the gallery of spectators that they were free to remain in the courtroom, but there would be no disturbances. Court was still in session. Bailiff Quinn, to assure order, rose and assumed a position in front of the bench facing toward the gallery. Officers of the Baltimore Sherriff's department assigned to the courthouse positioned themselves on either side of both defendants and at courtroom entrances.

At 3:05 the conference concluded; the Judges, defense and prosecution counsels returned to the courtroom. Chatter in the gallery ended. Those who had left the courtroom returned and took their seats or stood quietly in the back of the chamber. Judge Gorter nodded to Bailiff Quinn, who then asked for order. Gorter handed the folded sentencing verdicts to Clerk of the Court Richard McKindless, who returned them to Jury Forman Edward McCauley.

Just as the day before, McKindless rose and asked the jury if they had agreed upon a unanimous sentencing verdict for each of the convicted defendants. Ed McCauley answered, "We have."

McKindless turned to John Smith and ordered him to stand and face the jury. Rotating back to the jury, McKindless asks: "Gentlemen of the jury, how say you? Guilty of murder in the first degree with capital punishment or guilty of murder in the first degree without capital punishment?"

Ed McCauley, already standing, answers in a resolute voice: "Guilty of murder in the first degree—without capital punishment."

As John Smith, showing no emotion, sits down, there is a sudden buzz of conversation throughout the gallery. Judge Gorter, striking his gavel several times, orders quiet.

McKindless turns to Charles Carey and orders him to rise and face the jury. When asked with or without capital punishment, Ed McCauley responds: "Murder in the first degree—without capital punishment."

Noticeably relieved, Carey smiles at his attorney Milton Altfeld, who pats him on the shoulder as he takes his seat.

Again, the gallery begins to stir. Judge Gorter orders quiet.

McKindless, addressing the defense (lawyers and prisoners), asks that they stand and face the judges.

Judge Gorter, speaking to both defendants begins: "A jury of your peers has convicted you of Murder in the first degree—without capital punishment. We (looking first at Judge Bond and then at Judge Duffy) concur with the jury's verdicts as just."

Then speaking to both defendants, Judge Gorter says: "You, John Smith, and you, Charles Carey, have been convicted for your part in a dreadful crime. It is this court's determination (Gorter looking at each of his fellow judges—Bond and Duffy nod back in agreement) the jury has been merciful. Each of you are hereby remanded to the Baltimore City's Sherriff's department to be brought forthwith to the Maryland Penitentiary, where you will spend the remainder of your natural lives. There, in God's eyes, you may find redemption."

There was some cheering in the courtroom. Gorter struck his gavel and ordered quiet and for everyone to remain still until the Sheriff's deputies handcuffed and removed Smith and Carey from the courtroom. Gorter then dismissed the jurymen thanking them again for their service. After the jury and Judges Gorter, Bond, and Duffy left the courtroom, Bailiff Joseph Quinn announced that the present case before the Supreme Court of Baltimore was concluded.

There was an eruption of conversation as courtroom 600 began to clear. Out on Battle Monument Square, the restless throng of watchers, hearing the news of a sentencing verdict, broke into earsplitting applause. Some reporters and a few photographers raced to the Calvert Street side of the building hoping to get a final look at a shackled John Smith and Charles Carey as the black jail wagon hauled them away. As Smith and Carey were ushered the several yards from the courthouse to the jail wagon, John Smith turned to a band of correspondents and said, "I would have rather had the rope."

Disposition of Jack Hart

On Wednesday, September 28, as the Carey-Smith Trial was underway, although they did not disclose it publicly, Robert Leach, Courtenay Jenifer, and Herbert O'Conor decided—for the reasons discussed on September 22nd in Leach's office—to offer Jack Hart the deal his attorney, Oscar Bermau, proposed—first-degree murder without capital punishment. In the plea agreement, Hart was to be condemned to life in the Maryland Penitentiary. Following the Socolow trial, scheduled to be held in mid-October, he would be sentenced by Judge Gorter.

A component of Hart's plea deal was that if called, he would testify as a State's witness in any of the Norris case trials. Hart accepted. So, on September 28th and 29th, Jack Hart was in the courtroom (under guard) with his attorney, Oscar Bermau, ready to testify if called upon by the prosecution. Hart was never called.

Disposition of Benny Lewis, Allen N. Buddy Blades, George Heard, and John Fats Novack

After the Carey-Smith trial, the members of Hart's gang not directly involved in the murder of William Norris pleaded to the lesser charge of "accessory before the fact" and were sentenced to various stints in the Maryland Penitentiary ranging from three to five years.

Disposition of Walter Socolow

C. Gus Grason, Walter Socolow's attorney, announced that his client asked for a jury trial. Grason was assisted by W. Gill Smith and Jack Hart's attorney, Oscar Berman. Ever since his capture in New York City, Socolow stuck to his claim that he was innocent. Grason was able to secure a change of venue. Socolow's capital murder trial began on October 15th, in the Circuit Court of Baltimore County. Courtnay Jenifer led the prosecution, assisted by Robert Leach, Herbert O'Conor and Timothy Andrews, Assistant Baltimore County State's Attorney.

Newspaper reporters flocked to the Historic Towson Courthouse to report on the last trial for the Murder of William B. Norris. Because of the kidnapping of Socolow from Justice Martin's courtroom in New York City and O'Conor's escape back to Baltimore with Socolow in tow, Walter Noisy Socolow's trial drew a national audience. Everyone in America wanted to know if the nineteen-year-old boy, purported to be the trigger man in the killing of William Norris, would be the only member of Jack Hart's gang to be executed.

Socolow's trial lasted five days. Frank Allers and John Keller were State's witnesses. Keller testified about being with Socolow in Harry Wolf's house on August 18, 1922—the night of the crime. New York police detectives Christopher Kelley, Cornelius Browne, and James Gegan testified about the arrest of Socolow in New York and what he had to say afterward.

When called, Harry Wolf said it is not true that Walter Socolow and John Keller were ever in his house. He was ill that night when Detective Hammersla showed up. Wolf maintained he told Hammersla the truth—no one, except for himself, was in his house on the night of August 22, 1922.

When called by the defense, Hammersla stated he never suspected Socolow or any other member of Hart's gang was in Wolf's house.

Historic Baltimore County Courthouse

Former Precinct Captain John Leverton testified he had no knowledge that Walter Socolow or John Keller were ever in Harry Wolf's house. He testified, "I never, for one minute, believed Keller's ridiculous story."

The prosecution was unable to present another witness to confirm that Socolow and Keller were in Harry Wolf's house on the night of the crime.

Despite Socolow's claim he was not the shooter, H. Courtney Jenifer, Robert Leach, and Herbert O'Conor made an indisputable case against Walter Socolow as the man who murdered William Norris.

On October 20, 1922, Walter Socolow was convicted of murder in the first degree. C. Gus Grason, however, was able to persuade the jury that the real villain was Jack Hart. "Walter Socolow," Grason told the jury, "is just a teenager, who would have never been involved in the robbery and murder had it not been for Jack Hart."

On October 21st, like Charles Carey, John Smith, and Jack Hart, Walter Socolow was sentenced to life in the Maryland Penitentiary.

Results of the William Norris Murder Case Trials

On January 14, 1923, Jack Hart—who pleaded guilty to "murder in the first degree" to avoid the death penalty—was sentenced to life in prison. Hart's conviction effectively closed the book on the highest profile murder case in the United States. No other homicide (or in fact any criminal delinquency) would capture such national interest until September 1934, when Bruno Richard Hauptmann was arrested for the kidnapping and murder of Charles and Ann Lindbergh's twenty-month-old son, Charles Jr., on May 12, 1932. Hauptmann's trial lasted from September 2 to February 13, 1935. Although claiming his innocence, Hauptmann was found guilty and sentenced to death in the electric chair. He was executed on April 3, 1936.

Although Carey, Smith, Socolow, and Hart received life sentences, the criticism of these nationally tracked high-profile murder trials was that—despite the preponderance of evidence—none of the defendants received the death penalty.

Leach and Jenifer, nevertheless, satisfied with the prosecutions, admitted that it would have been a stretch for twelve jurors (in the Carey-Smith and Socolow trials) to agree on the death penalty when only one defendant was actually guilty of murder, and he (Walter Socolow) was a teenager.

Because of the national dragnet, the courtroom kidnapping of Socolow, O'Conor's dramatic getaway from New York to Baltimore, and Jack Hart's claim that "no jail could hold him," recollections of the Norris case lingered in the public consciousness for years.

44

FOLLOWING THE NORRIS CASE TRIALS

Charles Country Carey and John Wiggles Smith

The Smith-Carey trial was the warmup to the main event—the anticipated prosecutions of Jack Hart and Walter Socolow, who had, during the summer of 1922, been the two most wanted fugitives in America.

John Wiggles Smith and Charles Country Carey, convicted of murder in the first degree, were sentenced to be confined in the Maryland Penitentiary for life.

In 1927, Charles Carey stabbed and killed an unarmed prison guard. Herbert O'Conor indicted Carey for first-degree murder. Carey was convicted and sentenced to death. He was hanged in the courtyard of the Maryland Penitentiary the following year.

In 1940, for health reasons, John Wiggles Smith, who said he preferred the rope rather than spending his life in prison, was transferred to the Maryland Correctional Institution in Hagerstown, where he worked in the prison bakery. He died there of natural causes in 1946.

Walter "Noisy" Socolow

Walter Socolow, beginning with jury selection on October 16, 1922, and throughout his trial, maintained his innocence.

The *Baltimore Sun* headline on October 20th, read:

"Socolow, On Witness Stand, Says He Took no Part In Robbery and Murder of Norris"

In rebuttal to John Keller's testimony, Harry Wolf—in an effort to help himself more than Socolow—testified that Walter Socolow never told him that he (Socolow) shot Mr. Norris on August 18th, the day of the crime, in his Pikesville home.

O'Conor proved correct when he predicted that if Socolow took the stand in his own defense, he would seal his fate as Norris' killer. Socolow's trial went to the jury that same afternoon (October 20th). The following day the jury came back with the verdict: Guilty of murder in the first degree.

During the sentencing hearing, Gus Grason successfully argued that Walter was still a teenager under the influence and whims of Jack Hart. "If anyone deserves to be hung—hang Jack Hart—not a naïve boy who did what he was told by the man responsible for the robbery and murder." Socolow, skirting the scaffolds, was sentenced to life in the Maryland Penitentiary.

During his confinement, Socolow was given a job in the prison print shop. For the next twenty-three years, Socolow became a skilled printing press operator and was considered an exemplary prisoner.

Because of a manpower shortage during World War II, Walter Socolow, at 42 years of age, was paroled so he could go to work for the *Baltimore News American* as a pressman.

In 1970, Socolow was discovered dead in his boarding house room by a coworker after failing to show up for the evening shift. He was 67 years old. At his funeral service, Walter was remembered by his *News American* colleagues as a well-liked, law-abiding citizen.

Jack Hart

Baltimore Sun – January 14, 1923

Jack Hart's Prison Mugshot (1923)

HART RECEIVES LIFE SENTENCE IN NORRIS CASE

Three Others Sent to Prison for Life…

Harry B. Wolf Disbarred as Lawyer as Outgrowth of Killing…

The *Baltimore Sun* article recaps the robbery and murder of William Norris on August 18, 1922, on Madison Street at the intersection of Park Avenue. To avoid the death penalty, Hart pleaded guilty to Murder in the First Degree. Like Smith, Carey, and Socolow, Hart was sentenced to life in the Maryland Penitentiary. Hart's wife, Kitty Connelly, who visited her husband whenever permitted, attended the sentencing hearing. She broke into tears when "Life in Prison" was read to a packed courtroom by Judge Gorter.

During his confinement in the Maryland Penitentiary, Hart was the ringleader in six prison break attempts. He was successful twice. In 1924, he bolted by way of a bathroom window considered too narrow for a man to squeeze through. He was captured a month later trying to visit Kitty. From then on, their love affair captured the romanticized newsprint empathy, similar to Bonny and Clyde, who would become infamous lovers eight years in the future. Jack Hart, the bandit, willing to risk freedom to spend a fleeting moment in the arms of his starry-eyed lover.

Hart escaped again in 1929. He managed to cut through three locks of a solitary confinement cell, release another prisoner, shimmy through a ventilator shaft to the roof and rappel to the ground with a rope made of bed sheets. This time, Hart wasn't so easy to find. Neither was Kitty, who disappeared from her mother's Highlandtown house only to materialize days later. The police did their utmost to keep track of Kitty Kavanaugh Connelly, who despite being watched, proved elusive.

In January 1930, Kitty became seriously ill. On March 30, 1930, Kitty Kavanaugh Connelly died due to a massive abdominal infection. During her final delusional hours, Kitty called out for Jimmy. She was 29 years old. Kitty's Uncle Joe attended the service at the William Cook Funeral Home on April 3rd where he spoke a few comforting words about his niece and loving goddaughter. Following the service, Kitty was buried in the Archdiocese of Baltimore's New Cathedral Cemetery in West Baltimore.

The whole affair turned into a bizarre spectacle when hundreds of false mourners, along with a sizable contingent of police, showed up hoping to catch a glimpse of or capture Jack Hart. Hart never appeared.

Hart was captured in 1933 and returned to the Maryland Penitentiary. Because of illness (thought to be lung cancer), he was paroled in 1955. He lived out the last months of his life at his brother's home in New Jersey. Hart was 68.

Joseph Kavanaugh Company

Joseph Kavanaugh was never called to answer for being in the whiskey business with Jack Hart. As of 2020, run by old Joe's generational offspring, the Joseph Kavanaugh Company was still in business.

Harry B. Wolf

Harry Wolf was tried for obstruction of justice before a five-judge panel of the Supreme Court of Maryland. He was found guilty. Wolf was fined and sentenced to probation with no prison time.

Wolf appealed and lost. Because of his felony conviction, he was disbarred by the Maryland Bar Association overseen by Association President Edgar Allan Poe, a descendant of the poet. Wolf was pardoned in 1935 and reinstated to the Bar in 1940.

Harry Benjamin Wolf was a long way from giving up dabbling on the edge of maleficence. Several years before the Norris case and until it was uncovered in 1937, Wolf and several lawyer colleagues devised a scheme whereby mentally-ill female inmates housed at Maryland's Rosewood Mental Hospital were hired out as housekeepers. Wolf and his solicitor chums collected most of the money, camouflaged as legal fees.

Using *habeas corpus* writs, Wolf was able to have mentally deficient inmates released into his or one of his associates' guardianship. Once discharged, these women (mostly without families) would be lent out as housemaids. Compelled to live in unfamiliar and often uncaring circumstances, these defenseless women were in many cases abused physically, mentally, and sexually, sometimes abandoned, left to fend for themselves on urban streets.

One way or another, this (if not illegal) immoral and heartless business venture (that took advantage of a flaw in the application of writs) went undetected until Leo Kanner, a psychiatrist and social activist, uncovered and exposed this legal defect in 1937.

The practice of mistreating or effectively enslaving the mentally ill through the use of a writ or other means was brought to a legislative end. Herbert O'Conor, Maryland Attorney General at the time, was a driving force in exposing the abuse and recommending legislation that was passed by Maryland's Legislature and signed into law by then Governor Harry W. Nice, a Republican who defeated Albert Ritchie's run for a fifth term in 1934.

Harry Wolf died at his Pikesville home on February 17, 1944. He was 64. Wolf's ability to circumvent prison time and influence politicians had a deleterious effect on Robert Leach's zeal to continue as Baltimore City State's Attorney. Leach would keep this to himself right up until the 1923 election, when he announced that he would not seek a second term.

Baltimore City Police Captain John Leverton

Baltimore Police Captain John Leverton was not charged. There is no record of him after January 1923.

Frank Stinky Allers

Despite being the main State's witness and receiving partial immunity, Frank Allers was held over in the Maryland State Penitentiary to stand trial for a robbery he committed on June 8, 1922, two months and ten days before the robbery and murder of William Norris. On December 7, 1922, Allers was indicted by a Baltimore County Grand Jury and prosecuted by Courtenay Jenifer for breaking into the home of Thomas and Lula Hooper and stealing a large cache of imported whiskey and champagne.

He pleaded not guilty, but was convicted and sentenced to ten years in the Maryland Penitentiary. His sentence was to be served concurrent with his limited immunity (Norris Case) sentence of ten years. The second conviction made Allers ineligible for parole. He served the full ten years.

In his (Hooper) trial, Allers' attorney argued that he had been given limited immunity by Robert Leach and Courtenay Jenifer for being a State's witness in the Norris case and this immunity should carry over to the Hooper case. He accused Leach and Jenifer of conspiring against Allers by not notifying him that the Norris case limited immunity agreement did not extend to the

Hooper case. Allers' appeal was denied. He was to be released on Monday, September 25, 1933. The night before, Allers was murdered (stabbed multiple times) while returning to his cell from the penitentiary dining hall. The killer was never identified.

John Squeaky Keller

Seventeen-year-old John Keller was sentenced to two years in a low security prison. In 1924, Keller was arrested again for theft but found innocent. There is no record of John Keller being convicted of another crime or what happened to him after 1924.

Buddy Blades and Johnny Jubb

Buddy Blades never implicated Johnny Jubb. Jubb was not prosecuted. Robert Leach regretfully determined he did not have enough evidence to convict Blades or Jubb of conspiring to commit the robbery of the Hicks Tate and Norris Company payroll. Blades only spent two years in jail as an accessory. Leach let it be known that he would, with more definitive evidence, have indicted Blades for capital murder. However, the men Captain Burns, and Lieutenant Hammersla believed were responsible for setting up the Norris robbery got off easy. Neither Blades nor Jubb appear (again) in police records.

New York Supreme Court Justice Francis W. Martin, Jr.

After the Socolow incident, Justice Francis W. Martin became an apolitical judge. He disassociated himself from Tammany Hall and avoided being tagged with political affiliations. Martin built a reputation as an impartial, universally fair jurist. He was especially tough on mobsters tried in his court.

In 1935, Martin was appointed presiding justice of the appellant division and was a delegate to the 1938 New York Constitutional Convention. He served as a justice on the New York Supreme Court until his unexpected death, at his home, on January 1, 1947.

JOHN VONEIFF II

New York Governor Nathan L. Miller

Governor Nathan L. Miller lost his bid for a second term. His most significant accomplishment was the establishment of the New York City Transit Commission, which effectively took control of New York City's transportation infrastructure out of the hands of Tammany Hall, the New York Mayor, and City Council. This legislation, Miller believed, cost him reelection.

Miller was replaced by Al Smith, who Miller had defeated in 1920. Alfred Emanuel Smith sought the Democratic nomination for President of the United States four times. He was successful once. Smith lost in a landslide to Herbert Hoover in 1928. He blamed his defeat on being Irish Catholic.

Miller became general counsel for United States Steel. He nominated his friend, Herbert Hoover, for president at the Republican Convention in 1928 but never again sought political office. He died in New York City on June 26, 1964, at the age of 84.

Fleet W. Cox

Fleet W. Cox a former Assistant United States Attorney, was selected by newly elected Baltimore City State's Attorney, Robert Leach, to be his deputy in 1920. Cox felt blindsided when Leach announced that he would not seek a second term and backed Herbert O'Conor as his replacement. Cox, who considered himself more qualified than the twenty-seven-year-old O'Conor, thought he had been unfairly passed over for the Democratic nomination to succeed Robert Leach. Even so, he made it known that he would like to continue as O'Conor's deputy after O'Conor was elected Baltimore City State's Attorney in 1924.

Although O'Conor respected Cox, he nevertheless wanted to appoint his own deputy. He chose Roland K. Adams, a partner in the Baltimore firm of Johnson and Adams. After O'Conor appointed Adams, Cox resigned. He relocated to Washington,

D.C. and went on to practice law in the capital, where he was a sought-after criminal lawyer.

Fleet Cox died of cancer on Saturday, January 8, 1927. He was buried in his family's private cemetery in the town of Hauge, in Westmoreland County, Virginia, near the mouth of the Potomac River. Cox was 56 years old.

Robert F. Leach, Jr.

In 1923, only three days before the deadline for filing to be a candidate, Robert Leach announced that he would not seek a second term as Baltimore City State's Attorney. His reason was an eagerness to return to private practice. Behind the scenes, Leach had become disillusioned in his ability to successfully prosecute organized crime and political corruption. In truth, Robert Leach was an apolitical man in a political job. Robert Leach threw his support behind Herbert R. O'Conor to be his replacement.

Bob Leach died on August 28, 1946, at Johns Hopkins Hospital, after lingering for two weeks following a massive cerebrovascular accident (stroke). He was 73 years old. In tribute to Mr. Leach, Criminal Court was adjourned for the day.

Leach was eulogized by Chief Judge W. Conwell Smith and Baltimore City State's Attorney J. Bernard Wells, whom Leach had brought into the State's Attorney's office along with Herbert O'Conor not long after he took office in 1920.

Wells said, "*I feel that under his direction, the office reached its pinnacle of efficiency in the prosecution of crime in this city in any time. He set the standard, which his successors have tried to emulate.*"

Wells brought back to mind "the gang of bandits who held up and killed William B. Norris, a Baltimore contractor, and robbed him and a clerk of several thousand dollars in August 1922." He underscored Leach's determination to stamp out corruption in all its forms.

In 1939, newly elected Governor Herbert R. O'Conor, in honor of his service to Baltimore City and Maryland and in gratitude for his unwavering support, rewarded his former boss with the position he modestly sought, Maryland State Librarian, a post Robert Leach proudly held until his death.

H. Courtnay Jenifer

After serving five terms as Baltimore County States Attorney, Courtnay Jenifer joined the United States Army's Judge Advocate Generals Corps. He was involved in the prosecution of war crimes following World War II. Jenifer returned to Baltimore County (near Towson) where he practiced law until his retirement in 1960. Courtney Jenifer died of heart complications, in 1964, at the age of 72.

William F. Broening

In addition to being Baltimore City State's Attorney twice, William Broening was elected Mayor of Baltimore twice, 1919 to 1923, when he was defeated by Howard Jackson. Borening reclaimed the office in 1927, but was turned out by Jackson again in 1931.

In 1930, during the midpoint of his second term as Mayor, Broening won the Republican primary for the office of Governor. He ran against Albert Ritchie who was running for an unprecedented fourth term. Broening was soundly defeated.

Howard Jackson, who was a staunch party rival of Albert Ritchie, would remain Baltimore's mayor until 1943. As much as anything else, Broening—like President Hoover on the national stage—lost the confidence of Baltimoreans after the stock market disintegrated on Black Thursday, October 4, 1929, often refer to as the first day of the Great Depression.

After Broening's harsh criticism of O'Conor on Friday, September 22, 1922, over the kidnapping of Walter Socolow, he abruptly

changed his tune. It wasn't surprising. Public opinion, especial-
ly in Baltimore City, came down overwhelmingly in favor of
O'Conor. By Tuesday, September 26th, the day after Governor
Ritchie sent his response to Governor Miller, Broening was all
in on the return of Socolow to Baltimore—no matter the means.
In interviews, he was complimentary of O'Conor, Commissioner
Gaither, and the police officers who rounded up Jack Hart and
his gang.

Following his defeat by Howard Jackson in 1931, Broening remained politically active but never again ran for office. He became a Mason, an Elk, an Odd Fellow, and was elected a Supreme
Representative of the Knights of Pythias—fraternal orders dedicated to humanitarian causes. William Broening died on October
12, 1953. He was 83 years old.

Iris Millman and Dorothy Livingston

Iris Millman sold her apartment building in March 1923 and
disappeared. Dorothy Livingston also vanished about the same
time, not long after her husband was convicted and sentenced to
20 years in federal prison.

Whether Iris and Dede left Washington D.C. together or separately is unknown. Neither was identified during the Norris trials. It took eight years before an investigative reporter identified
Dorothy Livingston as Leach's unnamed informant. Until then
she was identified only by the initial "L." Iris Millman was never actually known other than by the initial "M" (The name Iris
Millman, for this story, is a pseudonym).

Charles D. Gaither (circa 1917)

Charles D. Gaither

Charles D. Gaither served as Baltimore City Police Commissioner from 1920 to 1937. He had intended to be a career army officer. Gaither fought with distinction in the Spanish American War as commander of the Ninth U.S. Volunteer Infantry and then the Fifth Maryland Veterans Corps. After the war, he remained in the Army and was eventually promoted to Brigadier General and given command of the celebrated First Maryland Brigade that fought in Belgium during World War One.

When Albert Ritchie was first elected Governor in 1919 (assuming office in January 1920), he recruited Gaither to become Baltimore City's Police Commissioner. (Until 1978, the Baltimore City Police Commissioner was appointed by the Governor, not the mayor).

Gaither managed his department with military acuity. Throughout his 17-year administration, he was steadfastly supportive of his officers and detectives. Out of loyalty and affection, subordinates referred to him as "General" rather than Commissioner.

Due to age and declining health, Gaither resigned in January 1937. He died ten years later on March 29, 1947. Gaither was 87.

George J. Henry

Following the Norris case investigations, Gaither elevated Henry to serve as Deputy Commissioner and promoted Captain of Detectives Charles Burns to take over as Chief of Detectives. Upon Gaither's retirement, Henry sought to be appointed commissioner. Republican Governor Harry W. Nice, who had defeated Albert Ritchie in 1935 to become Maryland's fiftieth governor, chose his political ally, William Lawson. Henry left the police department. Also a former Army officer, George Henry, like Gaither, was deemed an accomplished Deputy Commissioner.

Charles Burns – and the Men of the Norris Squad

In 1922, following the Norris case, Captain of Detectives Charles Burns replaced George Henry as Chief of Detectives after Henry was promoted to Deputy Commissioner. With the exception of Charles Burns himself, all of Burns' Norris taskforce—Charles Kahler, William Murphy, Harry M. Hammersla, and James Comen—remained Baltimore City police detectives until their retirements. Little of their history, outside of the Norris case, is known. The investigation of the robbery and murder by Captain Burns' unit was deemed an example of effective police (team) work.

Charles H. Burns died on March 9, 1933. He was 57 years old. Although noticeably ill with what was thought to be a severe cold for the better part of three weeks, Burns stubbornly refused to take time off to recuperate until five days before his death. Burns died surrounded by his family at his 718 Woodington Road (West Baltimore) home. The cause of death was listed as succumbing to the corollaries of pneumonia. In announcing the death of Chief of Detectives Charles H. Burns, Commissioner Gaither said: "The Police Department has lost one if its most courageous officers. A man whose service to the public was absolutely preeminent in his makeup…"

Albert Cabell Ritchie

Albert C. Ritchie died unexpectedly at his home, on February 24, 1936, a little over a year after he was defeated by Republican Harry Nice. Ritchie was running for a fifth term as Maryland's governor. His funeral was private, but thousands of mourners attended a memorial service held after a public outpouring to say farewell to the man who had been (and would remain) Maryland's longest serving governor. On that occasion, Stuart Janney eulogized his longtime friend and law partner.

Ritchie was governor of Maryland for 15 years (January 14, 1920–January 9, 1935). He did not remarry after his divorce from Elizabeth Baker in 1916. The couple never had children. Ritchie is interred next to his parents in Baltimore's Greenmount Cemetery.

A conservative Democrat, Ritchie was a champion of states' rights for which he attained national prominence. For this reason, he was a vocal opponent of the 18th Amendment and the Volstead Act. In 1932, because of his national standing, Ritchie was advanced by conservative Democrats to be the Democratic nominee for President of the United States. Failing to achieve the nomination, he was asked by Franklin D. Roosevelt, who won the nomination, to be his running mate. Ritchie declined.

Throughout his governorship, he endorsed and funded improvements in secondary education including equal education for underprivileged children, an initiative headed up by Stuart Janney. Ritchie was an early advocate for the conservation of the Chesapeake Bay and began the overdue rebuilding of Maryland's transportation infrastructure. He built a reputation as a law-and-order governor who was especially tough when it came to political corruption or defending civil rights.

Although Ritchie was a popular governor whose business-like approach modernized government in Maryland, prominent members of his party believed he had held the office too long.

He was encouraged to run for the United States Senate, a seat he would have easily won. Ritchie, however, had no interest in being a senator and believed, because of his popularity, he would be elected to a fifth term in 1934.

Despite predictions that Ritchie would win, when the election results were tabulated, Harry Nice—who Ritchie defeated in his first run for the governorship in 1919—was the victor, prevailing by a narrow margin to become Maryland's 50th Governor.

Ritchie never got over his 1934 defeat. He returned to private practice, as a senior partner in the firm (Ritchie, Janney, & Stuart) he founded with Stuart S. Janney in 1903. Although Janney left Ritchie's cabinet in 1928, he continued as an intimate advisor to the Governor throughout the remainder of Ritchie's tenure. After Ritchie's 1934 defeat, he and Janney practiced law together until Ritchie's unforeseen passing in 1936. Albert Ritchie was 59 years old.

Stuart Symington Janney

On February 27, 1896, two young men, Stuart Symington Janney and Osmun Latrobe, born into two of Maryland's most prominent families, disappeared without a trace. Stuart and Osmun had been inseparable boyhood friends. Stuart, who graduated from Johns Hopkins University, like his father, planned to be a lawyer. Osmun, after graduating from the University of Pennsylvania, intended to follow in the footsteps of his great grandfather, Benjamin (who designed the United States Capital and the Catholic Basilica on Cathedral Street in Baltimore) and become an architect.

Ninety miles south of Florida, the Cuban revolutionary army was fighting for its freedom from Spain. There was widespread sympathy in America for the Cuban people that inspired a pervasive movement to expel Spain from the Americas by enforcing the (1823) Monroe Doctrine.

As he was leaving Leach's office on Friday September 22, 1922, Colonel Janney warned O'Conor about the unforeseen consequences of foolhardy decisions. Sometimes, he cautioned, such spontaneous choices work out—and sometimes not. What Colonel Janney didn't reveal to O'Conor after the meeting in Robert Leach's office, was the spontaneous decision he and Osmun Latrobe made the afternoon of February 27, 1896.

Without telling anyone, Stuart and Osmun boarded a train to Jacksonville, Florida where, ten days later, they embarked on a seagoing tug (named *Three Friends*) that was bound for Cuba with volunteers (soldiers of fortune) anxious to join the rebel army. The *Three Friends,* overloaded and tossing in a stormy and turbulent sea, missed the designated landfall by several miles and began to offload a hundred yards from a Spanish fort.

The rebels sent to meet the *Three Friends* were led by an American volunteer by the name of Frederic Funston, whose father was a United States congressman from Kansas. Proving himself a bold fighter, and because of his father's influence in Congress, Funston was elevated to the rank of colonel in General Morlot's revolutionary army.

Seeing the *Three Friends* was off course, Funston's attachment raced along the craggy coast, in the midst of a fierce downpour, to intercept and assist their new volunteers and retrieve essential supplies. When they arrived, the tug's four large skiffs were already unloading men, ammunition, weapons, and sundries while the captain did his best to steady his vessel some 50 yards offshore.

Suddenly, appearing out of the mist, a Spanish gunboat rounded the peninsula and opened fire. Janney and Latrobe, who had remained onboard to help unload, found themselves in the last skiff being rowed to shore. As 30-caliber shells tour through its deckhouse, the *Three Friends* fled into a fog bank and out to sea.

Lookouts, stationed on the fort's ramparts, spotted the landing. A company of Spanish dragoons, with fixed bayonets, charged the rebels on the beach. A fierce, hand to hand, battle ensued. Janney and Latrobe, wielding castoff rifles as clubs, found themselves in the midst of the bloody melee.

The fort's Spanish commander, misjudging the size of the rebel force, dispatched only a company of soldiers that quickly found themselves outnumbered. Within 15 gory minutes, the rebels overwhelmed their assailants. With dead and dying Spanish dragoons littering the tempest swept beach, Funston's insurgents gathered their wounded and, with mule drawn carts laden with supplies, headed for the shelter of the island's densely forested interior. It was an unanticipated baptism Stuart and Osmun would speak little of but privately recall for the remainder of their lives—a single transitory event that would cement their friendship.

Thirty-four years later, on the occasion of the 1932 United States Amateur Golf Championship Dinner, Colonel Osmond Latrobe—who remained in the United States Army and was serving as a military advisor to President Hoover—spoke about his boyhood playmate, who was the tournament's honorary chairman. Throughout his life, Janney was an enthusiastic and accomplished horseman and a talented amateur golfer. In 1932, the most prestigious golf championship of the era—the United States Amateur Championship—was held in Maryland. The tournament committee, looking to recognize one of the country's most prominent citizens, chose Stuart S. Janney as Honorary Chairman.

"Colonel Janney," Latrobe told USGA officials, golfers, patrons, and guests that included Governor Ritchie and Baltimore City State's Attorney, Herbert O'Conor, "served with distinction in three wars. He was an insurgent in Cuba, where he attained the rank of captain in the Cuban Revolutionary Army. He was commissioned a captain in the United States Army during the Spanish American War, where he was engaged in the hardest fighting. He volunteered to lead a brigade in World War I, where, as a lieutenant-colonel in Maryland's own 313 Infantry Division, Stuart led his command in the charge that captured the town of Montfaucon, north of Verdun in the Arden Forest, a decisive battle in that terrible war. And he was fortunate, as many were not, to return home where he serves his fellow countrymen with unwavering devotion."

In 1903, Stuart Janney founded a law firm with his law school classmate Albert Ritchie. From then until Ritchie's passing in 1936, they were close friends and professional colleagues. When Ritchie became governor 1920, Janney was his chief cabinet secretary and advisor. Janney headed up many of Ritchie's programs including Maryland's Department of Welfare, Educational Committee, Commission on Law Enforcement, and the Airport Commission among others. As Commander of the American Legion, Janney successfully lobbied Congress to release pensions for World War I veterans. He headed up the Boy Scouts of America, served on the boards of Johns Hopkins University and the United States Fidelity and Guaranty Company.

Stuart Symington Janney passed away on April 11, 1940—eight years after he was Honorary Chairman of the 1932 United States Amateur Golf Championship. He is buried in the Saint Thomas Episcopal Church cemetery in Owings Mills, Maryland. On January 11, 1939, he was a guest of honor at the inauguration of Herbert R. O'Conor as Maryland's 51st Governor.

Herbert R. O'Conor
(State House Annapolis, MD)

Herbert R. O'Conor

Jack Hart and his band of thugs never gave the slightest thought to the consequences of robbing a prominent businessman on Madison Street. It was just another hit. No one would get hurt and the members of his gang would all be a little richer. This wasn't the first time Hart went after an easy target. As it turned out, it would be the last. By the evening of August 18, 1922, Jack Hart and the members of his gang were on the run. The robbery and murder of William Norris turned into the biggest national crime story of the decade. Everyone in America found themselves captivated by the search for Jack Hart and Walter Socolow and the trials to follow.

The members of Jack Hart's gang were far from the only individuals whose lives were influenced by the robbery and murder of Bill Norris. Certainly, life for Mable Norris and her three sons was never the same. Nationally, everyday citizens became aware of the toxic outcomes related to Prohibition, organized crime, and political corruption, especially in America's largest cities.

No one's life was more transformed than that of Herbert R. O'Conor. Before the Norris case, he was a 25-year-old, fresh out of law school, unknown junior prosecutor. After the kidnapping of Walter Socolow from Justice Francis Martin's courtroom, on September 21, 1922, everyone in America knew his name. O'Conor could not have imagined his fateful ascent to political prominence.

In 1923, three days before the deadline to file to be a candidate for elective office in Maryland, Robert Leach announced that he would not seek a second term as State's Attorney for Baltimore City. Leach also made it known that despite his youth, he supported Herbert O'Conor as his replacement. O'Conor won the democratic primary and then the general election in a landslide.

When O'Conor took over on January 6, 1924, Baltimore was still considered a city overrun by armed gangsters. Over the next ten years, O'Conor's relentless criminal prosecutions—underpinned by Commissioner Gaither's Baltimore City Police Department— changed the city's reputation for the better. Baltimoreans attributed this sense of security to the man who brought Walter Socolow back to Baltimore to face justice.

In 1934, at the urging of Governor Ritchie, O'Conor ran for Maryland Attorney General. His election was never in doubt. O'Conor assumed the office of Maryland Attorney General on January 6, 1935. Robert Leach's explanation for O'Conor's stellar showing came down to the same reasons he appointed him an assistant state's attorney in 1921 and entrusted him with the Norris case in 1922. "O'Conor," he said, "was always effective and honest. After he brought Walter Socolow back to Baltimore, everybody knew his name and liked what they saw."

The biting columnist H. L. Mencken, monitoring O'Conor's time as Maryland Attorney General, said, "The only man in Annapolis who has shown any capacity for his job is the Hon. Herbert R. O'Conor, LLD., the Attorney General.

In 1938, the support of a popular American president, Franklin D. Roosevelt, on top of his already statewide approval left little doubt who would be elected Maryland's 51st Governor. The current Governor Harry Nice, who defeated Albert Ritchie's bid for a fifth term in 1934, never had a chance.

O'Conor assumed office on January 11, 1939. He was the first Irish Catholic to become a state Governor, a long overdue achievement given that Maryland was founded in 1632 through a Charter granted to Cecil Calvert (a Catholic) by King Charles I to provide a religious sanctuary for all religions but to Catholics in particular, who, during the 17th Century, were being oppressed and persecuted in England.

Herbert O'Conor served two terms as Maryland's Governor. Roosevelt thought enough of Governor O'Conor to offer him the cabinet position of United States Attorney General and proposed nominating him to the Supreme Court. O'Conor declined these offers but according to his son, Jim O'Conor, some 60 years later, an alliance matured between his father and the President that lasted until Roosevelt's passing in April 1944. In addition to his duties as governor and Chairman of the National Governor's Association throughout the war years, O'Conor became a sounding board for the President.

In 1946, *Baltimore Sun* reporter Louis Azreal asked O'Conor, "How will your record as governor stack up?" Then Azreal, speaking for most Marylanders, answered his own question saying, "Your governorship will, I believe, be judged very well!"

In 1946, Herbert O'Conor was fifty years old. He had held political office (Baltimore City State's Attorney, Maryland Attorney General, and Governor) for twenty-two years during the two greatest challenges of the 20th Century, Great Depression and World War II. Despite his decision to step down as governor, in terms of holding a political office, he was still a young man. O'Conor never worked for a private law firm, and he had never lost an election. Politics was the life he knew. In January 1946, O'Conor announced that he would run for the United States Senate. On November 4, 1946, Herbert O'Conor was elected Maryland's junior senator.

As a senator, O'Conor argued for a return to fiscal parsimony in the operation of government departments, reduction of the growing national debt, and tax cuts to increase economic productivity. Along with tax cuts, he proposed exemptions (credits for dependents) for low-income Americans. He debated on the Senate floor: "It is imperative that the government immediately set about the business of putting its house in order." It had become, in O'Conor's view, "a question of the taxpayer suffering the consequences of governmental inefficiency and waste..."

Throughout his years in the United States Senate, it became clear that O'Conor was an independent voice. His son Jim said that his father explained that he voted for what he thought best for the country, not for any particular political ideology. He once argued...

"The most insidious movement abroad today is that which seeks to substitute the guarantee of security for the guarantee of liberty as the prime purpose of our republic. Security has a price and all of history proves it. Men who would be free cannot always be secure. Liberty is won with difficulty and eternal vigilance is the price. To grant security from economic ills, Government must have more and more power and money. Since power and wealth originally proceed from the people, the increase of power and wealth in the government must necessarily be followed by the decrease in the power and wealth of the people."

On Sunday, January 13, 1952, with almost a year remaining in his term, Herbert O'Conor announced that he would not run again. His statement, timed to hit the Monday morning editions, came as a shock to just about everyone, fellow senators, Democrats and Republicans alike, constituents throughout Maryland, friends, and family.

For 30 years, Herbert O'Conor had become a preeminent household name in Maryland with associated national standing. It was hard to accept that his distinguished political career was, so unexpectedly, coming to an end by his own choosing.

Although not making the reason for his decision public, O'Conor was, as his father before him, suffering the manifestations of heart disease. He suffered a series of minor strokes and at least one heart attack during his final year as a United States senator. His doctors at Walter Reed and Mercy Hospital advised him to slow down. His condition was serious. O'Conor's official reason for leaving the Senate was to join his son and namesake, Herbert, Jr., in the practice of the law. Even after leaving the Senate, however, O'Conor maintained a vigorous schedule.

In a 2020 interview, Jim O'Conor said that his father always believed if he had chosen to run in 1952, he would have been re-elected. "My father," Jim added, "never lost his enthusiasm for politics or his love of country. Retirement was a family decision."

Herbert O'Conor, like all public figures, wasn't faultless. Some of his decisions harvested ample disappointment. In the retrospection of the American narration, like those before and afterward, he reflected the times in which he lived, triumphs and warts alike.

But Herbert O'Conor's fidelity to his Catholic faith never wavered, nor did he diminish the providence of his political rise nor Sister Mary Romula's belief that within him blazed the inspiration to do God's will. His biographer Harry Kirwin wrote, "There was no bitterness in his thinking, nothing grim about his resolve. He was never too busy to help the lowly, forgotten, and unfortunate."

On Ash Wednesday, March 2, 1960, following church services and his regular weekly game of pinochle with lifelong companions, O'Conor drove home and parked his car in the garage. Eugenia heard the garage door open and close. When her husband failed to come into the house she called out, "What are you doing out there?"

There was no response. She found him near the doorway struggling to stand, unable to speak. Eugenia was able to get her husband inside, where he collapsed into a chair. She called their son Herbert who notified his brothers Jim, Gene, Bobby, and sister Patricia. When they arrived, although their father was unable to speak, he gestured that he recognized them. It appeared that he was regaining strength, and although unsteady, was able to stand. Recognizing their father was suffering another stroke, Herbert, Jim, and Patricia drove him to Mercy Hospital. Gene and Bobby remained with their mother.

Not long after arriving at Mercy, O'Conor lapsed into a coma. He never regained consciousness. On Friday morning March 4, 1960, Herbert Romula O'Conor died. He was 63 years old.

On Tuesday, March 8, 1960, a Requiem Mass was celebrated at the Cathedral of Mary Our Queen on Charles Street in North Baltimore. The Most Reverend Francis P. Keough, Archbishop of Baltimore and O'Conor's priest and friend, led the *Requiems*—the request for eternal rest.

Throughout the seven years after O'Conor left the United States Senate, he maintained a heavy workload. First, of course, was practicing the law with his son.

Charles P. McCormick, another workaholic and Chairman of McCormick and Company (the world's largest spice company, headquartered in Baltimore) was the founder of the "McCormick Unsung Hero Award" *that honors Maryland's high school athletes who did not make the headlines but whose "skill, courage, courtesy, good conduct and cooperation make the victory possible."*

From his days as Maryland's Governor, O'Conor never missed the annual dinner where he spoke about the importance of service to one's community and country. After the 1958 dinner, where two weeks before O'Conor had suffered a near-fatal heart attack, McCormick sent his friend a letter of appreciation. In part,

McCormick wrote, "In your busy life, I marvel at your stamina which enables you to take everything and still smile. I don't feel I could do it."

O'Conor's response was that nothing can be more important than inspiring America's young men and women to achieve in the public eye or silently as your award so clearly defines. "As long as the invitation stands," O'Conor told McCormick, "you can count on me to attend."

His family story was after all the fulfillment of America's promise. He was the grandson of Irish immigrants, who arrived in New York with nothing more than the hope to begin life anew in the laborious stone quarries of Texas, Maryland. Herbert O'Conor rose to be Maryland's governor during the darkest hours of the twentieth century and play a defining role, as a United States senator, in the nation's meteoric reawakening. It was a story he never hesitated, upon request, to impart to school children who he believed should know the declaration upon which the United States of America was founded.

On one occasion, in 1957, Rosalie L. Moody, a science teacher at Clifton Park High School in northwest Baltimore, asked him to tell her class what he considered to be the best definition of democracy. His reply is worth repeating.

"Democracy, as I see it, is that form of government under which, everyone without distinction of race, color, or creed, enjoys certain fundamental rights; and in the conduct of which it is possible for any citizen to attain ascendancy and leadership in direct proportion as his (or her) intellectual attainments and natural sagacity entitle such advancement. It permits and encourages freedom of discussion and the right of criticism and depends on a free press for the preservation of the right of free discussion. Democracy holds that government is constituted for the good of the governed. Democracy, as an ideal, favors rotation as opposed to long continuance in office. It is opposed to nepotism and its ideal in the matter of appointing state positions is a

system under which all have an equal chance to attain the post."

"I could go on, but the gist is here."

What was important to him, he conveyed to Mrs. Moody, *"is to know how closely your pupils' ideas on democracy coincide with my own..."*

During a convocation at St. Joseph College in Philadelphia where he received an honorary degree when addressing the graduating class, O'Conor said, *"...The leadership of this day must be devoted to the preservation of civil rights, the dignity of individual men and women, and the rights of minorities, cognizant, at the same time, that the liberty of a democracy does not include the liberty to destroy democracy."*

His own words, voiced during the first dark days of the Second World War reveal the enduring spirit of the boy who sang in the St. Paul's Parochial School choir, all those years ago,

> *...that by in large, life on this planet is what men and women make of it.*

Related Titles from Westphalia Press

The Limits of Moderation: Jimmy Carter and the Ironies of American Liberalism

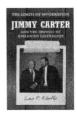

The Limits of Moderation: Jimmy Carter and the Ironies of American Liberalism is not a finished product. And yet, even in this unfinished stage, this book is a close and careful history of a short yet transformative period in American political history, when big changes were afoot.

The Zelensky Method
by Grant Farred

Locating Russian's war within a global context, The Zelensky Method is unsparing in its critique of those nations, who have refused to condemn Russia's invasion and are doing everything they can to prevent economic sanctions from being imposed on the Kremlin.

Sinking into the Honey Trap: The Case of the Israeli-Palestinian Conflict
by Daniel Bar-Tal, Barbara Doron, Translator

Sinking into the Honey Trap by Daniel Bar-Tal discusses how politics led Israel to advancing the occupation, and of the deterioration of democracy and morality that accelerates the growth of an authoritarian regime with nationalism and religiosity.

Essay on The Mysteries and the True Object of The Brotherhood of Freemasons
by Jason Williams

The third edition of Essai sur les mystères discusses Freemasonry's role as a society of symbolic philosophers who cultivate their minds, practice virtues, and engage in charity, and underscores the importance of brotherhood, morality, and goodwill.

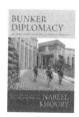

Bunker Diplomacy: An Arab-American in the U.S. Foreign Service
by Nabeel Khoury

After twenty-five years in the Foreign Service, Dr. Nabeel A. Khoury retired from the U.S. Department of State in 2013 with the rank of Minister Counselor. In his last overseas posting, Khoury served as deputy chief of mission at the U.S. embassy in Yemen (2004-2007).

Managing Challenges for the Flint Water Crisis
Edited by Toyna E. Thornton, Andrew D. Williams, Katherine M. Simon, Jennifer F. Sklarew

This edited volume examines several public management and intergovernmental failures, with particular attention on social, political, and financial impacts. Understanding disaster meaning, even causality, is essential to the problem-solving process.

User-Centric Design
by Dr. Diane Stottlemyer

User-centric strategy can improve by using tools to manage performance using specific techniques. User-centric design is based on and centered around the users. They are an essential part of the design process and should have a say in what they want and need from the application based on behavior and performance.

How the Rampant Proliferation of Disinformation Has Become the New Pandemic, and What To Do About It by Max Joseph Skidmore Jr.

This work examines the causes of the overwhelming tidal wave of fake news, misinformation, disinformation, and propaganda, and the increase in information illiteracy and mistrust in higher education and traditional, vetted news outlets that make fact-checking a priority.

Abortion and Informed Common Sense
by Max J. Skidmore

The controversy over a woman's "right to choose," as opposed to the numerous "rights" that abortion opponents decide should be assumed to exist for "unborn children," has always struck me as incomplete. Two missing elements of the argument seems obvious, yet they remain almost completely overlooked.

The Athenian Year Primer: Attic Time-Reckoning and the Julian Calendar
by Christopher Planeaux

The ability to translate ancient Athenian calendar references into precise Julian-Gregorian dates will not only assist Ancient Historians and Classicists to date numerous historical events with much greater accuracy but also aid epigraphists in the restorations of numerous Attic inscriptions.

Siddhartha: Life of the Buddha
by David L. Phillips,
contributions by Venerable Sitagu Sayadaw

Siddhartha: Life of the Buddha is an illustrated story for adults and children about the Buddha's birth, enlightenment and work for social justice. It includes illustrations from Pagan, Burma which are provided by Rev. Sitagu Sayadaw.

Growing Inequality: Bridging Complex Systems, Population Health, and Health Disparities
Editors: George A. Kaplan, Ana V. Diez Roux, Carl P. Simon, and Sandro Galea

Why is America's health is poorer than the health of other wealthy countries and why health inequities persist despite our efforts? In this book, researchers report on groundbreaking insights to simulate how these determinants come together to produce levels of population health and disparities and test new solutions.

Issues in Maritime Cyber Security
Edited by Dr. Joe DiRenzo III, Dr. Nicole K. Drumhiller, and Dr. Fred S. Roberts

The complexity of making MTS safe from cyber attack is daunting and the need for all stakeholders in both government (at all levels) and private industry to be involved in cyber security is more significant than ever as the use of the MTS continues to grow.

Female Emancipation and Masonic Membership:
An Essential Collection
By Guillermo De Los Reyes Heredia

Female Emancipation and Masonic Membership: An Essential Combination is a collection of essays on Freemasonry and gender that promotes a transatlantic discussion of the study of the history of women and Freemasonry and their contribution in different countries.

Anti-Poverty Measures in America: Scientism and Other Obstacles
Editors, Max J. Skidmore and Biko Koenig

Anti-Poverty Measures in America brings together a remarkable collection of essays dealing with the inhibiting effects of scientism, an over-dependence on scientific methodology that is prevalent in the social sciences, and other obstacles to anti-poverty legislation.

Geopolitics of Outer Space: Global Security and Development
by Ilayda Aydin

A desire for increased security and rapid development is driving nation-states to engage in an intensifying competition for the unique assets of space. This book analyses the Chinese-American space discourse from the lenses of international relations theory, history and political psychology to explore these questions.

Contests of Initiative: Countering China's Gray Zone Strategy in the East and South China Seas
by Dr. Raymond Kuo

China is engaged in a widespread assertion of sovereignty in the South and East China Seas. It employs a "gray zone" strategy: using coercive but sub-conventional military power to drive off challengers and prevent escalation, while simultaneously seizing territory and asserting maritime control.

Discourse of the Inquisitive
Editors: Jaclyn Maria Fowler and Bjorn Mercer

Good communication skills are necessary for articulating learning, especially in online classrooms. It is often through writing that learners demonstrate their ability to analyze and synthesize the new concepts presented in the classroom.

westphaliapress.org

Made in the USA
Columbia, SC
07 January 2025

49807440R00211